PRAISE FOR DiANN MILLS

DEADLOCK

"DiAnn Mills brings us another magnificent, inspirational thriller in her FBI: Houston series. *Deadlock* is a riveting, fast-paced adventure that will hold you captive from the opening pages to the closing epilogue."

FRESHFICTION.COM

"Mills's newest installment in the FBI: Houston series will keep readers on the edge of their seats. For those who love a good 'who-done-it,' *Deadlock* delivers."

CBA RETAILERS + RESOURCES

Mills does a superb job building the relationship between the two polar opposite detectives. With some faith overtones, *Deadlock* is an excellent police drama that even mainstream readers would enjoy."

ROMANTIC TIMES

DOUBLE CROSS

"DiAnn Mills always gives us a good thriller, filled with inspirational thoughts, and *Double Cross* is another great one!"

FRESHFICTION.COM

"Tension explodes at every corner within these pages. . . . Mills's writing is transparently crisp, backed up with solid research, filled with believable characters and sparks of romantic chemistry."

NOVELCROSSING.COM

"For the romantic suspense fan, there is plenty of action and twists present. For the inspirational reader, the faith elements fit nicely into the context of the story. . . . The romance is tenderly beautiful, and the ending bittersweet."

ROMANTIC TIMES

FIREWALL

"Mills takes readers on an explosive ride. . . . A story as romantic as it is exciting, *Firewall* will appeal to fans of Dee Henderson's romantic suspense stories."

BOOKLIST

"With an intricate plot involving domestic terrorism that could have been ripped from the headlines, Mills's romantic thriller makes for compelling reading."

LIBRARY JOURNAL

"A fast-moving, intricately plotted thriller."

PUBLISHERS WEEKLY

"Mills once again demonstrates her spectacular writing skills in her latest action-packed work. . . . The story moves at a fast pace that will keep readers riveted until the climactic end."

ROMANTIC TIMES

"This book was so fast-paced that I almost got whiplash. . . . Heart-pounding action from the first page . . . didn't stop until nearly the end of the book. If you like romantic suspense, I highly recommend this one."

RADIANT LIT

Visit Tyndale online at www.tyndale.com.

Visit DiAnn Mills at www.diannmills.com.

TYNDALE and Tyndale's quill logo are registered trademarks of Tyndale House Publishers, Inc.

Deadly Encounter

Cover design by Faceout Studio, Tim Green

Interior design by Dean H. Renninger

Edited by Erin E. Smith

Published in association with the literary agency of Books & Such Literary Management, 52 Mission Circle, Suite 122, PMB 170, Santa Rosa, CA 95409.

Library of Congress Cataloging-in-Publication Data
Names: Mills, DiAnn, author.
Title: Deadly encounter / DiAnn Mills.
Description: Carol Stream, Illinois : Tyndale House Publishers, Inc., [2016]
  | Series: FBI task force ; 1
Identifiers: LCCN 2016007630 | ISBN 9781496410979 (softcover)
Subjects: LCSH: United States. Federal Bureau of Investigation—Officials and employees—
    Fiction. | Government investigators—Fiction. | Murder—Investigation—Fiction. | GSAFD:
    Suspense fiction. | Christian fiction. | Mystery fiction.
Classification: LCC PS3613.I567 D435 2016 | DDC 813/.6—dc23 LC record available at
    http://lccn.loc.gov/2016007630

Printed in the United States of America

22   21   20   19   18   17   16
7   6   5   4   3   2   1

DiANN MILLS

DEADLY
ENCOUNTER

TYNDALE HOUSE PUBLISHERS, INC.
CAROL STREAM, ILLINOIS

TO STACY LeBLANC, AND ANIMAL LOVERS EVERYWHERE

ACKNOWLEDGMENTS

Randal DuPree—Thanks for helping me make gumbo and answering all my questions about Cajun culture and language.

Lori Johnson—Thank you for your friendship and your weapon knowledge.

Warren A. Johnson—Thank you so much for helping me to understand the shivah.

Stacy LeBlanc—Your role as an airport ranger for Houston's Intercontinental Airport helped me add a twist to my story. Your work with animals and answering all my questions about veterinarians made my story come alive with credibility. I so appreciate you.

Guy Gurley—Thank you for the brainstorming sessions. Your psychological insight gives my stories zip!

Dr. Richard Mabry—You always help me through the rough medical parts. Thanks for being my personal writer-doctor-adviser.

Kathy Walsh—Thank you for suggesting my Lab's name, Xena.

Kathi Wilson—You helped me so much with the real estate information. Thanks!

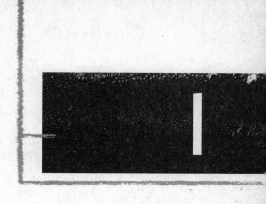

SATURDAY MORNINGS were Stacy Broussard's escape, especially when life slapped her with stress. No better way to unwind from the week than to ride her quarter horse on Houston's airport trail and enjoy nature. This morning promised to be the perfect distraction from a truckload of problems, from the anniversary of the death of her sister to seeking custody of a twelve-year-old boy. She looked forward to a lift in her spirit.

She pulled her truck into the Aldine Westfield Stables. As usual she was the first one of the airport rangers to arrive. Chet's pickup wasn't parked beneath the moss-draped oak, and he normally arrived before dawn. Strange since he took his responsibilities as stable manager seriously.

Finishing her latte, she grabbed her wallet and keys and stepped outside her truck to admire an incredible purple-and-gold sunrise. Not even an early morning aircraft landing disturbed her. She walked slowly to the stables, taking in the singing robins and the familiar humidity. The smell of horseflesh and straw tickled her nose.

"Good morning, boys and girls," she said. "Your friendly veterinarian is on the scene."

If anyone heard her, they'd declare her insane. Maybe so when she reflected on how much she preferred an animal's company to a human's. Except Whitt . . . the most fascinating twelve-year-old on the planet.

Stacy ambled past each stall until she reached Ginger's, greeting the horses by name, touching velvety soft noses, and visibly checking to ensure they were okay. Her pets looked healthy. Spending a few extra moments with Ginger eased the knots in her shoulders that no massage could ever eliminate.

She led Ginger into the stable area and grabbed a pitchfork to tidy up her stall. A strong horse smell and a little manure on her boots never hurt anyone. Being prissy was not one of her traits. When finished, she retrieved her mare's blanket and bridle from her tack box. Her cell phone alerted her to a text.

Sorry, Stacy. Got a sick baby. Won't b there.

No problem. Take care of her and give a hug 4 me.

She'd miss her friend this morning. The idea of a sick child sent a pang of loss and melancholy through her—and not just for what she didn't have. Who was she fooling? Reaching the age of thirty-five without a husband and children hadn't been her idea of the future. A quote sailed into her mind: *Want to make God laugh? Tell Him your plans.* Not going there. Not today.

Checking her watch, she pondered the whereabouts of her other partner and Chet. She saddled Ginger, adjusting the cinch twice. Another text landed in her phone.

Stacy, my in-laws arrived late last night. 4got 2 call.

After a soft sigh, she typed, **Enjoy the visit.**

Airport ranger guidelines stated volunteers were to ride in pairs or threes. This kept the rider safe if a situation arose on the trail, like in the event a rider fell or encountered a difficult person.

But what choice did she have? Chet hadn't made an appearance either. Who would ever know she made a solo ride? She closed Ginger's stall door and hoisted herself into the saddle. No point in abandoning this beautiful morning because of a single guideline.

"Let's go, Miss Ginger. We'll see if we can shake up a few squirrels."

She crossed the road and made her way to the entrance of the wooded area where the north trail around IAH began. An aircraft broke the sound of chirping birds and the peacefulness that had settled upon her. Right on time. The moment she turned Ginger into the brush area, another aircraft announced its departure. So much for the quiet.

She rode the inside perimeter of the fenced area. Nothing eventful to report—not even a piece of trash. As she made her way into a clearing, a squirrel scampered across her path. A ray of morning light filtered through the trees.

Ginger reared, catching Stacy by surprise. She pulled fast on the reins. "Easy, Ginger."

Her mare crow-hopped and reared again.

What had startled her? A snake?

Then she saw it.

A pair of legs stuck out from a bush approximately fifteen feet to her right.

Her heart hammered, and Ginger had to feel it. She struggled to control her own fear and the horse beneath her while her sights were glued to the man's lower extremities.

"Hello, are you okay?" When only the quiet met her, she dismounted and moved closer to where the man lay. Eyes open and vacant. Stacy had seen scowls like this before, but not on a dead man. He appeared to have defied his attacker in one last fit of anger before surrendering to death.

Blood pooled on his chest and trickled over his abdomen and left side. One—no, two horrible holes. The wounds looked fresh, perhaps within the last hour or so.

Terror rose, and she thought she'd be physically sick. She swung her attention in every direction, expecting someone to emerge from the tangled green terrain along the north section of Houston's Intercontinental Airport. She yanked her only permissible weapon from her jeans—a pocketknife—and opened it as if it would ward off a killer.

Why had she chosen to ride alone?

A yellow Lab snuggled near the body, her head resting on the dead man's chest. A leather leash from the dog was wrapped around the man's fingers. Five feet to the right, a blood-spattered motorcycle stood at attention. Securing the pocketknife in her palm, she lifted her phone from inside her jeans pocket and pressed in 911 while she continued to look over her shoulder.

"What is your emergency?" the operator said.

Stacy swallowed the acid rising in her stomach. The morning's heat didn't help. "I've found a dead body on the north trail that runs along the FM 1960 side of IAH. The nearest entrance is on Farrell where a sign designates the Houston Airport System equestrian security trail. My name is Stacy Broussard, and I'm an airport ranger volunteer."

"You're sure he's not alive?"

She bent beside the body and felt the side of his neck for a pulse. Nothing. "Very much so. He's lost a tremendous amount of blood from his chest and abdomen. I'm assuming gunshots."

"Do you know the man?"

"No, ma'am."

"Are you all right?"

"Shaken. I'm alone except for a dog lying next to the body. The animal's right front paw is bleeding, and I'm a veterinarian. She's not protective or aggressive." Stacy drew in a ragged breath. The dog rose from the body and limped to her side, while the leash stayed fixed in the man's hand. She rested her head on Stacy's knee.

"You're doing fine," the operator said. "I'll keep talking until the police arrive and I'm assured you're safe. How did you happen upon the body?"

Keep your head. You can get through this. "I'm a volunteer for the airport rangers. We ride horseback to patrol the outer perimeter of IAH and report any problems to the Houston Police Department. The man is in a clearing. I checked for a pulse, and I'm sure of his condition." She removed the leash from his hand and examined the dog's bleeding paw, a wound that would require a few stitches. The man wasn't as fortunate. "How long until officers arrive?"

"Only a few more minutes. You're a brave woman."

"I don't feel brave. How awful for this poor man." The victim's eyes would haunt her for a long time, maybe forever.

"Tell me more about the airport rangers," the operator said. "I wasn't aware Houston had such a service."

She's trying to calm me, divert my attention from the blood-coated body. "We're not highly publicized. Normally we find evidence of drugs or kids' inappropriate behavior. Never anything like this. And we aren't supposed to ride alone, but the other two volunteers canceled at the last minute. Our stables are close by." Stacy avoided staring at the body and instead concentrated on the injured dog. Her collar didn't have an ID. Had the animal been hurt while protecting her master?

"Are there any signs of a struggle?"

She peered around for what seemed like the hundredth time.

"There's a motorcycle, a Kawasaki. I suppose the plates won't be hard to trace." A strange object captured her attention in the shadow of the bushes. Boots? Shoes? "I see something unusual, but I can't make out what it is."

"Be careful. The police can investigate it."

No need to caution her. She was already frightened out of her wits. Sirens grew closer. "I hear them."

"Stay where you are until the officers arrive. They'll take over the situation."

"I'm sorry, but it might be another body or someone hurt. I have to see if someone needs help." She bolstered her courage and moved toward the questionable object. The dog followed her to the edge of the clearing, where a type of drone with four propellers was lodged in a fallen tree branch and bushes. A churning panic swirled through her. Had the dead man stopped a potential crime of blinding a pilot? "What happened here?" she whispered, more to herself than the 911 operator.

"Talk to me, Stacy."

"I've found a drone. A clear dome is attached underneath, and it's pointed toward the northwest end of the runway."

2

ALEX DROVE HIS JEEP along Farrell Road toward the crime scene on the north side of IAH. The narrow, potholed road slowed progress and elevated his impatience. An hour had passed since the Houston Police Department contacted the FBI with evidence indicating possible domestic terrorism. A woman had discovered a dead man. Tragic situation. But the clincher was she'd also found a two-foot-long, military-grade quadcopter.

"The woman who found the body is an airport ranger," his partner, Ric, said.

"That group is nothing more than wannabe cowboys playing a role they aren't equipped to handle. I doubt she ran off the shooter."

Ric chuckled. "You have a definite point of view."

"She could have been killed. Maybe this will scare off the volunteers. Have them do their community work at schools and hospitals instead of interfering with a bad guy's plan or an investigation. I've never been in favor of them patrolling the airport perimeter. Maybe those who are professionally trained law enforcement, but not those who are unskilled in weaponry."

Ric nodded. "I see where you're coming from, but it's a respected program, and the volunteers consider it their civic duty. They're subjected to thorough background checks and are required to take a mounted self-defense course."

"All I'm saying is we've seen the damage untrained people can do, destroying critical evidence that allows the bad guys to continue. I hope this isn't another one of those messes."

"Mr. Cynical, I'm right there with you," Ric said. "The 911 operator kept her on the line until the police arrived."

"My gut doesn't like any of this."

"My concern is the military-grade drone and the payload."

Alex swung a look at his dark-skinned partner, a man always in tune with the latest technology. "What are your initial thoughts, other than we need eyes on it ASAP?"

"Ask me after I've dismantled it and we're still breathing air."

Alex glanced at his phone's GPS map for the exit road off FM 1960. Couldn't get there fast enough. Their information set the quadcopter apart from a citizen's toy. He turned his Jeep right onto the farm road and in less than a quarter mile made another right to where several police cars were parked along a wooded area. A dark-haired woman stood beside a horse and a police officer. The woman was trim, jean-clad, wearing boots and a button-down light-green shirt. A yellow Lab lay at her side. She matched the description of the woman who'd found the body. "Let's get a history on her. What's her name?"

"Stacy Broussard, a veterinarian."

"Is she independent, or does she work for someone?"

"Independent. Owner of Pet Support Veterinary Clinic on the northwest side of town. Doctor of veterinary medicine. Graduated from A&M College of Veterinary Medicine and Biomedical Sciences.

A member of American Veterinary Medical Association and the Texas Veterinary Medical Association. I'd give you the acronyms, but you wouldn't remember them."

Ric's comment took the heat off the pressure. "Good call."

The two exited the car and approached the officer, who was talking with the woman. Heat and humidity assaulted them, typical Houston weather. Those working the crime scene must be miserable, and the woman who'd found the body had been there longer than all of them.

"Lead out, bro," Ric said. "I'll want to think through her answers."

Alex tossed him a grin despite the grave situation. "You mean form a theory that will most likely be different from mine." A few feet more, he took the initiative and stuck out his hand to the officer. "I'm FBI Special Agent Alex LeBlanc, and this is Special Agent Ric Price from the domestic terrorism division. HPD requested our assistance."

The officer introduced himself and Dr. Stacy Broussard. Her pale face told Alex she didn't find dead bodies often.

"I'm sorry your morning ride met up with a tragedy," Alex said. "We understand you discovered the body and the quadcopter."

He met cautious dark-blue eyes. "Yes, sir. And the dog here beside me."

He gave the Lab a momentary glance and noted the dog had an injured paw. "Once we've examined the crime site, we'd like to ask a few questions."

She glanced away. Fear or guilt? Alex shook off his suspicions. Not every woman was like the last one he got involved with.

"I have appointments at my animal clinic, and the officer has already interviewed me. Plus, this dog needs attention."

Alex plastered on his agent smile. "I understand, ma'am, but we have a serious situation here."

She tucked her shoulder-length hair behind her ear. Sweat beaded on her face, and her shirt was damp. "You're right. But I didn't witness a thing. Sadly, a man's dead, and I have no idea why."

"Sometimes additional questions can generate new evidence, especially when the mind wants to block out what really happened, such as what you've encountered today."

She lifted a brow. "I'm not in shock, Agent LeBlanc. My mind is working perfectly—I'm sorry. Didn't mean to sound uncooperative."

"The heat doesn't help."

"No, sir."

"We understand, and we'll do our best not to keep you waiting very long." He turned to the officer. "Can you keep Dr. Broussard company for a few minutes?"

Alex and Ric followed a narrow path into the thick brush and woods leading to a clearing where officers were sweeping the crime scene. Two sets of parallel fencing caught Alex's attention: one near the road and the second separating the airport property. The airport rangers rode between the two. Beyond the tree line was a field leading to the airport with a clear view of IAH's north side.

An officer stood by the body. No doubt the medical examiner was en route. As tragic as a murder could be, his and Ric's focus had to be on dismantling the drone.

They pulled on non-latex gloves and bent to the quadcopter still caught in the bushes. Ric rested his hand on his knee while visually scrutinizing it. "There's a serial number."

Alex snapped a pic with his phone and sent it to the FIG—Field Intelligence Group—for the drone's origin.

In less than six minutes, Ric had taken the device apart. "GPS controlled, touch screen module, small brushless motors, modular for easy assembly, carbon fiber blades, and other than the laser, no additional weaponry."

Definitely not the type kids flew in the park or Amazon used to deliver orders. Alex continued to snap pics while scenarios played out of what might have happened this morning. At this point, it looked like the dead man stopped a drone.

Ric pointed to the quadcopter with his pen. "The device has a snap-in modular design, wirelessly remote. Camera was destroyed when it crashed."

"Can it be repaired? It might give investigators a visual of what happened."

"Irreparable."

A text flew into Alex's phone. "The FIG ran the serial number. The Army reported it stolen three months ago. I'll request a full rundown."

"Which lends credence to the theory that a terrorist is behind this," Ric said.

Alex wanted details—now. "Failing is not listed in a terrorist's portfolio." He pointed to the laser capable of blinding a pilot. "Given the proximity to the north runway, this had the ability to damage an aircraft on its final launch." He peered at the three jagged bullet holes that had penetrated the quadcopter. "From the trajectory, whoever fired at the device was at a slight angle, about twenty feet below it. Looks like a 9mm."

"Like someone was trying to bring it down."

Alex stood and approached the officer by the body. Ric followed. "Do you know the type of bullet that killed this man?"

"A 9mm."

"Was a gun found near the body?"

"Nothing recovered yet." The officer gestured to a single boot print near the body. "From the size, it doesn't match the victim or the woman."

Alex knelt beside the print, snapping pics. Questions fired in his mind like a repeater. "Looks like a size 12, maybe 13. Had to be at least one more person in the clearing. Speculating here, but the man could have been killed to avoid identifying the drone operator." His gaze followed a path leading out of the clearing that had been swept with brush, eliminating footprints. He moved around the area, maneuvering behind bushes and trees, studying every angle of the crime, and looking for the weapon. Finding nothing, he returned to Ric and the officer.

"The motorcycle has blood spatters. Most likely the victim's, but if we're lucky, it's the third party's," Ric said. "Officer, did you run the plates?"

"Yes. It belongs to the victim, Todd Howe."

Alex scanned the scene, busy with law enforcement activity. "The victim rode his motorcycle through the gate and between the fencing in a restricted area. Not an impromptu venture on a Saturday morning."

"Unknowns and variables," Ric said. "Did the shots ending the drone's mission stop a potential plane crash?"

Alex blew out his apprehension for the innocent lives that could be caught in the crosshairs of a madman. Houston ranked second in laser strikes against aircraft. "The potential has me concerned about the safety of others." His mind centered on both crimes: the murder and the quadcopter aimed at the airport runway.

"We've put out enough material to combat those who claim ignorance." Since 2015, the FAA required drone registration for those over .55 pounds . . . but this was military grade.

"Drone operators aren't any better than snipers. No excuse for violators. This is our thirteenth laser target case this month."

"Threat is imminent until we catch who's behind it. My guess is an extremist militia group. Whoever's in charge didn't adhere to FAA regulations, which means our bad guy is looking at state and federal charges of murder and laser pointer violations. But I doubt he cares."

Ric walked back to the drone and picked it up. "Interesting to see what a fingerprint sweep from HPD shows."

"We've already lifted prints from the device," an officer said.

"Good. I'll place it in our vehicle," Ric said.

Alex stared at the path leading to the parked vehicles. "I want to know what happened here. What connects a dead man, a dog, a quadcopter, and a motorcycle?" Dr. Stacy Broussard might have more information, even if she wasn't aware.

"What's running through your head?"

"Do you think our airport ranger is involved?"

"Bro, why would she report the crime and stick around to talk to the police?"

"I haven't forgotten my last case dealing with a woman. I want every base covered."

3

STACY REPEATED EVERY DETAIL she could recall prior to and after discovering the body. Special Agent Alex LeBlanc posed countless questions, often repeating himself by rephrasing the query. Though she didn't mind looking at his all-American chiseled appearance and brown, nut-shaped eyes, she grew tired of the redundancy. The past hour in the humidity-filled air woven with Special Agent LeBlanc's questions, calls from animal owners requesting appointments, and an injured dog that required attention had readjusted her tolerance level. The image of the dead man refused to leave her alone. He surely had family and friends who'd mourn his passing.

He studied her. "Are you okay? Would you like to see a doctor?"

She shook her head. "How much longer will we be here?"

"A few minutes."

"All right."

"What was your first reaction when you rode into the clearing?"

She held her hand like a stop sign. "Sir, you've asked me the same thing three times. I don't know the man. Neither have I seen him before or heard his name."

"Do you ride this trail often?"

"This is the last time I'll answer that question. I'm sorry to sound uncooperative, but this has been the worst day of my life. I ride once a week for the airport rangers on Saturday mornings. As I stated earlier, I begin at six and ride until eight. The difference today is my companions had prior commitments, and I chose to complete my volunteer work alone."

"Which could have gotten you killed."

"My friends included, had they been here." Irritation capped her tone, and she no longer cared.

"I'd like their names, please." He'd run the information through the FIG to ensure her story was accurate.

"You don't believe me?"

"This is standard procedure for an investigation."

"Okay." She gave him the names of the two absent volunteers.

"Do you carry a concealed weapon?"

"I don't have a CHL, and we're not permitted to have a firearm in our possession while on duty, only a pocketknife." She pulled it from her jean pocket and showed it to him.

"We'd like to borrow it."

"Don't cut yourself." She bit her tongue to keep from releasing more sarcasm. "It means a lot to me, so I'd like it returned."

He nodded. "I've succeeded in angering you, Dr. Broussard."

She breathed out her weariness. "Yes, you have. Do you have any new questions?"

"Have you ever been arrested?"

"No. A ticket for speeding about three years ago."

"Have you served in the military?"

"No."

"Involved in an antigovernment organization?"

"No."

"Do you know the victim?"

"I repeat. No." She rubbed her face, trying to see the crime from his viewpoint.

"Did you see anyone?"

She blew out frustration instead of the words she'd like to use. "Look, I understand your questions are required. But explain to me why I report a crime, and you treat me as though I'm a criminal."

He frowned. "I'm not accusing you of anything, Dr. Broussard. The questions are to gather information while the crime is fresh in your mind."

Stacy handed him a business card. "Don't forget to return my pocketknife. It was a gift from my dad." She patted the dog's head. "She doesn't have a collar, and I assume she belongs to the deceased. I'll be back in a few minutes to take her with me. She'll be at my clinic."

"We have a kennel to house the dog."

"She needs medical care, and I doubt she can provide much evidence." She swallowed the mixed emotions tempting her to lose control. "I'll make sure her wounds are bandaged and look for an identification microchip. If I find one, I'll contact you." A media van parked across the road diverted her attention. She groaned. "I'm not talking to them."

He studied the cameraman and a woman walking their way. "No reason to talk to reporters. We'll make sure our media coordinator releases an accurate report." He bent to pat the injured dog, exposed far too long in the heat with a wounded paw. "I appreciate your help this morning."

That was a canned response. "Please give my condolences to the victim's family." She smiled at the helpful officer holding her horse's reins and hoisted herself into the saddle. Normally she worked hard to ensure everyone was happy and at peace with the world. But not this morning.

"Dr. Broussard."

What now? Her blood type? She pulled the mare to a halt and waited.

"I'm sorry for what you experienced this morning and my insensitive interview." He paused. "My mama didn't raise me to be rude." His voice slid to a familiar lilt.

"Do I hear Cajun?" Did he think this made his crude mannerisms acceptable? "Certainly in the name."

"A Berry boy." He was from New Iberia. A dimple deepened. "And you?"

"Southeast of Lake Charles."

"A McNeese grad?"

"Is there any other?" When he frowned, she figured him out. "Spoken like a true ULL fan."

"Played football for them. Do you have family there?"

"All of them," she said.

"Me too. Does this mean I'm forgiven?"

His eyes, with a hint of earthen mystery, probably got him whatever he wanted. She had cousins who thought they could turn on the charm and melt any female. "Maybe," she said. "Depends if you stay with the dog until I return in about ten minutes. The stables are at the corner of Richey and Aldine Westfield. Have a nice day, Agent LeBlanc."

"I suggest you reconsider your volunteer work as an airport ranger. As proven today, your life could be in danger."

She was committed to the program. "I can take care of myself without FBI interference." She trotted the mare toward the road with the determination to never talk to him again—except to retrieve the sweet Lab.

4

WHITT CONNECTED THE JUMPER CABLES to the positive and negative posts of the dead battery. Temperatures had risen in the garage to nearly ninety degrees, and that was with a fan, but Dad hadn't thrown the wrench or cursed and given up. He'd poured half a can of Coke over the battery's rust and eliminated much of the corrosion, and still the car refused to start. Dad attempted to engage the engine again, but it was dead.

"You need a new battery," Whitt said, hoping his suggestion wouldn't send Dad off the deep end. "I'll walk to Walmart and buy it."

"I'm trying to make this one last as long as possible." Dad stood back, his bare belly hanging over his jeans. "Rent's past due. Ain't nothing in the house to eat either. No way for my son to live." He stared at Whitt, his eyes free of the redness associated with alcohol and drugs. "Promise me you'll make something of yourself."

"Yes, sir, I will." Whitt wanted to believe Dad cared, and right now he showed genuine concern. But the facts proved otherwise.

He adjusted the clamps on the battery posts. "Want to crank 'er up and see if the blasted car starts? You might have the magic touch."

Whitt opened the door with a squeak and twisted the key. Nothing. Not a single turnover. If it had started, Dad would be in a decent mood until tonight. . . .

"What am I missing, Whitt? You're the genius." Dad chuckled. "Who would ever have thought I'd father a kid with a higher IQ than both of his parents."

Most times he considered his intelligence a curse. "Oh, you're smart, Dad." He stepped from the car. "Could it be the alternator?"

"Nothing wrong with it. Already checked."

Whitt examined the wires to ensure they were tight. "I think we don't have any choice but to replace it."

"I need money." He glared at Whitt. "You have it, and this car won't start without a new battery."

He hesitated. Giving Dad money satisfied him for a little while. If Whitt thought he'd stop drinking, he'd give him every penny in his bank account.

"You do real good working for Miss Stacy, so hand it over." His face reddened when Whitt just stood there.

"She keeps it for me. I'll ask her when she returns from her airport ride." But Miss Stacy had told him not to give the parents money.

"What's wrong that you can't keep track of your own cash?"

"I'm saving for college."

"College? I didn't waste my time there, and I turned out just fine."

Whitt wanted to tell him that a pot-smoking drunk wasn't the career he wanted, but Miss Stacy had warned him about being disrespectful.

Dad slammed the hood shut, cursing as he stomped to the door leading into the kitchen.

"Want me to get you a Coke or root beer?"

Dad snorted. "There are two six-packs calling my name as long as your mother hasn't drank them up."

Whitt cringed. "When Miss Stacy gets to the clinic, I'll get the money. We could walk to Walmart together."

"Too late. I've had enough."

He'd head to the clinic before Dad unleashed his temper.

At the stables, Stacy unsaddled and brushed down Ginger before driving back to pick up the injured dog. She dreaded the next encounter with Agent LeBlanc. Each time she remembered how he used his Louisiana roots to soften her first impression of him, she wanted to shake her fist at him. Too handsome for his own good. One minute he seemed to care about what she'd encountered, and in the next he rattled off questions like she was a suspect.

At the trailhead, she saw the police officer and dog, but no FBI agents. No surprise Agent LeBlanc had abandoned the wounded animal. The man had frustrated her from the moment he opened his mouth. Her job often meant dealing with pet owners across a wide spectrum, from those who were over-the-top anxious about their animals to those who were almost noncaring about their welfare. Both could be challenging, and she often stuffed her feelings into a closet.

"Miss, the agents were called to the crime site. They offered their regrets," the police officer said. He gently placed the sweet female Lab onto the front seat of the truck, as though the animal were an infant. After thanking him, Stacy drove cautiously with her precious cargo to the clinic. On the way, she called Whitt and learned he'd been there since midmorning. She told him about finding an injured dog. But not the particulars of the circumstances. The boy would have a bazillion questions, and she wasn't sure how much to tell. He'd sold pet food and vitamins, scheduled appointments, and checked on the cat who'd undergone surgery for a tumor on his heart.

Whitt's dedication to the clinic filled her with gratitude. Too bad he didn't receive the same loving care at home. Both parents were AWOL from the nurturing scene, taking turns on HPD's blotter. She couldn't save every human and animal, only the ones placed in her path, and she was committed to Whitt and the animals.

She pulled into the parking section at the rear of the clinic, located in a strip center at the front of the subdivision. When she moved there ten years ago, her small ranch-type home was all she could afford. Her neighborhood, nestled between I-45 and the Hardy Toll Road, had been established in the sixties and was poorly maintained. Some of the people living there were dear friends. Others not so much. Although she could easily walk to work, early morning and late hours alone made it unsafe. The crime rate escalated at an alarming pace, and thoughts of moving nipped at her heels.

Whitt opened the passenger door of her truck. His wild, light honey–colored hair hung below his ears, and his serious gray eyes veiled with thick lashes would one day drive the girls nuts, if not already. He grinned, a lopsided appeal that would always melt her heart. Small for his age, but his intellect made up for his size. Every Cajun knew family was what really mattered in life, and he was the closest she had to one of her own.

"The queen and princess have arrived," he said. "I have the surgery room ready."

"That makes you our hero," she said, exiting the truck. "If you can manage our princess patient, I'll get the door."

He helped Stacy lift the Lab from the seat with the gentleness she'd instructed. "I have an eye on her paw. Poor thing," he whispered. "Don't see a tag on her collar. But she's remarkably clean."

"No ID unless I find a chip." Stacy struggled to open the clinic's door while balancing the Lab. "She looks to be about two years old."

They carried the dog inside and laid her on an examination table. "You need a name, pretty girl. Looks like you've been through a battle." His soft voice showed his love for animals, a veterinarian in the making.

"I like Warrior Princess," she said.

"Consider Xena. It's Greek, and it means 'hospitable.'"

"Perfect." She turned on the warm water to wash her hands.

"Did you find her on the airport trail?"

She nodded while scrubbing up. "She might have an owner." Better Whitt hear the circumstances from her than the news. "She was lying beside a dead man."

"Whoa, Miss Stacy. Seriously?"

"Yeah. I'm late because of the investigation, HPD and the FBI." She noted her trembling hands, not really aware until this moment how badly the discovery had upset her. "Let's fix up Miss Xena. I don't want to discuss how I found her."

"Sure. I can see by the way you're shaking that it was execrable."

His vocabulary wavered between kid and sending her to the dictionary. She dried her hands and joined the dog to allow Whitt to scrub up. "I'm calming down. My hands need to be steady."

"Take deep breaths."

She smiled and thanked him.

"Who was the dead guy?" he said.

"I don't know." She sprayed lidocaine on the wounded paw and gingerly cleaned it of debris and blood.

"But this is his dog, right?"

"I think so. The man had her leash in his hand." She clipped the hair away and cleaned the wound again. The cut was straight. Perfectly straight. As though deliberate. Who would do such a thing to an animal? "She has a gentle nature. Hasn't snapped or growled at me."

"Makes me wonder if this is the work of an animal abuser."

"Maybe the dog stepped on a piece of glass."

"Really?" Whitt stared at the wound. "How did the man die?"

He'd find out on the news, but she preferred to answer his question. "Shot in the chest. We may never know what happened this morning to him or the dog."

"Lots of missing pieces here. I'll need time to analyze it."

Whitt, and his way of dealing with life. "That's why I'm the doc and the investigators have their expertise."

"Did they ask enough questions to fill Fort Knox?"

"Yes, but I don't want to go there." The morning dropped back into her mind. "Don't be surprised if the FBI shows up at the clinic in the next few days. A drone was found in the bushes, and the FBI seems to think it could have had deadly implications so close to the airport."

He sighed. "I should have gone with you. Protected my favorite vet."

Best twelve-year-old in the country. "Not sure what you could have done."

He sank his teeth into his lip, and for a moment she feared he'd shed tears.

"Are you okay?" she said. "Because I am."

"Sure." He tossed a fake smile her way.

Her heart ached for him. "Looks like subs for lunch today. Thanks for directing emergencies to Doc Kent's clinic and handling things this morning."

"No problem." He laid a hand on the Lab's back while Stacy

reached for suturing materials. He turned his head away when she produced the needle. "I need a distraction. Tell me everything that happened this morning."

"Focus on what we're doing. I'll tell you what I can when we're finished." And she would.

"Oh, could I have seventy-five dollars?"

"Sure. It's your money."

"Dad needs a battery for his car."

The man needed to work. "Once we're finished, I'll give you the cash." No questions. No comments. Whitt knew how she felt about the matter.

After she loosely sutured the wound and Xena was resting, she gave him his request plus a little more to go after sandwiches down the street. She responded to phone and e-mail messages, but curiosity soon got the best of her, and she switched on her computer for the latest news.

A quick read revealed more had been reported than what she'd experienced, including the victim's identity—Todd Howe. The family must have already been notified of his death. Howe was the owner of a series of Green-to-Go restaurants in the Houston area. The laser connected to the quadcopter had been damaged when it was brought down by three bullets and crashed into the brush.

Her pic and name hit the bottom of the screen as the only witness.

But she hadn't witnessed the crime. Agent LeBlanc said he'd ensure an accurate press release. Looked like the media beat him to it. Her cell phone rang, and she responded.

"Dr. Broussard, this is the *Houston Chronicle*. We'd like a statement from you regarding the crime you witnessed at IAH this morning."

"I didn't see any crime. I reported one, so you're wasting your time." She pressed End. Before she had time to recover, her phone rang again. Concerned it could be important, she took a deep breath and answered.

"Glad we caught you, Dr. Broussard. This is Channel 5 news, and we'd—"

"Not interested." She turned her phone off.

Did being labeled a witness to the crime mean she was in danger?

5

MIDAFTERNOON, Alex and Ric left the airport trail crime scene. They'd rewalked the area with HPD officers and FBI agents in search of other drones or evidence pertaining to the murder. The gun that had killed Howe would have been a bonus. The positive to the whole crime was someone had taken down the quadcopter before it inflicted serious damage. They requested HPD's lab expedite the fingerprint sweep. The media had obtained the information from someone about the crimes, and domestic terrorism with a murder had hit the public's attention.

Shortly after three, Alex drove to the Howe residence for an interview with the victim's widow, Bekah Howe. The quadcopter was on the backseat of his Jeep.

"Do we have an update on Todd Howe?" Alex said.

Ric scrolled through his phone. "No military background. No priors. His restaurants specialize in vegetarian fast food. Kosher too. Todd received an MA in business from Purdue, and Bekah graduated from Texas A&M with a degree in communications. Both were born and raised in Houston. From the date of their marriage, they were wed after college graduation. Two sons, ages six and eight."

"Probably in the wrong place at the wrong time and got himself killed. Would you request the FIG for a full background including his financials?"

"Already sent it."

Alex wished his brain fired on half of Ric's cylinders. "You're always one step ahead of me."

"Depends on the time of day."

Alex knew better. "What else?"

"Kosher menu follows Jewish dietary laws. Also serves no meat. Smart marketing in reaching out to the Jewish and vegetarians."

"The one thing I despise about our investigations is the info comes in snippets. But this guy looks clean. We just have to figure out the quadcopter piece." Alex stared at the road, not seeing but remembering his actions earlier. Guilt smacked him hard. "I blew it with Stacy Broussard. Rude. I was so focused on trying to connect the murder with some scum operating a drone, intent on bringing down a plane."

"I agree. When it comes to women, you need counseling."

"Other than the woman who nearly wrecked my career, I'm confused."

"The woman you fixed me up with last weekend."

"Thanks. For the record, I never claimed your date was a beauty."

"Or had a dynamic personality. In fact, I took your word on, 'I think you'll like her.'"

"Okay, I owe you. Her name came through as a friend of a friend. Two strikes against me today."

"Used to be, you'd charm the socks off a woman."

Alex responded with a humph. "At least I have one redeeming quality with Stacy Broussard. We're both Cajun."

"You left the dog with the officer." Ric lifted a brow. "Considering she's a vet and loves animals? Here I thought you were playing hard to get since she's gorgeous and not wearing a ring on her left hand."

"I hadn't noticed."

"Right." Ric pointed to a street in an upper middle-class neighborhood inside the loop. "See if you can do a better job sympathizing with Bekah Howe."

"She just lost her husband and her kids' father." Alex pulled onto the residential street. An HPD vehicle was parked at the curb of a sprawling white brick ranch. "This is one part of our job I don't enjoy."

Inside the home, it was quiet. Too quiet. Alex and Ric met with an officer who escorted them to a living area where a frail woman sat on a sofa with her face buried in her hands. Faint sobs met his ears. An older couple sat on either side of her on the long sofa. A photograph of a Marine was on the coffee table in front of them, not her husband.

Alex introduced himself and Ric to Bekah Howe and placed their cards on the coffee table. "We are very sorry for your loss. If you don't mind, we have a few questions for you. The answers may help us find who ended your husband's life."

She gestured to a pair of chairs. "Please, sit down."

"Thank you." Alex and Ric seated themselves on adjacent chairs.

Watery, caramel-colored eyes met his. "I have no idea who would want Todd dead."

"Had he been in any arguments, or had he received any threats that you recall?"

"No, sir. Neither has there been problems with the restaurants or neighbors or anyone."

"Does he own a firearm?"

"Yes, he has a CHL for a .22, and he keeps it in the glove box of his car. I already checked, and it's there." She reached for a tissue.

They'd verify his registration and concealed handgun license later. "Do you own a yellow Lab?"

"No pets."

"How about your neighbors?"

"None that I know of have a Lab."

"Mrs. Howe, your husband had the dog's leash in his hand."

She sat straighter. "Although my boys would like a pet, I repeat, we don't have a dog."

He'd ask the agents who interviewed the neighbors to inquire about the Lab.

"I haven't told our sons yet about their father. The words muddle in my mind. How does a mother relay such heartbreaking news? The rabbi promised to help me. He took the boys for ice cream."

"Did Todd tell you where he was going this morning?"

"No, sir. He loved to ride his motorcycle. Said it was the urban cowboy in him, a way to relieve work pressures."

The older woman, who had the same caramel-colored eyes, grasped Bekah's hand. "These are my parents. I'm sorry."

The woman lifted her chin. "Why is the FBI involved in this?"

"We work the domestic terrorism division, and a drone was found near his body."

Bekah touched her mouth. "Is my husband being investigated?"

"Yes, ma'am." Alex gave her a moment to gain control. "Was your husband interested in drones?"

"He didn't have time for hobbies." She stiffened. "Neither was he a terrorist. Talk to our rabbi. Everyone who knew Todd will vouch for him. What a horrible Shabbat."

Alex had forgotten today was the Jewish Sabbath. "Why ride his motorcycle today?"

She shrugged. "He said he needed to get away."

"I see." He picked up the photograph of the Marine.

"That's my brother," she said. "He died in Afghanistan."

"I'm sorry. What about your husband's parents?"

"They're both deceased."

Sympathy poured through him for her losses. "No other family?"

"Todd has a sister in Dallas, but we haven't seen her for years."

Alex requested the sister's name and jotted it down. "Who is your rabbi?"

"Myron Feldman. We attend the downtown temple." She gripped her fist. "When Todd wasn't working, he spent his time with us, in the community doing volunteer work, or at the temple. His only excursions were the brief motorcycle rides and business matters."

"Did his business keep him away from home a lot of hours?"

"Every day but Saturday. He believed in hands-on management. Wanted to be on-site at a different restaurant every day to ensure quality."

How did his personnel feel about someone looking over their shoulders? Unless he helped them, easing workloads. Alex understood her emotions were spent, but he had more questions. "In the past year, have there been any incidents in your and Todd's lives that would have made someone angry enough to kill him?"

"Nothing." She swallowed hard. "I believe my husband was in the wrong place this morning. He must have seen something that caused his death. The media claims drugs were suspected because of the remote area, but that's ridiculous. So I'm agreeing to an autopsy conducted within our faith's guidelines. I don't believe it will desecrate his body. The results won't disprove speculation of him selling drugs, but at least it will show his body clean of them. It may take as long as six weeks to get the complete toxicology report, but I want the truth. As far as the drone, I've never heard him mention one."

"Did your husband express antigovernment sentiments?" Alex watched for her response. Only shock and grief.

"No, sir. Never. Not even when my brother was killed serving his country."

"Thank you, Mrs. Howe. The FBI will be in contact today to image all of your husband's electronic equipment, including computers, cell phones, iPads, etc."

"I understand, and I want to cooperate fully."

"If you think of anything that might be helpful, please let one of us know immediately. You have our cards." He stood and Ric joined him. "Thank you for your time, Mrs. Howe. Again, we're sorry for your loss."

She reached up from the sofa and took his hand. "Promise me you'll arrest his killer. Our boys deserve closure." Tears streamed down her face. "They need protection from whatever the media claims. I want his murderer found."

Alex believed in truth, and he'd find out what happened. "We'll do our best."

Once in Alex's Jeep, they drove to the FBI office.

"I'm interested in checking the blood type on the motorcycle against Howe's and the Lab's. Dr. Broussard said she'd contact you about a microchip?" Ric said.

"Right. I doubt she'll speak to me, but I'll check with her later."

"Be nice. I'm giving you a second chance. For whatever it's worth, you had the right touch with Mrs. Howe."

Adrenaline slowed, and he thought through the interview with Bekah Howe. "She has a tough road ahead unless we can provide her with a legitimate reason why her husband rode into a restricted area and was killed."

"True. Most of what we need will take a few days—follow-up for neighbors' insight, personnel interviews, hobbies, undocumented time, cell phone records, and anything else we can think of, including a talk with their rabbi."

"Okay, so once we deliver the quadcopter to the techs, let's check with known terror groups in our area. I don't want to point fingers until I dig into surveillance reports."

Dexter Rayken walked onto his patio, needing fresh air even if the heat stifled him. He closed the door to his home office, leaving the luxury of air-conditioning behind along with stacks of medical books and research material. The wife had given up on him long ago to organize his small domain. But the mess behind him wasn't what plagued his mind.

The crimes near the airport had the FBI and HPD scrambling. Murder and domestic terrorism hit the media's talking points and filled up media airspace. Alex worked that division, and he'd be knee-deep in the investigation.

For twelve years, Dexter had been a mentor to the young man. Well, Alex wasn't so young, but early thirties sounded better than the back side of sixty. Dexter first met Alex years ago at a biological symposium for senior college students in Louisiana. Alex approached him afterward with tons of questions. He'd been interested in the newly formed Laboratory Response Network—LRN, an arm of the CDC whose objective was to improve a national network of laboratories in order to better respond to bioterrorism. Dexter saw right from the start that Alex's love of investigation fit an active career, not one spent in a lab. Not long afterward, Alex's parents died, and Dexter stepped in to help him with the grief. He and Eva loved on the boy as though he were their own. Through time spent together and e-mails, Dexter persuaded Alex to seek out the FBI. A wise decision on Alex's part.

He pulled his cell phone from his pocket and pressed in Alex's number. Before the first ring concluded, he'd answered.

"Hey, Dexter. How's your Saturday afternoon?"

"Likely more relaxing than yours. Working the suspected domestic terrorism case?"

"That's what I do. Solving crime and saving the world."

He chuckled. "Earth needs help when a Cajun takes on that role."

"Ric will appreciate that."

"Is he with you?"

"Yes. On our way back to the office."

"I won't keep you."

"Actually, I could use some advice."

"Today's crimes?"

"Yes."

"You messed up an investigation?"

"Very funny," Alex said. "But you might be right."

He relayed a botched interview with Dr. Broussard. Dexter had heard her name in the news. Laughter in the background must have been Ric. "Your communication skills with single women need a little help. I understand why." The woman who'd broken Alex's heart had nearly destroyed him and his career. "That woman lied to you and threatened your credibility as an agent. But you found out the truth and put her behind bars. Don't forget that."

"I'm trying, Dexter."

"Don't place a barrier in front of solving a murder or putting the brakes on a domestic terrorism case. If she's innocent, she could need protection."

"And I need evidence if she's guilty."

"What's your gut tell you?"

"Not sure with my track record, but I'm concerned if she does have information, she'd not open up to me."

"Then make a friend."

Alex groaned. "I'd rather face a firing squad."

"You'll be a better man for it. The only way you'll get past it and restore your confidence is to learn from your mistake and move on. Talk to you soon."

6

SATURDAY EVENING, Stacy slowly stirred homemade chicken stock into the dark roux. She'd given it her undivided attention for forty-five minutes and added chopped onion, bell peppers, celery, and garlic. Browned andouille, bay leaves, and seasonings were ready. After an hour of low heat, she'd add smoked chicken to the roux and let it simmer for another hour. Mom had taught her well. Dinner wouldn't be ready until nearly eight, but it couldn't be helped if the taste she'd learned to appreciate was going to meet her expectations. Nothing like comfort food to ease the extreme stress. She'd much rather have spent the entire day in her boots and jeans racing Ginger.

A glance into the living room, where Xena rested on a dog bed, told her the animal fared well. Stacy couldn't bear leaving her alone tonight at the clinic after the trauma of today, and here she seemed right at home.

Whitt showered at his house and would be back soon. Gumbo

was his favorite, although she liked it a bit spicier than he did. Chances were he'd sleep on the couch next to Xena tonight. The boy chose every opportunity to avoid his house and often requested her couch. She welcomed his company. Having him near ensured his safety from parents who routinely abused him in one way or another. They lived across the street . . . when they were home.

Whitt had no idea she'd hired Leonard Nardell, an attorney who'd come highly recommended by her pastor. Obtaining custody was in the works after she learned the school had contacted social services about suspected abuse. Whitt's social worker was aware of her role in his life and had already run a background check. Reference letters had been written on Stacy's behalf, and all that remained was a judge's signature. At the very least, she had the credentials to be his foster mother.

Whitt's parents believed Stacy had made the call. They'd sign away their rights for fifty grand. More like fifty shades of greed.

The door opened, and Whitt stepped in wearing a grin and wet blond hair. "Miss Stacy, my stomach's growling just smelling the gumbo."

"Wonderful. 'Cause I'm making plenty."

He dropped a bundle of clothes onto a chair and hurried to Xena's side. "Do you mind if I sleep on your couch tonight? Xena might need me. We've an incredible rapport going."

"Of course. But you can take the spare bed."

"I'd rather sleep near her."

"Suit yourself. Don't forget we're having community church in the clinic's parking lot tomorrow morning."

"I'll be up early."

"Did you leave a note for your parents?"

"Sure. Haven't seen either of them since around nine this morning."

She internalized her frustration. A part of her wanted them to shape up, and another part didn't care. "While dinner's simmering, want to help me get things ready for tomorrow afternoon's carnival?" She pointed to a box of quart-size baggies beside neat piles of pencils, erasers, brochures about the clinic, a child's guide to pet care, and small bags of Skittles.

Whitt bent to Xena. "I'll give you plenty of attention later. Right now I have work to do."

Tomorrow afternoon's festivities for their subdivision would be in the clinic's parking lot after a community church service. Her job was to showcase her veterinary services and host animal owners in a petting zoo, providing their animals loved kids. Barbecue and hot dogs, watermelon, cookies and pies, and a whole list of other food and games were free for the community event. In the late afternoon, a softball game between the men and women wound up the day. The losers would serve ice cream to the winners.

The two worked fast to stuff one hundred bags. Although she didn't expect more than twenty-five families, sometimes friends and family members attended. She welcomed them.

Whitt was unusually quiet. She assumed he'd bring up her morning ride at the airport, but he seemed preoccupied.

"What's wrong?"

"Ah, nothin'."

"Nothing doesn't put a frown on your face."

He gave a halfhearted smile and sealed a bag. "Eviction notice."

"When?"

"Monday. Dad told me he hadn't paid the rent."

"We've been down that road before. I'll help you bring your stuff over here after the carnival and stash it in the spare bedroom." She'd call her attorney Monday morning. This could be the deciding factor for custody.

"Thanks. Hope social services doesn't hear about it."

She kept her composure. Becoming an instant mother would be hard. But she was a grown woman, and she'd been parenting Whitt since he was a toddler playing in the street. Guilt riddled her for not acting on his behalf long before this. If social services yanked him from his parents before the custody hearing, would they allow her to be his foster mother? The judge might not view her as appropriate mother material or the case could take weeks to finalize. For certain Whitt would run. His emotions hadn't caught up with his intelligence, and he feared social services' intervention. He'd been in foster care a few years ago and had a bad experience. The agency had been monitoring his care through the school for the past several months, so the custody hearing needed to happen soon. All matters for her attorney on Monday morning. She loved Whitt, a trait his parents didn't seem to have.

"I'm sorry. You're bigger than your circumstances."

"Wish I could live here permanently." He bore his gray eyes into her face, but she wouldn't tell him yet.

"We're together when you're not in school." His slumped shoulders tore at her nurturing spirit and changed her mind. "I've filed for custody. The hearing will be soon. When I can give you positive news, I will."

"I understand. No point being disappointed till I have something to be disappointed about."

He was wiser than most adults, sometimes a disadvantage. "How's the English lit report?"

"About there. I'll have it ready for you to take a look at on Wednesday. Not due for a couple more weeks. It's a comprehensive look at the poets who've won the Nobel Prize in Literature. I know I complained when you mentioned getting ahead with advance summer school classes, but the counselor told me on Friday that I can graduate at fourteen with college hours. What a concept—graduate from high school and matriculate into college before I can drive."

She smiled and ruffled his hair. "I'm so proud of you. Hey—"

The doorbell rang. "I got it," he said.

Lord, please not his parents. Selfish as it sounded. Most times when they stopped in, they were drunk or high and needed money from Whitt. She wasn't in the mood for a confrontation. "Are you sure you should answer it?"

"I'm not too worried. My guess is the parents have been drinking for hours."

"You could be right. Or it could be someone else. People have been dropping off items for the carnival since I got home."

"We'll get them loaded up. Bet I can do it myself."

Her garage was a dispensary for a popcorn machine, dunking game, cases of soda, grills, folding chairs and tables, dozens of potato chip bags and hot dog buns, and that was just her last count. Expensive on her part, but the families living in her neighborhood needed a celebration and an opportunity to make friends with each other.

Definitely too many things bouncing off the sides of her brain.

Whitt opened the door as she sealed up another bag of giveaways.

"I'm Special Agent Alex LeBlanc with the FBI. Is Stacy Broussard here?"

7

ALEX STARED INTO THE FACE of a gray-eyed boy who stood in the doorway of Stacy Broussard's residence. Her background hadn't indicated a son, but this kid wasn't budging. "I stopped at her clinic and saw it was locked up for the day."

"Is this about her airport ranger work?" the boy said. "Or finding a dead man?"

"Both. Is she available that I can speak to her?"

"Do you have ID?"

Alex pulled out his creds and handed them to him. "Is Dr. Broussard here?"

He didn't look up from examining Alex's identification. "This looks in order." He returned the ID. "She's been through enough for one day. Try contacting her during business hours. The clinic's website has her e-mail and phone number."

Was this kid legit? He didn't look over ten years old. "I understand your wanting to shelter Dr. Broussard from the trauma she experienced this morning, but my visit is important to solving a crime."

The kid crossed his arms over his chest and took a bully pose, rather comical. "If you think for one minute I consider this a gregarious house call, you've misjudged me."

Gregarious?

Stacy leaned in behind him and placed a hand on his shoulder. "It's okay. I'll talk to Agent LeBlanc. Today was tragic, and I need to help in any way I can."

"Are you sure? Unless he has a warrant, you have rights."

"I can handle it," she said.

The kid backed away. Stacy's slender figure now blocked the door, easier on the eyes than her self-proclaimed bodyguard. She wore clean jeans and boots—must be her standard attire. "Thank you," Alex said. "I won't take much of your time." He'd get this done and head home. "I attempted to call you."

"I turned my phone off."

"That's why I couldn't get an answer. I owe you an apology."

"You did so earlier today." She studied him with eyes that seemed to smolder a darker blue in the shadows. Then a playful smile danced on her lips. "Is this apology for your blatant lack of professionalism in the interview, insulting the airport rangers, or not staying with an injured dog until I returned?"

He disagreed with two of her complaints. Babysitting a dog wasn't in his job description, especially when he was staring down a murder and potential domestic terrorism. Neither did he believe in the airport ranger program.

"Which is it?" she said.

"All three. You could have been killed today, which would have meant two murders. And I'm sorry about abandoning the dog, but my partner and I were working the investigation."

She sighed. "The incident's over, and I accept your apologies. My pride and shock are a nasty mix. How is Mr. Howe's widow?"

He paused. "Grieving. Her parents and rabbi are with her."

She leaned against the doorframe. "The gripping reality of love is while the giver is free to embrace its joy, the chains of hurt bind tighter than any pain known to the soul."

A poet? "It fits her. Who wrote that?"

"I did."

A twinge of admiration swirled in him. She possessed a sensitivity not many women offered freely. "Well done. When I interview her rabbi, may I share those words?"

"That would be fine. If the situation is appropriate, I'd like to express my sympathy to Mrs. Howe, perhaps through her rabbi."

"I'll see what I can do and e-mail you with the response." He peered behind her in an effort to avoid the strange feelings she brought out in him, a peculiar familiarity that drew him back to his roots. "How's the dog?"

The kid snickered, breaking Alex's scrutiny of the feelings he had around the woman. "We named her Xena, and she's recuperating," the boy said. "Doing well."

He glanced at the yellow Lab with its bandaged left front paw. The dog wagged its tail as if to show she was in a happy place. "How bad was she hurt?"

"Straight cut that required a few stitches. She'll be fine."

"Can I pet her?"

"Have her sniff your hands first," Stacy said. "So far she's been gentle, Agent LeBlanc."

"Forget the formalities. I'm Alex."

"And I'm Stacy. My partner's name is Whitt McMann."

The kid narrowed his gaze. "Miss Stacy is like my mom, so watch it."

He hid a grin. "Yes, sir. My intentions are honorable."

She stepped aside for Alex to enter her home, and they walked to where the dog lay. He knelt with an outstretched hand. When she nuzzled against him, he stroked her head. Despite the day's ordeal, the dog seemed to be thriving in Stacy's care.

"Does she belong to the man I found? A scan confirmed no microchip implant," she said.

"No, and Mrs. Howe stated none of her neighbors own a dog matching Xena's description."

"Do you find it odd that the man holding her leash was riding a motorcycle?"

He caught her deep-blue gaze. "Yes, I do."

"I'm sure you'll get it all resolved. I can keep the Lab until her owner turns up. Can't imagine anyone abandoning such a beautiful animal." She bent beside Alex. "Looks like she's forgiven you too."

A timer went off and her attention flew to an open kitchen. "Whitt, would you stir the pot?"

"Yes, ma'am," the kid said.

Alex's stomach loudly protested its lack of lunch and dinner.

"Has it been a long day?" Her full lips curled into the same enticing smile. She'd probably offer him Kibbles 'n Bits.

"Yeah."

"Leads or an arrest?"

"Gathering intel and asking questions."

She laughed softly. "Your specialty."

He ignored the barb and stroked Xena. Genuinely friendly. "Do I smell gumbo?"

"You do."

"Scratch?"

"Is there any other way? I'd invite you for a bowl, but it has another hour to simmer."

"I can wait." It had to be as tasty as it smelled. "Ah, reminders of home, the *joie de vivre*, joy of life."

She tilted her head as though deliberating his request. "I'd chat, but we're getting ready for a community carnival tomorrow."

"I saw the flyer on the clinic door. I could help."

"We don't have a clown if you want to volunteer." There was the dancing smile again.

"I had that one coming."

"Alex, I believe you're wanting to interrogate me further and in my own home. What would your mawmaw say?"

He cringed at the thought of what his grandmother wouldn't say but do. "I'm starved. If a question pops up, I'll warn you."

"How gracious." Her tone indicated she didn't believe him. "I won't turn away an extra hand, even from a man who's yanking my chain."

Whitt peered up from stirring the pot. "Taking in another stray, Miss Stacy?"

Alex laughed. "You two have to be related."

"Nah," Whitt said. "I'm a neighbor and help out at the clinic."

Alex made his way to the stove and breathed in the aroma of spices and the reminders of home, specifically the cooking. "And you made it in a cast-iron pot."

"Dutch oven. My grandmother says it's the only way to make gumbo. She said God gave man Jesus to redeem their sins and gumbo to redeem their stomachs."

He laughed. "Mine would agree." He took inventory of the modest home, decorated in off-white furnishings that looked like someone had beaten them with a chain. She liked fake flowers and green things. And bird nests.

"What is it you want to know? Ask me nicely, help us finish with these bags, move a few items into my truck so I can pull it halfway into the garage, and I'll make sure you don't leave with an empty stomach."

"You drive a hard bargain, but okay." Something about the woman intrigued him, and it was more than those cute freckles on her nose and cheeks.

She handed him a plastic bag and pointed to the items on the kitchen counter. "Question one?"

"Has anyone contacted you about the crimes?"

She glanced at Whitt and frowned, but he waved her away. "Miss Stacy, you're not in the presence of a child unless you mean the guy in the sport coat packing a Glock."

Alex stuffed a brochure into a bag. "Are you always such a wise guy?"

"Yep." He grinned. "I'm twelve and have an IQ higher than most of my teachers. No, I don't want to be recruited into the FBI. I'm going to be a vet or a shrink. Haven't decided."

What had Alex gotten himself into?

"Whitt, behave yourself," she said. "I received calls from the *Houston Chronicle* and Channel 5. I declined them. That's when I turned off my phone. Now I have a question. Why am I now the only witness to Todd Howe's murder? Can I have the statement retracted to say I'm simply the woman who discovered the body? You'd mentioned the FBI issuing a press release."

She had a point. "Our press release will go out around seven thirty tonight. But I admit the first media report sticks in the public's mind. I'll do my best to clear it up."

"I'm not ready to be the next victim."

"Let me know if you're threatened."

"Great." Whitt huffed. "The FBI won't ensure her security after her name's smacked across the media? Does it matter she refuses to own a gun?"

Alex turned to the kid. "I understand your wanting to make sure she's safe."

"I'm looking out for her well-being, which you can't do unless she's been threatened, beaten, or killed."

Stacy clasped both hands on the kitchen counter. "Stop it, you two. The crime will be solved, and I'll be fine. I have more important things on my mind than someone thinking I saw a murder. Question two?"

"We'd like to have the clothes you wore today for blood traces."

She raised a brow. "Really. They're in the laundry. My boots have traces of horse manure."

Whitt chuckled, but Alex refused to glare at him. Puberty at its finest. "May I have them?"

She nodded. "Why not? They smell and have Xena's blood on them. Guess you're looking for DNA, which means I'm your leading suspect. Thrills. Question three?"

"Is there anything you haven't told me? Like frequenting a Green-to-Go restaurant?"

"Never been to one. Question four?"

"Do you own a handgun?"

"Whitt just told you I don't do guns. I carry a pocketknife, which you have. Question five?"

"No more questions. I'm ready to load your truck."

After squeezing what Alex believed had to be half the carnival supplies into the back of Stacy's truck, he washed up while she ladled gumbo with potato salad into huge bowls and set a plate of hot corn bread on the table.

"This is like home," he said. Even if he had to work for it. "Thanks."

Her spoon rested in the bowl, and her fingers wrapped around a glass of iced tea. Preoccupied with what? The crime or something else?

She shook her head. "Incredible."

He didn't get it and tossed her a quizzical stare.

"Consider today," she said. "Everything about it is insane, and now you're eating gumbo in my kitchen when I should have tossed you out on your rear."

He chuckled, but reality hit, and his gut twisted like an angry gator. The media's declaration that she was the only witness to Todd Howe's murder could put her life in danger. She was wading through a murky swamp. . . . Killers and domestic terrorists played for keeps.

8

ALEX FOUND HIS MANNERS, thanked Stacy for dinner, and helped clean up before leaving her home.

The media coordinator at Houston's FBI issued a press release about the morning's crime, and the report would be aired again on the ten o'clock news. It announced the FBI and HPD had formed a task force regarding Howe's murder and the quadcopter, labeling the case as possible domestic terrorism. Fortunately, the release indicated Stacy had found the body and nothing more.

Stacy had given him an earful about the merits of airport rangers. She'd marched into the volunteers' arena and waved her banner of citizen's pride and the number of drug busts attributed to the organization. She neither raised her voice nor embellished the facts, and he'd researched the group prior to knocking on her door.

"I'm proud to serve my city," she'd said. "I've been a part of the volunteer program for six years. And it was far better for me to ride into that scene today with Todd Howe's body than a drug addict who'd have stolen his clothes for a hit of cocaine."

"I won't argue any further about it, but you know where I stand. We could have found both your bodies today. The person operating that quadcopter was on a mission, a deadly one."

They'd sprinkled Cajun, the lifestyle, relatives, and great dogs into the conversation. He enjoyed her company, although Whitt tossed him poisonous darts all evening. Alex would have to increase his vocabulary to keep up with him. Just when the kid sounded his age, he'd use a ten-dollar word.

"What do your parents do for a living?" Alex had said.

A strange look passed over the kid's face as though he'd been caught stealing. "Whatever is necessary. They aren't home right now. Miss Stacy's often my babysitter."

Alex simply nodded. Earlier he'd observed her neighborhood had far too many abandoned properties, weed-infested yards, junk cars, repossessions, and broken windows. A handful of homes were the exception, as though defying the others. Stacy's brick ranch fell into the responsible category with upkeep and landscaping. He admired her willingness to rally the community with a carnival.

Once inside his Jeep, he pressed in Ric's number. Background noise reminded him that his partner was attending a family birthday party.

"Hey, bro," Ric said. "Hold on a minute. I want to take this outside. Do you have an update?"

"I suppose." Alex used his hands-free device and drove away from the curb before Ric got back to him. "Just came from Stacy Broussard's."

"Did you eat crow?"

"Gumbo. The real thing, straight out of my mawmaw's kitchen. And yes, I apologized. I doubt she's a suspect. She brought up the media naming her as a witness, but that was retracted by our office." Alex relayed the conversation. "Media has said nothing about a composite drawing or a suspect, so that's to her benefit."

"The estimated time of death is between five thirty and six this morning. She made the 911 call at 6:47. If whoever controlled the quadcopter and killed Howe reads the full report, he'll realize she's not a threat."

"I'll text her when we've finished and give her your insight."

"Is she afraid?"

"Body language showed some fear, but she denied it."

"Any leads on the second man?"

"His shoe size is a 12½ wide. No match with Howe. Did you see the Lab?"

Alex stared at the dark street. "She's doing fine. No ID chip. Can't be a stray with the circumstances."

"How did the dog get there? And if it belonged to the killer, why leave the dog behind?"

"We'll have the fingerprint and blood analysis in the morning. See what we have on file. And I have Stacy's clothes for DNA testing. The blood on her clothes is probably the dog's or even a trace of Howe's, but I want to be sure. One more thing," Alex said. "Her clinic is hosting a carnival tomorrow afternoon. I'm going to show up. Might offer to help."

"Thought you didn't believe she was involved?"

What were his conclusions? He liked the woman, was attracted to her striking blue eyes and dark hair. Her smile was incredible, but something about her mannerisms seemed off. "Remember the case we had a few years ago when our prime witness committed the crime?"

"Don't tell me you're still beating yourself up over that witness, bro. This isn't the same scenario."

"Dexter said pretty much the same thing today. Told me to move on. I promised myself I'd never be used like that again, especially by a woman. Today's crime has mastermind stamped on it. If the quadcopter was scheduled to blind a pilot and take down an aircraft, then the area had been staked out to ensure success, which should have occurred before she got there." His mind settled on the potential of hundreds of people meeting their death. "The airport rangers use the trail every Saturday morning. So did Stacy figure into the plan?"

"What about Todd Howe?"

"He's our variable. Howe either found himself at a crime scene while taking a morning ride, or he had a hand in something that went south. My gut tells me Stacy and Howe are innocent, but I've got to keep an open mind."

9

STACY WOKE EARLY SUNDAY MORNING. Sleep should have evaded her. Instead, exhaustion had drawn her into a perfect dreamworld, no nightmares about finding Todd Howe's body or a drone chasing her. Or the unexpected visit by Alex LeBlanc. The verdict on him balanced on a scale with his Louisiana charm on one side and his irritating opinion of airport rangers on the other. But he had called instead of texting about his partner's thoughts that she wasn't in danger. Nice gesture.

She glanced at the clock—5:30. Ten more minutes . . . The scent of coffee wafted from the kitchen, luring her to grab a robe.

Whitt had brewed a pot of coffee. What a sweet boy. Would he one day call her Mom? This neighborhood grew worse by the day. She'd been looking for a home and clinic site in a top-notch school district. Whitt deserved a fresh start, new home and school. With God's help, she could learn the mothering thing.

He must have heard her coming down the hall because a mug

filled to the brim and laced with cream sat on the counter. He grinned, a sofa pillow imprint on his cheek. She ruffled his bedhead hair. Was it wrong to love someone else's child and want him for her own? If so, she was guilty. She shoved aside a deep longing to hold him close. With what she'd read about twelve-year-old boys and their changing bodies and minds, she certainly didn't want to approach him as anything but a mother figure. When the adoption was final, she'd hug him long and hard.

"You're spoiling me," she said.

"After last night's dinner? You're crazy." He sobered. "You've been there for me when I was alone. You've encouraged me to be more, do more, and not be a product of my environment. You claim God has a purpose for me and urged me to not settle for less. Yeah, you push a few of my buttons, but it's for my own good." He wiped a dribble of coffee from the counter. "You don't make fun of me when I cry."

Stacy wanted him to have friends his own age. He hid behind his intelligence and humor, afraid other kids would find out the truth about his home life. Because of his small stature, he'd become the target of too many kids. In God's timing his life would improve. . . . Perhaps she could afford a Christian school, as long as it offered advanced classes. For that matter, she'd need to enroll in Christian parenting classes.

She carried her mug to Xena and examined the dog's paw. No swelling. Had to be a positive sign for the busy day ahead.

"Let me shower, and I'll make French toast and bacon."

He gave her a thumbs-up. "We should take Xena with us today. Neither of us wants to come home and find she's been suffering or eaten everything that is and isn't esculent."

"I agree, and we can keep an eye on her. The kids will love her. Do you think she could handle the petting zoo?"

"I'll keep her separate from the other dogs and not leave her alone. Gives me something to do." He sat beside Xena. "You know, having the FBI guy here last night was weird. What's up with that?"

She couldn't quite label the emotion in his voice. "He's doing his job, I guess. The crime is serious and unsolved unless there were new developments while we slept."

"Maybe he thinks you're hot," he said.

"He's not my type. Too opinionated. We won't see him again."

A car horn blared and Whitt groaned. When it didn't let up, he hurried to the door. "The parents are home and Dad's probably inebriated. Must have passed out on the horn again."

The child in him was hurting, when raw emotions surfaced and he couldn't use his mind to soothe his heart. "I'm coming with you," she said, grabbing her phone. The last time Whitt tried to get his drunken parents into the house, his dad blacked his eye. Time to call the police and pray social services didn't hear of it until he was officially placed in her care.

Whitt's attention swung to the time—6:05 on a Sunday morning? He opened Miss Stacy's front door to the ear-blasting sound belonging to his parents' battered Ford parked in his driveway. A screaming guitar from the eighties penetrated his skull. Paint-scraped dents, a broken passenger window covered with duct tape, and a dangling fender reminded him of the many times his dad had driven home high and out of control. He never let Mom drive, even when he was in worse condition. At least the car contained a new battery, courtesy of Whitt.

Whitt made his way to the driver's side, his insides burning at the thought of his scumbag parents. Why couldn't they drink at home? Dad's bloated cheek flattened the horn, mouth agape.

Totally out. Whitt glanced into the backseat for Mom's curled-up, undernourished body. Not there. Maybe she was in the house.

At least no one was driving by or walking the streets this early to spread the news. He hated it when word got out. The other kids were the worst. As if their houses didn't have secrets. Most of them didn't wear the battle scars like he did.

He jerked on the car door, ignoring its groans and Miss Stacy's pleas to let her help him. Pity was another thing he despised, and when he felt like this, his mind swirled with inadequacy.

"Whitt, you aren't alone," she said.

Her light scent of peach met his nostrils, fresh and new, representing how life should be. A home . . . A family . . . What was wrong with him that he'd been given this loser's hand? He used to dream about the parents cleaning up their dirt, but no longer.

He turned off the radio, then touched his dad's shoulder. The big man didn't budge. "Dad, the horn's waking the neighborhood."

He shoved an elbow into Whitt's chest and cursed. "Leave me alone. Have a little respect for a man's privacy."

Whitt rubbed where Dad's elbow hit him.

"Whitt," Stacy said.

"I got this." He tried to lift Dad's head and breathed in a whiff of his breath, reeking of booze and garlic. A syringe and hypo needle had been tossed to the floorboard of the passenger side. Even an idiot could figure out this scenario. "Get up or someone will call the cops."

"Touch me again, and I'll kill ya. You—"

What should he do? Would this work for or against the custody hearing? "Wish I had the fifty grand they wanted from you."

"Wait a minute. They told you about the money?" Miss Stacy said.

"Of course. Mom wanted me to apply a little pressure, see if you'd come through with the cash."

"I'm sorry," she said. "Never wanted you to find out."

"Look at it this way. Your attorney can use it to our advantage. The judge will think the parents can't be rehabilitated into the model mother and father."

Dad coughed. "When I get outta this car, I'm gonna beat you, boy, for talkin' family business."

"Whitt, I'm calling the police. He's violent, and you'll get hurt." Miss Stacy pressed in numbers on her phone. "This is Stacy Broussard. Ace McMann is passed out in his car. Yes, that's the horn." She gave the local precinct operator the address as if the cops hadn't been there enough times to have it memorized.

He bit back stinging tears, more embarrassed than afraid. Should he pick up the drug stuff? Dad would be furious later if he left it.

"Leave the evidence intact."

He whirled to face her. Had she read his mind? "Then what will happen?"

"Anything's better than this. My lawyer can use it to your benefit. You can't save them." Her words were kind, and he swallowed the familiar lump in his throat. "Your parents have to make their own decisions."

Whitt turned back to his dad in time to dodge a beefy hand. "Stop it. I'm trying to help."

"How will you explain a black eye to the police?" she said, her tone soft. The voice of truth.

He understood. No point in giving the authorities more ammo to stick him in a foster home. The horn blasted on. He opened the hood and disconnected the battery, his battery. He moved back to where Miss Stacy stood. Dad could get mean. "Where's Mom?"

"Caught workin' the street," his dad slurred. "Jail."

He sickened. Should have known on Thursday when she told Whitt if he wouldn't give her any money, she had no choice but to earn it.

"I'm sorry," Miss Stacy whispered. "I haven't forgotten the eviction notice. We'll get your things out of the house tonight after the carnival."

"Okay."

Days like this he wanted to escape this miserable life and run so far away no one would ever find him. Miss Stacy cared . . . talked to him like he had sense. Made sure he had decent food, clean clothes, and was given the positive feedback a kid needed. But even if she was awarded custody, the parents would still be across the street playing their addictive games and still sucking the life out of him and dragging Stacy into the consequences of their habits. They'd get someone to pay the rent—they always played on the sympathies of some poor fool. Waiting until high school graduation seemed like forever. Being on his own seemed even longer. What choices were there? Between the laws for the welfare of underage kids and the downhill spiral his parents were taking, he knew where this was headed.

If he could only fix the mess.

Sirens rose in the early morning air. The familiar drill. Closing the car door, he bolted toward Miss Stacy's home. Cops couldn't dump him into social services' lap if he wasn't around when they arrived.

10

ALEX SMACKED THE ALARM BUTTON on his phone as though it were a clock. Some called Sunday a day of divine rest, but he hadn't done the church thing since leaving Louisiana. A round of golf or sleeping until noon suited him better. . . .

Another day. This one had a to-do list a mile long.

Within moments, he'd ground coffee beans. Adrenaline pumped high. The pressure to end this case came the hardest from himself. Always did. The satisfaction kept him alive, excited. His mind whirled with the e-mail notifications that had wakened him in the early morning hours. He, as well as other agents, had received documents regarding domestic terrorist groups and extremists with fingerprints on stealing a drone or taking down public transportation. Of specific interest were militia extremists. Bulletins about the investigation hit law enforcement across the nation, and every airport in the country was on heightened alert.

Last night he requested Todd Howe's college records and past employment from the FIG. Agents in Dallas had interviewed his sister and learned she'd broken contact with him when he'd sold their deceased parents' home without her knowledge and invested the funds in the restaurant business. She had an alibi for Saturday morning.

Interviews with Howe's neighbors had started yesterday afternoon with nothing reported but shock and dismay from those who claimed to know him well. Todd held the man-of-the-year award from everyone the agents talked to, but Alex would reserve his opinion for now. Today and tomorrow agents would meet with his employees and add their testimonies to the mix. By then, they'd have his business and personal financials and his wife's background. Alex and Ric would take their findings and follow up if necessary.

As he reached for a mug to pour coffee, another e-mail sounded from his phone. Snatching it, he noted the update included the origin of the Army's missing quadcopter. Fort Benning had an ongoing investigation on the drone's whereabouts. To date, no one had been charged.

This day wouldn't start until he took it by the horns, and he hurried to the shower, carrying his mug of coffee.

Alex and Ric had an appointment with the Howes' rabbi this afternoon, a first for Alex. Would the rabbi stand up for Howe and his wife? He expected no less.

Water from the shower poured over him, hot and therapeutic. Last night the judge okayed an order to secure the Howes' cell phone records, which had Alex's attention for later on. Today's demands focused on the fingerprint sweep and the results of blood samples at the crime scene. And a trip to a carnival. He paused in his thoughts. Was he seizing a moment to see her? A part of him was concerned about the initial media report that claimed she was a witness. And she could have lied about what she knew about the case. Ah, but he didn't think so.

Two cups of coffee pumped caffeine into his veins, and two frozen sausage breakfast sandwiches warmed to perfection filled his stomach. The clock on the microwave displayed a respectable time, so he phoned the lab for the fingerprint and blood reports.

Moments later he sent the findings to Ric. The only fingerprints on the motorcycle were Todd Howe's, and the quadcopter had nothing identifying. Howe's body held dog hair and blood, probably his and the dog's. What were the chances the dog hair held the other person's DNA? He pressed in Stacy's number.

"Good morning, Alex. You caught me before I left for church."

"Have you bathed Xena?"

"Strange question, but no. I washed the wounded area when I treated her. Why?"

"I need a snip of her fur."

"I can retrieve some. Put it in a baggie."

"Perfect. Will you keep it with you? I'll stop by the carnival and pick it up." Now he had a professional reason to see her.

"Okay." She didn't sound happy, and he'd hoped after last night they could be friends.

The call completed, Alex checked off two items on his list. His phone buzzed with a text from Ric.

What time's the carnival?

2–6. I'm going @3. Wanna meet me there?

K. Send the address. B nice 2 Stacy.

Alex ignored him. **Don't 4get our appt with Rabbi Feldman after.**

K

A lot of hours between now and then. Alex left his apartment, a complex designed for professionals that contained shopping, restaurants, and medical facilities within walking distance. He exited onto Highway 290 and drove southeast to the FBI office. First on his agenda were the cell phone records, comparing numbers and matching them with names. The day stacked up to be a long one.

After an outdoor service in the clinic's parking lot, Stacy and Whitt helped stack chairs in preparation for the afternoon carnival. The church hour had consisted of a local nondenominational pastor delivering a message on the importance of walking with God, a guitar player who had a decent voice but sang through his nose, and twenty-one of the subdivision's residents chiming in with amens. Whatever the pastor had said bothered Whitt. She could feel him tuning out the message midway through the sermon. Difficult family situations had a way of pushing faith aside. She should know.

The sound of hammering and laughter surrounded them while booths and banners sprang up announcing games and activities.

"Thanks," Whitt finally said.

"For what?" But she knew. His intelligence continued to war with his emotions when it came to his parents.

"Are you going to make me say it?"

"What do you think? Express exactly what you're feeling." Her methods of raising him might be questioned by a psychologist, but she believed in facing challenges head-on. The sooner he learned how to manage them, the more successful he'd be tomorrow and the next day.

He stacked two chairs atop hers. "I hate my mom and dad, and I have no problem admitting it after church. If Jesus had been forced to endure my parents as His own, He'd have run from the cross. Forgiveness is a concept I can accept for people I don't know. Everything about the parents, who they are and what they do, is selfish. They never wanted me, per their words, and when I don't give them money, they are . . ." He stopped.

Stacy peered at him. "Keep going. I can handle it. God can too."

"He's going to send a bolt of lightning."

She stared up at the cloudless sky. "Then we'll both get zapped." She didn't agree with his hatred for his parents, but she accepted his feelings considering what they'd done to him. One of the hardest concepts to learn about God was that He understood hurt and grief.

"Every time they're gone, I hope they never come back." He blew out a ragged breath. "I want them to overdose, kill themselves. The only reason I tried to get Dad out of the car was so the neighbor kids wouldn't use it against me."

"Are you angry with me for calling the police?"

"Nah. Saved me from a punch in the face."

"Be honest, Whitt."

His eyes met hers, and she saw the well of hurt for one so young. She ached to see the pain removed.

"You are my real mom," he said. "Not always my friend 'cause you put my needs first. I might not like the police sirens in the neighborhood telling the world of the parents' stupidity, but I know it's because you care. I only hope today is the last time I have to deal with them." His face grew splotchy, and he hastily swiped beneath his eyes.

He spoke like an adult, yet his heart and soul needed to heal. "My lawyer believes we have a solid case," she said. "Before the court hearing, he'll need to ask you questions, and a caseworker from social services will be involved. The same woman you've dealt with before."

"She makes me want to throw up. I'm changing the conversation here. Nothing I can do about what I was stuck with anyway."

"What do you want to talk about?"

"I did some online searches last night about drone operators using laser beams to blind pilots," he said.

"How late were you up?" She shook her head. "Never mind. What have you learned?"

"According to the Associated Press, it's not unusual. The guys doing it think it's a joke. Arrests and fines haven't stopped them. The AP says they weren't terrorism actions, but you know me. I believe the stats are more on the other side. I'll send you my research sites."

"Okay. And we'll discuss this after I've analyzed the reports."

He grinned. "Let's get this carnival thing going, or we'll both still be here trying to figure out what happened yesterday."

Shortly before two, families trickled into the parking lot, now transformed into a carnival. A rental company erected a blow-up jump event for the kids. Pony rides were a new addition as well as the volunteer petting zoo. Animal owners were asked to stay with their pets for others to admire and touch. Whitt never moved from Xena's side. He demonstrated to families how to approach the dog, and they listened. Stacy's favorite twin girls imitated his careful instruction while taking turns holding their cocker spaniel's leash. Such cute little blondes. They'd be at the clinic this week. Meanwhile Stacy handed out the plastic bags and attempted to push aside the weekend's tragedies.

Mr. Parson limped her way. He offered a full-toothed smile, an updated version from the previous year's carnival. Dear man, loved kids and animals. Those traits made him a near-perfect human being.

"Afternoon, Dr. Stacy," he said, removing his ball cap. "Got ourselves a scorcher today."

"Sure do. Have you been keeping hydrated? Are you over the pneumonia? It's only been two weeks."

He patted his cap. "Yes, ma'am, to both questions. The heat will sweat out any that's left. I'm gonna mosey on over to Whitt. I see you have a new patient."

"Yes, a sweet Lab. They'll both want to see you." She handed him two bottles of water. "One for you and one for Whitt."

"I'll be here in the morning, the highlight of my day. Is the little tabby doing okay after his surgery?"

"He is."

"I'll bring your favorite blueberry muffins."

"Oh, thank you." She hooked her arm through his. "Let me introduce you to Xena."

Together they walked to the petting zoo. He went through the getting-to-know-you routine with Xena. The dog reached up and licked him on the mouth. Stacy laughed. This had turned out to be a memorable day, even with the obnoxious McMann using every foul word known to man when the police arrested him.

Then she saw Special Agents Alex LeBlanc and Ric Price walking her way. Why did one irritating man have to look so good?

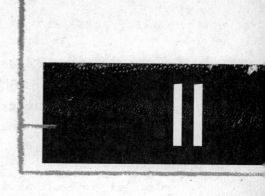

ALEX FAILED TO CATCH A WELCOMING SMILE from Stacy, and it bothered him. A twinge of rejection poked at his ego. He thought they were friends.

"She's not happy to see you, bro," Ric said. "Maybe she goes for the tall, dark, and handsome type. Non-Cajun. Or the older man keeping her company."

"I'm not here to impress." He donned his sunglasses in the glaring sun, but he hadn't missed the woman wearing boots and jeans.

"Ah, spoken by a man who's been rejected by a beautiful woman. Shall I show you how to win her over?"

"No thanks. I can handle Stacy on my own."

Their phones alerted them to an incoming text. Early interviews with four of Howe's restaurant managers indicated their boss insisted upon long hours without pay. In the past three years, each Green-to-Go had seen a new manager every eleven months or less. No stats were available yet on nonmanagement employee turnover.

"Conflicts lead to motive," Alex said, dropping his phone back into the pocket of his khakis. "How many of them hated Todd Howe's guts and wanted to bring down an aircraft?"

"That's a slim list. His managers despised him, but potential terrorism is a stretch. I'll make sure there's a priority on personnel backgrounds."

"Appreciate it. We need evidence to clear up this case. We'll need to talk to some of the employees."

"Right. I'll request the interviews, and we'll look at them later."

"I think our talk with the rabbi will be . . . interesting."

Ric nodded toward Stacy. "She's meeting us head-on."

"Stubborn Cajun," he muttered. But cute.

Ric snickered and held out his hand to her. She took it and smiled. So she had a favorite.

"Agent Price and Agent LeBlanc, this is a dear friend, Mr. Parson," she said. "He helps me out at the clinic."

"My pleasure, gentlemen." White hair peeked out from under a ball cap. "I'll mosey on over to the snow cones."

The older man limped away. Had to be in his nineties.

"What brings you here?" she said. "Gumbo? Oh, that's right. You want a sample of Xena's fur." She pulled a small plastic bag from her jean pocket and handed it to him.

"Thanks. Your carnival has drawn a crowd," Alex said.

"It's the subdivision's event, not mine." She gestured around the parking lot. "Volunteers work hard to ensure the families have a great time."

Alex refused to state the obvious—the small subdivision hit the bottom rung of lower middle class with more than its fair share of abandoned properties and foreclosures. Keeping the residents united contributed to a slash in the crime rate. At least on paper it looked doable.

When had he gotten so cynical? This afternoon families were supporting each other, an admirable trait.

"Would you like your face painted, Alex? Mickey Mouse or a dragon?" she said. "How about taking a seat on the dunking board?"

"Ma'am, he doesn't know how to swim unless a gator's after him," Ric said.

She leveled her sights on Alex, more like a challenge, but he caught a playful smile. "So why are you here?"

"Update on the case. Thought you'd be interested."

"You caught the killer?"

"We wish. Haven't made an arrest regarding the drone either. But we have the fingerprint and blood spatter results. Thought you might like to hear firsthand."

"You could have called or e-mailed, but I appreciate the personal touch."

Not a trace of sarcasm. He must have gained a point. "The only prints at the scene are Todd Howe's, and the blood belonged to him or the Lab. The DNA report takes longer, but I doubt if we have further questions for you."

"Perfect, since I've answered the same ones a half-dozen times. Xena will be happy to hear that she's been exonerated from the crime." The sun glistened off her lightly tanned face. "Last night's press release from the FBI helped me to sleep easier. Thanks."

Alex's sunglasses hid his burst in ego. "Glad I'm back in your good graces."

She lifted a brow. "I said 'the FBI.' Haven't figured you out yet. By the way, next Saturday I'll be riding the trails again and hoping all I find is a beer can. Airport rangers and the manager of the stables have promised to take a switch to me if I ever attempt a solo ride again."

"Smart friends. How's Xena?"

She whirled to where a crowd of children encircled a pen. "Very well. Bouncing back like a princess warrior. Whitt has her with the kids if you'd like to see for yourself."

"Sure," Alex said. "She's our only witness. Don't imagine you're a dog whisperer?"

"Not yet." She turned to Ric. "Why does your partner do all the talking?"

Ric lifted a brow. "Because I'm the brains. Can't have both."

She laughed and searched Alex's face. "So Ric communicates like Whitt?"

"Ric doesn't send me to the dictionary. The kid's brilliant." His dealings with the kid flashed across his mind. "Let me say hello to him and Xena before we leave."

"Stay the afternoon. We're having a softball game later. Plenty of food and drinks."

Crazy, but he actually wanted to hang around. "We have interviews, but thanks."

After checking in on Xena and having Whitt ignore him, Alex and Ric walked through the crowd before leaving.

Next stop was the temple, where Rabbi Feldman awaited them. A young woman led them to his office. The man wore a skullcap over graying hair, but he was minus the black hat and suit Alex believed was the general dress. He escorted Alex and Ric to his darkened office and opened the blinds to reveal one ancient artifact after another.

Ric studied a glass display case of antique oil lamps, an assortment of sizes and shapes. "I assume many trips to Israel?" he said.

"Three times a year." Rabbi Feldman beamed. "Gentlemen, take a look at the treasures unearthed below Jerusalem." He led them to another long glass display case where plates, bowls, and wooden goblets rested on black velvet.

Alex bent to look at an etched goblet. "You have quite a collection here. Impressive."

"It's taken me over two decades, and I'm always looking for new pieces."

"Do you collect scrolls?" Ric said.

The man smiled. "Facsimiles only, but I have several."

Since when was Ric an Old Testament scholar?

"My great-grandmother on my father's side was Jewish. My dad has her journal. Interesting legacy."

"What a rich heritage," the rabbi said.

"Absolutely. I regret I can't read Hebrew, an endeavor I intend to accomplish one day."

"You'll not be disappointed. When you're ready, I can introduce you to a couple of fine teachers."

Alex had never heard about Ric's heritage. New respect for his friend and partner mounted. The rabbi pointed to volumes of books, old and new, that were stuffed into a floor-to-ceiling bookcase.

"This is amazing." Alex peered at the books, all in Hebrew. Many appeared too fragile to touch.

"Thank you, but you didn't come to admire my obsession with antiquity," he said. "Todd's unfortunate demise has many of us grieving. Sit down, gentlemen, and we'll discuss what's on your minds."

"The woman who found Mr. Howe's body would like to pass on her condolences to his wife. I have her phone number if you feel it's appropriate."

The rabbi nodded. "Yes, of course."

Alex handed him a slip of paper with Stacy's contact information and her quote about love.

After they were seated on brown leather chairs, the rabbi pulled one from behind his desk and took an unassuming pose. "You want to know my perspective?"

"Yes, sir," Alex said. "We're looking for his killer and could use your insight."

He studied his hands as though contemplating how to begin or possibly praying. "What I'm about to say is not news to Bekah, though she'd not offer anything derogatory about her husband. Neither would she lie." He paused. "If you should choose to talk to her further, form your questions carefully, and please wait until the seven days of mourning are over." He smiled. "We Jews protect those we love."

"Are you saying her husband abused her?" Alex said.

"Oh no." He waved away his response. "I'm talking about his business practices." Rabbi Feldman leaned back in his chair. "A man wants to support his family in the best way possible, but not at the expense of offering others a decent living or treating them humanly."

The man confirmed the earlier manager interviews. "We heard he went through managers frequently."

"All employees. To say the least. At times one of our youth would apply for work, but it never lasted long."

"Can you give us specifics?"

He sighed. "My daughter worked for him until I asked her to quit. She didn't object."

Now he had Alex's attention. "What happened?"

"I'm speaking as a father. She was to work four hours on her first day. But when it came time for her to leave, Todd informed her of extra training which consisted of cleaning the women's and men's restrooms with a scrub brush until the areas met his approval. That was the first night. The second night, she was told to stay after closing to clean and disinfect the kitchen. The job took over two hours. The third night he told her the kitchen didn't meet his expectations from the previous night, and she had to clean it again. She called me. I picked her up. Todd refused to pay her for the extra hours, stating it was part of her training. My daughter said the other employees went through the same initiation."

"Do you think his business practices could have gotten him killed?"

"I'm not law enforcement. But the employee always had the option to quit. He paid minimum wage, and I understand he deducted bathroom breaks, chatting times, whatever he could." He smiled. "Trust me, I wanted to level him."

Not what Alex presumed from a rabbi. "Can't blame you."

"Is there anything else you can tell us?"

"Honestly, Agent LeBlanc and Agent Price, Todd was faithful in attendance and generous in giving of his time and money to the temple and his family. He may have weighed heavily on the scales of fair business practices, but nothing that I know of to warrant murder or a threat to airport safety. I assure you, he wasn't involved with terrorists."

12

MONDAY MORNING, shortly before 8 a.m., Alex met with Ric at the office. Reports flowed in from Todd Howe's friends' and neighbors' interviews while updated information on known extremists garnered their attention, but nothing concrete surfaced.

Ric took a long drink of coffee. "The murder and stolen quad-copter have sent us scattering in opposite directions, sort of like roaches when the lights flip on."

Alex nodded slowly. "Todd Howe, Stacy Broussard, a downed quadcopter, and a stray dog simmering on low until they blend together into something that makes sense."

He chuckled. "Gumbo on Saturday night made roux of your brains. Or is it the woman?"

Maybe the latter added spice, but he'd not let his partner know. "Everything about her, including college and work history, seems legit."

"Here's my theory. Stacy doesn't have a scratch on her. Whoever was behind the drone and murdered Todd hightailed it out of there without cleaning up their mess."

"Let's dig deeper to see if he had connections to Fort Benning. So far, their investigation hasn't revealed who stole their quadcopter. Low priority until we started digging."

Ric finished a breakfast bar and tossed the wrapper in the trash. "The Army's CID will be a driving force now that we're involved. But we need who's responsible now." Dark eyes peered into his. "Todd Howe looks like an innocent victim, but what sticks in my mind is that he rode into a restricted area. Was it random or did he have business there?"

Alex weighed his words. "The case is homegrown domestic terrorism, but I have another thought. Military extremists are usually anti-Semitic."

Ric ran his fingers through shortly cropped hair. "People can always be bought. And note he's dead. If I understand anything, it's prejudice. We'll see who's right when arrests are made."

"My focus has been on Bekah and Todd Howe—their backgrounds. Both are clean at this point. Our victim was a restaurant owner, ambitious and despised by his employees. Nothing in his records indicates unlawful activities. The only derogatory info we have on him are his managers' and Rabbi Feldman's testimonies."

"But motive could be there. People have killed for less," Ric said. "Financials are in order. Nothing suspicious for the past ten years. What else do you have?"

"I examined the Howes' cell phone records. Bekah's calls are okay. None of Todd's have our attention. Go figure, though. He'd left his phone at home on Saturday morning, and his contacts and calendar information have been erased. However, his phone records didn't raise anything suspicious, which makes me wonder why he erased them. To protect himself or his family?"

"Hard to say. He could have been having an affair," Ric said. "His business calls will take a few days to sort out. What's up for this morning?"

"One of the Green-to-Go managers has my attention." Alex positioned his computer screen for Ric to see. "Todd liked to party without his wife. This was posted by one of his managers who works at a Green-to-Go located around the corner from his office on San Felipe."

Ric took a look at Todd toasting a scantily clad blonde in what appeared to be a bedroom. "Bekah misjudged her husband." He glanced up. "Or maybe she knew about his extracurricular activities. Anything in her background or her parents' that we missed?"

"I didn't read anything but grief. Early this morning, I had her parents checked out, and they're clean."

"I'll spin a few cycles on this, but Saturday has more stamped on it than a Jewish boy who liked to party and met up with a bullet."

Alex nodded. "Believe me, I'm right there with you."

An hour later, Alex and Ric entered the Green-to-Go restaurant on San Felipe, where the breakfast crowd still lingered over coffee. The female manager whose photo appeared on Facebook stood at the counter, blonde and built. She was talking to a young man taking orders, who wore a green T-shirt with the name of the restaurant in white letters.

Alex walked to the pair. He displayed his FBI creds. "I'm Special Agent Alex LeBlanc, and this is Special Agent Ric Price. We'd like to speak to Elle Vieson."

She tossed a skeptical look their way. "What about?"

"Todd Howe."

"I've already spoken to FBI agents. Don't you guys compare notes?"

That hit Alex's frustration button. "We do, but some interviews require extra attention."

She flushed red. "We're in the middle of a rush. Later would be more convenient."

"Ma'am," Ric said, "murders are never convenient, at least not for the victim. Perhaps due to the sensitivity of this conversation, it should be held in privacy."

His partner wasn't always so talkative, unless annoyed.

Ms. Vieson led them to a small office in the rear of the kitchen. Once inside, she closed the door. "Have a seat. I assume this is about the Facebook post?"

"Would you show Ms. Vieson the photo she posted early this morning?" Ric nodded at Alex, which meant he wanted to observe and analyze the woman's responses.

Alex swiped to it on his phone and turned the screen for her viewing. "Is this you?"

She swallowed hard. Slumped in her chair. "I didn't post this." She tapped the screen. "It is me, but it's not."

"Please explain your answer," Alex said.

She dabbed beneath her eyes and closed them with a sigh. "I'm mortified. The embarrassment is beyond anything I've ever experienced."

An old expression from his Cajun roots surfaced at her drama-queen antics: *C'est tracas comme ça tous les temps.* It meant she was a pain when they needed answers now.

"Agents, I deny having an affair with my boss. Todd Howe was insufferable, and I'd never lower myself to his level or help him cheat on his wife." She leaned across her desk, revealing plenty of cleavage. "The miserable excuse of a man loved his wife."

"Love and having an affair are two different things."

"Not with Todd. Demanding. Egotistical. Cheapskate. But not a womanizer."

"Your Facebook post says otherwise," Alex said.

"Anyone can stick pics up there and make them look like me. See for yourself. I outweigh her by fifteen pounds, and that's just above the waist."

Alex pulled up the pic again. The body shape didn't match. "Are you implying the pic was photoshopped?"

"Duh. Read my lips."

Alex flashed his anger. "Excuse me? We're investigating a man's murder."

She dragged her tongue over her lips and scooted back in her chair. "I apologize. Gentlemen, I'm a recovering alcoholic and the woman in the pic is holding a glass of booze. I have a boyfriend who is already giving me a hard time about this. I tried to delete the pic, but someone hacked into my account and everything is frozen. Facebook told me the problem would soon be resolved, and then I could remove it. I have an idea who posted it but no proof."

"Who?"

"A kid who works here. He's been bragging about hacking into computers and playing tricks on people."

"We'd like to talk to him."

"Please, I'd rather handle it. Once I have confirmation, I'll call you. Todd had as many enemies as friends, which I'm sure you've learned. But even then, this is an attack against Bekah, and she doesn't deserve the backlash."

"So you're a friend of Mrs. Howe's?"

Ms. Vieson shook her head. "Only by reputation. Sometimes she came in with Todd or just with the boys. Very much a lady. Drop-dead gorgeous too."

Alex glanced at Ric, who made notes. "You mentioned he had enemies. We'd like those names."

She held up both hands, palms out. "When the other agents were here, I didn't mention anything about Todd's enemies. The man's dead, and I don't plan to join him."

Ric cleared his throat. "This is in strict confidence, Ms. Vieson. If you believe you're in danger, we need to have the information before someone else is killed."

"He was horrible to work for. But I don't know of anyone who'd want him dead."

Ric continued the interview. "What do you mean, he was horrible to work for?"

She hesitated. Why? Afraid or massaging the truth?

"Demanding and always adding to the manager's workload. At first, he asked for details of how many customers showed up at every meal and separate numbers for breakfast, lunch, dinner, and the after-eight crowd. Then he had us break it down to men, women, and children. Last week he added how many customers requested refills on beverages and which beverages included water. Once a week I had to stay late to ensure inventory matched his ordering records. All the restaurants have considerable turnover. The wait-staff's trial period is filled with unreasonable extra hours. I've been here for six months waiting to apply for a restaurant opening down the street from where I live."

No surprise Howe's employees despised him.

"Thank you." Ric typed into his phone. "Anyone threaten to do him harm?"

"You don't give up, do you?" She snorted out a laugh. "We thought he should be put out of his misery, but nothing spoken. He paid a bonus to those who reported other employees not doing their job."

"Are you saying any employee could be a suspect?"

She pressed her lips together. "I suppose."

Ric turned to Alex. "Agent LeBlanc, what additional questions do you have for Ms. Vieson?"

He showed her a pic of Stacy on his cell phone. "Have you seen this woman?"

"No." Not a muscle moved to indicate deceit.

"Did Todd receive any visitors here or did anyone ever stop in and ask for him?"

She crossed her arms over her chest and appeared to ponder his question. "Other than an occasional vendor, I'd say no. His office is located around the corner, but you probably already know that."

"Do you have an interest in drones?" Alex said.

"Are you kidding? I work all the time."

"What about your boyfriend?"

Irritation seared her features. "The only hobby he has is me. What are you looking for?"

Alex smiled. "Are you or your boyfriend antigovernment?"

"Freedom of speech is guaranteed by the Constitution. I might complain about the current administration, but I'm not out to make a statement."

He reached into his jacket and placed a business card on her desk. "We've posed a number of questions, and we appreciate your cooperation. If you hear or see anything that can help us, please contact us immediately. Don't forget informing us of your findings about the Facebook post."

She nodded. "Am I a suspect?"

"Not at this time." Alex considered saying those who had motive were all under suspicion.

"I have an alibi. I was with my boyfriend." She jotted down a man's name and where they were when Todd was killed. "There is something more." She wrung her hands. "It's probably nothing. But Saturday night around midnight when I locked up to leave the restaurant, I saw a man standing on the corner facing Todd's office. I drove away, then circled back around. Not sure why, except I was suspicious after his death. The man had walked to the rear of Todd's office and was attempting to enter. I flashed my headlights, and he took off running."

"Did you see his face?"

She shook her head. "Wore a hoodie. He was a little overweight."

"Are there security cameras in the area?" Alex said.

"The one from Todd's office should have caught him. I can give you the security company's phone number." She opened her drawer and handed them a business card with the contact information.

"Thanks, Ms. Vieson. Appreciate your cooperation. We may ask you to identify the man."

"Whatever you need."

While Alex drove from the restaurant to the FBI office, Ric requested a search warrant for Green-to-Go's security footage. Some companies cooperated without the document, but they had the legal right to ask for it. Within the hour, they had the footage . . . of a man who'd successfully avoided the security cameras.

13

A MIDMORNING RAIN riddled the windows of Stacy's clinic as she typed the previous few days' activities into her computer. This way she had a journal with stats, including money spent on vendors for the carnival. The event had been fun but expensive. As much as she despised giving up on her subdivision, Whitt needed a safer place to live—so did she.

The time caught her attention. She should have contacted her attorney by now. Using the clinic's landline, she phoned Leonard Nardell.

"Mr. Nardell, this is Stacy Broussard. I have new information regarding the custody hearing." She relayed the eviction notice for today and Mrs. McMann's arrest for prostitution. She continued with Ace McMann's early Sunday morning episode and arrest. "Do you have a court date?"

"We do. Looks like a week from Wednesday, 9 a.m. at the family court building on Congress Avenue. Afterward, you and Whitt will be able to celebrate. I know the judge, and this hearing will be only a formality."

She sighed relief. "Thank you. I want this over and adoption proceedings started."

"Matters of law take time. Are you still contemplating a move?"

"Yes. Once the adoption is filed, I plan to sell my house and relocate the clinic."

"Good. Stay put for right now. The judge could view your relocation of the clinic and move as unstable. But I know your area, and I can't blame you for wanting out of there."

"Mr. Nardell, I won't do a thing that might jeopardize the hearing."

"Wise decision. I read you had an eventful weekend."

She inwardly moaned. "Media got the word out."

"I wish you'd have consulted with me before the FBI's and HPD's questioning."

"Never crossed my mind. I had nothing to hide. Media contacted me, but I refused to make a statement."

"Wise move. Right now you don't need any more attention. If anything escalates, let me know. You're under enough stress."

She hung up the phone and typed the court date into her online calendar. Where was Mr. Parson? She could set her clock according to the elderly man's daily arrival, and he always phoned ahead if he feared he'd be a minute late.

"Them dogs wait for me to walk 'em," he'd said repeatedly.

Over an hour had slipped by without a word from him, and she hoped his health hadn't dealt him a nasty blow. Nearing ninety-one years old, Mr. Parson complained of aching bones and a nagging cough. She pressed in his number on the landline and listened to his voice message. Worry assaulted her. If he didn't contact her by noon, she'd ask Whitt to mind the clinic while she paid him a visit.

A jingle alerted her to someone entering the clinic, and she longed for the familiar leathered face. "Mr. Parson?" She hurried down the hall to the front reception area.

She stopped the moment she recognized the man—Ace McMann, wearing a red face and a permanent scowl, dripped water on the floor.

"Where's my boy?" He smelled like sweat and alcohol, the stench coming from the pores of his skin. "There's a padlock on the house."

She clutched her cell phone in her lab jacket and took a quick look to press Record. She moved to where the man leaned on the counter. "Whitt's at school."

"I'm not stupid. This is summer." He spoke low . . . and frightening.

"Whitt's attending summer school, remember?"

"You're lying. He's smart."

"He's getting extra credits so he can graduate from high school early."

"You're filling him with stupid ideas. Want to get him away from me and his mother." He sneered. "I need the key to get in the house. Whitt leave it with you?"

"Neither he nor I have a key."

He swore, calling her vile names. "Oh, the old lady forgot to pay the rent again. Are you ready to hand over the fifty grand for my kid?"

She wouldn't have to. Not only did she have the McManns' history, but the school had provided enough ammunition for them to lose custody. "Selling children is against the law."

"I admit he ain't worth much, but I guess he could clean your cages like he does now."

Her temper would get her into trouble if she didn't find a way to curb it soon. "Whitt is highly intelligent. He plans to enter college much sooner than other kids his age. His ambition to succeed will take him far."

"Whatever. When will he be here? I need money."

"He doesn't have any."

"I know you pay him to clean up. Why else would he hang around?"

How about a breather from your abuse? "His earnings go directly into a savings account."

"You—"

"Cursing me doesn't change a thing. Whitt's a fine boy, and you should be proud of him."

"Maybe, if he'd take care of those who brought him into the world."

"He didn't have a choice of parents." She wanted to ask how Ace had gotten out of jail so quickly but thought better of it. Since he was in his driveway when she called the police, he could have gotten his bail reduced.

"I asked when he'd be here." His voice rose and she detected a slur. "Won't ask again."

"I told you he's at school. Please leave now." She pulled her phone from her pocket as though it were a weapon.

He picked up a glass bowl of doggy treats and sent it shattering to the floor. "I'll leave when I see my boy and get what he owes for his keep."

"How do you figure he owes you? He's twelve years old." She cautioned herself again to control her temper.

"My business, and you got your nose where it don't belong."

"You've been drinking. Either leave or I'll call the police."

"You're going to wish you'd never been born." He scoured the clinic, narrowing his gaze into every corner. "Hate to see this burned to the ground with them animals in it. People might be upset to have their animals barbecued." He stumbled to a painting of a mother collie and her pups. Sneering, he pulled it from the wall and smashed it against the floor. "Ask Whitt what he gets when he crosses me."

"Is that a threat?"

"Take it how you want. A little gasoline would send this up like a torch."

"Think about this—Whitt works here sometimes. Do you really want to burn the clinic with your son inside?"

"That's his problem. He has a bed at the house."

"Not when you don't pay the rent."

"Where he's at ain't my business unless I need money."

McMann's admittance was vital for the judge to grant her custody. "Anything else you'd like to say?"

"Yes—I'm tired of you spending time with my boy. You want a real man? I can oblige anytime. Right now is just fine. We can use one of those tables for operating on animals."

"Enough of your filth." She took a step back to call the police.

He yanked the phone from her hand and threw it across the room, pieces flying everywhere. "I'm leaving, but I'll be back. You tell my son he'd better bring me what's due." He slammed the door behind him.

Stacy walked across the room to gather the remnants of her phone. McMann didn't realize her security camera had caught him in action, along with audio. She'd send the video on to her attorney. . . .

The rain had stopped by the time Stacy greeted Whitt after school. The police had filed assault charges and arrested Ace at a bar two blocks down. The video of his actions sealed his fate in jail, and hopefully he'd be incarcerated through next week's hearing. Whitt's mother was facing her third prostitution charge, and when she was in the picture, she ignored her son. At least Whitt had been spared his father's temper and the scene when he attempted to hit a female police officer. Stacy had witnessed the assault and recorded the officer's name for her attorney.

She'd decided not to tell Whitt about his father's arrest, but the broken picture of the collie and puppies stirred his curiosity. Especially with a broom and dustpan in her hand.

"How did the picture break?" He whirled around. "My dad is the one responsible for this mess, isn't he?"

Her heart ached for him, but lies solved nothing.

"How did he get bailed out of jail? Never mind, probably his supplier."

"He's on his way back there."

He took the broom and dustpan from her. "I'll do this. Are you hurt?"

"I'm fine. Just a little shaken. How about you sweep and I'll dump?"

His lips quivered.

"You make your decisions, and he makes his. When he's not drinking, he treats you fairly."

Whitt nodded. "Happens rarely. The problem is he loves his addictions more than me."

"That's not true. The drugs and alcohol have him chained. He's in a prison."

"He chooses to be there, and I hate him and Mom for it."

"I understand. But I want you to see that those we love who hurt us shouldn't be despised because then we become imprisoned by the chains of hate. I don't want you destroyed by any poison."

"Is this about God too?"

"Yes. He's bigger than our problems."

Whitt shook his head. "Not yet, Miss Stacy. The concept of a heavenly Father who might resemble my dad turns me against church talk. I'm sorry."

"I'm not giving up."

He smiled. "Thanks."

Thoughts of her own parents swept across her mind. She missed them, and yet she held back. Her calls to them were once a month on a Monday evening. Twelve minutes long. Her heart wanted to tell them of her love, but the past stuck in her throat, choking the life out of her relationship with them. She and Whitt had much in common. . . . Both carried the burden of responsibility at a young age, powerless with circumstances beyond their control. They enslaved themselves to ugly feelings.

She comforted herself that soon he'd be in her home, where dysfunctional behavior was an occurrence of the past. The moment the thought left her mind, she chastised herself. Self-centered actions were a part of every human being, but she could provide love, faith, traits that had escaped his parents. Faith was something she needed to practice more, not use Jesus as a drive-by solution to life's misfortunes.

"You're quiet," Whitt said, walking back to the clinic's kitchenette. "Upset with me, or haven't you told me all that transpired?"

"Sorry. How's school?"

He laughed. "Trig had me a little bored, but learning foreign languages is fun. We're doing a play in Spanish a week from Friday. Wanna come?"

"Sure. Remind me a few days before with the time."

"Okay. Is Mr. Parson walking one of the dogs? I asked him yesterday to let me take care of Xena." He stacked ham and cheese on wheat bread.

"He didn't show up today. I called, but it went to voice mail."

"Leave a message?"

Oh, his meticulous way of handling detail. "Three messages. No response. Would you keep an eye on things while I make a quick trip there?"

"Do you need to ask?" He squirted mayo onto his bread. "He complained of a headache last night during the carnival teardown, and he's really old."

Stacy had enough pressures without adding the failing health of a dear old man. She grabbed her keys. "I'll be right back."

"Text when you're there."

"I can't. Dropped my phone, and it's in pieces. Do me a favor and find out how late the Apple Store is open tonight, and we'll run by and pick up a new one."

Whitt shook his head and handed her his cell. "Take mine and call on the landline when you find Mr. Parson. It scares me when I think of your handling life without my assistance."

Would he ever concede to being a child? "I squeaked by before, so I can do it again. My organization skills are a little lax, but I'm doing better."

"A little?"

She laughed.

"Ignorance is not bliss."

She laughed again and he joined her.

A few moments later, she parked in front of Mr. Parson's home. His car was in the driveway. When he didn't answer the doorbell or her knocking, she turned the knob and stepped inside. "Mr. Parson? This is Stacy. Are you okay?"

Blinds were open, and a blue-green aquarium hummed. His small, tidy home reminded her of everything uniquely him—family photos, A&M paraphernalia from his great-granddaughter, his deceased wife's hobby of embroidering pillows, and his stamp collection. A hint of Old Spice. Yet no sign of Mr. Parson, and she called to him twice more. He had acute hearing, so if he were there, he'd have responded. Unless . . .

Dread washed over her. She walked through the living area and into the kitchen, where a full glass of orange juice rested on the counter. The house layout meant the bedrooms would be down the hallway to her right, and she ventured there while repeatedly calling his name.

The first bedroom contained a treadmill and weights. She smiled at the many times he'd bragged about his four-mile-a-day cardio and four-day-a-week weight-lifting program. A small bath was empty, and she even pulled back a shower curtain to ensure he hadn't fallen. Before entering the second and last bedroom at the end of the hall, she called his name. But no answer.

Her heart pounded violently against her chest. Perhaps finding a body on Saturday and Ace McMann's threat had deemed her officially paranoid.

She glanced at his bed and moaned. Mr. Parson's head hung over the edge. She rushed to his side, but his open eyes were gone to this world.

"Mr. Parson," she whispered. "Tell me you're all right. Please."

Squeezing her eyes shut to stop the flow of tears, she checked for a pulse. None. Acid rose in her throat, and she forced it back down.

This would be the second time in three days she'd alerted 911 to a dead body.

14

EARLY TUESDAY MORNING, Alex met Dexter at Starbucks near the FBI office to report he'd made amends with Stacy. Not that the conversation was necessary, but his mentor had been like a father to him since he'd lost his parents in a car accident. Alex could never repay the Raykens' support and encouragement in the past and present.

Dexter had worked several years for the CDC and then the LRN and was now the director of the Houston lab.

"I apologized and she accepted it," Alex said.

"Is evidence stacking up for or against her?" Dexter said, taking a bite of a cinnamon chip scone.

"For, I think. She's clean, and I like her."

He raised a brow. "So the suspect is attractive? Does that make you want to run?"

"A marathon. But she's keeping her distance from me."

"She's not pleading, 'Help me, save me, marry me'?"

Alex frowned, but the question deserved a response. "You're harsh, but no. She's active in her church and community. Independent from what I've seen." He took a long drink of his coffee. "I promised you I'd never date a woman who was involved with a case until arrests and charges were filed. I'm asking you to keep me accountable. Friendship? Yes. A relationship? No."

"You got it."

Alex had a brief flashback of the woman he thought had been innocent. She perjured herself on the witness stand and was found guilty of dealing in illegal weapons. She'd sworn her love to Alex until the truth was exposed.

"Alex?"

He smiled. "Yep."

"A lesson learned. 'The truth is like a lion; you don't have to defend it. Let it loose; it will defend itself.'"

"She's Cajun."

Dexter nearly choked on his scone. "The good Lord has something grand in store for you."

"I've thought the same thing. We'll see when the truth surfaces."

Dexter reached for a metal tin on the floor. "Eva sent chocolate chip cookies. I told her a man of your age outgrows those things."

"Never," Alex said. "Let me have one and I'll dip it in my coffee. And tell her I'll take her cookies as long as she bakes them."

Alex approached Ric at his cubicle. "I'd like to walk the crime scene again, then stop in at the Aldine Westfield Stables. Although Stacy's riding partners checked out, we haven't talked to the stable manager." He glanced at his watch. His stomach growled but it was only eleven. "There's a Whataburger close to where we're going."

"You're on." Ric grabbed his phone. "You drive, bro."

While on the road to the northern outskirts of the airport, Alex tapped the steering wheel of his Jeep and replayed the interview with the Howes' rabbi. "Do we have additional info on Rabbi Feldman?"

"Hold on." Ric pressed into his phone. "So righteous he's sterilized. Feldman despised what Howe did to his daughter, but the rabbi was with his family the morning of the murder. Before you say another word, the report's in on Elle Vieson and her boyfriend."

"Anything we can use?"

"Of course not," Ric said. "They were seen together Saturday morning having breakfast alone at The Egg & I on Memorial Drive. After we left her, an employee admitted to Vieson that he was responsible for the Facebook prank. Seventeen years old, and she fired him."

"We're eliminating suspects, but I'd feel better with more progress." Alex swung onto the road leading to the airport trail. He pulled into a spot beside a new white Lexus. "Familiar car?" he said.

"No."

Could be anyone.

They exited the Jeep and took the path toward the crime scene. On Saturday he hadn't noticed how very green the area looked. The crime and humidity, along with a few million mosquitoes, deterred his appreciation of nature.

His mind turned to the reason he and Ric were there, and he zoomed into alert mode. Other agents had checked with the airlines for threats, but there had been none. If Saturday had been successful, it would have been a surprise attack on innocent people.

The two entered the clearing.

A woman knelt where Todd Howe had fallen.

15

"MRS. HOWE," Alex said. "We're sorry to disturb you."

Bekah slowly turned to them but didn't move from her kneeling position. Several roses were strewn on the ground where her husband's body had been discovered.

Two more times Alex called her name. Grief sometimes paralyzed its victims.

"Agent LeBlanc and Agent Price?"

"Yes, ma'am," Alex said. "Is there something we can do for you?"

"I'm talking to God about Todd." She stood and wiped brush and dirt from her black skirt and white blouse. "I wanted to leave these flowers. Red roses were Todd's favorite. I was praying as I placed each one on the ground." She held a single rose and stooped to leave it with the others.

"Is there anyone we can contact? You shouldn't be alone."

"I'm fine." She closed her eyes and lifted her face to a clear sky. "I hadn't visited where it happened, and I wanted to see where he died."

"Have you been here long?"

"I'm not sure." She continued to stare upward while tears streamed down her face. "Wish I could have been with him in those final moments. Held his hand. Whispered my love before he breathed his last." She lowered her gaze to the roses. "It's pretty here. Peaceful when a plane isn't roaring overhead. When I arrived, squirrels were scampering about."

"Yes, ma'am. Had he shared this place with you?" Alex poured tenderness into his words. He sympathized with her anguish and saw no reason to be callous. Yet the question was important if her husband had been acquainted with the area.

Red-rimmed eyes met his. "No, sir. I called the police officer who first notified me on Saturday, and he gave me directions. Todd liked to take different routes on his bike. Usually he preferred a country setting, which is why I'm not surprised he was found here among the trees." She pressed her lips together as though fighting for control. "Am I in the way of your investigation? I can leave."

"Not at all. Agent Price, do you see any reason why Mrs. Howe shouldn't stay?"

Ric took over the conversation. "Perhaps we're the intruders. We're exploring the crime scene and talking through scenarios. Saturday was noisy, and solace is vital to thinking through evidence."

She nodded. "So many people have been at the house to sit shivah. I'm ashamed to have left, but I thought I'd break down and never recover. I looked in the mirror, and I wasn't supposed to do that either. What's wrong with me? My sons need their mother. I've always followed our practices. Faithfully. The mourners will be disappointed when they discover I'm gone. They mean well. Everyone does. Want me to eat. Recite the kaddish prayer. Listen to them talk about good times with Todd. Encourage me to do the same. But I want to forget, grieve in my own way."

"The mourners are there to comfort you," Ric said. "A blessing during this sad time. But they aren't the ones going through the incredible loss."

Alex listened to Ric, wishing he had the empathetic skills of his partner. His parents had the ability to minister to others, but Alex had believed their methods were weak—giving what they had to a widow they didn't know, or to a man who was drunk and wouldn't remember their generosity. Now he regretted not paying attention. Bekah Howe hurt, and he wanted to do more than arrest the person who killed her husband.

"Mrs. Howe, this is not a time to be alone. Allow those who want to help be your support. Let their memories of your husband touch your heart," Ric said.

She smiled with water-filled eyes. "Yes, I will. Thank you for your understanding."

"Yes, ma'am."

"I've been here long enough. Agent Price, Agent LeBlanc, I'm glad you stopped by."

"You're welcome."

She focused on Alex. "I haven't forgotten your promise to find the person who did this to my family."

He hadn't promised her, just said he'd do his best. But it was a commitment, and he'd honor it. "Law enforcement across the city are working together to find your husband's killer."

She reached for a tissue in her pocket and touched it to her nose. "Agent LeBlanc, I intended to contact one of you, but with so many people at my home, I couldn't focus." She drew in a light sob. "I received a call on my cell phone for Todd last night. Let me retrace my steps. I had his cell phone forwarded to my cell. The number wasn't recognizable, so as advised by our family's lawyer, I pressed Record on the phone before I answered. I'd been doing this in case the information was business related and I'd need it as reference in

the future. A man wanted to speak to Todd. He said it was important. I explained what happened. He said whoever popped Todd did
the world a favor because he was a worthless idiot. When I asked
his name, he hung up."

"And you have no idea who the caller was?"

She shook her head. "The voice was vaguely familiar. But I can't
remember where. He really frightened me."

"Can we listen to the recording?" Alex said.

"Yes, but the phone is at home. This is so horrible," Mrs. Howe
said. "The man hated Todd. Why would my husband be in contact
with such a vile person?"

Alex and Ric walked Bekah Howe to her car. Alex showed her
a photo from the footage obtained through Green-to-Go's security
cameras. "Does anything about the build of this man remind you
of someone?"

She peered at the photo. "I don't think so. Wish I could help you."

"Mrs. Howe, once we have your phone, we'll trace the number
and run the recording through voice recognition software to see if
we have the man's identity in our database."

"You mean this man might know who murdered my Todd?"

"Possibly."

She touched her stomach as though nauseated. "Come by later,
and I'll give you the phone."

"We'll assign another agent to make that pickup. Will it interfere
with shivah?"

"Finding his killer takes priority. Others will not agree, but I
don't care. I'm grateful for all you've done. I'll be home shortly."

Alex waved as she drove away. "Makes me wonder who the real
victim is."

"If Todd Howe had another cell phone on him, most likely a
burner, the killer could have confiscated it," Ric said.

"Which brings us back to the question of why he was in that clearing."

"Whether he's innocent or involved in a crime, Bekah Howe has to assemble the pieces of her life and look to the future."

They took the path that wove in and out of thick woods, then back to the clearing and the crime scene.

Alex bent in the same spot where Bekah Howe had left roses. "At least two people were a part of Saturday morning's murder: Howe and the killer. The same weapon that brought down the quadcopter is the one that killed Howe. But who operated the quadcopter?" He stood, his mind continuing to speed over the various scenarios. This wasn't a competition. His and Ric's skill sets collided on a regular basis, but their success rate showed high stats in solving crimes. They'd figure out what happened here. "All we can do is stay on this until we have solid answers. Nothing happens by chance. We have likely homegrown terrorism and a murder."

"That was a lengthy analysis for a Cajun."

"I do have my intellectual moments." Alex stared at the field toward the airport. He glanced back at where Howe had been found. The area had been searched repeatedly. Nothing had surfaced.

Moments later, they climbed into Alex's Jeep en route to the Aldine Westfield Stables. The temp read 99 degrees, and the air-conditioning seemed slow. "Nothing in this case makes sense. Stacy found a dead man, a dog, and a drone. Sooner or later we'll get inside the warped mind of whoever's responsible for the murder and the quadcopter. We simply need to stay on it."

16

EARLY AFTERNOON SHADOWS had set in when Alex and Ric entered the Aldine Westfield Stables. The smell of horses mixed with hay met Alex's nostrils and transported him back to his boyhood days in Louisiana. He hadn't ridden in years, and he missed the freedom of a powerful animal lunging beneath him.

A white-haired cowboy greeted them and explained he oversaw the stables. "The name's Chet. How can I help you?"

Alex introduced himself and Ric. The agents displayed their IDs and gave him their cards. "We understand the airport rangers keep their horses in these stables."

"Yes, sir, they do. This is their headquarters."

Alex took his usual lead. "What can you tell us about the organization? We're investigating the murder of a man found Saturday morning and a stolen quadcopter with the capabilities of blinding a pilot. One of the riders discovered the body."

Chet narrowed his gaze. "Oh, you mean Stacy Broussard. Hated that for our cowgirl. Been meaning to call her, see how's she doing."

"I'm sure she'd appreciate it. We're curious as to why she was alone."

Lines deepened across his brow. "She knew better. Should have reached out to someone or me when the other two riders canceled."

Alex whipped out his notepad and pen. "What can you tell us about them?"

"Sure. The three rodeo queens, I call 'em. I remember one had a sick young'un, and the other had unexpected company."

Confirmation from Stacy's testimony. "Thanks. Is there anything else we should know about the airport rangers?"

"Gentlemen, follow me, and I'll give you a tour." Chet led them to an office marked Private. After pulling a ring of keys off his belt chain, he unlocked it, gestured them inside, and pointed to a map on the wall. "This here's the airport's perimeter, covering about thirteen thousand acres. The rangers are volunteers who patrol the area. They come from every walk of life—housewives and college students to civic leaders and those trained in law enforcement. I'm one of them, retired gas and oil man, and we're dedicated to increasing airport security. Those who are interested in serving the community complete an application and are thoroughly screened before being accepted into the program. They ride in pairs or threes." He peered over his wire-rimmed glasses. "That's why last Saturday was unusual."

Alex still had a problem with the whole concept. Stacy hadn't convinced him, but he'd not mention it.

Ric cleared his throat. "How are the volunteers scheduled?"

The man pointed to a bulletin board on another wall above a desk. "It's printed out and tacked up here, but they can get their times online." He gestured to a computer on the desk below. "Sometimes they use this too."

Ric read the schedule. "Looks like the riders maintain the same schedule and trails."

"Yes, sir. It doesn't vary much since most have jobs and other responsibilities. They enter any changes online and work it out among themselves if there's a problem. But life happens, as it did on Saturday." He rubbed the back of his neck.

Did Chet blame himself for Stacy riding into a crime scene?

"Is the website security protected?" Ric continued.

The man shrugged. "I don't know much about computer technology or what you mean."

"I'm sorry." Ric smiled and glanced at the computer. "I was wondering if anyone could see the schedule."

"It's private, sir. I suppose a hacker could find out in a flash who was riding and guesstimate when and where the rider would be on the trail."

"My thoughts too. Do you mind if I attempt to access the secure site?" Ric said.

The man held up his hand. "Go for it. If you can figure out how this could've been prevented, my hat's off to you. I mean, Stacy being there by herself and having to deal with a dead body is nothing we want repeated."

While Ric sat at the desk, Alex turned to the man assisting them. He shifted from foot to foot. "Chet, I'm curious." He captured the man's attention to figure out why he was uncomfortable, to either reassure or identify some form of guilt. "Do you blame yourself for Dr. Broussard being alone Saturday morning?"

He released a sigh. "Yes, sir, I do. I slept past the alarm and didn't get here until she'd already left. If I'd been on time, I'd have ridden with her." He paused. "At least been able to take over the unfortunate situation."

Everything about Chet's body language also spoke of sincerity and regret.

"You obviously value her friendship, and I encourage you to

support her." Alex bent over Ric's shoulder and watched him click the Members Only tab on the airport rangers' website. The page asked for a password.

Ric's fingers sped across the keys. One day, Alex would request a tutorial. "Does the password change on a regular basis?" Ric said.

"I think it's always the same. Too many people need it."

"Thanks." He typed on.

"Can you get into it?" Alex said.

"Working on it, bro. I'm trying the most common ones first."

"What are you using? *Airport*? *Horse*? *Saddle*? *IAH*?" Alex said. "*Rider*? *Stable*?"

"Been through those and anything resembling them." He tilted his head and typed in *122003*, the date the airport rangers were organized. "Bingo." He glanced at Chet. "Sir, I'd like to talk to whoever's in charge of the website because the password is too obvious."

"I'd be glad to. Our web guy is retired and a volunteer. This is one mess."

Alex handed him his notepad and pen, and Chet jotted the name and phone number. Most likely Ric would contact the webmaster, and Alex the two women volunteers. "Have you noticed anything unusual, a stranger on the grounds or a phone call asking about the rangers?"

"I get those kind of things all the time, but nothing I recall that a feller would question. I can call if I think of something." He studied their cards. "Special Agent LeBlanc and Special Agent Price, the airport rangers are my friends. I don't want to see bad press or any of 'em hurt. So whatever I come across, you'll be the first to know. God and country and Texas."

Alex hid a grin. "Thanks for your help."

Ric stood and aimed his attention at Alex. "Do we have all our questions answered?"

Alex nodded and the two agents shook Chet's hand.

Once in the Jeep and facing the beginnings of rush-hour traffic, Ric sighed deeply.

"Let me have it," Alex said.

"Here's my overview of what we've learned. Todd Howe rode his motorcycle into an area on the trails posted for equestrian riders, specifically the airport rangers, and he's murdered. Stacy rode the trails by chance without her partners, stumbled onto the body, the quadcopter, and a dog. She reported it. Exonerating her makes sense to me. We have nothing solid to locate who stole the quadcopter or who murdered Howe. Bekah Howe receives a threatening phone call from a stranger. Then we learn the airport rangers' website is easily hackable, providing the volunteers' unique schedule."

Alex stopped behind a string of brake lights winding along the road. "Back to Stacy. What if she and her friends had ridden upon Howe's body? Would that make any difference in our case?"

"At this point, I don't see how. The 911 call would still have been made."

"Then we're back to ground zero." Alex drummed his fingers on the steering wheel.

"Bro, we've pored over the same dilemma since Saturday. Let's find out who called Bekah."

17

STACY WANDERED THROUGH THE CLINIC on Wednesday morning. Visitation for Mr. Parson would be tonight and Thursday, and his funeral on Friday afternoon. She missed watching him shuffling about, listening to him greet each animal, and joining in his aged chuckle. His special kinship with animals and children made him a favorite among whoever visited the clinic. He was most surely in heaven, for she'd never seen a man with faith in motion like his. Faith . . .

She believed, but for many years, her faith had been a Sunday ritual that didn't trickle into today's problems. Memories of when her prayer life and closeness to Him took priority pounded at her heart until she listened to what God was saying. Forgiveness was a choice, an act of obedience. Eight months ago, she took the first step to reestablish a relationship with her parents. The break had been her choice, and now the reuniting must be hers too. Time to change her monthly habit and call more often. Like Mr. Parson, her parents wouldn't be around forever. She picked up her cell phone. It rang twice before her mother answered.

"Hi, Mom, this is Stacy. How are you doing?"

"Wonderful at just the sound of your voice."

She smiled. "Dad busy in the garden?"

"That he is. The tomatoes this year are huge."

"Save me a couple when I'm there at the family reunion."

Mom sobbed, and Stacy swallowed her own emotion. "Can't wait to see you."

For once she felt the same—scared but wanting her parents in her life. So much to say and yet it would take a face-to-face. "Mom, I saw a great photo of you and Dad on Facebook. Was it taken at the crawfish festival?"

"Yes. And I found your veterinary clinic there too. You are more beautiful than I remember."

She missed her. "I need to go, Mom. Got an appointment in a couple of minutes. Give Dad my best."

"I will." Mom paused. "I love your calls."

"Good. Because I don't want to stop. Bye, Mom. Love you." She clicked off the call before hearing if her mother would respond the same way. Taking a deep breath, one filled with stress and satisfaction, she turned to pull out the chart for the cocker spaniel's upcoming visit.

The time read 10:35. Her ten o'clock with the cocker spaniel and the sweet family who owned the dog was normally punctual. Since the girls were out of school, maybe the owner had forgotten. But another appointment had been scheduled for eleven, a sometimes-difficult macaw. Stacy pressed in the tardy pet owner's phone number, and the woman answered on the third ring.

"Dr. Stacy, I'm so sorry. I meant to call earlier. The twins have the flu, and it's been a tough morning. Can we reschedule?"

"Of course. A week from tomorrow at the same time? I'm closing Friday afternoon for Mr. Parson's funeral."

"Perfect. If everyone here is healthy, we'll be at the service. Thank you for your understanding. The girls love your clinic, and they really wanted to come today."

"Hope they feel better very soon."

The woman sighed. "They're running fevers, body aches, vomiting, and feeling miserable."

"Oh, I'm sorry."

"My fear is they were contagious at the carnival."

"Or someone there infected them with a nasty virus."

Stacy said good-bye. Summer vacation and dealing with the flu hit low on her chart for any child.

The colorful scarlet macaw arrived a few minutes early. True to the bird's reputation, he attempted to bite her several times. Odd how such a beautiful red, yellow, and blue bird could have such a deplorable temperament. But she was determined to make a friend out of him.

After the macaw and its owner left, she glanced at the clock. Whitt would arrive soon. He'd inquire about how she was doing with her new iPhone, and she'd done little but look at a few apps that he'd loaded. Unopened mail from earlier lay on her desk, and she ripped into each envelope, sorting the junk from those things requiring her attention. Whitt had been after her to handle paperwork immediately so he could organize her desk. She smiled at the thought of him devising ways to show his affection. His love language was having things done for him. In turn, he chose the same for her.

An envelope from the health department caught her attention, and she opened it, knowing her license and state regulations were in order.

Ms. Broussard,

Health concerns in your subdivision indicate a potential problem with the water tower supply to your homes and businesses. Consuming the contaminated water leads to flu-like symptoms. Until the source of bacteria has been identified and treated, please cease from using tap water for drinking, cooking, bathing, and watering vegetable gardens. This includes pet care. The request is effective immediately.

We regret the inconvenience, but for the health and safety of every person in your neighborhood, kindly adhere to these regulations until further notice.

For additional information, you may call or e-mail us at the contact information in the letterhead. A representative will assist in answering your questions.

Sincerely,
Houston Health Department

How strange. She reached for the landline on her desk and called the number. A man identified himself as from the health department.

"I just received a letter indicating a water problem in my subdivision. Can you provide guidance for those of us who live and work here?"

"Yes, ma'am. We apologize for the disruption, but flu-like symptoms have been reported in epidemic proportions in your neighborhood. We've isolated the problem to what we believe is your water supply."

"When was the water tested?"

"I'm not privy to those dates."

Why hadn't she heard about an outbreak of flu until today? The twins had been her first notification. No one at the carnival spoke about the illness. "I understand. My subdivision consists of many residents who are not financially able to purchase water. Has any provision been made for them?"

"Not to my knowledge."

"What is the contaminated zone?"

"Just your subdivision and the strip center where your veterinary clinic is housed. We're encouraging residents to consider temporarily relocating until the problem is resolved."

"And who's paying for this?"

"We're not able to say. Perhaps churches and community organizations will assist the unfortunate."

"Have you seen this neighborhood?" Her mind raced with how much bottled water would be needed for residents to continue living in their homes. She could help a few but not everyone. "What about Volunteer Houston? Would one of the organizations under their umbrella help?"

"We've contacted them, and they refused. Their guidelines state the mayor must declare an emergency before they can get involved. We've received several calls today regarding this matter. Again, we regret the hardship for your community. Please check back for updates." The man expressed his sympathy and clicked off.

Stunned, Stacy deliberated her next move. Mass panic would erupt among the residents unless they were provided viable options. She phoned neighborhood friends to see if they'd received the same letter, which they had. Several small children and elderly suffered from the symptoms outlined in the letter.

She contacted a friend whose family attended her church.

"My sons are really sick. I called my husband about the letter. He's been talking about moving out of the neighborhood, and this new development sealed his decision. It's not safe here," the woman said.

Had the water infected a myriad of people? It certainly seemed so.

Gossip would spill over into anger and very soon rage. A meeting with the residents would help, and she could hold it here at the clinic. One of the local churches came to mind, but the residents who weren't believers might shy away. Foremost she needed a representative from the health department to conduct an orderly and informative session.

How quickly could she make that happen? A call back to the health department eased her mind. The man demonstrated a willingness for a spokesperson to conduct a meeting. He'd pass along Stacy's inquiry, and she'd be contacted before the end of the day.

"Thank you."

The phone clicked in her ear, and her stomach swirled with acid and too much coffee. How would she spread the word about this meeting? She knew from experience that obtaining phone numbers for her neighbors was nearly impossible and e-mail a futility. She'd request official letterhead for credibility. The most efficient way to alert people would be to go house to house with flyers and speak directly to them. Not pleasant when some of the residents were hostile. She was a dog lover, but the canines trained to discourage visitors had her respect. The two-legged deterrents were worse.

Did she have a choice when she wanted to protect others from an epidemic originating in their water?

Alex opened his iPad to the *Houston Chronicle* and accidentally swiped on something that took him to where the obituaries were noted. He wouldn't have paid attention except he saw a photo of the old man he'd met on Sunday at the carnival. Mr. Parson had been found dead in his home on Monday afternoon by a neighbor. The highly decorated man had fought in the Korean War and earned a

Purple Heart for his valor. He'd risked his life to enter a combat zone three consecutive times to pull out wounded soldiers and was shot in the leg during his last trip. No wonder the man limped.

He should call Stacy to offer his condolences. She'd had her share of deaths recently. Or was he fishing for an excuse to talk to her? Maybe an e-mail, but then he'd not hear her voice. Or a text . . . Friendship only.

He chose to text.

Sorry 2 hear about Mr. Parson.

Busy day ahead. Every airport in the country was on elevated threat alert. Airlines grumbled about business and wanted Homeland Security to redefine the threat, but the caution remained until the persons behind the theft of the quadcopter had been found.

A text soared into his phone. **Thnx. Hard 2 believe he's gone.**

Cause of death?

Assumed heart attack. I found him. Sad.

Alex groaned. How unfortunate for her to discover two bodies within a few days. He pursued the investigations of stopping those who caused death and destruction. But the average person left such repulsiveness locked outside their front door.

Sorry. R u ok?

Will b.

Whitt ok?

Quiet

Alex didn't know much about the kid except he appeared close to Mr. Parson.

Bummer. Take care. Why hadn't he asked her out?

Thnx again.

Get your courage on. **Would u want 2 have coffee sometime? 2nite?**

U r kidding!

I'm serious.

Am I still a suspect?

Alex pressed in her number, and she responded on the first ring. Her voice held the lilt that transported him back to family and home.

"Coffee, not an interrogation, to get to know each other better," he said. "Purely platonic." Who was he kidding?

"Can I have the request in writing?"

"Do you want the director to sign it?"

"I'm teasing, Alex."

He chuckled. "You got me on that one."

"Any arrests?"

"Not yet. Running down leads. So what about coffee?"

"Alex, I'm not dating material. Life is extremely complicated, and the situation with Whitt is . . . demanding."

"Is he in trouble?"

"No." She sighed. "Can't believe I'm telling you this." She explained the past several years with the boy, his parents' mistreatment, and her filing for custody. "His parents are unfit in every sense of the word, but I'd not tell him that."

"When's the hearing?"

"Next week. My lawyer doesn't see a problem, but I'll feel better when it's over. Both parents are currently in jail."

"I'm sure you've given this a lot of thought."

"Of course I have." Her voice rose. "I'm sorry. No excuse for bad manners."

"Can I call you later this afternoon about coffee, and we can take Whitt with us?"

"Guess I haven't deterred you."

"Whitt might object, but I'm still interested in friendship."

"Really, *couillon*?"

She'd called him a crazy fool in Cajun, and it touched him in a way he couldn't put words to. His mother had referred to his dad with the same endearment. "Ah, yes."

"My schedule's unpredictable and leaves little time for social activities, and then there's Whitt. Have you ever been married, Alex?"

"No." She did have her blunt side.

"Neither have I. The parenting thing is frightening. I'm prepared to make mistakes, but taking the first steps of a friendship sends up flares."

Did he want to continue seeing her, knowing the little professor was part of a package deal if things developed after the case closed? "My life is not my own either. I can be called out on a case day or night and have to cancel plans at the last minute. Some women can't handle the unpredictable, and I understand. It's obvious you care for Whitt, and I hope everything goes smoothly for the hearing."

"Appreciate it. Think about what I said before you decide to call again."

He laughed. "Yes, ma'am. And I'll get back with you." He ended the call, wondering if he'd officially lost his mind by asking out a woman who most likely would be raising a twelve-year-old. Alex had been a handful at Whitt's age, and his behavior didn't improve until he entered college and found an interest in the FBI.

His gut told him to walk on. Ready-made families were for guys who had nine-to-five jobs. And he'd done exactly what he'd told Dexter wouldn't happen.

18

WHITT STOPPED AT A CONVENIENCE STORE on the way home from school and purchased a can of Mountain Dew. He allowed himself one soda per week on Wednesdays. The rest of the time, he drank tap water. Except in the morning when he mixed coffee loaded with chocolate creamer and syrup to counteract his habit of reading until 2 a.m. He'd taught himself to speed-read—it only heightened his craving for more knowledge. Weird, but his desire to learn about the world, past and present, helped him survive the chaos of his parents and bullies who used their fists instead of their brains.

He stepped out of the store and popped the top. After a long citrusy swig that jolted his toes, he studied the decline around him. The area could use a renovation, but not many cared about mowing yards and planting flowers. Too many of them, like his parents, were more interested in dulling their senses to forget their miserable existence. But not all, and his mind swept through a few names and faces of respectable families. Unfortunately none of them had kids his age who were interested in science and world events.

Why think about a friend when Xena listened? No fears the warrior princess would broadcast his nurturing-challenged parents from the rooftops or inform a well-meaning adult who'd make a report to social services. Mr. Parson had listened, and Whitt respected him for his sound advice to work hard in school and make something of himself.

"Give to this world a gift that can only come from you," Mr. Parson had said. "Discover a cure for cancer or a way to bring Jesus to the world. But above all, be a loving husband and father to your family."

"I promise," he said. "I'll make you proud, more than anyone ever imagined. Sometimes I think I want to be a vet like Miss Stacy, and other times I want to be a psychologist or a surgeon. But whatever I choose, I'll have a PhD after my name by the time I'm twenty-one, and I'll be working on another one."

A tear slipped over his cheek, and he brushed it away. Wasn't fair about Mr. Parson, the one man he trusted now zipped out of his life.

On his twelfth birthday, the older man gave him $150, said a man always needed an emergency fund. Whitt referred to it as disaster relief and deposited it in the bank. Now Mr. Parson was gone, but Whitt still had Xena.

He loved Miss Stacy too much to reveal all of his inner thoughts—the nightmares and memories that boiled pure hate and rage. She might not want him anymore.

The custody hearing couldn't happen soon enough. He could log on to her computer and learn more since he'd memorized how she changed her password on a weekly basis, but accessing the device without her permission seemed wrong, like stealing. Not cool, and he refused to go there unless it was critical. In case the judge ruled against him, he'd established an escape route with a place to start over miles away from here. The CDC's website gave him valuable info about emergency preparedness. Following their guidelines, he'd assembled his disaster supply kit and kept his eyes and ears open.

By habit, he glanced at his backpack. Risky to stash money there, but he'd inserted a secret compartment where no one could find it. Over six months ago, he'd developed a plan after social services made a house call. At the time Mom was sober and played the role. She wanted Whitt around because he had the only steady income. He gave her a little on occasion, not because he owed her but because she threatened to call the agency to pick him up.

Whitt's plan had foolproof stamped on it. He just hoped he wouldn't have to put it into action.

Stacy watched Whitt ride into the parking lot from school and chain up his bike. Soon he'd be her son, and they'd be a little family. She craved an opportunity to love him completely as a mother. If the judge chose to award custody later to his parents or someone else, he'd always have her love.

He entered the clinic, wearing his familiar grin.

"How was school?" she said.

"Good. I finished the edits on my English lit paper. I'd like for you to read it. Any feedback would be welcomed." He reached inside his backpack and handed it to her.

Not sure why he wanted her to read it, yet the thrill of reading his work gave her a sense of pride, and she cherished every word. "Excellent job," she said. His written communication skills, including grammar and punctuation, far exceeded her skills. But now she was versed in the styles of the poets who'd won the Nobel Prize in Literature.

"What suggestions do you have?" he said.

Quick, Stacy. She returned the paper. "You have an extra space in the header."

He nodded. "Contentwise."

"Organized. Informative. Will this be an online submission to the teacher?"

"Yes. The hard copy is for you."

"A photograph of each poet? Or for a contemporary one, a link to a recording of the author reading his work?"

He gave her a high five. "I'll get on it. How was your morning?"

"Fairly quiet."

"Does that mean your new phone is operational?"

"It is. Do you feel okay?"

"Perfecto. Why?"

"Just checking. Some of the kids who were at the carnival have the flu."

"I'm healthy." He slid a sideways glance at her. "What has you stressed? Are you sick?"

"I'm good."

"Something's wrong because I see little squiggly lines in your forehead."

She drew in a breath. If she kept the health department's recommendations from him, he'd find out or worry about whatever was bothering her. She handed him the letter.

He read and folded it neatly before returning it. "What actions have you taken?"

She told him what had transpired with the phone calls.

He paced the reception area of the clinic. "Why wouldn't they talk to each resident about the potential danger? Release a statement to the media? Put up posters? Take out newspaper ads? Talk to pastors and schools? Where's their community-minded spirit and communication skills?" he said. "From what you've told me, they're shoving the problem onto our shoulders. Like, 'Don't use the water, and we're sorry for the inconvenience.'"

"I'll learn more when the representative contacts me." She pointed to a notepad. "My questions are here, and I'm sure you have additional ones."

He scrunched his forehead and read her scribblings. "If it were me, I'd contact the local media and get them out here. Channel 5 has the most viewers. Suggest they interview residents and hear what we're up against. Three reasons why—number one, it could expedite the health department's involvement. Number two, the news would show how our community desperately needs help, and number three, it takes some of the burden off those who care about our little neighborhood."

"You're a genius."

He grinned. "So it's been said. You'd have come to the same conclusions." He nodded toward the back of the clinic. "I'm starved. Did you bring the leftover brisket?"

"With buns, chips, and ranch dressing."

"Stupendous. Have you eaten?"

"Go ahead. I'm going to make a few calls first."

Whitt leaned against the wall. "Since Saturday, one mess after another has clogged your head. How can I help?"

She blinked back the wetness. "Be yourself, and pray things resume to normal."

"Not too normal. The custody hearing is hovering like a storm cloud."

"God's will, Whitt. Although I'm anxious, the scales are balanced on our side. How about saddling up on Sunday afternoon and taking a long ride together? It'll be hot, but we can take the horses to a tree-lined trail."

"I'm all over it."

"Figured so."

He shifted uncomfortably. "By the way, on the way home from school, I saw a man nailing up signs—'Cash for your house.' I wonder how many people in our neighborhood will take him up on the offer after the health department letter."

"If he'd invest some dollars and flip the houses, I'd help him."

He laughed. "Hope the parents' landlord is the first to sell out."

"Me too." Poor boy. Once he'd loved them, but they'd crumpled any trace of affection. One day she and Whitt would have to face issues squarely and deal with the pain. But not today. *Change the subject.* "How was school?"

He shook his head. "Reverting to an old topic doesn't make the problems disappear. But I'll play. I finished math early and did the assignment for tomorrow."

"Good."

"Has the FBI guy called you?"

"Why?"

"Because he's interested, and I'm looking out for you."

Oh, Whitt. There's no need to be afraid of someone not wanting you in the picture. "He called to let me know there's nothing new about the case."

"Did he ask you out?"

"Why would he do such a thing?"

"Your face is red."

She gave him a feigned sideways glare. "Please."

"So are you going out?"

She lifted her chin. "I informed the agent that you and I are a package deal."

His eyes softened. "You don't have confirmation yet. Putting your life on hold for me isn't necessary."

"Let me be the judge of what's important in my life."

"Okay. I'm going to eat." He disappeared into the break room.

Her little man did a better job of avoiding emotional confrontations than she did.

"Miss Stacy," Whitt said, walking into the reception area again, "what time are visiting hours at the funeral home?"

"Seven to nine o'clock."

"One more thing I need to get behind me."

She ached to make Whitt's world an easier place, but he refused to address his deepest hurts, the ones only God could heal. She'd left hers at God's feet and prayed soon Whitt would discover his need for the ultimate Father, the One who'd never disappoint him.

Life had become far too tangled.

19

WEDNESDAY NIGHT, Stacy met Channel 5's TV station reporter and cameraman in the parking lot of the clinic. The well-dressed blonde in her early thirties smiled and extended her hand. Stacy recognized her from the evening news, a popular figure in Houston. The cameraman whipped into action, apparently preparing to use the clinic as a backdrop for the interview in the parking lot.

How very strange that a few days prior, she'd hosted a carnival here where families were entertained and enjoyed each other's company. Since then Mr. Parson had died and residents were becoming sick with flu-like symptoms from the water. But at this moment, she could handle only one of the problems plaguing her community, that of the health department warning them not to use the water while offering no alternative. She hoped her plea would bring a solution to the residents, other than moving to another location until the correct chemicals addressed the problem. Although nervous, she believed this was the best way to support the residents.

"Stacy Broussard?" When she nodded, the reporter introduced herself as Kathi Scott. "Thank you for agreeing to the interview. Do you have the health department's letter?"

She handed it to her, and the woman read the contents.

"I've never heard of the health department making such demands without offering assistance. For that matter, I'd think the Centers for Disease Control might have been consulted. Peculiar." Ms. Scott stared out at the street. "Would you excuse me for a moment? I want to call the station for clarification." The reporter made her way to the van.

Stacy waited in the heat. Whitt preferred to stay out of the public's eye, a wise move on his part. When Ms. Scott returned, she no longer wore a smile. "I've been asked not to cover this story until we have confirmed the letter's contents," she said. "Could I have a copy?"

"The one you have is a copy. I don't understand what's going on."

She smiled with what Stacy had come to recognize as professional courtesy. "My supervisor wants to talk to the health department. It's likely the notification is a hoax. Which is still a story for us to report but from an entirely different angle."

Cajun anger lifted the roots of her hair. She inhaled to keep from exploding. After all, it wasn't the reporter's fault. "Several of the residents received the letter. I phoned the number given on the letterhead. Twice. A representative was supposed to call me this afternoon to schedule a meeting. I expressed the need for residents to have a defined plan. Look around you—this isn't even middle-class America."

"Were you contacted?"

"No. I assumed they were busy."

Ms. Scott pursed her lips. "I'm really sorry, but we have to verify the sender. I should have asked you to fax me the letter beforehand, and then we wouldn't have wasted each other's time. This is a serious implication about the water's contamination, and the health department doesn't operate this way. They'd be swarming the area offering assistance and providing solutions."

"So you think the letter's a fraud even though people are sick?"

"I'm not sure, but our station prides itself on fair reporting based on facts."

Was she insinuating Stacy had lied? Trying to get media attention? For what? "Have you heard of anything like this before?"

"Not to my knowledge."

"Who would do such a thing? A desperate bottled water company?"

"I have no idea, but I do know this. Once we have the truth and this goes live, whoever sent the letter had better hide under a rock." She lifted her shoulders and drew in a breath. "But a hoax doesn't address the flu." She pulled her phone from her shoulder bag. "I do have a contact at the Laboratory Response Network. The director's a great guy, and if the water's been tested for disease, he'd know." She pressed in numbers. "This is Kathi Scott from Channel 5. I'd like to speak with Dexter Rayken."

Stacy waited while the reporter explained the situation.

"Thanks for taking the time." Ms. Scott ended the call and focused on Stacy. "Nothing's come through the LRN."

"This doesn't make sense." Stacy crossed her arms over her chest. "Would you use the water?"

"No. I'd be packing my suitcase."

She couldn't blame Ms. Scott for verifying the facts. If Stacy's mind wasn't so scattered, she'd have done the legwork prior to contacting the TV station.

20

STACY WOKE ON THURSDAY MORNING after a restless night deliberating the likelihood that she and other residents had received hoax letters regarding water contamination. The problem was worse than she'd imagined. If the threat was real, how long would the inconvenience last? If it was someone's idea of a prank, rowdy folks would be out for blood. Such was her neighborhood.

A few answers sounded good.

Late yesterday, after Kathi Scott from Channel 5 drove away with a promise to call back, Stacy and Whitt visited the funeral home. Mr. Parson had so many people paying their respects, but she welcomed the crowd. The two didn't stay long because they were both exhausted. On the way home, she purchased fifteen cases of water to drink, brush teeth, cook with, and use in the clinic. Actually, she'd bought out what Walmart had left in stock, which said others were on the same wavelength. Before coming home, they unloaded ten cases at the clinic. But what about bathing and laundry?

"I suppose you could call the pastor," Whitt had said last night. "See if we can shower there in the morning. We can load my bike into the truck, and I can ride to school from his house. This is worse than camping."

"I thought you enjoyed camping when we took some of the kids from church."

"When it's my choice, and the camping sites have water. I really hope someone ends up in jail over this."

She'd wanted to take herself and Whitt to a hotel, but reality and logic nixed the idea. Too many would view the action as inappropriate. Plus, if the letter was a deception, she'd be spending money needlessly and inviting vandals. No matter what path she chose, someone would criticize. The future had snakes slithering around her ankles.

At this very minute, she must spring her body into action for whatever Thursday demanded. Time to face the day. The enticing aroma of coffee captured her attention, and one more time she thanked God for the boy who'd stolen her heart. When the judge awarded her custody, she'd take him shopping for a new laptop. The one he used was a refurbished model that gave *slow* a new line in the computer dictionary. He needed tennis shoes and jeans and a haircut. She'd given him a bicycle for his birthday and wanted to do much more, but she feared purchasing even the essentials might meet with disapproval from social services, as though she were bribing him. So hard to discern how much or how little to contribute to his life when she wanted to do it all.

Her feet hit the floor, and she tied her robe securely around her waist. Odd, she was a little dizzy. She made her way down the hall to the kitchen. Once at the clinic this morning, she'd pull up the health department's website and find out for herself what was going on. Why hadn't she done that yesterday afternoon instead of panicking like a woman on hormone overload? There had to be a test for her own water to show its purity.

She paused at the entrance of the kitchen and watched Whitt add a half cup of chocolate syrup to his coffee. Some bits of him were all kid. "I'm buying stock in Hershey," she said.

He lifted a brow in greeting. Secretly she referred to him as Little Einstein.

"Do you have the right blend?"

"Sweet, chocolaty, and full of caffeine," he said. "I'm ready to leave whenever you are."

"Let me get us breakfast."

"Got it handled. We have cranberry pecan English muffins and bacon. I'll ready them for consumption while you pack your gear for the day."

"Thank you, sir." She wanted to laugh, but he was serious. When the mess of their lives was over, she'd encourage him to be a boy, not a mini adult.

Xena wagged her tail, and Stacy bent to pat her. "You are such a blessing to me and Whitt." The dog followed her back to her bedroom. Her cell rang, and she hurried to lift it from her nightstand charger.

"Dr. Broussard, this is the health department," a man said. "You left a message about needing a rep to speak to your subdivision. I apologize for not getting back to you. We had a series of emergencies that delayed us."

Reservations coiled around her. "A return call yesterday would have eased my mind in view of the water contamination scare. What is your name?"

"Jake Johnson. This is not a scare."

She wrote his name on a scrap piece of paper. "I must admit I have a few doubts."

"About what?"

"The validity of the letter. It's highly unlikely Houston's health department would make such an announcement without having media backup, a press release, and solutions for the residents."

"I assure you our claims are viable with serious health implications. Would you like for me to come by your clinic on Monday?"

"Today is preferable. Residents need answers as soon as possible. These people are not financially able to check into hotels."

"I'm sorry, but we are still in the midst of an emergency."

"Friday?"

"Impossible."

"Saturday?"

"We don't work on weekends."

"Really? When people's health is an issue?"

"I'm sorry. Today's situation takes priority."

"What's the critical issue? Media hasn't reported a problem."

"Neither have they done so with your polluted water. We've learned some information communicated to the public can lead to near hysteria."

"Like you've done in our subdivision. I'd like to speak to your supervisor."

"She's not available."

"If I drive to your office, who will I talk to?"

"That would be me, Dr. Broussard. We're managing the best we can." Jake verified the clinic's address.

"I'd like your supervisor's name."

"We can discuss that when I'm there at nine thirty on Monday morning."

Stacy fumed, while misgivings spread through her mind. "Please bring a copy of the water testing report regarding our tower, and I'll invite a few of the residents."

"Most certainly. We want to answer questions and help you determine a path forward."

"Bring your supervisor. This situation has been handled poorly."

"I'll talk to her. She's quite busy."

"Then I'll make a personal—"

He ended the call before she had an opportunity to tell him she'd be at the health department's front door if answers and solutions weren't provided soon.

She placed her phone back in the charger. The smell of bacon met her nostrils, reminding her the day ahead demanded full attention. She and Whitt ate breakfast, showered at her pastor's home, then chatted with his family until it was time for Whitt to ride his bike to school and her to drive to work.

At 8 a.m., she opened the clinic and began the morning. Only Xena remained in her care, and with the freedom, Stacy let the Lab keep her company. The dog had the sweetest temperament, and Whitt had quickly grown attached. They both loved her.

Shortly before nine, a short, round man entered the clinic without an animal. From his white shirt, khaki pants, and briefcase, she figured he was peddling animal supplies.

"Can I help you?" she said.

"I'm looking for Stacy Broussard."

"I'm she."

He handed her a business card—Walter M. Brown Investments. "I represent an investor who is interested in purchasing property in this community. I understand you own your home and lease the space here for your clinic. We're prepared to make you a cash offer for your property."

She'd paid cash for the home and would sell when she was ready. "I'm not interested."

He snorted. "I understand, but with the health department's

mandate about the water problem, we're prepared to offer residents a way to recoup from the loss of value certain to come."

"The theory that our water is causing illnesses hasn't been confirmed."

He leaned over her receptionist counter, reminding her of Ace McMann taking a threatening pose. Apprehension crept through her. At least a four-foot-high barrier stood between them.

"Dr. Broussard, I believe you and the residents have been officially notified about the bacteria polluting your water. Waterborne diseases plague the world. In your community, children and adults are battling flu-like symptoms." He held his fist up, punctuating every word. "How long can people hold out when loved ones are ill? What if they die?"

"You've rehearsed your spiel quite well," she said. "I'm not impressed. The letter arrived yesterday. Without verification, I refuse to jump onto your bandwagon. To assume our water isn't pure or that it's causing people to be sick is a mistake." She eyed him curiously. "Or is this what you're planning, to take advantage of innocent, frightened people?"

He stepped back. "I resent your insults. I represent an investor who is reaching out in a gesture of goodwill."

"Why? If the water is a problem, why would anyone be interested in the homes and land?"

"Because ultimately the city is responsible. Until it's rectified, my investor can wait it out."

"What plans does the investor have for our little subdivision?"

"I'm not privy to future projects. I'm not sure he has made a decision."

"How did you learn about the water?"

"Public knowledge."

"Really? Who's the informant?"

"I believe Channel 5 stopped by the clinic yesterday with Kathi Scott. Was the TV station interested in helping the folks here like my investor?"

Anger tramped through her body. "Are you the one who posted signs about paying cash for houses?"

"I am."

She bit her lip to keep from lashing out even more than she'd already expressed. "Your investor didn't waste any time."

"No, ma'am. Opportunity knocks. If we can't do business, then I'll be on my way. Contact the number on the business card to speak to me directly."

"I think you're full of garbage. I'm really disappointed in your investment firm attempting to capitalize on the less fortunate, so, Mr. . . . ?"

"Smith."

She huffed. Why was she not surprised? The more she learned, the more she smelled a bag of lies. Jake Johnson from the health department and Mr. Smith. "Thank you for stopping by, but I'm not about to promote your propaganda." She took a breath. "If you are correct in your claims, I'll be happy to apologize for my rudeness."

His smile was . . . slick. "I have several appointments today in your neighborhood. Thank you for your time." He walked to the door. "Don't imagine your clinic will stay in business when folks move out. Hate to see you file bankruptcy."

"I'm sure it would distress you immensely."

"Even if you learn the water's safe, who would ever be interested in purchasing property here?"

Ace McMann threatened to burn her to the ground, and now

Mr. Smith indicated her clinic would be ruined. Time for a fact-finding mission.

As Mr. Smith left the parking lot, she wrote down his license plate number. First on her agenda was pulling up the official website of Houston's health department.

She spoke to a Mr. James Nisse and explained the situation. Two minutes into the conversation, she learned the people of her subdivision had been duped.

"If the health department suspected a problem with your water, we'd have people there immediately," Mr. Nisse said. "The public needs to be aware of possible criminal activity. If you'll give me your address, I'll be there in the next hour to handle this unfortunate incident. In the meantime, I'll contact HPD for their assistance."

"Thank you so much. Finally I'm getting help and answers." She sat at her desk and stared at the landline. Another thought came to mind, and she typed into her computer for a large, nationwide real estate company with offices in Houston. Finding their number, she called for possible commercial real estate information. They were unaware of a developer interested in her subdivision or the surrounding area. A certain amount of trickle-down information occurred at the highest level of management among real estate companies, but they knew nothing.

So why had someone chosen to scare those in her neighborhood, and were they connected to the investment company buying out the home owners?

Dexter concluded a conversation with James Nisse, who wanted to know if he'd heard anything about a water hoax on the north side of town. In view of Kathi Scott at Channel 5 making an inquiry the previous evening, he wanted to handle this personally. He'd first heard Dr. Broussard's name on Saturday when she found a body. This was Alex's case and the woman he'd talked about. Picking up his phone, he called the veterinary clinic, and a woman answered.

"Dr. Broussard, this is Dexter Rayken, director of the Laboratory Response Network. I spoke to a representative from the health department, and he relayed an unfortunate incident about the water tower in your neighborhood."

"Yes, sir. It appears we've been victims of a water hoax, and now an investment company is approaching home owners. A man from the health department should be here shortly, and I've been assured HPD will be involved. Another problem that seems to coincide with it is an outbreak of flu."

"James Nisse is a good man, and he'll help resolve the issues. When this came to my attention through Channel 5 last night, I failed to contact you. I'm truly sorry."

"Apology accepted. I feel foolish to have been so vulnerable. If you don't mind, what is your role with the city's health department?"

"Dr. Broussard, your questions show your concern for yourself and others affected. The LRN is a federal network of laboratories to assist with public health concerns. Our organization tests all possible contaminants for the CDC, FBI, and other agencies. I suggest you continue to work with the Houston Health Department and law enforcement to resolve the problem. However, if you have further questions or concerns, please take my personal number to contact me." He gave her his cell number. "No one should live in fear of water contamination."

"Thank you, sir. I appreciate your taking time to reassure me."

Dexter said his good-bye and e-mailed James and Alex as a follow-up. Whoever was responsible for the scare deserved to be in jail.

21

WHITT PEDALED HIS BIKE to the clinic after school, eager to hear every detail about the health department's assessment of the water problem. His concern for Miss Stacy mounted. She already struggled to keep all her balls juggling in the air, but no one could maintain a stressful pace for very long without eventually crumbling. If she did, he'd be dropped back into the system.

He was selfish, but he couldn't help it. Miss Stacy stood for the things he'd always wanted . . . a home and someone who cared.

Late into the night, he'd read about waterborne diseases. A host of protozoal, bacterial, parasitic, and viral infections were water transmitted. The majority had flu-like symptoms, like those reported from the sick kids in his neighborhood. If the reports about their water were the real deal, a lot of people would be sick. Some might even die. The names of the diseases and how they affected people were characteristic of incidences in third-world countries, not in Houston, Texas. The thought of biological warfare hit him hard.

The people in his neighborhood were the poor who couldn't afford to move and those who'd knife you for your shoes. Neither deserved to die. Miss Stacy had always insisted upon the value of life.

You're overreacting, overthinking, overanticipating again. He rode his bike as though getting to the clinic faster would produce positive results. Once he locked up his bike, he dashed inside.

"Miss Stacy?"

"Back here. Xena and I are discussing the possibilities for lunch." She sounded optimistic. Happy. He relaxed.

With purposeful strides, he joined her in the office. "You must have extraordinary news about the water problem."

She glanced up into his face. "Depends on how you look at it. The spokesperson from the health department called me."

"What did you learn?"

She scratched Xena behind the ears. "They apparently don't have time for us until Monday."

"We're at the bottom of their totem pole."

"I'm teasing. There's more. I went online and phoned the number for Houston's health department, and guess what I discovered?" Anger burned in her dark-blue eyes. "We received a bogus letter. Officials from the city are going door-to-door, speaking with residents about the hoax. From all indicators, our water is fine. I've called or sent an e-mail to those residents we have addresses for and given them the real health department's phone number. I received a call from the LRN, and the director gave me his cell phone number if problems persist. In the meantime, I've agreed to cooperate with local authorities and meet Monday morning with the originator of our letter." She lifted her chin. *"Jamais de ma vie."*

He'd heard the Cajun phrase enough to understand the meaning—he'd never heard anything like this in his life either. "Wait a minute. . . . Are you putting yourself in danger?"

She shook her head. "Already have it handled. The moment the person suggests he or she is employed by the health department or admits to sending the letter, a police officer back here will make an arrest."

He bent to love on Xena. "Why go to all the trouble? Let someone else handle it." His mind shifted into reverse. "What would anyone have to gain by spreading lies anyway? I mean, if we had oil beneath our homes, maybe."

"I investigated potential building projects too." She told him about the real estate investment company wanting to pay cash for homes, and her futile effort to find out what a developer wanted with their property. "The problem is I don't see a connection to those sick with flu."

"Flu can break out anywhere. He's using it to his advantage. I don't like the idea of him having appointments with residents."

"Right. I also learned he's not doing a thing wrong by offering them cash for their property. It's a legal transaction."

"By preying on people who're afraid? Miss Stacy, you know he's using scare tactics and making dirt-low offers. I bet he sent the letters."

"Maybe so. Which is a huge reason for me to do my part on Monday. Maybe the investment company plans to build something here and wants to keep it secret."

"The city's had a proposed Grand Parkway in the works for a long time, and the construction would bring in jobs." Questions skipped across his mind. "But I'll look into it."

"In the whole scheme of what's happened to upset our lives, the biggest priority is getting custody of you. Pushing for adoption—"

His insides did a flip. "You never told me about adoption."

She blew out her exasperation. "Sorry. My thinking's jumbled, and I really wanted to ask you about it in a sit-down conversation. But it's in my plan if you're okay with it."

"Of course I am! Having you for my mom would be awesome."

She smiled. "Then we'll pray for the judge's wisdom. The fraudulent letters about the water and the alarm it's caused are deplorable, but it's not the most critical issue in our lives. We can't take on the problems of the world. Those who have expertise in bringing down lawbreakers will take care of this."

Whitt didn't like the string of coincidences, underhanded business tactics, and lies. From the lines across her forehead, she had worries that rose to a frightening level. One more time, she was trying to protect him from the realities of life. "This won't be over soon," he said. "Too much is at stake and whoever's responsible has gone to a tremendous amount of trouble."

The possible repercussions from her setting up the bad guys yanked at his fear factor. He'd read the Bible tonight to build up his points with God.

Please protect Miss Stacy.

22

ALEX GRABBED HIS PHONE and met Ric in the hallway. Techs had identified the voice of the man who'd called for Todd Howe, a man who'd done time for land fraud. This wasn't information to convey over the phone.

"Is Bekah expecting us?" Ric said.

"She is, and I told her we not only had the name but also have a photo. She said she might have additional information for us."

Alex and Ric were escorted inside the Howe home by an older woman who introduced herself as a friend. Bekah soon appeared. Her dark skirt and blouse hung on her like a scarecrow's, and her hollow cheeks rivaled a horror movie. Wasn't anyone taking care of her? What were these people doing if not helping her through this tragedy?

"We can talk in Todd's office," she said. "Would you like something to drink?"

"No, thank you." Alex wanted to take her to dinner, fill out those bones. She'd wither away to nothing if someone didn't give her a reason to live.

"How are your sons?" Ric said.

Good man.

"They are managing. I appreciate your asking. Please, follow me." She walked to a room on the left and opened the door, indicating for them to enter.

Todd's large office was typical—rich hardwood floors, a massive desk, and a built-in bookcase. From the randomly placed three chairs, the seating arrangement was a new addition. She was the last one to sit.

"Mrs. Howe," Alex said, "do you mind if our conversation is recorded?"

"Of course not."

He pulled up a photo and handed his phone to her. "This is Lynx Connor, who has been confirmed and identified through voice recognition software as the man who phoned asking for Todd."

She clasped her mouth and stared at the photo. "He's the man I suspected from the footage you showed me. I planned to give you his name."

"Do you know him as Lynx Connor?"

"Yes, he's a business associate of Todd's. Have you questioned him?"

"The FBI is seeking to locate him. He used a burner phone when he contacted you. What can you tell us about Mr. Connor?"

"I never cared for him. Rather crude in his language. Actually I wouldn't have learned his name if I hadn't found a slip of paper in my husband's suit pants. I check his pockets before the cleaners pick them up."

"How was Connor introduced to you?" Nothing about the man had been found on Todd's devices or phone records, indicating he must have used burner phones when they communicated.

"Todd said Mr. Connor lived in LA and owned a real estate investment company that also had an office in Houston. Mr. Connor would come by the house all hours of the day and night to tell Todd about commercial opportunities. My husband used him for possible restaurant expansion sites."

"Seems odd the man made house calls instead of picking up the phone or communicating electronically."

"I asked the same thing, but Todd claimed it was necessary for discreet conversations."

"Were you privy to their discussions?"

"No, sir."

"Weren't you curious?"

"Not at 2 a.m. or when I was busy with the boys or running our home. In hindsight, I should have insisted on being a part of those meetings. Gentlemen, I will never again fall under the heading of sheltered or protected." She paused. "We have security cameras inside our home, and I can provide the link for you to view."

"Perfect." Alex pieced together a marriage that left more than communication out of the relationship. "How long had the two men been doing business?"

"Hmm. A couple of years. Maybe longer."

"Thank you for your help, Mrs. Howe. Agent Price or I will be in touch."

"Mrs. Howe," Ric began, "before we leave, I'd like to speak sincerely with you regarding your health. Your sons are Levi and Elijah?" When she nodded, he continued. "They need you. Their father is gone, and you have the tremendous role of filling both shoes. But if you don't take care of yourself, they will be orphans."

Her eyes pooled. "I realized my failings this morning when I dressed."

"Promise us from this moment on, you will eat, rest, and find the strength to take each moment as it occurs."

She drew in a deep breath. "You and Agent LeBlanc are more than investigators. You have become friends. I promise, just as I made the same vow to God earlier today."

23

LATE FRIDAY AFTERNOON, Alex battled the traffic as he left the office. Dumb decision to venture into Friday's midafternoon rush hour. People were hurrying home from a short workday or following up on early weekend plans, and the result was bumper-to-bumper traffic, brake lights, and impatience.

Alex despised the lack of progress in the case. Dead ends had plagued him last evening and today, leaving a taste of bitterness and frustration that added acid to his disposition.

Unfinished work on the case could be done at home, including probing deeper into the relationship between Todd Howe and Lynx Connor. Alex needed think time. Then he would run his thoughts by Ric. His partner took evidence and simplified it like a math formula, shoving theories into Alex's mind that he'd never considered. Together they were able to dissect crimes effectively.

Domestic terrorism waved the highest flag, and homegrown offenders had his vote. This weekend he'd spend hours poring over evidence and backgrounds to help the FBI put boots on the ground to end this mess. And hope Lynx Connor was brought into custody and persuaded to talk. Although, with the way this case had gone, Connor probably had nothing to do with any of it.

Alex lifted a bottle of water from the cup holder and drank deeply while the vehicles in front of him crept ahead. An image of Stacy Broussard refused to leave him alone. Every time he decided she was too complicated for his style, her face or something she'd said took over his thoughts. He refused to call her with his misgivings, but he wanted to. A relationship, or friendship as he should term it, hadn't interested him in months. Maybe longer.

He wanted a woman who challenged him, not a yes-sir type. Stacy had those qualities along with beauty and a depth of intellect hidden behind those blue eyes and cowgirl image. Determination and a heavy dose of stubbornness made her that much more attractive. Cajun roots were a plus too.

Alex turned up the radio's volume to hear the latest out of Washington. Never positive, but always information he needed to know. His cell rang in the middle of a commentary about the latest threats to Israel.

"Special Agent Alex LeBlanc."

"This is Whitt McMann. Do you remember me?"

He smiled, despite being interrupted from the news flash, and turned down the radio. "Yes. You're a friend of Stacy Broussard."

"Right. Our subdivision has been hit with threats about our water system being contaminated. The residents received letters supposedly from the health department . . ." Whitt went on to explain the letter's contents, Stacy's attempt to obtain clarification, the investment firm offering cash for property, and Houston Health Department's denial along with Stacy's contact with the LRN. "She tried to find out if our subdivision was the site of any building programs. Couldn't find a thing. A hoax."

"The situation isn't under the FBI's jurisdiction unless we're asked to get involved." Alex needed to follow up with Dexter about his e-mail.

"I realize your boundaries, and your specific division is domestic terrorism. My concern is she's agreed to set up the ones who sent the letters. I'm worried about her safety. She has the license plate number of the man representing the investment firm."

A twinge of alarm met him. "I'll take it and run a check."

"Thanks. I also called a pro bono attorney, but no one would talk to me because of my age. My question is how reliable is the Houston Police Department at keeping her from getting hurt?"

"Is an officer accompanying her? Or is she wearing a recorder?"

"HPD plans to be in the back of the clinic and make an arrest when the conversation incriminates the speaker."

This kid and his vocabulary. "Our police department is one of the finest in the country. The officer will have her back."

"But there is an element of risk in the takedown, right?"

"There's always that possibility."

"Would you talk to her? I personally don't think this is a smart move. She has no martial arts skills, no means of defending herself."

"I'd be glad to. I'll call and see if she opens up."

"What about an impromptu visit? You're a pro at showing up unexpectedly."

Alex chuckled. "When would you like for this to happen?"

"Tonight. No gumbo, though. Usually we grill burgers and watch a movie on Friday nights."

There went his evening alone with his thoughts and waiting on a call from LA. "Okay, I can do this. I like my burger medium rare. What's the movie?"

"It's an old one called *High Crimes*, one of my favorites. Miss Stacy questioned the rating's kid-friendly status, but I've seen it all. Anyway Morgan Freeman, Ashley Judd, and Jim Caviezel are the stars. Released in 2002. You might like it. Lots of intrigue and deception."

Alex should recruit this kid. "I think I remember it."

"Oh, bring flowers. That's always a good touch with a woman."

Alex laughed. "Thanks. Does she have a favorite?"

"Yellow roses, and for bonus points, popcorn-flavored Jelly Bellies."

"Where do I find the candy?"

"Candy store at the mall near us. About seven thirty okay?"

"Sure. Are you playing matchmaker?"

"No. You'll be there as an investigator. I'm not even sure I like you yet. Got my own trust issues going on. But I think of myself as Miss Stacy's bodyguard."

"Tough role for a kid." Another question rose in Alex's mind. "What's the name of the investment firm?"

"Walter M. Brown Investments. They have a website and a contact tab, but not an address. Looks like a shell company to me."

Once more the kid was one step ahead of him. "Appreciate the heads-up. I should have time to check it out before picking up flowers and candy."

"Channel 5 is reporting the fraud on the six o'clock news tonight. But money talks, and Mr. Smith is writing checks."

"If he's doing anything illegal, he'll get caught. I guarantee it."

"Thanks for helping me keep her safe." Whitt ended the call.

Alex laughed again. Youth, bluntness, and obviously a mind that never shut down.

Was Stacy a magnet for trouble? In the last week, she'd been hit with a boatload of grim encounters, and none had been resolved. He'd always heard troubles came in threes, and she'd met the max.

The agent in him probed the various possibilities. She lived in an area many Houstonians would prefer to see bulldozed or totally refurbished. He sent a request to the FIG concerning Walter M. Brown Investments.

Thirty-five minutes later when he pulled into his apartment complex, he had his answer. The license plate was listed to a woman who'd reported the car stolen. The firm was a shell company, as Whitt suspected. But this one had a paper trail a mile long.

24

FRIDAY EVENING, Stacy parked her truck in the garage and turned off the engine. Never had she been so glad to see a week come to a close. The alleged Mr. Smith had stopped by the clinic earlier that morning and informed her three families had accepted Walter M. Brown Investments' cash offer for their homes, and six others were considering the deal. Fortunately Whitt had already left for school. Or had Smith watched him pedal away and chosen then to pay her another visit? The prices the home owners were accepting were far lower than market value, and she told him so.

"Hard times demand hard prices," Smith had said. "This afternoon I'll be speaking to several owners who rent out their properties."

"They'll be making a terrible mistake. Our water's fine."

He smirked. "Damage's already done. Regardless of what is proven or revealed, the owners want to unload their property."

She pointed to the door. "Leave now before I call the police."

He waved and left, squealing his tires in the parking lot like a disgruntled teenager. Today he was driving a different vehicle, but by the time she hurried outside to read the plate number, he'd already driven off.

Then the 1:00 funeral drained her of what little emotional control she had left.

Mr. Parson received military funeral honors. The dear man had outlined his service in detail and given his requests to his son months prior to his death. An honor guard of four Marines performed a powerful ceremony that included folding the American flag and presenting it to Mr. Parson's oldest son. The music was a patriotic and faith-filled commemoration to a highly decorated Marine. The service concluded with a Marine playing taps and not a dry eye in the church. Hers and Whitt's included. Afterward, Whitt wanted to spend time at her house alone, and she understood his need to work through Mr. Parson's death.

Now all she wanted to do was shut the world out and relax with Whitt. He'd offered to put together a salad, bake potatoes, and grill burgers. She'd make brownies to go with vanilla ice cream, or the other way around. She preferred a balance of hot gooey brownies covered with mountains of vanilla ice cream, drowning her woes in indulgences that would add inches to her thighs.

For a week she'd endured one horrific event after another. It almost made the custody hearing next Wednesday a breath of fresh air. Almost. She refused to cease praying until the judge signed the papers.

She ventured into the kitchen and noted an extra uncooked hamburger patty on a platter. "Did you forget one?" she said to Whitt, who was chopping up cucumbers and red bell peppers for the salad.

"I'm really hungry and thought I might want another one later."

He already had the brownies in the oven. Did he think he had to earn her love?

A nudge to call her mom swirled around her head and landed in her heart. She wanted to tell her about Whitt, but with all that was going on and the exhaustion weighing on her body, she'd wait for the next conversation.

They ate while watching the six o'clock news on Channel 5. Kathi Scott reported the water fraud incident and gave residents a number to call at the health department. Finally resolution to a few headaches. But Smith's words slammed against her brain. No matter what happened, owners would want to unload property. Who'd ever want to live here where it was dangerous to step outside your home at night? Although the water problem was a hoax, some people would never forget it.

After they'd eaten and loaded the dishwasher, she and Whitt settled into their Friday night routine. She slipped the DVD into the player and grabbed an afghan to snuggle up on the couch. Xena lay at Whitt's feet, and it was blissfully, wonderfully peaceful.

The doorbell rang. She moaned and glared at the door.

"I'll get it." Whitt rushed to his feet. He had more energy than she'd ever own.

"Check who's there first."

"Yes, ma'am." A moment later the door creaked open. "Hi, Agent LeBlanc. Looks like you're armed to see Miss Stacy."

Armed? She shook off the afghan, paused the DVD, and stumbled to the door. Alex grinned. In one hand he carried a vase filled with a dozen yellow roses and baby's breath, and in the other, he clutched a bag of popcorn Jelly Belly candies. He handed both to her. She inhaled the sweet rose scent. "Thank you so much."

"You're welcome."

She sent an accusatory look at Whitt. "I sense a conspiracy here. Whose idea was this?"

"Mine," they both said.

She laughed and gestured Alex inside. "We're ten minutes into *High Crimes*. From the looks on your faces, you two probably wrote the script." Now to figure out why Whitt wanted Alex to pay a visit, especially when the man would have called her if he'd truly been interested.

"Have a seat, Alex. The afghan is mine, so hands off."

"Yes, ma'am." He sat rather stiffly.

"Coffee or lemonade?"

"Coffee. Black."

"Typical," she said on the way to the kitchen.

"How so?"

"High-profile law enforcement types always drink their coffee black. That way they can cap it and dash out into the cold, cruel world to solve a crime." She reached into the cabinet for a mug and whirled around to find Alex behind her. She jumped.

"Didn't mean to startle you."

She smiled. "Tell me why you're here. I'm really tired, and I know Whitt put you up to this. Can't be about last Saturday." Realization rained on her. "He called you about the health department mix-up."

He nodded and took the full mug she extended to him. "He mentioned a sting operation. I learned that Walter M. Brown Investments is a shell company."

"For what?"

He tilted his head, probably forming an appropriate reply. "Not sure because this one isn't easily traced."

"My life goes from one nightmare to a huge stressor that has me on overload." She took a breath, the kind that usually calmed her. "What else can you tell me?"

"Mr. Smith is driving a stolen car."

"This morning he had a different one. But I missed catching the license plate number."

"No problem. He's stretching his luck. Whitt's concerned about your safety in helping HPD."

She tossed a glance into the living room, where Whitt was sorting through DVDs. "He's a bit over-the-top. I'm simply having a meeting with a person at the clinic. The only difference is a police officer will overhear the conversation."

"I can still hear you," Whitt said. "I'm not over-the-top but a conscientious citizen."

"Close your ears." Her gaze fell on the uncooked hamburger patty. "Grill the burger for Alex, since that was your original intention."

"Yes, ma'am. Medium rare?"

Alex nodded and watched him walk onto the patio. "You can file tonight as an unorthodox interview." He waited until Whitt closed the door leading outside to the patio and grill before continuing. "Ever done this sort of thing before?"

"No." She rummaged through her mind for words to change the intensity of the moment. "Want to give me a couple of tips?"

He frowned. "How about be careful, and do you want to go through with this?"

She poured a cup for herself and added cream. "Seriously, I'm fine." She leaned back against the counter and faced him. "The flowers and candy are very thoughtful. The popcorn Jelly Bellies are delish."

"I wouldn't know."

"I'll let you sample mine."

"And deprive you of your treat?" He pulled out his phone. "Can you look at a photo?" When she agreed, he navigated to Lynx Connor's pic.

She drew in a sharp breath at the recognition. "He's the man representing Walter M. Brown Investments, wanted me to sell my home. In fact, he's put up signs to pay cash and has been meeting with home owners to buy their property. Using the water hoax as a scare tactic."

"We have a BOLO out for him. When was the last time you saw him?"

"This morning shortly after Whitt left for school. He claimed to be meeting with more home owners in the afternoon."

"Hold on a minute while I notify the office." He typed into his phone. When he finished, a slight smile met her. "Thank you. He's been identified as an associate of Todd Howe's."

"The murder is connected to the water scheme?"

"Possibly."

"Alex." She touched her throat. "I'm waist-deep in a horrible crime."

He studied her color-stricken face.

"Can you arrest him?"

"Only question him. It's not against the law to use a pseudonym, capitalize on gossip, or pay cash for property."

"That's disheartening."

"But he has rights too. Stacy, I promise this will soon be behind you."

She saw a hint of interest in his gaze that shook her. "You don't have to stay."

"But the movie is supposed to be one of Whitt's favorites."

"Oh, he primed you." She pressed her lips together, a bit nervous to be alone with him even with Whitt there. But she wanted to know him better.

He took a long drink of his coffee. "So you hear it from me first, earlier this week Ric and I talked to the manager of the Aldine Westfield Stables. Said his name was Chet. He gave us the tour."

She paused, a surge of anger rising from the soles of her feet. "I thought I'd been cleared?"

"You have. Every detail of Saturday's case has to be visited. Nothing personal, okay?"

She sensed her face growing hot. "Learn anything new?"

He slowly nodded. "The members-only section of the airport ranger website isn't secure."

"Does it matter?"

"Only when a hacker can determine when and where a volunteer is riding and a man ends up dead. Add the quadcopter piece."

He'd made his point. "I'll insist stricter security measures are used. I'm an officer for the group. Is the investigation headed toward interviewing all the airport rangers?" Sarcasm laced her words, and she didn't apologize for it.

"We want to talk to a few. By the way, I saw you're on the schedule tomorrow."

"I am."

"Mind if I join you? Chet said he'd have a gentle horse for me to ride."

She should have known Alex had his bases covered. "With two other women?"

"I've already talked to them, and they said I was welcome. I have their coffee preferences so I won't come empty-handed."

"*C'est tout finis.*"

"That's it. You're finished?" He translated her Cajun and laughed. "Do you mean I'm irresistible?"

"Please."

The back door opened and shut. "Hey, you two. A movie is calling our name," Whitt said. "And we have brownies and ice cream for dessert."

"I smelled them the moment I came in," Alex said. "With or without nuts?"

"Without," Stacy said, almost wishing he'd be gone by then.

So much she wanted to know about what the agents had discovered, but she couldn't ask with Whitt privy to every word. What more had Alex uncovered about Lynx Connor?

Tomorrow she'd probe deeper.

Sunday she'd rest.

Monday she'd do her part in stopping those who were spreading lies about their water.

Tuesday she had an appointment with Mr. Nardell to go over the court details.

Wednesday was the hearing. Then she'd move on to whatever was going to blindside her next.

25

SATURDAY MORNING, Alex stopped at Chick-fil-A and loaded five large coffees with the fixings, breakfast sandwiches, and orange juice into carryout containers—the OJ because women liked the healthy touch. As he maneuvered his Jeep to the stables, the smell drove him nuts and his stomach rumbled.

He removed the lid to one of the coffees and took a sip. Sleep had evaded him last night. Being around Stacy distracted him far too much, and now he was heading to the stables to ride the airport trail with her and her friends. He told himself this was in the name of investigating an unsolved crime, but he enjoyed the side benefits.

Shortly after 1 a.m., Pacific time, the LA office had picked up Lynx Connor at LAX airport, arriving from Houston. He lawyered up at his arrest. His interview would be a priority not only for California and Houston but for all the nation's FBI offices. Alex wanted an opportunity to question him, but he'd have to settle for his responses from the LA office. Connor could have been in Houston during the time of the murder. Did the man wear a size 12½ shoe and own a 9mm?

Alex parked and grabbed the cardboard container of drinks and bag of breakfast items. He made his way to the stables. The mixed scents of animals and hay took him back to boyhood days. Now to find out if distributing Connor's pic there provided more information. Long shot, but he'd been surprised before.

Chet had a gelding saddled for him. Alex handed him a coffee and a breakfast sandwich. From the wide smile, he'd pleased the man.

Shortly thereafter, Stacy and the other women parked alongside Alex's Jeep. She introduced Marie Albert and Leslie Ott, the two volunteers she normally rode with, and he presented his breakfast tokens. One more time, he received extra points for his Cajun charm.

"Please, *couillon*," she said.

"What did you call him?" Chet said.

"Cajun for a 'crazy fool,' but it's not bad. Rather sweet." He lifted a brow at her and chuckled.

She marched into the stables, giving Chet and the other two women a laugh. Strange, he hadn't wanted to impress a woman in far too long. Maybe when this case was over, he'd ask her out for dinner instead of coffee or showing up unexpectedly at her doorstep. Or having two other women chaperone.

While the women saddled their horses, Alex showed Connor's pic to Chet and the women. None had seen him before. He found Stacy alone.

"I have some news," he said. "Lynx Connor was picked up by the LA office."

Her shoulders eased. "What a relief."

"I'll keep you posted with what I can."

She tilted her head. "I understand."

The ride relaxed him, although at times the sound of approaching aircraft broke the solitude. The outdoors and the horse beneath him gave him more of an understanding why the airport volunteers were eager to do their part.

Not that he totally supported them.

They rode past the crime scene, and he picked up on Stacy's tense reaction.

He rode closer to her. "Breathe and relax," he whispered.

"It's raw, remembering it again. Was I targeted to find the body since this is apparently connected to my subdivision?"

He had the same theory, but more evidence was needed. "We'll find out the truth. Given enough pressure and his increasing charges, Connor could provide answers today."

"You're just trying to make me feel better, but I appreciate it."

He thought of her poetry. "Have you written out your feelings? That might help."

Her blue eyes flashed to his, warm and vulnerable. "I could try."

He'd touched on her creative side, and that seemed to bother her a little. How well he empathized with those conflicting feelings of wanting a person to know him completely but being afraid of getting hurt. How would she respond if she knew he could read her?

Stacy's mare snorted and reared. Alex's horse spooked too, and he gripped the reins.

A rattlesnake slithered across the trail in front of them and disappeared.

Stacy's mare's front legs lifted again, sending Stacy into the brush. The mare took off running toward the busy road.

Alex attempted to calm his dancing horse while worry slammed against his mind. "Stacy, are you all right?"

The two women dismounted and hurried to Stacy's aid, while he rode the whirlwind with the horse beneath him. His horse stilled, yet continued to tremble. He patted the gelding's side, coaxing the horse to relax. "Is Stacy okay?"

"We're not sure yet," Marie said in a gentle Hispanic lilt. "Looks like she got the wind knocked out of her."

"Call an ambulance." Alex dismounted and wrapped the reins around a sapling. He wanted eyes on Stacy.

"I'm okay," came a familiar voice.

A rustle in the bushes snatched his attention. Stacy's horse trotted back onto the trail and nuzzled against her cheek.

Stacy reached up to pat the mare's neck. "Sweet Ginger, you should never run onto the road. You could have been killed."

Alex knelt at her side. "What about tossing her rider?"

"The rattler scared her."

"Right. Where do you hurt?"

"I'm in one piece, other than bruises."

"The last time you broke your arm," Leslie said. "I should know—since I was with you."

Stacy peered at Alex. "Help me up?"

"No way." He scooped her up into his arms, and that's when he realized his heart had taken a huge dip. "Do you hurt?"

Her face flushed red. "Not at all. I . . . I can ride now."

Back at the stables, Alex unsaddled and brushed down the gelding, then made his way to Stacy's side.

"Is your day busy?"

She brushed her mare without giving him eye contact. "Appointments at the clinic. I'll open back up at noon. Will the FBI issue a press release about the water fraud?"

"I'll check. Since we've connected a couple of dots with Connor, the update would calm your neighborhood and certainly help negate signing a hasty buyer's agreement." He frowned. "The whys are like walking through a maze blindfolded." Bekah had stated that Connor recommended properties for future restaurant sites. A whole subdivision made little sense, especially given its location. Why Stacy? What was the common denominator?

She caught his attention. "I see worry lines. Whitt and I will be on our best behavior until this is settled. No crusading or knocking on doors to deter home owners from selling out. But I do want to know exactly how Lynx Connor is connected to Todd Howe."

"Me too. Your bodyguard better keep you in line."

"He will. Too much like a little man instead of a boy who needs to experience life."

"When's the hearing?"

"Wednesday afternoon."

"I'll make sure a prayer is sent your way."

Her eyes indicated surprise. "A Christian?"

"I believe in God. Was brought up in church. I accepted what I heard but never understood what it meant. Working on it."

"Hard to live a Christian life and hard not to rely on God. Which is it?"

"Another poem?"

"Yes." She looked at the brush. "Alex, you and I—"

"Might kill each other if we attempted a relationship."

She stepped back, shying away from him, unlike the Stacy Broussard who spoke her mind with ease. "Exactly."

"Don't know until we try—when this is over."

Chet ambled their way and took the mare by the reins. "I've got her from here." He nodded and walked away.

She spun a combination lock, lifted the lid of a tack box, and pulled out her purse. "Is it worth the effort?"

For some crazy reason, he wanted more than friendship between them, the three of them, Whitt included. Bizarre thinking when at times, he'd doubted her truthfulness in the crime. Wanting to trust her didn't make her innocent. Especially when he considered his track record.

"This case has me as a person of interest, and if you proved that I was an accomplice, you'd look like a fool."

He'd look like more than a fool if he fell for a criminal. Been there.

"The timing's off." She walked toward her truck.

He watched her, slumped shoulders telling him she was disappointed. Her phone rang and she pulled it from her pocket and answered. She stopped and her body stiffened.

Bad news?

Stacy slowly turned toward him. Did she need his help? He wasn't taking any chances and took long strides her way. He reached her and she handed him her phone.

"This is your department," she said, her fingers shaking. No one could force fear into their system. "I don't take threats lightly."

"What happened?"

"A man told me to stop interfering or the worst was yet to come."

Alex hit reply on the number, but it simply rang. No voice message. "Was it the man who handled scheduling a spokesperson about the water?"

"He sounded similar. Earlier this week he gave me the name of Jake Johnson."

"I'll run it."

If she was part of a murder, a drone operation, and a plan to buy up property in her neighborhood, she wouldn't have identified Connor or volunteered to help the police. Time he confirmed his feelings about her innocence. Reaching into his pocket, he pulled out her dad's pocketknife. "This is yours."

She took the knife. "Are you saying you believe me?"

He took a deep breath. "Yes."

She slipped the knife into the back pocket of her jeans. "For whatever it's worth, I'm sincerely grateful."

He saw the fright in her eyes. "To help you, I must know if anyone is upset with you."

"Ace McMann warned me the clinic could be burned down, but he's in jail. So is his wife. Lynx Connor informed me my clinic could go bankrupt, but he's in custody. I remember the number he gave me, but it's not the same as the man who just called me."

Alex texted the FIG with both numbers. "Remember what I said earlier? Soon this will be over."

"I've never backed down from anything, but between last Saturday and this craziness with the water, I want to take Whitt somewhere and hide." She bit her lip. "Alex, how does all of this fit together? And why me? I'm not wealthy. I don't have any power over people. I don't even know any of those who are involved."

"But there has to be a reason why you've been singled out. We have to keep probing. What about your clients? Unhappy pet owners? Church members? Neighbors? The owner of the strip center?"

She shook her head. "No one. I can't think from reliving it all. I have no one to suspect or even a reason why the incidents are anything more than coincidences. Which is impossible." She stared into the barn, her eyes dazed.

"We'll shake it up and see what rolls out. The phony letter about the water used flu symptoms to garner the residents' attention. That aspect was in motion approximately the same time as Todd Howe faced his killer." Alex paused. "Howe and Connor had been doing business for the past year or so." He needed to talk this through with Ric.

"If I were penciled in to find Howe's body and the drone, and my neighborhood was the subject of a water hoax, what's next? And why?"

Good question. "Looks like those pulling the strings are either dead or successful in keeping their IDs hidden. It's only a matter of time for Jake Johnson."

She rubbed her temples. "I want it over now."

Her cell rang again, and he still had the device in his hand. "Your caller hasn't finished his lecture. Answer it, and I'll listen in."

"This is Stacy. Did you forget something?"

"You're keeping company with a man who'll get you hurt," the voice said.

She nodded at Alex, signaling it was the same man who'd called a few moments before. She swallowed hard. "Who?"

"The FBI agent who makes house calls."

"Since you're watching me, what's your name?"

The man laughed. "Does it matter? What's important is I know yours . . . and the kid who hangs out at your house and clinic."

"What do you want from me?"

"Mind your own business. Sell your property, and everything will be fine." The call ended.

Alex studied the area around them. Woods and brush could easily conceal the caller. But what was behind this?

"I need to get to the clinic," she said.

"Is Whitt there?"

"Yes." She shoved her phone into her jean pocket. "I'll call him on the way, not to scare him, but to have him lock up until I arrive."

"He'll have questions."

"He always does. Those can wait until later. I can't let him hear panic in my voice."

Alex had an idea. "I'll call a police officer friend to keep an eye on the clinic. And I'm following you."

26

ALEX DROVE HIS JEEP far enough behind Stacy's truck to locate a tail. But his precaution didn't bring anyone to the surface. He'd request permission to run a tracer on her cell phone and the clinic's landline. In the meantime, he learned the numbers Stacy had given him were from burner phones. No surprise there.

Someone didn't want her talking about the water hoax. But why? The other residents would surely pass on the info. Nothing had been mentioned about her finding Howe's body. Were the two related? The caller referred to Alex as the FBI agent. Obviously he was a threat to their scheme that now looked like covering up fraud.

Once at the clinic, he met Stacy at her truck. She trembled, and he couldn't fault her for being apprehensive. "Are you okay?"

"Will be soon." The feigned enthusiasm in her voice spilled over into his suspicions. She touched his arm. "You're going way beyond an agent investigating a domestic terrorism case. Whitt pestered you for some of this, but you didn't have to agree. I know it, and I appreciate what you've done." Her blue eyes pooled, and she brushed away the wetness.

He leaned against her truck. "For the record, no one maneuvers me into doing things. I've helped because I wanted to." He wanted to touch her, but his instincts said she'd back off. "Remember, this is the agent who's interested in a certain veterinarian and a twelve-year-old boy."

She breathed in deeply. "We are stubborn Cajuns."

"Glad you agree. I'd like to search the clinic for a camera or listening device."

She tilted her head. "Sure. My home, too, if you think it's necessary."

"Has to be the first time you haven't disagreed with me. I'll mark today on the calendar."

She smiled. "The day's not over yet."

They walked to the rear door, and she unlocked it. Whitt sat at the receptionist desk with Xena at his feet and a laptop before him. "Hey." He grinned. "You're early. Hope the ride was easy."

"A picnic," she said. "Did you have a good morning?"

"Sold a few pet supplies and scheduled two checkups before your call to lock up. Filed papers, cleaned a bit, and learned more about shell companies and how Walter M. Brown Investments could be a front for another company. Illegal of course. Understand, not all shell companies have an ulterior purpose, but this one has already ridden the train of unscrupulous activities."

Alex chuckled to offset what she must be feeling. "I'm sure you could educate me."

"And I'm sure you have access to more information on the FBI's secure site than I'll ever find online."

"Count on it. Can't fool you. I'm going to check the clinic for a camera or listening device."

"Need some help?"

"Maybe a few screwdrivers, a Phillips head and flathead?"

Whitt scooted off the stool and disappeared down the hallway.

"While you two are busy, I'm going to return phone calls," she said. "Xena, you can keep me company." The Lab limped after her. "By the way," she called, "I'll be ordering subs for lunch. What would you men like?"

"Lots of meat and cheese," Alex said without hesitation. Once he finished here, he had tons of work to do. He'd call Ric on his way home from the clinic to pick his brain with the updates.

Twenty-five minutes later, while standing on a ladder, Alex found a minuscule camera located inside an air-conditioning vent. This hadn't been placed here by an amateur.

"Stacy, do you have a minute?"

Her slim figure quickly appeared with Whitt beside her. "What've you found?"

He held a finger to his lips and held up the tiny camera. A moment later he disconnected the feed and dropped it into his pocket. There could be something the techs could trace. "That was the source of your caller's intel. It's—"

"What caller?" Whitt said.

"Later," she whispered.

"This transmitted audio and video to a remote location." He shined the flashlight around the area for any other devices. Satisfied he'd located the only one, Alex climbed down the ladder. "I have a whole string of questions." He reached into his other jean pocket for his phone. "I'd like to record this. Makes it easier when Ric and I go over it."

"You want to know who's been in here to plant this," Stacy said.

"Right." He pressed Record.

"Whitt and I have the only keys to the clinic. I have a monitored alarm system and a security camera. I haven't been notified of any abnormal activity. But I can give you the alarm company's info and my personal code so you can check with them."

"The camera footage has my attention. I'd like to take a look."

She walked him back to her desk and brought up the feed on her computer.

He sat at her desk and typed into the program. "I want to set the parameters for the times when the clinic was closed, going back about six weeks. I also want the FIG to analyze it. This may take a while."

She shook her head. "I have no idea how this could have happened."

"Unless the alarm and security camera were hacked and disabled long enough for the device to be planted," Whitt said.

"He's right. The driving dilemma is how, why, who, and when." Alex noted the modest furnishings and equipment. She eked out a living but little more. Her background indicated a savings account that allowed her some ease in her budget, but her choice of location didn't offer an abundance of clients. Still, someone was interested in her every move. Alex studied her.

"Whitt, would you pick up the sandwiches?" she said.

"So you and Alex can talk about what's going on like I'm a normal kid?"

"Yes."

He let out an exasperated sigh. "Figures."

She handed him twenty dollars and a coupon. "I have Cokes here. Don't talk to strangers and make sure you have your phone."

"Has my dad or mom been released from jail?"

"Don't think so."

Whitt paced the floor. "The parents are always up to no good. If it's a fast buck, then they're on it. Dad would bust a few heads, and Mom would do what she does best. But neither of them is smart enough for this." He stared out at the parking lot. "A pro could hack into the security system, open the door, and insert the camera. Wouldn't take ten minutes. The right person might charge a couple of grand."

Alex hoped someone snatched this kid for the FBI because he had a mind like a steel trap.

Whitt headed to the door. "About what you and Alex are hiding from me? You know I'll find out the truth."

"And Stacy might tell you," Alex said. "But she's stubborn, and the more you pester her, the more she's going to hold back."

Whitt appeared to be satisfied and left the clinic for the sandwiches.

"I suppose I'll fill him in after we eat," she said. "Alex, I'm not anyone's competition or enemy. This doesn't make sense."

"You haven't recalled the right person." He laid the screwdrivers on the receptionist counter. "We'll resolve this and get your life back to normal. I'd like to check your home before I call it a day."

"Whitt can take you once we've eaten."

When the boy returned with lunch, the threesome ate in the back of the clinic. She insisted upon keeping the door locked, and they were officially closed. But Alex sensed her fear, and from the looks Whitt tossed her way, he believed the same thing.

"Whitt, I want to tell you what Alex and I discovered. The man who tried to buy my home, he . . ."

Alex listened to her explain in adult language what they'd learned about Lynx Connor. "That's it. We won't be bothered with an investment company buying out our neighbors."

"So Connor's being held in LA and has already spent time in prison for land fraud." Whitt touched the side of his mouth, yellow with mustard. "If Howe and Connor were working together, Connor might have eliminated his partner."

"That's a theory," Alex said. "We need evidence to charge him and the motivation for the murder, and we need to figure out where the quadcopter fits." Why did Alex feel like Whitt was the agent? "One more thing," Alex said. "I urge you to seek protection until this is over."

"I'm not running from another person," Stacy said. "The threats are just talk."

"Would you like a list of the people who are on death row or doing life for murder? We have testimonies of them threatening their victims," Alex said, his temper creeping into his tone.

"Miss Stacy, listen to Alex. You have no means of defending yourself. We've gone over your refusal to own a gun or take a martial arts class. This isn't upper-middle-class America, but a crime-infested roach trap. I know you look at the exceptional people here as the norm, but they are few. Too many crimes have pulled you into their clutches. Somewhere along the line, you've enticed a criminal to use you like a chess pawn."

"Whitt, no. I'm not hiding, and don't ask me again. Either of you. I'm not having a bully think he or she can scare me into hiding behind a bodyguard. I can take care of my responsibilities."

Whitt's bewildered gaze looked like he didn't recognize her. Alex had seen women play the heroine before, and it seldom ended well.

He couldn't arrange protection without her permission. How did she fit into a criminal's plan?

27

SATURDAY EVENING, Stacy dumped a load of towels into the washing machine and added detergent before setting it into whirling action—or agitation. This was normal life. Sometimes boring. Sometimes disgusting. But always safe. Had she made a mistake in refusing protection?

She glanced down at her bare feet and painted toes, a mix of hot pink, melon orange, and emerald green. Alex said it was the first time he'd seen her without her boots. She smiled despite the circumstances. The third time he'd been in her home, and she . . . didn't mind. How did she really feel about him? Not now. Too tired to weigh the advantages and disadvantages of a relationship with Special Agent Alex LeBlanc.

He'd left shortly after five o'clock, and—hallelujah—he hadn't found a device in her home. The man took on her troubles while investigating a murder possibly tied to domestic terrorism. His effort made her feel weak. For sure he'd left here to dive into resolving the horrible atrocities linking her and now Whitt to serious criminals. How could he work through the garbage of the world and keep his sanity? That's why she preferred animals.

Except she liked Alex. A little.

And she loved Whitt. A lot.

She yawned. Every day brought new challenges, shadows of fear darkening her life. Now she could add paranoia to the list. Howe, Connor, and the strange caller plagued her waking and sleeping hours. If her body wasn't replenished soon with much-needed rest, she'd not be able to sort laundry.

Whitt leaned against the doorway. "I'll cook tonight. Pasta and salad okay?"

Tears filled her eyes, and she turned so he wouldn't see. "Perfect. Thanks. I'm going to bed early."

"Me too." He picked up a towel she'd dropped and slipped it into the washing machine. "I heard a dozen homes are under contract by the investment company. Not sure about the rental properties."

Her stomach rolled with the news. "Instant gratification and cash talks."

"True. Have you heard new numbers on those sick?" he said.

"The contagion factor is growing. How about you? Any symptoms?"

"No. I'm healthy."

A relief. "Do me a favor and stay that way."

He saluted her and she smiled. "Miss Stacy, I'll get the water boiling for pasta before I change my mind and whip up peanut butter and jelly sandwiches."

"Raspberry chipotle jelly," she said.

"Seriously?"

"And a glass of milk. Should take five minutes."

"You're on. We need our brains in gear for whatever comes tomorrow, and I'm talking about church. You're the best one to talk to Him. The God thing will have to wait until I can concentrate."

"But you need God now. We both do."

"I don't plan on dying anytime soon. I've been reading the Bible and checking facts with archaeological finds and ancient writings. Antiquities prove much about the historical nature of the Bible, but I'm not there yet."

"What weighs the heaviest on your mind?" She forced the aching in her body aside. This could be the moment Whitt chose to step forward in faith.

"Faith. When it all comes down to the God thing, the person chooses out of trust. That's where I'm stumped. I want to see, touch, and feel a sovereign God."

"We all do, Whitt." The woman inside her who wanted to be his mother longed to draw him close, tell him to enjoy his youth and not be burdened with life until grown. To trust God, even when he doubted. "You are so incredibly gifted with wisdom, but reliance on God requires faith."

"I'd trade any wisdom and my IQ for a new beginning."

"God can provide that. Honestly. I doubted God for so many years after my sister died. He doesn't make our lives easier, but He does promise to be with us."

"I'll consider the discussion after a judge's signature."

"You can have a relationship with Him regardless of a judge's signature."

He shook his head. She considered talking more about what faith required. Frankly they were both too exhausted for a heart-to-heart about anything more than dinner and ten hours of sleep.

An hour later, after repeatedly checking the locks on the doors and windows like she'd become obsessive-compulsive, Stacy closed the blinds in her bedroom and crawled beneath the sheets. Her mind bounced from the nightmare of riding into the clearing and finding a dead man, the vile Lynx Connor taking advantage of a lie about their waterborne disease, the strangeness of Howe and Connor as business partners, and the reality of someone gaining entrance into her clinic and monitoring her actions. The part of her she couldn't deny nudged her to rid the demons chasing her and Whitt. But her performance-oriented personality couldn't make this go away. . . . Not since living in Louisiana and her sister's death had she sensed such despair.

She longed for relief and answers.

Finally her body gave in to a deep sleep.

Alex munched on pizza while his thoughts of the day pushed around his brain. Stacy could have been killed today when Ginger tossed her. Life had no guarantees, and that reality pressed him to focus on God and the eternal perspective of his own life. He looked at his cell phone, deliberating a call, which meant swallowing his pride. Tossing aside his misgivings, he pressed in Eva Rayken's number.

"I knew it was you," Eva said. "Felt it in my heart."

"I've eaten most of the cookies and not thanked you for them."

"You have now. Are you being careful?"

He pictured her in jeans and a T-shirt, wearing more jewelry than most women owned. "Yes, ma'am. I do have something to say." He didn't give her time to respond or he'd lose his nerve. "For a lot of years, you and Dexter have encouraged me to get back with God. I regret I left Him behind in Louisiana."

"Oh, Alex, that's a lot for you to admit."

"Don't I know it. Stubborn Cajun meets more stubborn God. Meant to tell Dexter the other morning. Anyway, I'm into Scripture."

She sniffed. "Wonderful. You know we love you like our own son."

"The sentiment works both ways. Talk to you soon."

Long after most people were asleep, Alex brewed a fresh pot of coffee and studied his legal pad filled with notes and circles. He'd phoned the office and filed an update about his and Ric's case, including the false letter from someone posing as the health department and the resulting problems which linked Howe, Connor, and Stacy—but nothing to the quadcopter.

He focused on the bureau's web of information. Five years ago, Connor was arrested and served two years for land fraud. Looked like he was at it again. But why the risk for property that was seemingly worthless? The dilemma was burning brain cells.

Rubbing the weariness from his eyes, he examined the autopsy report one more time. Close range. Howe probably knew the man to let him get close enough to kill him. This wasn't a random act of violence. Could Connor be the shooter? The man's residence was in California . . . Howe's in Houston. He requested a security camera check from the tech agents in LA for a video linking Connor and Howe.

Alex glanced at the time: 11:45. Would Bekah Howe still be up? She responded on the third ring. "Mrs. Howe, this is Special Agent Alex LeBlanc. I apologize for the late hour."

"That's okay." She sounded groggy.

He mentally kicked himself for his spontaneity instead of logic. "I've disturbed your sleep. Again, I'm sorry."

"Have you found Todd's killer?"

"No, but Lynx Connor has been brought into the LA FBI office for questioning. My partner and I'd like to stop by in the morning around ten. We won't take up much of your time."

"Can you make it nine? I planned to take my sons to breakfast and on to the zoo."

"We'll be there. Thank you." After disconnecting the call, he texted Ric with a suggested breakfast place and the appointment with Bekah. Ric responded immediately.

Will be there. I know u claim 4 hours sleep is enough, but 1 day it'll catch up.

I'm about less sleep and solving crime. :)

U r wired on caffeine.

Right. C u in a.m.

Going to bed crossed Alex's mind, but thanks to the coffee jolt, he had energy to spare. He grabbed his laptop and eased into his recliner. What were the circumstances surrounding Connor's previous land fraud? And where did Howe fit? Was he innocent, like his wife wanted to believe? Or had he gotten in over his head in an act of terrorism?

28

STACY WOKE FEELING RESTED and ready for the day. Falling asleep at seven o'clock with the sun still high in the sky replenished the deficit in her sleep bank—a Whitt saying.

Sunday . . . the Lord's Day. She looked forward to worshiping and forgetting about her own woes for a while—immersing her heart in the most important factor of her life instead of herself and the ever-growing grocery list of problems.

As on every morning, she smelled the enticing aroma of coffee beans drawing her from bed and to the kitchen. She wrapped her robe securely around her waist and opened the bedroom door. Sweet Whitt was frying bacon. Breathing in, she also smelled cheese grits. He could outcook her any day of the week.

"I think I'm in heaven," she said on her way to the kitchen.

Whitt glanced up from the counter. "Morning." He rolled up waxed paper covered in flour and tossed it into the trash. A pan of biscuits sat ready to bake. "Coffee's ready," he said.

"I followed my nose." She peered at the biscuits. "Is there cheese in those?"

"Yep. You know me. I love cheese in everything." His bed head gave him the softened features of a boy.

"You must have slept well."

"Amazing. Which is why I'm into breakfast. Mushroom and spinach omelets suit you?" He pointed toward the stove. "Tried a new recipe, sort of a Tex-Mex hollandaise sauce. Tossed in a jalapeño and cilantro."

"Are you writing these things down? I mean, Whitt, you could write a cookbook."

"Thought about it. Even thought about gearing it for kids and having an enhanced e-version with links to YouTube showing how to prepare the dishes in terms they'd understand."

She laughed, and it felt wonderful. "In your spare time between earning your bazillion doctorates, you can work as a chef."

"Maybe. I have until I'm fourteen to decide. Maybe longer. Then again, I could have more than one career."

She ruffled his hair. "And you'll be successful at all of them."

After pouring them coffee and lacing his with chocolate, she walked to the living room and opened the drapes. Early morning sunlight streamed in like a promise for a better today and tomorrow. Xena followed her, nuzzling against her legs.

"I'll get the newspaper while my coffee cools," she said.

"Where are your shoes?"

"I won't be long."

"The last time you went barefoot to retrieve the Sunday paper, you stepped on a broken beer bottle tossed the night before."

She raised a brow with a teasing grin. "Must I?"

"Breakfast is on the line."

She slipped into flip-flops by the door. "You drive a hard bargain, but my tummy's growling."

"Can I have the sports page first? Astros won another game last night."

"The sports page will be all yours."

Warm, humid air met her. This was home. A lonely oak in her front yard branched out to shade pink-and-white impatiens. In August, the Broussard family reunion in Louisiana would kick off a day of fabulous food and fun. She planned to take Whitt if all went well at the hearing.

Stacy walked down the driveway and picked up the thick *Houston Chronicle*. By habit, she observed Whitt's home across the street. The McMann house had a lock on the door, and the grass needed to be mowed. Usually Whitt tended to it without any prompting, but not when his parents hadn't paid the rent. As she walked back to the house, she pulled the sports section out from the paper, ready to hand it off to Whitt, when an envelope with her name on it caught her attention.

Odd. She'd paid for the newspaper until December 31. After that she'd renew it for online access. As she tore into the envelope, four photos of Whitt tumbled out onto the driveway. She bent to pick them up, her insides churning, much too common a physical reaction these days. The first one was him riding his bike to school, the second of him leaving school—dressed in different clothes. The third photo captured him at the carnival, and the fourth was him outside their front door. That photo had a message written across the bottom in red marker: *Sell or regret it.*

She stared at the photos, holding her breath and sensing her world crumbling around her. The words in red letters paralyzed her thinking.

Bloodred.

Threatening red.

The color of the red on Todd Howe's blue shirt.

Think. Be brave, Stacy. This is the work of a bully. Stand up to these cowards. Don't cower.

"What's wrong?" Whitt said from the doorway.

The thought of sheltering him, keeping him naive crossed her mind, but he didn't have the mind of a child. "A visitor left me an envelope in our newspaper. It has four photos of you." She would not resort to tears.

He frowned and approached her, wearing the much-older Whitt expression on his young face. "Come inside. I want to grab a pair of gloves and take a look at them."

"Hadn't thought about fingerprints." With a cleansing breath, she followed him into their home.

Whitt opened the pantry and retrieved a pair of non-latex gloves, the same ones used at the clinic. He slipped them on and studied each photo as though looking for who'd snapped them. Finally he viewed the last one. "Jerk."

"I was thinking of a less civilized description."

He slipped the photos inside the envelope and returned it. "We need to talk about what to do next."

He wouldn't see her break down when she was the mother figure.

"Breakfast is just a few browned biscuits away. We'll eat and discuss a solid plan. Neither of us can ignore the threats any longer, or we'll become FBI statistics."

His choice of adult words demonstrated his stress. She tried to smile for his sake. "I'm going to fight back."

"I expect no less, Miss Stacy, but we have to be intelligent."

"I know."

If the person who'd done this was watching, he'd be thrilled with her near-panic response.

Whitt handed her a mug of coffee, and she sat at the counter. "Thanks."

"I'd like to take a look at them again."

"Is it necessary?"

"I might remember seeing something unusual."

Whitt was right, so she handed him the envelope. He spread the photos on the counter and peered into each one with no expression on his face. "This person is a professional. I know when these were taken, and I don't recall anything out of the ordinary." He lifted his gray eyes to meet hers. "I learned a long time ago to be in touch with my surroundings. Bullies can jump from behind bushes."

"And you have a solution?"

"Take a deep breath. That's what I do when I'm tossed rotten eggs. I consider options in my head, but you might want to write them down. Imagine you'll want to pray."

"Do you find that a weakness?" She caught his attention.

"This God the perfect Father thing still has me conflicted. Nothing's changed there." He reached into a drawer and pulled out paper and pen. "This will help—I promise. Would you do one thing for me?"

"Of course."

"Contact Alex. Tell him you agree to a protection detail from HPD or the FBI. You've been threatened again, and it's time to respond logically. I know the pics are of me, but it's only a cheap way to get you to cower. By refusing to unload your home, you'll be facing worse retaliation. He can advise you on whom to contact and how to word what's happened. He can probably arrange the protection."

The truth made her head throb. Whoever wanted her home

had resorted to cheap shots. Her precious boy realized this too—he simply didn't want to appear selfish and make demands of her.

Moistening her lips, she formed her thoughts. "After church, I'll call Alex and agree to whatever he suggests. In the meantime if anyone mentions me selling, I'll tell them I'm giving it serious consideration. I'm not sure about following through with the proposed meeting in the morning with the fraudster. That's a question for Alex."

"Thanks. I can relax now."

She smiled and pushed caring into the gesture. "Whitt, this is bigger than anything we've ever faced. It's wrong of me to burden you with this crisis when you should be enjoying life as a twelve-year-old."

"I promise you, I'll do my best to act like a kid—later."

The buzzer on the oven signaled the biscuits were done. Breakfast. A normal event. But she was scared of the next minute and the next.

29

SUNDAY, ALEX AND RIC MET at The Egg & I for breakfast at 7:30 before driving to Bekah Howe's home. After ordering more eggs, bacon, sausage, and pancakes than they'd ever eat, Ric eyed him with a chuckle.

"What time did you crawl into bed?" he said.

"Three thirty." Alex rubbed his bristled chin. "My mind wouldn't shut down."

"Connor talking yet?" Ric said.

"No. IAH security cams show him arriving in Houston the day before Howe was killed. Nothing more since he lawyered up. Claims he doesn't own a 9mm, but he wears a matching shoe size. Plea bargaining under consideration. Says he has information that could get him killed."

Ric frowned. "Don't tell me we're buying a plea out?"

"Time will tell." Alex paused while the server unloaded their plates of food. "Thanks." He waited until she'd disappeared before continuing. "Another thought, and you received the report early this morning too. Howe's business calls checked out as well as his personnel backgrounds. Neither do his financials raise a red flag."

"No one has a foolproof plan. Could be something is lurking beneath the layers of a spreadsheet. Is the investigation there ongoing?"

"Absolutely. We have to dig deeper."

"Bro, something brought them together. The one thing we can't control is a criminal's behavior." Ric downed a large orange juice. "But we can think like them. What do you suppose Howe and Connor were really up to?"

"I feel like we're spinning cycles with the current dogged approach to this investigation." Alex could hear the frustration in his words. "I have definite matters to check into today, plus wherever your mastermind takes you. If nothing more surfaces about Howe, I'm changing my strategy and focusing on whatever's out there about Connor. Take it for what it's worth. In my opinion, he killed Howe, just as sure as I'm sitting here."

Ric studied him. "Sleep would clear the cobwebs. If you're right, he could have run from the scene."

Alex toasted him with his coffee cup. "Maybe. Sure would like to find the gun." He rested the cup beside his plate. "Have we checked to see if Howe used personal or business storage units?"

Ric picked up his phone. "A question for his wife. I'll make a reminder so we don't forget." He held up a finger. "I'm sending a request to check if Howe traveled through LAX. If Connor made trips here, possibly Howe reciprocated."

"Good call. Where did Howe store restaurant supplies? Don't think he'd be stupid enough to hide drones with illegal payloads there, but if he had the only key and wasn't anticipating getting caught or killed . . . Nothing in the law says a man can't own drones. The shell company."

"What?"

Alex shook his head. "Thinking out loud. We've uncovered Connor's involvement in a shell company, and the same company could hold stashed money from Howe. The other thing plaguing me is how a flu epidemic slipped into the plan."

"As in not a coincidence."

"Right. It's a virus." Alex's mind sprang into action.

"Where are you going with this?"

"Probably nowhere. I'm twisting an idea that has a vicious endgame."

"Like the neighborhood was deliberately infected with flu?" Ric raised a brow. "Any doctors' reports?"

"No. Do you see a doctor when you have the flu?" When Ric shook his head, Alex continued. "We complain and take something over the counter. Most of the residents there don't have insurance. Seeing a doctor is a luxury."

Ric stared at him, obviously thinking. "I'm just speculating too. The water hoax is connected to cash for property right after flu-like symptoms appear. But the health department tested the water on Friday and nothing surfaced."

Alex set his fork down. "So where does Stacy fit into the picture? I keep wrapping my brain around the same crazy scenario. Stacy is caught in the middle of what she found at the crime scene and the water hoax. So far Connor and the water hoax have a role. Did he hack into the airport rangers' computer system and orchestrate things so Stacy would find Howe? Why? Why the quadcopter? And what does any of it have to do with a run-down subdivision? A report from the CID would help tremendously."

"She and the boy need protection after the call yesterday and someone accessing her clinic."

"Oh, I tried. But she refused."

"She's upset the wrong people. They're watching her, which means they could strike at any time. How about using Whitt as leverage? Would she agree for his sake?"

"I'll check on her later today and toss that idea out there."

"No wonder you were up late."

Alex rubbed his forehead. "She makes me crazy with her bull-headed determination to take care of everything herself."

Ric laughed.

"What's so funny?" Alex scowled.

"I think she's gotten under your skin. Stubborn Cajun meets stubborn Cajun. Will they get together or drown each other in the bayou?"

"Very funny." He picked up the salt and pepper shakers. The problem was Ric had hit on the truth. He thought back over holding her in his arms after she fell from her horse. She had placed his heart in a vulnerable condition.

Either Bekah Howe was one of the most naive women on the planet or beneath her gracious and innocent exterior she was a skillful liar. Alex hadn't decided yet.

The three sat at her kitchen table, sipping coffee. More caffeine than Alex needed. At this rate, he'd have a full-blown ulcer by the time he reached his next birthday.

"Did your husband have a personal assistant or secretary?" Alex said.

"No. My husband felt having a woman in close quarters would cause others to talk. He didn't like others knowing about his business either."

Todd Howe might have broken the law, so violating a moral code too wasn't an impossibility. "I see."

"I have a key to his office if you'd like to take a look. Police officers searched it right after his death, and I'm sure they sent you their findings. My understanding is there was nothing there to show my husband had any illegal dealings."

"We have HPD's report, but we'd still like to see for ourselves where your husband worked."

She stiffened. "If something is found, I insist on being the first one notified."

Bekah Howe had reached deep and found a little gumption. "We'll do our best. What about storage units, personal and business?" Alex said.

"Those keys are on the same ring as his office. We use Public Storage for personal items, and he also used the same company for business at another location. I'll give you the entrance codes for both facilities, and if you need for me to sign permission forms, I will." She glanced into the other room, where her two young sons were watching TV. They were beyond earshot.

How much did the boys comprehend about their father, and what were the kids at school saying? The innocent always suffered the most, whether in grief or possibly learning derogatory information about their father.

She dabbed at her nose with a tissue. "I told you previously that I'd do anything to help find my husband's killer, and I meant it." She turned to Ric. "But my mind says I've been very foolish. Todd reassured me of his love for us and God right up to the time he left on the motorcycle ride that got him killed. Were his words a lie?"

"Mrs. Howe—" Ric's gentle tone seemed to relax her tense facial muscles—"we're doing everything we can to find out why your husband met such a violent death and to uncover the truth behind his and Lynx Connor's dealings."

She nodded. "No need to spare me any longer. I'm preparing

myself to meet the public straight on about Todd's inappropriate traits, including how he treated his employees. Yes, I knew he treated them unfairly, but I justified his actions, believing he knew best. Rabbi Feldman told me the woman who found his body wanted to express her condolences, but I haven't felt much like talking to anyone." She lifted her chin. "I must be strong for my sons."

"We have to be brave when life gives us hardships." Ric pushed back his coffee cup. "Have you shared everything with us?"

"Yes, sir."

Ric turned to Alex. "Agent LeBlanc, do you have any more questions for Mrs. Howe, or can she take her sons to breakfast and to the zoo?"

Alex leaned across the table to show his sympathy. "One more thing." While they talked, a question had emerged. "Did your husband own a private plane?"

"Yes, a Citation jet. Todd has taken us on family trips because we can go almost anywhere."

"Did he use it for private or business trips?"

"Both. It's hangared at Hooks Airport."

"Mrs. Howe," Ric said, "you say your husband owned the plane. Our investigation hasn't revealed an aircraft."

"He used my maiden name. Todd said his accountant urged him to build up assets that put my credit in good standing."

Had this been another part of Todd Howe covering his trail of possible crime?

"What name did he use?" Ric continued.

"Rebekah Shaw. How soon before the media learns of this?" She touched her fingers to her lips. "They can twist information in the name of truth."

"They can also shed light on matters to give us peace."

"I keep praying the truth will cast honor on Todd's name—the light, as you said. I'll get you his keys now. I'll also give you the plane's tail number. Todd told me the number was essential in the event of a crash." She stood from the chair. "I've been shielded from the harsh realities of life by my father and Todd. I want to weather this catastrophe and be a source of comfort to my sons. But every step forward sends me back three."

Ric cleared his throat. "My partner and I are huge advocates of counseling."

She focused on her sons in the other room again. "Rabbi Feldman's recommended it too. I'll make the necessary arrangements. Excuse me while I find Todd's keys."

Bekah Howe disappeared, leaving Alex mentally processing the case. The elusive pieces flew by, and when he grasped one, several more sailed by.

What if Howe had no knowledge of the quadcopter until that fatal Saturday morning?

30

STACY COUNTED FOURTEEN PEOPLE IN CHURCH. Never had she seen the attendance so low. Usually their small start-up church ran about eighty attendees. The pastor announced the flu bug had bitten many of their members and asked those present to keep the ill in their prayers. Small groups were canceled as well as Sunday night's organization meeting for the Labor Day picnic. But in the intimate gathering, she silently admitted her prideful nature and asked for her relationship with God to be restored and stronger than ever before. She wanted her parents in her life—full-time. She prayed for Whitt, for him to acknowledge his need for a heavenly Father who'd never fail him.

On the way home, Whitt turned to her. "What are you going to do if someone stops by the house with a checkbook?"

"I'm thinking we should spend the day away from home and the clinic. We'd originally planned to go riding, but I think a more public place is safer. We could take Xena to the park. Enjoy the beautiful weather." The saying "She could run but she couldn't hide" crossed her mind. The envelope found this morning made her even more determined not to play a criminal's game.

"Okay, as long as you talk to our FBI friend first. I'd like to see a police officer parked in front of our house before we go to bed tonight."

She wanted privacy for that conversation, but Whitt understood persistence, and he wouldn't let up until she contacted Alex. Once in her driveway, she reached for her phone and pressed in his number. It went straight to voice mail.

"Alex, this is Stacy. I'd like to reconsider protection for Whitt and me. I'm not sure how to proceed, who to contact, or what to say." She swallowed a lump in her throat. "I found an envelope in my morning newspaper containing four photos of Whitt. I was instructed to sell or regret it. Call when you have an opportunity. We're leaving the house for the day, going to do fun stuff in public places."

She dropped her phone into her purse and leaned her head back against the truck's seat. The paralyzing grip on her heart returned in full force.

"Keep the pics with you," Whitt said. "Alex will need them to test the ink and see if they can lift prints." He held up a finger. "If those were printed at a store, there might be an identifying mark on the photo paper. From the store's location, they could check security cameras."

"You always make incredible sense."

"Keeps me sane."

His voice tugged at her nurturing instinct. "You are not to leave my sight."

"The ultimatum goes both ways."

She shoveled courage into physical movement and opened her

truck door. "Okay, we'll change clothes, load up Xena, and drive through Sonic for a picnic lunch. When we have our orders from Alex, we'll do whatever the man says."

"Promise?"

"Yes." She had no choice when it came to her precious boy.

31

ALEX PHONED HOOKS AIRPORT and explained the FBI's interest in the aircraft owned by Rebekah Shaw. "We have the owner's permission to search the plane. Will you be there this evening around six thirty?"

"I can be. Has the aircraft been used for illegal purposes?" a woman said.

"We have no evidence at this time," Alex said.

"My name is Taylor Freeman, and I'll be here until after ten thirty."

At Todd Howe's office on San Felipe, the two agents wore disposable gloves as they inspected the highly organized files, from employees to vendors. But nothing connected him to Lynx Connor. Alex searched the desk, running his hand along the sides and around drawers for a hidden compartment. Nothing surfaced but a splinter.

Ric explored an oversize closet filled with paper products. "Howe was one cheap guy. The quality of toilet paper, napkins, and paper towels is the worst."

"He was a businessman. Gotta cut corners wherever you can."

"Customers expect to pay for the best, then they're cheated. Even in the bathroom."

"You don't eat toilet paper."

"Very funny. I'm telling you, a man who shirks on these things can't be trusted." He shrugged. "Truth is the guy was crooked."

"Doubt if his choice of paper goods got him killed, despite how others feel about one-ply versus three-ply."

"Depends on how deceit leaks into other parts of a man's life."

Alex stood from the desk, his mind questioning every aspect of Howe's life. "Do we have a list of his vendors?"

"It's in our files. Company backgrounds checked out."

"Salesmen too?"

Ric pulled his phone from his pocket and typed. "Done."

An FBI team arrived to sweep the office, but Alex sensed they wouldn't find a thing.

When the team completed their work, it matched HPD's previous conclusions. The fingerprint team stayed while other agents joined Alex and Ric at the address given for the personal storage unit, ten by fifteen, organized like Howe's office. It would take hours for agents to search through the belongings. The containers were of highest plastic quality that ensured water and insects didn't take residence. Howe took every precaution to protect the belongings of his family.

"My interest isn't here," Ric said. "Howe was too smart to leave evidence among toys, a crib, kids' clothes, and what looks like unopened wedding gifts."

Alex lifted the lid of a box labeled *Mother Howe's china*. Each piece was packed in a separate storage container, and he moaned at the thought of going through it all. "This could take three days. My vote's to leave the items for the search team and check out the business storage." He tore off his gloves.

"Meet you there."

The address for the Public Storage was a central location for the Green-to-Go restaurants. The two agents arrived at the same time.

"Now to find out what's behind the orange doors," Alex said, slipping into another pair of gloves. He unlocked the ten- by twenty-five-foot unit and raised the door. He snapped on a light. As expected, efficient organization in the same type of sturdy containers stacked in alphabetical order. Huge black letters marked boxes of cooking utensils, display cases, several tables and chairs, and whatever else Howe deemed necessary to store.

Ric bent to a box labeled *Future Expansion* underneath three containers. "This could hold a few answers," he said. "Future plans need money to finance them."

Alex helped him move the boxes until they could pull out the one that had garnered their attention. Ric lifted the lid and set it aside. He pulled out a leather file folder and handed it to Alex. "We've got a lockbox here—small, rectangular." He examined it closely. "It's heavy. One of those keys from Bekah might unlock it."

Alex riffled through the ring until he found two small keys. "Try these."

When neither fit, Alex glanced at his phone and saw Stacy had left a message. The call time lined up with his moving boxes, and he'd missed the call because he had his phone on vibrate. He'd listen to her message after talking to Bekah Howe.

The widow responded on the first ring.

"We're at the restaurant storage unit," Alex said. "Your husband had many items stored in the same type of plastic boxes as your personal unit. One of the containers is marked *Future Expansion*. Inside is a rectangular lockbox for which none of the keys fit. Are there any other keys in your possession?"

"No, sir, and I've never been to that unit."

He wasn't surprised.

"You have all the keys," she said. "Take the lockbox with you. When it's opened, I want to know what's inside immediately. Todd claimed to have overextended himself with the last restaurant. But he must have changed his mind, or rather Mr. Connor persuaded him."

"FBI teams are at his office and your personal storage unit. They'll conduct their work there. The task won't be completed today."

"Conversations with Todd stalk me, and if anything comes to mind, I'll contact you. Is that okay?" She paused. "Yes, honey, we can get lemonade."

When she returned to the call, Alex thanked her for her cooperation. It sounded sterile, but he meant it. "Enjoy your time with your sons, Mrs. Howe." The phone clicked silent. "I hate what Howe is putting his wife and family through. He may be innocent of anything illegal, but his business practices left room for improvement."

"Obviously he didn't care."

"Interesting to learn what really motivated him." Alex turned to Ric, who was rummaging through other containers. "Find anything unusual?"

"I'm looking for more than industrial-size cans of food." Ric stopped in the middle of the unit. "How do you take a can of peaches and make it taste like it's fresh picked from the tree? Aggravates me when he advertised fresh, organic, and kosher foods."

Ric still felt betrayed by Todd's choice of food and supplies.

"Cutting corners. Neither his wife nor his rabbi knew the real Todd Howe. Hold on a minute. I have a voice message from Stacy. She called earlier, and I missed it." He listened and relayed the contents. "I'm wondering if the man who contacted her yesterday had an agenda and was aiming his efforts at a twelve-year-old." The thought fired up Alex's temper while he feared for her and Whitt's safety.

"Has she indicated any other residents have been threatened?"

"Who would admit it?"

Ric nodded. "When loved ones are targeted, tough decisions weigh in the balance."

"I'm calling her now." Stacy answered on the first ring. "Where are you?"

"Memorial Park."

"Any problems?"

"Don't think so. I'm not beyond thinking we could have been followed, and someone could be snapping photos. I hate this disturbance to Whitt's life. But I'll not risk him getting hurt when he's under so many other pressures."

She was like a she-bear when it came to the kid. "Can you meet me at the FBI office on Highway 290 in two hours?"

"Yes."

Her agreement was rare. "I'll put in an immediate request for protection." He hesitated, wanting her and Whitt safe without delay. "I suggest driving to the office now. I'll feel better knowing you're okay until I arrive."

"We have Xena."

"No problem. We'll handle the situation."

"Alex, you're busy, and I've made a pest of myself. I'm sorry to have bothered you."

"Wrong. We're friends, and this is my job. Text me when you leave Memorial Park, then when you reach the office. If you suspect anyone is tailing you or you're afraid, do not hesitate to contact 911. Don't let Whitt out of your sight."

"He and I have already made that pact."

Alex chuckled to relieve the tension on the other end of the phone. "The pics are in your possession?"

"In my purse. Whitt figured you would want to analyze them."

"That's my boy." Too late to retract his words, but no harm done.

"My phone is signaling an incoming call, but the number's unfamiliar."

"I suggest answering."

She responded to the call. After clicking back to Alex, she reported that it was a telemarketer.

"Can I talk to Whitt?" he said.

"Why?"

"He's an extra pair of eyes to keep both of you safe."

"All right. Hold on a sec. Whitt, Alex wants to talk to you."

A rustling met Alex's ears. "Yes, sir."

"Have you seen anything suspicious?"

"No, and I'm looking."

"Good. Ask Stacy if you can hold on to her phone in case of an emergency."

"I have my own phone. Already added your number."

"Great. I'd like to talk to Stacy." A momentary shuffle, and she returned to the line. "Don't take any chances," he said. "Call me as soon as you arrive at the office."

32

LATE SUNDAY AFTERNOON, Alex drove to the FBI office while munching on fries and chicken nuggets. He and Ric had left instructions for the search team to take however many days necessary to complete sorting through the Howes' personal and business storage units. The job was tedious, but those agents who worked the division were incredible.

The lockbox sat on the passenger side of the Jeep. Ric had family obligations, and Alex had the remainder of the afternoon and late into the evening scheduled at the office. He regretted not recording the call made to Stacy yesterday. As with Connor's message, voice recognition software could have provided a name. Two priorities fought for first place: securing Stacy and Whitt with a protective team and learning the contents of the lockbox. Since talking to her, he'd learned HPD would supply protection detail.

He steered his Jeep into the FBI's parking section and grabbed the rest of his food and the lockbox. After downing his meal and depositing the metal box with an agent who'd use bolt cutters to open it, he hurried to the reception area, where Stacy and Whitt were reading from their cell phones. They stood and greeted him— she with a smile and Whitt with a measure of respect.

"Where's Xena?" he said.

"We took her to the clinic rather than inconvenience you," she said.

Those she'd angered would have no problem hurting a dog, but he'd not mention it. By this evening, he'd have the three of them under HPD's capable care. "Police officers will be ensuring your and Whitt's safety."

She stiffened. "We've had a little change in plans."

Irritation scoured at his nerves. His gut told him whatever she said wouldn't meet with his approval. "Which is?"

She stared at him with a stormy, don't-cross-me look. "We'd like our lives to be as normal as possible. If it fits within protection guidelines, we'd like to request someone to watch the house and clinic and ensure Whitt is safe going back and forth to school. But not inside my home."

He digested what she was saying. So much better than he'd anticipated. "I see no problem with those conditions. But how about a vacation?"

"Now is not the right time." She maintained eye contact. "I'm concerned my house or clinic would be torched since I refused to sell. Makes sense for someone to destroy my home and livelihood in my absence."

He chose another angle. "Have you thought through your home enveloped in flames with you and Whitt trapped inside?"

A muscle twitched beneath her eye. "With assigned officers, the potential is unlikely."

He rubbed the back of his neck.

"I've told Whitt that if this doesn't meet with your approval, I can hire private security."

Alex blew out more irritation. How could one woman be so charming in one breath and exasperating in the next?

"Alex, I'm a fighter." She folded her arms over her chest. "Leaving my home for a vacation means I risk losing what little I have."

"Are you considering Whitt's welfare?" He started to inquire about the judge's reaction to her decision in light of the custody hearing, but with Whitt listening to every word, he changed his mind. Surely she'd thought through the repercussions of losing the court battle.

"What kind of role model would I be if I showed him how to take a coward's stance?"

Alex slowly turned to Whitt. "Your thoughts on the matter?"

He arched his shoulders, amusing if the situation had been different. "We discussed this after we left the park. I'm not afraid. Spend an hour with my dad when he's mean drunk, or some of my parents' loser friends, and nothing will ever scare you."

"Danger is not acceptable no matter the circumstances." Alex lifted a brow. "There are other factors to consider."

"You mean the meeting with the scammer in the morning?"

"That's one of them."

"I want to be part of the solution by contributing to a speedy arrest," she said. "If successful, we'll rest easier. Those at fault for the chaos will be behind bars."

"What about the threat to Whitt?"

"He's why I want trained professionals to watch us at all times."

His phone alerted him to a text from the agent with the lockbox. He'd successfully broken it. Alex's attention darted like a bad case of ADHD. "All right, Stacy." He hoped she wasn't being naive with her decision. Fear did crazy things to people.

"Thank you." She smiled. "We're going home."

"You could wait here a little longer while I handle a matter. I could give you a personal escort and have another agent drive your truck."

"No thank you." She lifted her chin. "We've already taken up too much of your time. Will you text or call when the arrangements are made? Or if you have a number, I can do it myself."

"I've started the ball rolling. Should have security lined up by the time you arrive home."

"Perfect." She gathered her purse. "I nearly forgot to give you the photos."

Alex extended his hand. "I'll run a few tests here and get back to you. The man who called you yesterday morning at the stables used a burner phone."

"Smart, aren't they?" He caught a brief sparkle in her eyes.

"Not as smart as the FBI. It's only a matter of time."

"I know, Alex. I just want to ride my horse or go fishing with Whitt."

Within ten minutes, he was watching her and Whitt leave the building and take the steps down the small hill, through the gate, and on to visitor parking.

Shake it off, Alex. They'll be fine.

Prioritize . . . He'd check on the contents of Howe's lockbox. Deal with it, then on to Hooks Airport.

He met the agent in a work area where the padlock had been cut.

"Back to you, Alex," he said. "But I'm curious. This belonged to Todd Howe?"

"Correct." He walked to the table where the box sat for his scrutiny. After tugging on gloves, he opened the lid and removed a manila envelope. He pulled out a paper document—proof of an offshore account in Andorra and a deed to a condo there.

Had Todd Howe planned to leave Bekah?

33

ON SUNDAY EVENING, Stacy and Whitt met two plainclothes police officers who would be working the night shift in an unmarked car parked at the curb. Both men were in their forties, and their age gave her a measure of comfort. She and Whitt also learned the names of the two officers assigned to the day shift. Whitt googled each officer's name and gave her a thumbs-up.

Trust came at a premium, and after the deception from those posing as health department officials and Lynx Connor posing as a rep for an investment company, she wanted a background completed on everyone she met.

"I hope this is only a twenty-four-hour or less gig," she said. "I'm ready for an arrest." She didn't want to mention her role in setting up whoever was behind the water problem.

"We'll be outside all night watching your home, Dr. Broussard," one of the officers said and gave her his card. "This has my cell number."

She took it and smiled. "I really appreciate what you're doing."

The officers headed to their car, and she dead bolted the door.

"I'll cook tonight," Whitt said.

Chef Whitt. He wanted to make her life easier, while she was determined to do the same for him. "Let's do it together, but you choose the menu."

"Chicken-corn chowder and seven-grain bread."

She gave him a high five. "And we'll eat while watching a movie. Not a crime show."

"Are you sure? We could figure out who the bad guys are in our mess before the cops or the health department or the FBI makes another move."

"Dreamer. I want animation so we can laugh."

His smile faded. "This week will be tougher than the last."

"Custody hearing on Wednesday and your Spanish play on Friday." She pulled out the recipe book for the chowder.

God, help me through this week. I'm scared, really scared.

Late Sunday evening, Alex drove to David Wayne Hooks Memorial Airport, his mind rippling in far too many directions, reminding him of dropping a stone into water. Although he admired the ever-increasing circles, the same analogy in a crime ground at his waking and sleeping hours. As always, he sought to grab the next piece of evidence to end the ripple effect.

The day had been filled with new pieces of evidence that pushed him on past the exhaustion phase with adrenaline more powerful than a triple espresso. The FIG had been given the Andorra bank account and condo information. Bekah claimed to know nothing about either one. Now to wait until he and Ric had the particulars.

An offshore account wasn't illegal, but the funds pouring into it could have been obtained by fraudulent means.

At the airport, he took a few moments to scan the area, noting more hangars than when he'd been there a couple of years ago. New expansions made the airport desirable for private owners and companies, a plus for northwest Houston and the surrounding communities. He entered the office of Gill Aviation and introduced himself to Taylor Freeman, friendly and professional.

"Here's my card," Alex said. "If anyone contacts you about Rebekah Shaw's plane, I want to be notified immediately."

"Yes, sir," Ms. Freeman said. "Earlier you had questions about the aircraft."

"I'd like to take a look at the flight plans going back as far as you have record."

"There's no requirement for pilots to file a plan unless they are flying under instrument flight rules during bad weather. In those cases, they want to be in constant contact with air traffic controllers. If good weather prevails, there's no need to file."

"If the pilot did file one, I assume you'd have the information."

"Right. Pilots have the option of doing so either by phone or online. I can look it up by the pilot's name, but the critical piece of information is the tail number of the plane."

"I have that." Alex jotted down the number Bekah had given him. "Do you check the pilot's name for identification?"

"No. The purpose of the flight plan is not to keep tabs on a plane, which of course can be accomplished, but to give us some idea of where to start looking if a plane fails to show up at its destination. Our chances of rescue increase if we have an idea of the general route." Shortly thereafter, Ms. Freeman peered up from her computer. "We have no flight plans with the tail number of the aircraft."

"From what you've told me, am I correct to assume a pilot could fly from this airport without speaking to anyone?"

"It's possible as long as the pilot's landing at airports that have no control towers. Our country is full of private airports. But not here. A pilot cannot land without communication to a controller at our tower. But he doesn't have to give his name."

"Passengers are at the pilot's discretion?"

"Yes."

Todd Howe had his transportation plan intact if he was using the plane to meet with anyone secretly. The more suspicious activity uncovered about Howe, the greater Alex's concern for Stacy and Whitt. "I'd like to view the security cameras."

"We'll need a subpoena for that."

Alex had hoped she'd skip the formality, but apparently not. "I'd like to take a look at the aircraft. I have the keys."

"That I can do."

He followed her to the hangar where the Citation was stored. Everything appeared to be in order. What he'd suspected had been verified. Todd could come and go with anyone who wanted to climb onboard.

Now to see how much Lynx Connor revealed.

LA FBI sent Connor's interview at 1:30 a.m. Central time. Agents confronted him with conclusive evidence, and he confessed to posing as a representative of the health department, falsifying the water hoax letters, and duping the residents of Stacy's subdivision into selling their property.

Connor offered no motive for his crimes. He denied knowledge of Todd Howe's murder and the theft of the military quadcopter.

"Why talk to us now?" an LA agent said.

"You offered a plea bargain, and I don't want to spend more time in prison."

"But you have more information, Mr. Connor. You've neglected telling us about Walter M. Brown Investments."

"I've told you everything I know."

Alex wanted to face Connor himself. He offered just enough to keep agents interested . . . but not enough for a plea bargain.

34

MONDAY MORNING Stacy startled at the sound of her alarm alerting her to a workday. Although she'd fallen asleep instantly after the *Penguins of Madagascar* movie, her body craved more. She rolled over, her mind tossing around the prospect of police officers making an arrest while she slept. What a wonderful answer to this nightmare . . . She and Whitt could shake off the past and ease back into a normal life.

Rolling back the blanket, she forced herself out of bed—and wished she could crawl back in. Her head pounded and her body ached like an old woman's. Profuse sweating and chills made her wonder if she had a fever. Please, not the flu. She'd hoped to escape the virus raging through her community. Rarely did she catch anything. Her theory was she'd grown up with mosquitoes and every other disease-carrying insect, and her body staunchly fought the worst of illnesses. Besides, she didn't have time to mess with being sick or going to the doctor. Burying her face in her hands, she rubbed her temples.

First on her list for the day: Whitt needed to see her healthy and happy. She made her way down the hall, following the aroma of coffee.

"Morning," she said as cheerfully as her throbbing head would allow.

Whitt peered at her, then poured her coffee. "Miss Stacy, are you okay?"

She smiled her thanks and wrapped her fingers around the mug for warmth. "I'm fine. A little tired after our excitement."

"More like an onslaught of weapons of mass destruction." He grabbed a chocolate chip English muffin, split it, and popped it in the toaster. He searched her face again.

"What?"

"Your face is flushed. Not much of a healthy glow."

She laughed. "No makeup and in my robe? Are those words for your almost-foster mother?" *Concentrate. You can do this.*

"The flu is spreading in our neighborhood." He reached to touch her forehead, but she jerked back.

"I'm okay."

"You're sick. You even smell sick."

"Thanks, doc. For your information, I haven't taken a shower." She wiggled her nose, but the attempt at humor only brought a scowl from him.

He sighed. "Look, in the last few days, I've learned about my dad threatening you at the clinic, social services and your lawyer wanting to question me, the phony water department and invest-ment company buying up property here, the sting operation this morning—a bunch of stuff. Add to that, two cops are watching your house. Actually, you probably left out more than I've observed because you didn't think I could handle it."

He was so right. "Your point?"

"You keep rubbing the back of your neck. If you haven't contracted the flu, stress can make you sick. As I just stated, you have garbage stacked everywhere. Not sure how you handle it all."

"I might have a slight headache."

He reached into the cabinet beside the bottle of vanilla and box of salt for the Tylenol. Flipping the lid open, he dumped two into his hand and handed them to her. "This is selfish. But permanent custody of a kid means taking care of yourself. I'm supposed to stay after school. Can't take a test until after one, so I packed a lunch."

"Testing out of Spanish four, and just so you know, I'm in charge of making your sandwiches."

"Right. You're sick and you want to unload germs on yummy meat and cheese? But I can cancel the test and reschedule—"

"Not on your life. If I have a fever, then I'll make a doctor's appointment for this afternoon."

"Promise?"

"Who's the adult here?"

He raised a brow. "Don't go there, Miss Stacy, or I'll have to toss the IQ card." On the other side of the vanilla lay the thermometer. He set it next to her coffee mug and stared at her. "You look awful." He placed his plate and knife into the dishwasher. "I've already talked to the day team of officers, and one of them will follow me to school. They came prepared in separate cars. You'll take the Tylenol and your temp?"

"Yes." She pointed to his backpack. "Don't forget your tools for the day. And thanks for helping out this morning. Tomorrow I make coffee and breakfast."

"Your coffee's strong enough to slice it with a knife, and you burn the bagels."

Once he left, she swallowed the pain reliever and decided to wait a half hour before taking her temp. She took a shower and let the spray run cold—another way of ensuring her body heat registered 98.6. If only she didn't feel so rotten. The muscle and joint aches were dragging her under.

After drying off, she popped the thermometer under her tongue, closed her eyes, and listened for the digital click. It read 101.5.

Moaning, she phoned Dr. Maberry's office. The kind gentleman had been her doctor since she moved to Houston. Thirty-five-year-old women weren't supposed to run a fever like a child. She scheduled a one thirty appointment for this afternoon. Her calendar indicated a Pomeranian suffering from a possible ear infection would be at the clinic around 11:30. That gave her ample time to do her part in ending the water hoax, and she'd return from the doctor before Whitt arrived home from school. The good thing was she had her bodyguard in case the situation at the clinic got sticky.

By 8:30, the police officers were in the rear of the clinic within earshot of whatever transpired. At 9:20, the door opened and a tall man in jeans entered the clinic with a bulldog on a leash. Could he be the man they were looking for? Why the dog?

"I'm new to the community," he said. "Mind if I look around, check out your pet supplies and food? Cookie-Buttons is particular."

Cookie-Buttons was a male. "Certainly. If you have any questions about pet care, I'd be happy to help you."

"Dr. Broussard," an officer called from the rear. "Don't let him fool you. He's one of us."

She burst into laughter, the stress lifting like a bag of rocks. "Good one."

"His name is Oscar." The man patted the dog.

She bent to the dog's side and let him sniff her. "Beautiful animal."

Nine thirty became ten o'clock, as the undercover officer and his dog lingered. She phoned the number on the letter, the same one she'd used previously. It simply rang with no voice mail. The deception crew must have learned about the sting. They could have been watching the clinic since early morning and figured out the plainclothes officers were not there for a pet check. This had been a huge waste of everyone's time and energy.

The morning dragged on uneventfully, and Stacy found herself looking forward to the doctor's appointment in a weird way. She felt too bad to phone the woman with the Pomeranian when she failed to keep her appointment. Whitt took priority this week, and she needed to be game-on for Wednesday, and flu was notorious for sticking its claws into the sufferer and hanging on. Stuffing her keys into her purse, she moved slowly to the parking lot. The officer assigned to her today would follow, and she almost asked if he'd drive her. But that would be awkward, embarrassing. Her best friend, Hannah, was on a mission trip, or she'd ask her for a ride.

For sure, Stacy needed an injection and a boatload of medicine. Too much going on to risk not being 100 percent. . . .

The custody hearing. Nothing would stand in her way of that battle.

35

WHITT ACED THE SPANISH FOUR PLACEMENT TEST. When his quizzes and daily work had hit 100 percent each time, his teacher suggested testing out. One more class under his belt.

He unlocked his bike and noted the police officer parked across the street. His stomach growled, reminding him of the leftover turkey and cheese in the clinic's fridge. Next time, he'd pack fruit and chips with his sandwiches.

Two guys he recognized as trouble blocked his entrance to the street. Incorrigible. Sophomoric.

"Hey, loser. Where ya going?" the tall one said, a ninth grader who'd taken summer school to make it to the tenth grade.

"None of your business." He stared into the kid's eyes and hoped he and his sidekick left him alone. The idea of the police officer rescuing him made him physically ill. It would only make the next time worse.

The tall kid sneered and exposed rotten teeth. "Trash like you needs to learn how to respect others."

Whitt clenched his fists. "Respect has to be earned."

"Big talk for a popcorn shrimp. You need to learn some manners."

"And you think you have some?" He'd gotten into a few fights, but Miss Stacy didn't know about them. Why tell her when she'd be disappointed? She'd assess the situation and determine she'd messed up when he made his own choices. He might not be bulking up as fast as he'd like, but he could hold his own and dodge the hits. But there were two of these guys.

"Shrimp, we're talking to you." The tall kid stood over a foot above Whitt.

"What do you want?" The bullies' backs were to the officer's car. From there it would only look like three guys talking.

"Cash. We know you work at the animal place. Hand it over."

He figured as much, but he was through with people demanding money from him. "Don't have any on me."

The stockier one grabbed Whitt's handlebar. "We'll take this. Looks like it's in good shape."

No way would they get his wheels without a fight. Miss Stacy had bought it for him two months ago on his twelfth birthday. "I'll bring money tomorrow."

"Now," the tall kid said. He laughed with the stocky one. "Cash or the bike. You choose."

"Got a few twenties in my backpack," Whitt said.

"Then get it. Don't have all day here."

He'd heard those words enough times. Unzipping his backpack, he dug deep to find the can of Mace. Yanking it out, he sprayed both guys in the face. The tall kid screamed like a girl and lunged blindly at him. The stocky kid swore and released Whitt's bike.

He jumped back to avoid their fists.

Leaving the two guys behind, he didn't want to think about

what would happen when he met up with them again. The officer hurried from his car, but Whitt just waved and raced to the clinic, Mace in one hand, and his backpack slung over his shoulder.

Bullies existed in every community, but this neighborhood had a 90 percent crime rate, as huge as their foreclosures. Miss Stacy claimed if she got custody, they'd have to move. He wanted to believe the adoption would be reality too. Couldn't happen fast enough.

At the clinic's parking lot, her truck was gone. Weird. He couldn't remember the last time she'd left the clinic alone during business hours. But she'd been sick this morning. He used his key to unlock the door and stepped inside, with the officer right behind him.

"Whitt, what happened back there?" The officer had a fatherly look about him.

He had no intention of providing details. "Two guys wanted the stuff in my backpack."

"The next time you might not be so lucky."

"I'll worry about it then."

"Have you thought about learning martial arts? Won't need Mace when you can fight with your body."

Respect washed over Whitt. He'd spent his life dodging and mistrusting men, and this guy offered encouragement. In his head, he knew not every man was like his dad, but trusting took guts. "I will. Thanks. You understand I couldn't have you running them off."

"Right. A man has his pride."

Whitt grinned.

"I received a call from my partner, and Dr. Broussard dismissed our protection detail, but I wanted to see you home from school."

The sting this morning must have led to an arrest. Relieved, Whitt turned to the officer. "Okay. That's the best news today. I mean, the officers must have made an arrest. I'll get the whole story as soon as she returns."

The officer handed him his card. "Call if you need anything."

The officer drove away, leaving Whitt alone with his own worries. Concern for Miss Stacy pelted his mind. Remembering he hadn't turned his cell phone on after the test, he checked for texts and voice messages. A text indicated she had a doctor's appointment and would be gone until around two thirty or three. It was now 3:45.

She must have had a quick errand to run. He checked on Xena and gave her water. No other animals were at the clinic, and clients were canceling because of sickness. Hard to take a pet for an exam when the owner didn't feel well enough to drive. No surgeries were scheduled either. His mind stayed fixed on Miss Stacy. They'd been foolish not to take more precautions against the flu. Although washing hands and staying away from those who were sick was the best preventative against a virus, it might not have helped in her case. At least he didn't have any symptoms. That way he could help her.

The light on the office phone blinked a message. When he checked the online scheduling, he learned she hadn't kept any of her day's appointments. The woman who owned the Pomeranian had been detained and been a no-show. She'd left three frantic messages apologizing and cried through each one of them. He'd return her call as soon as he figured out what was going on.

He pressed in Miss Stacy's cell phone number. No response, but he left a message.

She must be really sick and resting at home. For once he wished she had a landline there.

He locked up and pedaled the short distance through the subdivision to her home. After discovering an empty house, he hurried back to the clinic. Where was she? His heart took a dip. This wasn't like Miss Stacy. She always kept him informed.

Whom should he call? She had friends at church, but who would have any clue about her doctor's name? Not exactly what he figured as church talk. He made his way to her desk, a mess of disorganization. Every time he put papers and files in order, she destroyed his efforts. Ten minutes later, he found a stack of business cards and sorted through each one until he found a doctor's name, an internist. He pressed in the phone number.

"My name is Whitt McMann, and I'm trying to locate my foster mother." The words slipped out without much thought. "Her name is Stacy Broussard. Is she a patient there?"

"You're Dr. Broussard's foster child?"

"Yes, ma'am. I go to summer school and just arrived home. She wasn't feeling well this morning and mentioned seeing a doctor. I thought she might have scheduled an appointment with Dr. Maberry."

"Hold on a minute."

He put the phone on speaker and sorted papers—a stack each for client files, invoices, bills, and the carnival.

The receptionist returned. "Whitt, Dr. Broussard is in the hospital."

His stomach jolted. "Why?"

"She fainted while here, and we transported her by ambulance to the Woman's Hospital."

"Why there?"

"Dr. Maberry has an affiliation at the Woman's Hospital."

His nightmares had hit. "What's wrong with her?"

"She's been admitted for testing."

Miss Stacy believed in straightforward communication. "How sick is she? Is it flu?"

"I'm not at liberty to say. I suggest you contact your social worker to make arrangements for your care."

A viselike grip clamped onto his heart. "I'd like to give social services solid answers."

"In view of your age and not being family, it's against our guidelines to give patient information. However, we can make an allowance for your caseworker."

"Did Miss Stacy make those recommendations?"

"No. She didn't mention you."

"Okay, thanks." He slid the phone into his shorts pocket and eased into her desk chair, an ergonomically correct variety. He'd insisted upon the design when he noted her poor posture. Life was so much easier when people were predictable.

Calm down. She'll be fine.

Social services . . . Would they find out she was in the hospital? Would it affect the hearing?

Self-pity smacked him in the face and he berated himself. Miss Stacy's health came first, before him or any program designed to enhance society's castoffs. Why couldn't the receptionist have given him the diagnosis? She'd said testing. Didn't the doctor know why she'd fainted?

A scratch pad seized his attention, and he quickly scribbled the hospital's name. He handled critical matters best when he had his thoughts on paper.

1. Call the hospital.
2. Ensure everything at the clinic is in impeccable order.

That always pleased Miss Stacy.

3. Search her house to see if she left a note.
4. Find a way to see her. The bus line might be the best option.

Calling an adult teetered on first-class idiocy. They might contact social services, and he'd be drop-shipped into a home with a dozen other kids. Been there, done that when he was eight. Taking a breath, he found the number for the hospital.

"Are you family?" the woman on the other end said when he requested information.

"I'm her son."

"I'll connect you with the nurses' station."

Couldn't someone give him a straight answer?

"Can I help you?" another female voice said.

"I'm worried about my mom. Her name is Stacy Broussard. What I've learned is she fainted at the doctor's office and an ambulance transported her there. I have no idea if she's been admitted or is still in the emergency room."

"Your father?"

"He's not in the picture."

"She's been admitted and is currently sleeping."

"What about tests?"

"We're following her doctor's orders. Please, hold on a minute."

Panic raced through his body. The nurse seemed to take forever before returning to the phone. "You're Whitt?"

"Yes, ma'am."

"Dr. Broussard said if you should call, to not worry. She forgot her cell phone at home."

Whitt wanted to scream. The correct grammar was "not to worry." He had to gain control of his emotions, the one part of him he found difficult to understand. "Can I talk to her?"

"I'm so sorry. I'll let her know you called. Are you at home?"

"I will be shortly. Tell her I'm taking care of the clinic first."

Normally he'd spend time with Xena, but all he could do was walk her and make sure she had food and water. The thought of taking her with him crossed his mind, but not until he had questions answered about Miss Stacy. Xena's wound had healed nicely, but he still wanted to apply a topical antibiotic. She planted a sloppy kiss on his face as though she understood his apprehension. He shook off the urgency of finding a way to visit Miss Stacy until she called. Locking up the clinic, he rode his bike to her home while forming the appropriate response to the woman who owned the Pomeranian. He'd encourage her to contact Doc Kent without explanation, the veterinarian Miss Stacy referred clients to when she had a full schedule. Once inside the home again, he found her phone on the nightstand beside the charger and plugged it in.

She never forgot her phone.

What could he do? His stomach twisted. Must be the worry over Miss Stacy.

Kitchen.

Yes.

Every woman appreciated a spotless kitchen. Give him something to do while he waited for her to contact him.

Their pastor would suggest praying, so he tried that. But he and God weren't on the best of terms. Maybe Whitt's opinion would change after the hearing on Wednesday.

How could she get custody if she was in the hospital? Would the judge be lenient?

His thoughts were honest, and yet he sensed guilt and worry fusing into something horrible.

Her phone rang, and he hurried to answer it. The screen read *Alex LeBlanc.* "Dr. Stacy Broussard's phone."

"Whitt? This is Alex. I wanted to check on how the protection detail is going."

"She dismissed them."

"When?"

"Sometime while I was at school."

"Do you know why?"

"I assumed the officer made an arrest." Nagging suspicion bubbled like he'd be sick.

"To the best of my knowledge, no one showed up this morning. Is she around so I can talk to her?"

"No. She's . . ."

"Whitt, what's wrong?"

"She's in the hospital. I just found out."

"Where?"

"Woman's, near the Medical Center. Look, I don't know the problem. She wasn't feeling well this morning. I think she had a fever. Guess it's the flu spreading around." He caught his breath. "The hospital isn't informative."

"Do you have someone to drive you there?"

Whitt sank onto the side of her bed. "I'm checking the bus line." He thought she'd have called by now.

"Would one of her friends take you? Your pastor?"

"Her best friend is on a mission trip in the Dominican Republic, and the pastor isn't my favorite person." Whitt had overheard him telling Miss Stacy that she wasn't equipped to take care of a nearly grown boy who reeked of bad genes. "I'll walk to a bus stop."

"No need. I'll swing by and get you."

Whoa. What's his angle? "Why?"

"As a friend."

A bazillion synapses fired out of control. But he needed to make sure she was okay. "I'll be ready."

36

STACY ATTEMPTED TO OPEN HER EYES. So much of the day blurred no matter how hard she fought to reconstruct it. Her head throbbed worse than when she'd chosen to call the doctor. Nausea swept through her. The idea of having to seek medical attention and embarrassment over the no-show on the sting had caused her to cancel the protection detail. Why had she made such a foolish decision? Who was protecting Whitt? The memory lapses and poor judgment must be a result of her fever. No excuse when she loved him, when motherhood meant sacrifice.

Struggling with a flash of earlier today, she remembered driving to see Dr. Maberry. She'd given him her symptoms. What happened then? Oh, he'd ordered an injection and instructed her to fill two prescriptions and go home to bed. She'd made her way to the reception area when dizziness overcame her, and she couldn't shake it. She awoke in an ambulance, the sirens howling like a swamp witch. A white-haired female paramedic adjusted an IV. The woman reminded her of an aunt in Louisiana. What happened afterward muddled her brain—someone took blood, machines, more sleep, and horrific nightmares.

Whitt. He must be in a state of panic, worried sick. She had to contact him. She forced her eyes open, to leave the world of confusion behind.

A hand held hers firmly, and a sweet boy's voice whispered her name. How long before his voice changed and cracked? Would he start a growth spurt soon? When would he tower over her? Her mind wandered toward darkness.

"Miss Stacy, are you awake?" Whitt said. "Can you hear me?"

She battled with eyelids that felt like they were superglued together. "Yes. So sorry to alarm you." She drew in a breath and hoped she didn't get sick. "I'm in a hospital, right?"

"Woman's Hospital, near the Medical Center."

Shadows dimmed the window. "What time is it?"

"Eight fifteen," he said. His voice sounded tight as though he'd been crying.

"I'm okay." Had she been sleeping all that time? Why couldn't she remember? "How . . . how did you get here?"

"I brought him," a male voice said.

Alex? She was drifting. What strain of flu attacked a person like this? The agent leaned over Whitt's shoulder.

"Thanks." Her lips were so dry. "Hope you stay healthy."

"No problem. I'm a strong guy."

"Miss Stacy, I'm a strong guy too."

"How are you feeling?" Alex said.

Be strong. "Like running a marathon."

Alex chuckled. "Dr. Broussard, are you aware lying to an FBI agent is a federal offense?"

"A hospital is pretty close to a jail. Solitary confinement."

"Ha." Whitt squeezed her hand. Poor boy wore fear of psychological pain like a battle scar.

"I imagine the doctor's running tests," she said.

Her boy trembled. "Alex and I are waiting on him now. He assured us he'd be here before nine."

"Then I can go home?" She glanced at the IV bags dangling from a pole. "These are nearly empty. Can I have a couple of prescriptions and more blankets? I'm freezing."

Whitt released her hand and stepped away.

Alex turned to her boy. "She'll be fine. Once the doctor gets here, he'll discuss her test results and how he plans to treat her."

She needed to comfort Whitt. "I've let you down . . . Sent the police officers home. I have to get better before the hearing." Speaking zapped what little strength she had left.

Whitt whirled back to her. "We're in this together, remember? The judge will look differently at you in the hospital than the parents in jail." He shrugged. "Maybe you don't have to appear. Maybe the attorney and social services have the evidence they need for the judge to make an informed decision."

The words of an adult from one so young. She'd call the attorney first thing in the morning. "It's only Monday. A lot can happen by Wednesday."

"Do you mind if I stay here tonight?" Whitt's voice took on the edge of a little boy pleading. "Nothing big for school tomorrow."

She reached for his hand and blinked back the incredible urgency to sleep. He needed her as his mother, and she wanted him as her son. Her thoughts failed to translate into words, and she drifted into darkness.

37

AT 9:20 P.M., an older man stepped into Stacy's private room, and Alex introduced himself. Whitt had paced the floor for the past hour, watching the doorway, then Stacy, and back to the clock. The kid cared for her in a major way. From what she'd told Alex, Whitt hadn't experienced nurturing at home, and she filled the void.

The man with thinning gray hair and glasses stuck out his hand to Alex. "I'm Dr. Maberry, Dr. Broussard's physician. Are you family?"

"Friend."

He eyed Whitt. "You're her foster son?"

"Yes, sir. How is she?"

Whitt didn't hesitate to deceive the doctor. What else would the kid do to protect himself?

Dr. Maberry walked to her bedside and checked the two IV bags. "Has she been awake?"

"For a few minutes around eight," Alex said.

"Actually it was a total of six minutes before she went back to sleep," Whitt said.

If the situation hadn't been so grim, Alex wouldn't have swallowed a chuckle. "Can you give us an update on your findings?"

Dr. Maberry smiled, the same professional expression Alex tossed out when he wanted to make those around him relax. Being on the receiving end didn't soothe his qualms. The bottom line? Alex believed Stacy was battling a serious illness, and the doctor hadn't reached a diagnosis. Whitt perceived it too.

"Dr. Broussard's tests are inconclusive at this point," the doctor said. "Her white blood count is high. Along with the fever—"

"How high's her temp?" Whitt said.

"Currently at 102.2. She's been nauseated. Her liver, spleen, and lymph nodes are swollen. We'll need to keep her for further testing and treatment."

Whitt eased around to the opposite side of Stacy's bed, where she slept seemingly unaware of the doctor's presence. "So you don't know what's wrong? Modern medicine offers little assistance in the face of whatever has made her ill?"

"Son, we have a team of doctors reviewing her case and believe it's a flu strain, but it's not confirmed."

He pointed to the IVs. "What's in there?"

The doctor studied him.

"Sir, I'll understand your answer. I've been researching."

Alex nodded. "Trust me, he will."

"All right. Normal saline and I'm trying broad-spectrum antibiotic coverage until we have a positive culture."

"Is she getting worse?" Whitt's voice trembled.

Dr. Maberry rubbed his forehead, the gesture revealing Stacy was headed further downhill. "We're doing everything we can to keep her comfortable and support her natural immune system. She's a strong woman and can fight this thing."

"What else are her symptoms telling you?" Whitt said.

The kid was persistent, but they were getting answers.

"Possibly rheumatic fever."

"That's unusual. Anything else?"

"As I said, further testing is required. She mentioned flu had been rampant in your community, and she may have contracted a bad strain."

"I want to stay with her." Whitt raised his shoulders. "Nurses can't be in here every minute of the day or night."

Dr. Maberry crossed his arms over his chest. He studied Whitt before turning his attention to Alex. If the doctor thought Alex could help him ease out of Whitt's request, he'd better come up with another plan. "Those exposed to her could become ill."

"I can handle a little flu," Whitt said. "He's a friend. Hasn't been around her much. Not vested in the relationship."

Alex faked a cough to muffle his laughter. "Doctor, do you recommend a twelve-year-old spend the night?"

"Is anyone at home to care for him?"

"Not to my knowledge," Alex said.

"No, sir," Whitt said. "I'd be alone."

"Your choice, but you need to abide by hospital rules. No friends, loud music, that kind of thing."

"Yes, sir. I'm very responsible."

"I'll be making rounds in the morning. The hospital will notify me if anything about her condition changes. If your behavior is inappropriate, you'll be asked to leave."

When the doctor left, Whitt paced the room. "Now to find someone who can watch the clinic." He snapped his fingers. "I'll call another vet who helps her out. Worry for Miss Stacy has me scattered." He peered up at Alex. "I have the situation under control."

"I'm glad to hear it." Alex wrestled with his own world and how to deal with the woman and unusual boy who'd stumbled into his life. He pulled out his wallet. "You'll need to eat, and although hospital food is the worst, it's the best I can do."

He made eye contact with Alex. "I have money in my backpack."

"You might need it later." Alex handed him forty dollars. "I'll check on you tomorrow."

"Thanks, Agent LeBlanc. Appreciate you . . . bringing me here and the loan."

Alex hesitated. The kid was scared. Inside his supercharged brain was a little boy. "I'm Alex. Anyone I can call? Her family?"

Whitt stared into her sleeping face, smooth and untouched by the turmoil around her. "Mostly it's just me and Miss Stacy and the animals at the clinic. Her best friend won't be back for another three weeks." He offered a grim smile. "I could check her contacts since I have her cell with me. Lately she's been calling her mom in Louisiana. According to her, neither parent has been to Houston. Sorta sad when you see her giving to people and animals without expecting anything in return." He drew in a sob. "I'm afraid she's not going to make it. She'd ask me to pray, but God and I aren't at the point of talking."

"Whitt, God always listens."

He frowned. "Whatever."

Alex sensed the boy's fear moving toward hysteria. The only person who'd reached out to him was desperately ill. A high IQ never matched fragile emotions. Dexter and Eva would suggest he pray with Whitt. Not a bad idea. "Would you like for me to pray with you?"

Whitt raised a brow. "You and Miss Stacy have the faith thing going. No, I don't need you to pray with me. Too awkward, and I'm not sure God's the answer."

"He's always the answer. Would you like for me to stay awhile? You could sleep a few hours."

Whitt walked to the window and looked out at the next building. "This makes no sense to me."

"The doctor will figure it out. Her resistance could be low, and she simply needs rest and meds to fight it."

He faced Alex. "Not Miss Stacy. You. Is this a game to figure out if she's hiding information about the murder, quadcopter, and water scare?"

He understood Whitt wanted someone to blame, to unload twelve years of anger. "No ulterior motive."

"What about the first night you came to the house?"

"Initially that was fact-finding. The gumbo and company came as a bonus."

"She told me about your invitation to coffee and how she informed you that we came as a package."

"We discussed it."

"You tossed in the towel because of me."

"Not necessarily. I'm a totally in or totally out man. Do you have a problem with me in the picture?"

Whitt's shoulders lifted and fell. "Not sure. Makes me nervous. The final picture could be . . . devastating."

"Accepting a package involves a commitment to the contents."

"Not for everyone. Parents are supposed to take care of their kids."

"Preconceived ideas can destroy the truth in others."

"And only the strongest survive." He picked up Stacy's limp hand. "When will you have the DNA results from her clothes?"

Did Whitt know something or was he only changing the subject? "Another week. Takes a while. Why?"

"I really wanted everything wrapped up about that Saturday before the custody hearing. The social worker assigned to me is . . . biased, rude, and views me as subhuman. She might look at the case and say something ugly about Miss Stacy to change the judge's opinion."

"Why would she do that?"

He sighed. "She and I had an argument. When the school

called me into the office, she was there. I told her to mind her own business."

Whitt's adolescence and insecurity shouted from his every word. Social services were his advocate, not the enemy. "Sounds like a bad experience has turned you against those who are dedicated to the care of kids."

"Not this woman. She stuck me in a foster home with four other kids. The so-called foster dad ruled with an iron fist and the Word of God. The foster mom cleaned up after him."

"Were they reported?"

"Yeah, and the kids removed. I went back home to the same disaster."

The male figures in his life had used power and control to make their point. No wonder he shied away from Alex and God. "I'm not like the men who've disappointed you."

Whitt nodded. "I've met a couple of good guys. I'm watching you to see if befriending me is your inroad to Miss Stacy."

Alex studied him. "Deceit has a way of slapping you in the face. Not my style. Trust has to be earned—a cliché—but if a relationship with Stacy and you is in my future, we'll have to trust each other."

Whitt's attention moved to Stacy. "One minute I'm worried about her, and the next it's all about me."

"Understandable, Whitt. We can talk about this when she's better. You ought to sleep a few hours while I'm here."

"Doubt if I can, but I'd welcome the company."

Alex might have made a little progress with Whitt. . . . On the other hand, Stacy's pallor resembled a corpse's. The time had come to put aside his own issues with God and plead for her healing.

38

ALEX WOKE IN THE WEE HOURS of Tuesday morning to the sound of his phone signaling an incoming message. He snatched it from the hospital nightstand before it woke Whitt and Stacy. She slept hard, but the boy's restlessness and constant checking on Stacy revealed his concern. Poor kid. Alex sympathized with his plight. She was his mother figure, and he'd do anything to keep her safe. After losing his own mother as a young adult, Alex loved Eva Rayken for helping to heal his heart.

A report flowed in regarding the CID investigation at Fort Benning. They named two enlisted men who'd stolen the quadcopter. One man had been arrested, but the second was AWOL. The serviceman in custody, Private Luke Wilcox, refused to talk.

In the dim shadows and muted sounds, Alex put together what little had been uncovered about the quadcopter: stolen from Fort Benning by two enlisted men, who in turn sold it to someone. It ended up in the vicinity of the Houston airport, shot down and full of holes from a 9mm. A dead man was also found nearby, killed by a 9mm bullet. According to the dead man's family, he didn't own a drone.

Who purchased the device from the Fort Benning men?

What was the intended use?

How did it end up in the clearing?

Who fired the shots into the quadcopter and why?

He'd text Ric, knowing he'd be up with the same report, but nothing could be resolved. They'd work on it later at the office.

Alex yawned for the third time since he'd started a conversation with Ric. Caffeine hadn't jolted him awake yet, and he'd been drinking Coke and coffee since five this morning. He grabbed the bottle of water on his desk and took a long swig.

"Not much sleep last night?" Ric said.

"Didn't get home until after two."

"Hot date?"

"Hardly." He explained the whole flu and hospital thing with Stacy and Whitt. "She slept most of the time. Probably unaware of anything else. Whitt attempted to wake her a few times, but she was unresponsive."

"How's he handling it?"

"Not good. Actually, I'm right there with him."

Ric hesitated. "Is she going to make it?"

"Been wondering the same thing. Whitt said he'd call after the doctor made his morning rounds. She hadn't shown any signs of improvement when I left. Temp was over 102." When Ric jammed his hands into his pants pockets, Alex questioned him. "Something's churning."

"When did the flu start?"

Alex's thoughts sped. "People started getting sick after the carnival. Remember the elderly man we met with Whitt? He passed soon afterward. Supposedly a heart attack. I want to revisit Sunday afternoon once we learn more about Stacy's illness. But I have two thoughts. One, the photos of Whitt were placed on her driveway while Connor was in custody, which means we're looking at another person. Two, were those who've contracted the illness at the carnival too?"

"Bro, I bet Whitt could help us."

"We can take a run by the hospital after he calls."

A report from the FIG drew his attention. "This is what I was looking for," Alex said. "I'm hoping the security camera from the vet clinic shows who broke in and planted the recording device." He read through the analysis. "About four weeks before Howe was killed, someone disconnected the camera remotely for thirty-seven minutes. Meaning that same person hacked into the alarm."

Before Ric could respond, Alex's phone rang: Stacy's cell. "Special Agent Alex LeBlanc."

"This is Whitt," the kid said weakly. "Wanted to give you Dr. Maberry's report."

From the muffled sound of the kid blowing his nose, the doctor hadn't given him positive news. "Testing is inconclusive. He's keeping her another day. Maybe more. Fever remains high at 102.5."

"Is she awake?"

"Off and on, like last night. She fell asleep while the doctor examined her."

"Has she ever had anything resembling this in the past?"

"Not that I can remember. I've known her for years."

"Hold tight. The doctors will have this diagnosed soon."

"Yes, sir."

"Were the other people who are sick at the carnival?"

"Yes. I've already concluded someone there was contagious and infected everyone. Nothing like a mind on overload to conjure up the worst." He paused, and Alex envisioned him fighting to be strong.

"What else have you discovered about her symptoms?" Alex wanted him to feel useful and not to budge from the hospital.

"Flu makes the most sense, although it's a severe case. An older person or a child might not survive. I'm concerned about bronchitis and pneumonia. When she was awake earlier, I asked if her chest, sinuses, or ears hurt. She said no, and I reported it to the nurse." He sighed. "With her immunities down, I'm really worried."

Poor kid. His world leaned toward the edge of a cliff. "Those trained in the medical field will turn this around."

"You're talking to a kid who overthinks everything, but thanks for the encouragement. I want to ask for a medical book and make a diagnosis. At least I'd be contributing instead of going crazy. Man, I'm sorry. Using up your FBI time. Talking too much."

"I wanted to know about her, as a friend, and how you're holding up."

"She's the only mom I have. A great lady. Does the Jesus thing and helps others. She's solid." He hesitated. "I'm watching her for allergic reactions or bad side effects to the treatment Dr. Maberry prescribed. But it's also a bit early for any of those things to occur."

"Whitt, you're a smart kid, and I'm sure you have everything managed expertly with the clinic and home, but here are a couple of suggestions."

"I could have missed something. Hold on while I get my list." A moment later he told Alex he was ready.

"Contact Stacy's attorney and explain the circumstances. Let him know you're at the hospital with her 24-7, and a friend is bringing you a change of clothes and looking out for you. Make sure whoever is taking care of the clinic can continue until at least

Monday next week. Call her parents. There may be something in the family's health history that could help the doctors."

"Hadn't thought of family backgrounds." He sighed. "I already forwarded the clinic's calls to the other vet."

"Good. Have you eaten?"

"I will when I work through the list."

Whitt was afraid to leave her. His stability had been seized from him, shaking him to the core. "When we hang up, get a to-go order at the cafeteria. Remember, you have money in your pocket. Eat healthy stuff, not junk. You can make calls between bites."

"If she wakes up and I'm not here—"

"Leave a note. My partner and I will be there before noon."

"Okay. Are you calling social services?"

"We can discuss what's best later. Let's take one step at a time." The kid couldn't take care of himself, and Alex had a responsibility to report the situation. He didn't think Whitt would run, but intelligence and fear heated with emotions could cause a person to take drastic steps.

39

STACY SENSED more people than Whitt occupied her hospital room.
What time was it? She tried to move, and her whole body ached.
Enough of this. She had to get home. Too much work to do. The
custody hearing . . .

"Whitt, are we alone?" Her eyes attempted to focus on the dear
boy close to the bed while light streamed into the room. He touched
her shoulder. She cringed at the incredible pain, and he jerked back
his hand.

"Sorry. Alex returned and brought his partner. The FBI is upon
us again." His shot at humor caused her to smile.

That's right. Alex had spent the night at the hospital. "More
questions, gentlemen?" Might as well joke about it.

"Just checking on you," Alex said.

"I'm good. Ready to go home. What time is it?"

"Ten thirty."

"What's the verdict? Will I live?"

"I'm sure you will." Alex's smile didn't match the apprehension in his voice. "You, Whitt, and I have a date at Starbucks. I hear he's a double chocolaty chip Frappuccino fan."

"I look forward to it." Would their time together really happen? Moistening her lips, she dug deep for strength to continue talking. "Thanks for stopping by. Alex, I need someone to call my attorney about—"

"I handled it," Whitt said. "Told him you were sick, but I didn't say 'hospital.' Didn't think he needed to know. He said with the preliminary work completed on our case, he'd see about getting the judge to approve custody without our presence. And if there's a problem, he'll reschedule the hearing. Since the parents are still in jail, I don't know who'd protest except social services. Doc Kent is taking care of the clinic until he hears differently. I found your mom's number in your phone contacts and called her. A little weird but she was nice. Your parents will be here in the morning."

Mom? Dad? Stacy closed her eyes. Dear Whitt. Dad would be the perfect role model for him. Maybe Dad would take him fishing. "What did you tell her?"

He shrugged. "A strain of flu had you hospitalized. I asked about family health history and mentioned your symptoms. She didn't have anything to report. I told her a trip here might make you feel better."

A tear slid down her cheek. "You covered the bases."

"Sure."

The ways she'd disappointed others with this untimely hospital stay dashed into her heart. "I need to get out of here. I'm afraid I've ruined our custody celebration, and what about your play on Friday? In my sleep stupor, did Mrs. Howe call? I've never told her how sorry I am about her husband's death."

"No, she didn't. Now don't get all girly on me. The hearing's in the bag." Whitt had confidence in his words, but the uneasiness was there too.

"Oh, Whitt. I do love you so much." She touched his hand resting on the bed, although contact against her flesh stung. His hand was cold. "Would someone give me the doctor's report? Flu is Tylenol and a prescription for Tamiflu. I feel like every breath is borrowed time." Exhaustion spread through her. No energy. But desperation for answers caused her to crave more strength than her body offered. She glanced at Ric. "Are they keeping something from me?"

He moved to her side. "Dr. Broussard, I'm not a medical professional, but I understand your concerns. Looks like the young man here is doing a fine job of taking care of you and your veterinary practice."

"Yes, he is. I just want to go home." Then she remembered. "Have you received Lynx Connor's confession and solved the crimes from that Saturday? Found out who threatened Whitt?" She gulped.

"No, ma'am, nothing affirmative on either count," Ric said. "But we're on it."

So much easier to keep her eyes closed. "Alex, I need a favor."

"Sure."

"Not for me. Whitt." She took a breath. "Thanks. You've done so much. I . . . can be stubborn." Her mind shadowed. "If I don't make it, help Whitt."

"I promise," Alex said without hesitation.

Her precious boy whispered, "No, Miss Stacy. This is just flu. You're going to pull through this."

She nodded, but the words wouldn't form audibly. She peered into his serious gray eyes and silently vowed not to abandon him like his parents. She'd fight these symptoms and win.

40

DEXTER CONCLUDED the day would be long the moment he received the blood test results for Dr. Stacy Broussard. This wasn't a rare case of canine brucellosis that had affected a human, but a genetically engineered strain, designed to inflict damage. His first call was to James Nisse.

"We have a potential biological problem," Dexter said and revealed the test results. "Dr. Broussard has come in contact with brucellosis, and the public needs information immediately. We've never dealt with this strain before. According to her physician, she's very ill with flu-like symptoms."

"When I talked to her last week, she indicated others in her community were experiencing flu symptoms."

"Let's hope her case is isolated, but my concern is otherwise. I'll send a response team to her clinic. Begin testing canines in her care and search files for those she's seen in the last few months. James, we'll get protocol into place. I'll contact the FBI now." He glanced at his watch. "Can you meet me at the Woman's Hospital in one hour, say eleven thirty?"

"Of course."

"I'll contact her physician, inform him of the findings and that we're on our way."

"Dr. Broussard may be able to help us expedite the communication process," James said.

"Or she may be too ill." Dexter concluded the conversation and phoned Houston's FBI director with the findings. On the way to the hospital, he called Alex. "Has your supervisor contacted you?"

"No. What's going on?"

"Dr. Stacy Broussard has been diagnosed with a genetically modified human brucellosis, likely contracted from a canine. The FBI director will release a statement before the day's complete."

"I'm at the hospital with her now. Is the strain airborne?"

Dexter blew out a sigh. "Not usually. Airborne contagion is extremely rare, but not an impossibility, especially with one that's been genetically engineered. Canine brucellosis in its singular form is transmitted through contact with the infected dog's bodily fluids."

"In short, you don't know what you're dealing with until further testing."

"Right. I'm meeting James Nisse from the health department at the Woman's Hospital. Her physician will have met with her by then."

Stacy watched Dr. Maberry enter her hospital room, wearing a mask. He opened a cupboard and pulled out a handful of masks. After distributing one each to Whitt, Alex, Ric, and her, he requested they place them over their mouth and nose. She must be highly contagious. He wore the same unreadable features, and she wanted information now.

"Stacy, I need to talk to you." He pushed his glasses up his nose. No emotion. "We've found the source of your illness."

The doctor gave no indication of promising news. "Shall I brace myself?"

He studied her as though forming words for a huge disappointment. "It's called human brucellosis. You're acquainted with canine brucellosis."

"The disease is extremely rare, and I use every precaution." Shock rippled through her. "It's a bacterial infection that dogs normally transmit sexually. There isn't an available cure. This is what has made me so sick? Could this be a case of false testing?"

"Stacy, we're positive. Unfortunately this is a strain we've never seen before."

Clenching her fist, she geared herself for what she feared would be potentially devastating. "What do you mean?"

"A strain that's been genetically engineered to be five times more powerful."

"Recombinant DNA." Whitt lightly touched her arm.

"Exactly," the doctor said. "Our first concern is taking care of those infected and preventing the disease from spreading to others." He shook his head. "Then learning why someone would develop the disease, which is the reason the health department and the director of Houston's LRN have been called in. Representatives will be here shortly."

She'd talked to the LRN director about the water fraud. The laboratory used CDC protocol. Fear coursed through her. "Explain this to me."

"If you've been infected, others will be or are too. There's a real risk of extreme contagion."

"Oh no," she whispered. The carnival on Sunday flashed across her mind . . . the men, women, and children who'd attended the event. Those who were sick. But the dogs in her care were healthy. Except Xena. She'd never tested the Lab. A single dog could infect the others. . . . Her gaze flew to Whitt. A lump the size of a golf ball formed in her throat. "Someone needs to contact the dog owners who were present at the petting zoo. I think four total and Xena makes five."

Whitt picked up the phone. What about Mr. Parson? Xena had licked him in the mouth. Had Stacy's neglect caused his death? "Wait. Whitt, how are you feeling?"

"Just tired, Miss Stacy. I'm okay."

"Fever?"

"Nah."

"Please, have the doctor examine you while he's here." She flashed concern at Dr. Maberry.

"This is a serious matter, Whitt," the doctor said. "We have no definitive indication the disease is transferred from humans, but until we have that confirmed, we're initiating precautions. Those entering the room must wear a mask and gloves. Your door will remain closed. Procedures will be posted outside the door. Any visitors who suspect they are ill, have heart problems, diabetes, cancer, compromised immune systems, etc. will not be permitted. That also means anyone under the age of sixteen and the elderly. Whitt, I'll need to run a blood test on you."

Whitt laid the phone on the bedside table. "Look, I don't have insurance or money."

"I'll take care of it," she said.

"Only if I can pay you back."

"It's not necessary."

Whitt trembled. "Are you finished so I can call Doc Kent? Or do you have other questions for him?"

"Please contact him, now," Dr. Maberry said.

Panic rose. She refused to ask if this strain produced a death certificate because preliminary indications weren't available. "What about an antibiotic? For animals, we use multiples." Her mind swept over the cases where owners chose long-term antibiotics and isolation of the animal rather than euthanasia—the latter she'd never recommend. "I encourage you to check with the AKC Canine Health Foundation. New strides are made every day."

Dr. Maberry hesitated. "That was one of my calls. There isn't a cure. To treat you, we'll change to a combination of streptomycin and doxycycline. If your body reacts positively, then we can use it on other patients who are infected with the same strain."

"Intravenously, injections, or pills?"

"Injections."

"Will you alert the residents of my neighborhood?"

"The health department is handling the notification."

"When can I be released?"

"Your temperature is 102.5. Does that answer your question?"

She drew in a sharp breath. "If the strain has been altered, how does it affect the incubation period? Ultimate prognosis?"

"Unable to determine at this time."

What kind of future was ahead of her? Animals aborted and had to be isolated. That was no life for a human. "Like a dog, I could live with this forever?"

"Stacy, we can discuss long-term prognosis when we have a consensus from the experts studying the disease. You could respond, then have a relapse, or the symptoms could continue. We also have no idea how effective the drugs will be in treating this modified strain of brucella." He stared at her chart, obviously in shutdown mode.

"I'm sorry to upset you, Dr. Maberry. Reality is I have no idea how to cope with this. On a much smaller scale, I deal with not having the resources to cure animals. When that happens, I feel helpless and angry at the same time."

His gaze lifted to hers. "People have varying reactions to bacterial infections like this. One could be introduced into an area, and some would have no reaction at all. Others experience a few symptoms and they're back on their feet. And others become very ill. Like you."

Before she could question him further, Whitt interrupted. "Excuse me. I have Doc Kent on the phone. He wants to talk to your doctor." Whitt handed the phone to Dr. Maberry, who walked into the hallway with the phone.

"What did he say?" she said.

"Mostly listened. Told him about the possibility of Xena carrying a strain of the disease. If she has it, we're looking at a critical situation."

Her thinking was muddled with the fever. What Dr. Maberry wasn't saying about the infected spoke the loudest . . . Children and older people. Those whose immune systems fought an ongoing battle with disease. Why would anyone develop such a despicable thing? Closing her eyes, she fought the extreme fatigue settling on her. But she couldn't sleep until questions were addressed.

When the FBI agents left the room, she reached for Whitt's hand. The movement sent pain coursing through her body. "I won't give up."

"What can I do to help?" he said. "I can't make you well and nothing else matters."

That's when his dam broke, and she was powerless to comfort him.

"I love you," he said. "You're my real mom."

41

ALEX RODE ON THE PASSENGER SIDE of Ric's Camaro to lunch. One minute he focused on the case, and in the next he wrestled with the genetically engineered human brucellosis.

"When I analyze all that's happened since Stacy rode into the clearing, this looks like a crazy scheme with her as a pawn," Ric said.

"When you figure it out, I want to be the first to know. A murder, a stolen quadcopter, a water hoax, a plan to purchase apparently worthless property, and now a bacterial infection that could be deadly."

Ric shook his head. "I'm sending a request to LA to question Connor about the latest development. His plea bargain is sounding better, except if he killed Howe or left a disease-carrying dog in Houston, he gets a get-out-of-jail-free card."

"The money from buying worthless property isn't worth the risk of a murder charge."

"Something is. Do you want to talk about the personal side of this?" Ric said.

"Not sure I can put my thoughts into words. Separating the case from the woman has become a hurdle."

"Obviously you have feelings for her and Whitt."

"I guess. How did I allow this to interfere with my ordered life?"

"You're human, and despite the woman who attempted to draw you into her crimes a few years ago, you've developed a bad case of Stacy Broussard."

"When you put it that way, it's less ironic."

"It is what it is."

Alex's heart plummeted to his toes, and he tossed his attention to his partner. "You think she's dying."

Ric stared at the road. "How long can she maintain the high fever?"

He'd prayed for her, but God could have other plans for her. "There are several doctors on it."

"All right. Bro, I need to ask you something, as a friend. Real personal. Have you two been intimate?"

Alex stiffened. "That *is* a personal question, but no."

"Hey, just thinking about you catching the same illness."

"It's okay, and I'm fine. More concerned about Whitt. He can't live at the hospital. There's a custody hearing tomorrow, and he and Stacy were supposed to be there, but her attorney says their absence is not a concern."

"If the attorney fails to convince the judge, social services will want to be reassured he's okay. Do you think he'd take off?"

"If a decision goes against him? No doubt in my mind. And considering his intelligence, he'd find a way to beat the system. He lied to Dr. Maberry about being her foster son. I asked him to tell the attorney that Stacy's in the hospital, but he chose otherwise. He has guts." Alex wanted to trust the kid, but his actions jarred the trust level. "I gave her my word to look out for him, but it might not be something he'd want."

"Would he steal from her to get away?"

"I hate to think so. He genuinely cares for Stacy. Hard to fake it. His voice takes on a certain reverence when he talks to her, even when he's teasing." Alex reviewed the conflicting emotions he'd seen and heard from the kid. "Whitt's a good kid. But what did you observe?"

"Nothing and everything. She's his meal ticket and a roof over his head. He could have easily lied to her and us about matters pertaining to this case."

Alex groaned. He really liked Whitt, wanted to see him overcome his bad parenting. "Let's keep an eye on him. I'm not discounting anything, but it's a far stretch to think he knows anything about these crimes."

"She's sick and the kid's worried about himself and her. If you were Whitt, how far would you go to ensure your world was okay?"

"I'd say and do those things that would guarantee my comfort zone." Alex snapped his fingers. "I haven't ordered a background on his parents. There could be a connect in this, and I've ignored it. According to Stacy, they wanted fifty grand to sign over custody of Whitt. Currently both of them are in jail."

"And Whitt?"

Alex glanced up from typing into his phone. "I talked to his school counselor this morning. Great kid. No problems. School records point to his high IQ. Way ahead of other kids his age."

"What are the numbers?"

"147 plus."

Ric startled. "Now the reference to the little professor makes sense. At times today he sounded like a boy and other times a thirty-year-old."

"He's enrolled in summer school for high school and college

credit classes. On track to graduate at fourteen." Alex paused. "I don't want to think of him using his intelligence to outsmart law enforcement."

"He's responsible for his own decisions."

"I'm praying he uses his intelligence for the betterment of the world."

"Since when did you pray?"

Alex stared at the street. "I was brought up in the faith. Left it, and now I'm trying to find my way back. Doesn't mean I have solid answers."

"All right. My granny will be happy to hear it. She's the praying type. So you were raised in church?"

"I think I was born there. Grew up and decided if being a Christian was all about doing and sweating for Jesus, then I had better things to do."

"Now?"

Alex kept his gaze on the street. "The road to heaven isn't paved with how many times I mow the church's yard or have perfect attendance. I entered the FBI to find a better way to serve the world. Now I see it's a mixed deal." He swallowed.

"You aren't comfortable with this conversation," Ric said.

"I'm doing better."

"Switch gears. You know, I don't want to see Whitt head down the same tracks as his parents. He has too much potential. But the choice is up to him."

"Honestly I appreciate it. Keep asking the tough questions. I need an objective voice."

42

WHITT HAD ALWAYS THOUGHT HE WAS SUPER BRAVE. Super brain. Super whatever. He'd faced bullies, been beaten until knocked unconscious by his dad—while Mom watched—wished they were dead, spent nights alone, planned how to run away, wanted to save the world from itself . . . But he hated needles. And the huge woman wearing a mask and standing over him planned to take enough blood from his body to fill six vials. Would he have any left?

"You're a bit green," the lab tech said. She could hold him down if he attempted to flee.

"The news about my foster mom is tough."

"Whitt," Miss Stacy said from her bed, "look at me while she draws blood. I know needles bother you."

"A big strapping boy like you?" The lab tech chuckled.

Everyone had their nemesis.

He obeyed. No point in throwing up all over himself while the goliath lab tech rubbed alcohol over his inner arm. Next came the rubber band restricting circulation. He wished Miss Stacy hadn't embarrassed him in front of the woman. True, he couldn't watch while she drew blood from the clinic's animals or gave injections. The idea of hurting one of them scraped against his heart and stomach. Weird, a few years ago he'd thought about cutting the brake line on his parents' car. Imagine the blood from a car accident. That's when Miss Stacy started taking him to church. The God and Jesus stuff hadn't grabbed him yet and might never, but he'd always go with her to church because it made her happy. Truth was he'd go anywhere with her to escape his parents. He loved her and always would.

Miss Stacy chatted on to divert his attention. She shouldn't attempt conversing when she was already weak. "The pastor is picking up your school assignments and bringing them by. Your teachers said they'd include Wednesday's work too."

"What did you tell them?" He wished the lab tech would get it over with.

"The truth. I'm in the hospital, and you chose to stay with me."

He refused to respond. The idea of someone running to social services was worse than a needle. "Will the attorney contact you when the hearing is over? I mean, I expect him to inform us."

"Of course. He knows we're both anxious."

"All done," the lab tech said.

His attention flew to the six vials. "You drew the blood you needed? Whew. I kept waiting for the little prick."

"I'm an expert," she said. "Do you want a gold star?"

"No, ma'am, but if I can talk to your boss, I'd recommend a raise."

She giggled, sort of little girl like, which was strange considering her size and age.

A knock on the door seized his attention. Always the fear of social services, men and women who claimed to have an understanding of kids. The woman assigned to him was overworked and couldn't remember his name. She called him Wyatt.

Two men filled the exit. Suits. Ties. But wearing gloves and masks. These could be the men Dr. Maberry spoke about. His heart plummeted to his toes.

"Are you looking for Stacy Broussard?" the lab tech said.

The suits entered the room. The first man was silver-haired, but not as old as Dr. Maberry.

"I'm Dexter Rayken from the LRN," he said. "This is James Nisse from Houston's Health Department. We're here to talk to you about the possibility of human brucellosis being transmitted to you from a dog carrying canine brucellosis."

"I'll help however I can," Miss Stacy said. "I talked to both of you a few days ago about water contamination in my neighborhood. A hoax." Her color likened to the white sheet and blanket.

Whitt fumed. She'd been prepared to sleep, and now she must focus on the suits.

She inhaled deeply. "Mr. Nisse, representatives from your department were at my clinic within an hour of my call. I saw you on Channel 5 news. Thank you for educating my neighborhood about the water fraud. Mr. Rayken, I valued your call."

"Glad to help," Rayken said. "Grim circumstances, but I believe a man's been arrested in conjunction with the problem." He walked toward her bed. "Dr. Broussard, we understand your need to rest, and we'll make this as quick as possible." He pulled out his phone. "You've been briefed on the severity of this strain of human brucellosis."

Briefed? Was the guy ex-military?

"Yes, sir. Dr. Maberry explained the seriousness."

"We have the forms granting us permission to enter your veterinary clinic and do a complete sweep of its contents and test any animals. I'd like your cooperation, although we don't need your signature to conduct the investigation."

"Just do it." Little lines around her eyes revealed the intensity of the disease raging through her body. Miss Stacy explained that her animals' records were on her computer and how Doc Kent was in the process of testing a dog she'd found on Saturday. "My concern is our subdivision held a carnival a week ago. We had a petting zoo. Plenty of people could have been infected there." She moistened her lips. "But you'll find everything in the clinic is up-to-date."

"I'm sure everything is in proper order. We'll take over with Dr. Kent." He stared at Whitt. "You are not to leave this room without a mask. Keep this in mind—if you have the disease, you'll be occupying a bed too. I'm sure your mother will agree." He shoved a twinge of kindness into his words, but Whitt had experienced it all. Nothing short of pulling a trigger would stop him from implementing what he felt was right, and he hadn't decided if staying here was the best choice. Depended on what happened at the custody hearing.

"He's not my son," Miss Stacy said. "He's a neighbor, and I take care of him when his parents are busy."

Why had she told this suit his status? The meds must have distorted her thinking.

"Where are they now?" Rayken said.

"In jail."

He frowned. "Do you have legal custody?"

"I'm in the process. In fact, I should know tomorrow."

Rayken turned to James Nisse. "Make a note to get social services involved." He turned to Whitt. "Only as a temporary measure."

Whitt inwardly moaned. A nightmare . . . One more lit fuse on the bomb threatening to explode his hope of a family.

"Do you want my attorney's name?" She pointed to her purse, and Whitt retrieved it. She reached inside and handed Rayken a business card.

Whitt needed to make plans before anything else happened. The lab tech, who hadn't left the room, laid a hand on his shoulder. "It'll be okay," the woman whispered.

Nothing would be okay if social services managed his life. Selfishness washed over him, but he couldn't stop it.

Rayken glanced at the lab tech. "Are you finished here, ma'am?"

"I have an order to draw blood from Dr. Broussard."

"Please step into the hall. I'll let you know when we've completed our discussion."

"I have a job to do." The three-hundred-pound woman rose from the chair. "Perhaps you can talk while I handle her medical needs. I'm cognizant of patient confidentiality."

Whitt stifled a laugh at her sarcasm. At least his mask concealed a grin.

"Go ahead." Rayken shook his head. "Epidemics aren't pretty."

It could be more than an epidemic . . . bio or chemical terrorism. Horrible.

The woman moved to Miss Stacy and pulled out her equipment.

"I'd like to recover at home," Miss Stacy said.

"Impossible until your fever is gone. Dr. Broussard, you are in no condition to relinquish medical care. Leaving the hospital could mean . . . death." He drew in a sigh, and compassion spread over what Whitt could see of his face. The change in persona frightened Whitt. "A mother didn't make it. Three additional people have been hospitalized—two are children."

"Who died? Who is in the hospital?"

"Dr. Broussard, it's important for you to relax and let your body heal. We have no vaccination, no cure, for this strain, and need I remind you it's five times stronger." He shook his head. "Please, your temperature is still over 102. For your own sake and the boy's, do all your medical team asks."

"I understand. What about the other people in my neighborhood?"

Rayken took her hand, a gesture Whitt hadn't expected. "When you're well, you can help others. We're working now with the health department to educate them, test them and their dogs. Every TV and radio network in the city will air our public health emergency report. We'll find a way to stop the contagion and treat those who are ill. Our best bet is a combination of antibiotics."

This part interested Whitt. He'd read about the CDC online, but he craved clarification. "Mr. Rayken, can you explain how your organization works? I live there too, and I'm sure I know those who are ill."

The man stared at him for a moment. "Young man, I wish I had the time to give you the information, but Mr. Nisse and I have a lot of work to do." He reached into his pocket and pulled out a card. Taking a pen from inside his suit jacket, he jotted down something before handing it to Whitt. "Research our website about our policies and protocols. Write down any questions, and I'll do my best to answer them as soon as I have a breather."

"Thank you, sir."

"Part of our role is to provide reliable, consistent, science-based assistance in public health emergencies." He glanced at Miss Stacy, whose eyelids were drooping. "You'll read about our various responsibilities and how we work with other organizations."

"I assume the AKC Canine Health Foundation is involved now," Whitt said.

"We contacted them earlier." He glanced at his watch, and Whitt knew he shouldn't detain him. "I'm a dog lover," Rayken said. "I hate the thought of my buddy contracting a disease for which there's no cure. Granted, our concern is for people, and nothing stands in the way of finding a cure and an end to this infection, but I feel for pet owners too."

Whitt attempted to cover his emotions. "Puts the researchers and workers in a difficult place." He studied Miss Stacy. Her eyes were closed and her features softened. "Have you considered a theory that AKC researchers unknowingly developed and released the disease?"

"We have people on it. Son, to be honest, the strain was probably developed to spread contagion."

He remembered Mr. Parson. "An older man who volunteered at the clinic died last week. Could he have been infected?"

"Had he been ill?"

"He was ninety-one years old and suffered from a failing heart. Diabetes too. If he'd been infected, the disease attacked him within hours."

A tear slipped from Miss Stacy's eye and trailed over her cheek. She wasn't asleep, just too weak to contribute to the conversation. Whitt hurried to her side with a tissue and lightly dabbed her cheeks.

"Do you have a list of those in attendance?" Mr. Nisse said. "The health department needs to contact them."

"We do. We had everyone register at the entrance gate. The list is on Miss Stacy's desk, in a green spiral-bound notebook."

"Another thing, Whitt, if the dog we're speaking of is—"

"I've already thought about what the authorities might do, more testing. Even putting Xena to sleep."

"I'm sorry. Hope it doesn't come to you losing the dog."

He needed Stacy to survive today and be his mom. *God, do You hate me? Why is my world a nightmare?* There. He'd admitted the horror causing his head, heart, and body to ache.

Miss Stacy drifted off to sleep within minutes of Dexter Rayken and James Nisse's visit. Maybe the doctors had made a mistake or the antibiotics prescribed to Miss Stacy would kill the infection.

Whitt accessed the Internet through the hospital guest services and navigated to the LRN website. He read about the actions people could take when there were no or limited supplies of drugs and serums—nonpharmaceutical interventions, or NPIs. To Whitt, the recommendations to slow the spread of germs were no-brainers, like washing hands, covering the mouth during coughs and sneezes, and staying home when sick. For those people who might be among others who are contagious, they recommended changing regular seating patterns on public transportation, or refraining from public gatherings like schools, churches, and businesses. Whenever possible canceling mass gatherings or postponing events to reduce the contagion. The LRN's work was mostly behind the scenes, testing and helping to find solutions.

Stacy's phone alerted him to a call, interrupting his reading. The attorney's name registered on the screen. He snatched it.

"Whitt McMann answering Stacy Broussard's phone."

"This is Leonard Nardell, Dr. Broussard's attorney. Is she available?"

"She's asleep. Is this about the custody hearing?"

"I'm sorry, but the information is for Dr. Broussard. Would you have her contact me at her earliest convenience?"

Should he wake her? He glanced at her anemic face. "This concerns me. I have the right to know my fate."

"Son, I know she's very ill, in the hospital, and the long-term prognosis is unknown."

He fought nausea. "Was the judge informed?"

"Yes."

His heart slammed against his chest. "Social services?"

"Your caseworker was notified. Please have Dr. Broussard call me."

✻

At the FBI office, Alex ended a call with Dexter. His friend had expressed grave concern about the deadly infection spreading quickly, and they discussed the value of exhuming Mr. Parson's body for an autopsy. A press release within the hour would reveal the LRN's involvement with Houston Health Department and Human Services, HPD, and the FBI. What motivated the bad guys?

"While the health department specializes in ensuring people receive accurate information so they can make healthy decisions, I'm concerned about a panic," Alex said to Ric. "We both know the neighborhood is filled with people looking for a reason to riot. The news is bad, no matter how well it's stated. My control side is kicking in at the thought of what fearful people will do until a serum is developed or a combination of antibiotics cures the disease."

"Bro, we're offering the public concrete steps to minimize fear," Ric said.

"Like staying inside their homes and not coming out for anything? Who's going to make a milk and bread run?" Alex tapped his finger on the desktop. "I know the necessities will be provided for those people. The real issue is emotional support, and we don't have many model citizens living there."

"The people will rally and cooperate—"

"But how many more will die or be infected before then?" Alex raked his fingers through his hair. "What I now suspect is Stacy was set up to find the Lab. Those who are behind this banked on her not abandoning a wounded animal, and it wouldn't have mattered if her riding partners had been with her. She was targeted to do their dirty work—infect her community with canine and human brucellosis. Then they'd buy the property at ridiculously low prices. If we could figure out what's so valuable about the run-down subdivision, where the quadcopter fits, Todd Howe, and Lynx Connor, we could wrap this up."

"We will. The plans for the Grand Parkway are on hold, so there goes that theory, and the FBI hasn't unraveled Connor's shell company yet."

Their phones alerted them to updates. They grabbed their devices and read. Lynx Connor had agreed to talk in exchange for protection. They'd receive a transcription tomorrow morning.

"Better news on that front," Alex said. "He claimed to fear for his life." He zeroed in on the time. LA agents had scheduled the interview in fifteen minutes. The case had gotten way too personal—Stacy, Whitt, Bekah Howe, his city, national security, possible terrorism . . . He read the second update. "More positive news. The DNA testing on Stacy's clothes contained no traces of Todd Howe, only the dog's DNA."

Ric peered into his face. "The dog that might kill her."

43

WHITT KNEW WHAT MUST BE DONE and wrote her a note. For months, the appropriate words had sailed in and out of his mind. But what flowed from the pen now was exactly how he felt.

> *Dear Miss Stacy,*
>
> *Thank you for all you've done for me. No one has ever given me care and concern like you have. Love for me shows in your eyes, and I've memorized the special sparkle meant only for me. We've laughed together, and you've comforted me when I've cried.*
>
> *You taught me about life and God, and because of you, I'll not forget to look for Him.*
>
> *I could list the things you've purchased for me with the dollar amount, but this note isn't about things I can touch. This is about the heart, and I have difficulty expressing those things.*
>
> *Miss Stacy, this is good-bye. Risking social services walking into the hospital room and placing me in foster care is worse than death, and only you know I'm not exaggerating. I have*

to leave the city and find a way on my own. You know me well enough to understand my emergency exit plan has been in existence for months. I can take on life and determine my place, obtain an education, and fulfill my dreams of helping others in some capacity unique to my abilities.

I hope when your mom and dad come to visit, you're able to fully reconcile with them. I have no idea what the problem is between you, but I hope for your sake it's over. Maybe someday I'll meet them.

I saw you cry when you read this from Emily Dickinson. I want to live up to these words.

If I can stop one heart from breaking,
I shall not live in vain;
If I can ease one life the aching,
Or cool one pain,
Or help one fainting robin
Unto his nest again,
I shall not live in vain.

When you were delirious, you said to me: mother and son come from the heart, not from a piece of paper signed by a judge. I'll never forget those words.

Love,
Whitt

P.S. Tell Special Agent Alex LeBlanc that I appreciate him, and I'll mail him the forty dollars once I get settled.

He folded the paper in thirds and wrote her name on the front. He slipped it under her cell phone with her name sticking out.

Once on his way, he could pick up a prepaid phone and keep her posted on his welfare. Glancing into her peaceful face, he whispered a prayer for her recovery and forgiveness. Abandonment rang like a sour note in a concerto. As much as he despised his parents for discarding him, he was doing the same to Miss Stacy. Perhaps Alex would step in and be her friend.

No wonder God dealt him a continuous bad hand. He wasn't worth the trouble.

Whitt rose to his feet, already missing her. Watching the nurses' desk, he slipped down the hall and to the stairway exit. No one even looked his way. The bus would stop outside the hospital in six minutes.

Once he found a seat on the bus, he relaxed slightly. Maybe he should have stolen to the lab and tried to find his vials of blood before they tested it. Yet the risk of getting caught negated the idea. He was healthy. No reason for alarm.

He'd memorized his escape plan, and when dread hit him in the middle of the night, he recalled every detail. Foolproof. No one would ever find him. He'd hide out for around five days, then hitchhike to Arizona, using a random trail. Eventually he'd reach an orphanage for illegal kids who crossed into the US, continue with his education, and take his GED so he could begin college as soon as possible. Although his light hair and gray eyes would never pass for Hispanic, he'd purchased brown contacts from a sleaze in their neighborhood and hair dye weeks ago to counter the identity problem before leaving Houston.

Whitt's first stop was to free Xena from the clutches of Doc Kent and the researchers. Although rescuing the dog poked a hole in his logic, he feared she'd be destroyed. Xena had been his friend, and he couldn't walk away. Leaving Miss Stacy was low enough. Thoughts of the dog infecting others bothered him, but if need be, he'd live a solitary life for a while. Right now, he had to get away before they were apprehended by well-meaning people.

Shaking off the consequences of his actions, he headed to the nearest ATM to draw out three hundred dollars. The other six hundred dollars left in the bank belonged to Miss Stacy, since she'd signed on the account, fed him, and bought so many things. From there he'd purchase a phone.

Success meant he had to move fast. The clinic would be flooded with health department types, but not Miss Stacy's house, not until the investigators discovered he'd escaped. No one had reason to be watching the rear, where an unlatched window awaited him. A change of clothes, a little food and stashed items, dye his hair and insert the brown contacts before heading to the back roads. A surge of confusion seized him. Had he made the right decision? Would she hate him?

The note to Miss Stacy indicated he'd leave Houston when in truth, he had a destination just outside of the city until the authorities gave up searching for him and assumed he was dead. Statistics showed runaway kids often disappeared, and he intended to be one of those who were gone without a trace.

Stacy opened her eyes in the darkness of the hospital room, her body much too warm under the pile of blankets. After shoving them aside, she pressed the nurse call button. Could her prayers have been answered, and she was on her way to healing?

She looked for Whitt. "Are you in the bathroom?" Maybe he'd gone to the cafeteria.

The nurse stepped in. "How can I help you?"

"Would you mind taking my temperature? I'm no longer experiencing chills, and I'm more alert."

"That would be wonderful news. I'll be right back." She stepped into the hall and returned within moments to pop a thermometer into Stacy's mouth. "Dr. Broussard, your temperature has dropped to 99.9. I'll contact your doctor immediately. The combination of antibiotics seems to be working."

Thank You.

Stacy wanted to sleep, but joy filled her. "Tell him I want to go home. My parents are arriving in the morning."

"You are still very ill. Your doctor will want to keep you until a cure for the disease has been found."

"But look at my temp."

"That only means the antibiotics have lowered it, not that you've been cured."

"I have important matters to take care of. I allowed this problem of human brucellosis to spread because of my negligence. I'm not spending another day here when I can help others."

The nurse smiled gently, shook her head, and bid her good night. Stacy reached for her phone and texted Alex.

Fever down to 99.9.

Within three minutes he responded. **I'm doing a Snoopy dance.**

She laughed. **Do 1 4 me. Please pray 4 others.**

Will do. C u soon.

She laid her phone on the nightstand and that's when she saw the note.

44

IN THE EARLY HOURS OF WEDNESDAY MORNING, Whitt huddled under a small tent. While reading about various camping supplies, he'd found the perfect fold-up tent that could be easily condensed for instant travel. Although he and Xena were squashed, he didn't mind. Once the sun went down, the heat eased a bit. Here in the woods of Montgomery County, where years ago his grandpa McMann had shown him the beauty of nature, he could hide for the next five days. By then, authorities and volunteers would have given up, and he could head north for a while and on to Arizona a few days after that. Getting across Texas was his worst obstacle. Everywhere authorities would be looking for him.

He patted Xena, and she plastered a wet kiss on his face. He no longer cared. If she infected him with the disease, no big deal. Depression had hit big-time, and the only person who'd given him hope was gone. The one thing his social worker had been right about was the suicidal tendencies. After Miss Stacy became more involved in his life, those feelings faded away. But now he was on his own, and he feared they'd come back.

Did it really matter whether he had brucellosis?

Promptly at seven o'clock, he fed Xena a packet of nutritious dog food. From his own stash, he ate an apple and a protein bar. When he'd purchased the tent, he'd also bought pills to purify the worst of water. The problem was finding a source. For now he had a stream about thirty yards from his site. His fingers wrapped around a pocketknife, which he'd use for protection against snakes and whatever or whoever threatened them. Not much different from hiding in a closet during one of Dad's drunken temper fits. He'd never had the courage to use it before, but now he was older. Smarter. More desperate.

No point checking his burner phone when he had poor connectivity out here. Besides, he needed to conserve his battery. A big drawback, but he believed those looking for him would think his techy mind couldn't survive without the world of knowledge. He'd prove them wrong, and he'd succeed.

A twinge of a headache plagued him, and his stomach tossed. No need to worry. Caffeine withdrawal.

Now to rest with Xena.

Stacy called Alex after reading Whitt's note.

"I'll get law enforcement notified immediately, and put out an Amber Alert. Would either of his parents know where he went?"

"Probably not, but it's worth a call."

"I'll make sure they're questioned. What about the results of his blood work?" Alex said.

"Sometime this morning." She refused to think about Whitt already infected.

"My guess is he wouldn't have gone to your home. Too obvious. What about friends?"

"He's a loner, Alex. Too many reasons to list."

"His note indicates he's leaving the city. I'll notify the bus station and check Metro's cams. He left his phone . . . Smart move on his part to leave it behind so we couldn't track him. Make sure Doc Kent is notified. I'm concerned Whitt might do something foolish, like nab the dog."

She sighed. "He's very attached to her."

"Dexter Rayken might have already picked her up. Besides, the clinic would be locked up. If you'll give me Doc Kent's personal number, I'll call him to check on Xena's status."

She gave him the number. "I'll hold on." How had life gotten so muddy? She reread his note. *Whitt . . . Where have you gone?*

"Stacy—" Alex's voice pulled her from her thoughts—"I've spoken with Doc Kent. He doesn't have Xena. Dexter Rayken had sent a representative from the LRN to pick her up. But someone removed her without his knowledge."

"Who?"

"Good question."

"Had he seen Whitt?" she said.

"No. He's isolating every dog in his care and running tests on them. He has my cell number if Whitt shows up. Get some rest if you can. I'll be in touch."

After the call, she lay awake until morning broke across the sky. If only the beautiful purple, pink, and gold came with a promise. The fever hadn't returned, and she was going home as soon as her parents arrived. She'd called them in the wee hours of the morning with the good news. The reunion she'd prayed for was happening, and not like she'd ever imagined. But life had so much unpredictability.

News would hit Houston about a disease-carrying Lab and a twelve-year-old-boy who might soon contract a disease that could cause his death.

When would the tragedies end? Guilt pelted her spirit for not testing Xena, a stray dog who should have received thorough blood work.

Shadows appeared in the doorway. A tall lanky man without a hint of slumping shoulders and a petite round lady. She heard her name, a sweet lilt of home, deep and rooted in the bayou.

Was she hallucinating? "Mom? Dad?"

The two familiar figures stood still, as though waiting for a sign, a welcome. Dare she take the first step since she'd been the one to choose to leave?

She'd chosen to forgive in her heart, but to see them, feel their arms around her . . .

"Can we come in?" Dad said. How she'd longed to hear his low rumble. He held up a mask. "We have these."

"Oh yes, please." She opened her arms and they hurried to her side. She hugged them both at the same time. The scent of Polo cologne and roses embraced her. Tears flowed, and she wanted the moment to last forever.

"I didn't expect you for hours," she said. "Didn't someone tell you about the precautions?"

"Didn't ask," Dad said, swiping beneath his eyes. "We couldn't wait a moment longer."

"I'm so glad. Neither of you have changed a bit."

"You're as beautiful as ever," Mom said. "But your dad and I have added a few wrinkles. I expected that sweet boy to be here."

Stacy explained Whitt's absence and how the city was out looking for him.

"Poor dear." Mom shook her head. "He's scared. If he'd just waited, your dad and I could have looked out for him until you're better."

"I'm going home, you know."

Dad furrowed his brow. "Your doctor released you?"

"Nope." She lifted her chin. "I'll sign myself out. I don't care if I have to go to his office every day for a shot."

"Such a stubborn Cajun." Dad's eyes twinkled.

"I get that honestly." She swallowed a huge lump of emotion. "I'm so glad you're here, and I'm sorry it took this for us to see each other."

"God works in His own ways," Mom said.

She nodded. "He does."

Dad pulled up chairs for Mom and himself. "I've been preparing this speech, so while we wait for the doctor to release you—"

"You don't have to do this," she said.

"Seriously, I want you to hear my heart. Your mom's too." He took a deep breath. *"Ma petite fille."* Dad's voice brought back the little girl in her, riding on his shoulders. "So proud of you takin' care of animals, even if one of them has made you sick."

"Thanks, Dad."

"Thinkin' back over all those times you hid animals in your room. The times you pulled fish from the line in my bucket and tossed them back. Mercy, remember the snakes and alligator you cried about until I returned them to their own home?"

"I do. Haven't changed much."

"It's been thirteen long years, and not a day goes by that God doesn't kick this Cajun about not chasing after you when you left after college."

She sobbed. No way to stop the flow. "Dad—"

"I need to say this. You blamed yourself for your sister's death, but KaraLee was born with a heart defect. If anything, your mama and I are to blame. We left you alone with her that summer while we worked. A little girl of twelve should never have so much responsibility."

"You had to pay for KaraLee's medicine."

"No excuse. We were simply too proud to ask others for help."

Now he sobbed. "When I look back, I think we all believed she'd get better, that God would heal her, and He did. Just not the way we wanted. Took me years to get over my bitterness. Blamed myself. Believed I didn't deserve you either. After a bout with pneumonia, I told myself family meant love. You started callin' and warmed my heart. I was fixin' to drive up here soon and see if we could talk. Put the past behind us. See if you'd give this old man a few minutes to love on you. Tell you how sorry I am. Can you forgive me, *cher*?"

More tears filled her eyes. "I'm sorry for never calling, never coming home for a visit. When KaraLee died, a bit of my heart went with her. Yes, I blamed myself. I was so full of shame." Her thoughts tumbled to the afternoon when her sister had grown worse. Stacy had phoned the ambulance and Mom and Dad, but none of them would arrive for thirty minutes. She'd run to a neighbor for help, praying for God to save her sister, but when Stacy and the neighbor returned, KaraLee had died.

"*Cher*, I love you. The more time that passes, the harder it is to make amends with those we love. Took my preacher to shake me up a bit. He told me you'd accepted Jesus as your Savior two months before God took KaraLee home. I was so wrapped up in work and the constant fear of her death that I ignored you, never talked to you about God's ways being higher than ours."

By this time, Stacy's nose ran with liquid sentiment. "Dad, you're here now." She sniffed. "I have a guest room, and the last I checked, the food in the fridge is okay." She glanced into Dad's wet, leathered face. "Are you still as good with animals as you used to be?"

"I am."

"Good. I'm going to let you help me at the clinic. I want to open it up to the public so people can test their dogs. Provide information about canine brucellosis."

"Can't wait to see my little girl in action."

45

ALEX WATCHED THE TIME while completing dreaded paperwork—8 a.m. and they hadn't received the transcript of Lynx Connor's interview. Of course, it was only six in LA. He couldn't keep his mind off Stacy and Whitt. Researchers much smarter than him were working on a cure for the powerful strain of brucellosis infecting humans. Regulating the spike of fever was promising, but only a stabilization if the symptoms persisted. In the meantime, he doggedly worked a case containing far too many unanswered questions.

Law enforcement had been unable to locate Whitt or Xena. Neither had anyone reported seeing the pair. He'd phoned Stacy twice since their initial conversation to see if the kid had contacted her. The search had gone statewide, and because of the contagion, media was broadcasting the unfortunate situation across the nation.

"He can't hide from the city's law enforcement for too long," Ric said.

Alex glanced up to see his partner leaning against the doorway. "I know, but I'll feel better when I know he's safe. Might want to shake his teeth out."

Ric shook his head. "Not sure appropriate discipline is your strong trait as a parent."

The words sobered him along with the growing thought of a family with Stacy and Whitt. He reached for his coffee, as bitter as finding a dead body.

An e-mail from the LA office landed in his in-box. Attached was a video allowing the agents to read Lynx Connor's body language. "Now we can find out what he said during the interview."

Alex moved his chair so Ric could view the screen. The video showed two agents sitting opposite a table with Connor and a well-dressed man in his fifties, obviously Connor's attorney.

An agent opened the conversation. "We understand you've agreed to help us solve specific crimes in Houston, Texas. Among them is the murder of Todd Howe. In turn, we will provide protection as needed until arrests are made."

"Yes. I'm concerned for my life." He gripped his hands on the table.

Real fear or a ploy for sympathy?

"Yes, sir. Would you begin by giving us your name and contact information?"

After Connor gave an LA address, the agent moved on to the case's legal ramifications.

The second agent, a female, interrupted the questioning. "Mr. Connor, the zip code you gave us for your address doesn't match what we have in our records."

Connor dragged his tongue over his lips. "I'm nervous, okay? So I transposed a number. You have it right."

Alex jotted down his confusion under possible deceit.

She typed into her phone. "The house number is not a part of the zip code."

Connor's attorney conferred with him.

"I apologize. I confused my former address with my present."

"What is your current correct address?" she said.

"The zip is correct, but the apartment number is 1103 Building D."

She nodded for the male agent to continue.

"Are you married?"

"Divorced."

"Children?"

"No."

"Were you acquainted with Todd Howe?"

"Yes. We worked for the same person."

"Todd Howe was the owner of four Green-to-Go restaurants in Houston, Texas. You've listed 'self' as your business consultant employer. Neither of you give another company or individual name."

Connor glanced away, then back to the agent. "We were private contractors."

"For whom?"

"Russell Phillips, owner of Phillips Security here in Los Angeles."

"What did you do for him?"

Connor snorted. "Whatever he told us. Isn't that obvious? He pays big bucks."

"Are you still employed by Mr. Phillips?"

Connor shifted in his chair. "I suppose."

"Either you are or you aren't."

"I am. At least he thinks so."

"Do you know who killed Todd Howe?"

"Only speculation."

"Did you kill Todd Howe?"

He startled. "No. I called his widow after his death looking for him."

The agent, a seasoned interrogator, opened a file folder. "Mr. Connor, covering your tracks doesn't make you innocent. At the moment, you are a person of interest in the death of Todd Howe."

The attorney lifted his hand to protest, but Connor stopped him. "I did not kill Todd."

The agent leaned back in his chair. "I think you did."

Connor stiffened, convincing Alex he'd committed the murder.

The agent continued. "How well were you acquainted with the deceased?"

"We worked together on a few projects."

"Specifics, Mr. Connor. Neither of us wants to be here any longer than necessary. Describe your relationship with Todd Howe."

"We met socially and conducted business."

"Ever been to his home?"

"A few times."

"Did you like him?"

Connor sneered. "What kind of question is that? We weren't touchy-feely, if that's what you're asking. Shared a few drinks."

The agent eyed him. "Have you ever flown in the Howes' private jet?"

"Yes."

"How many times?"

"Didn't count them."

"What were your destinations?"

"Social, pure social. He showed me the countryside."

"Interesting. Who placed the video and listening device in Stacy's clinic?"

"Todd Howe."

"Why?"

Connor rubbed his face. "Howe wanted to find out what went on at the vet clinic, to see if she'd catch on to the water hoax and the diseased dog. Be one step ahead of her. So he hacked into her alarm and security camera system and planted a camera and recording device."

"The neighborhood is not known for its real estate value," the agent said. "What made the property so valuable?"

"A future building site." Connor held up his hand. "I wasn't told the type of company."

"Was it worth posing as the local health department, using a shell company, and stating the water had been contaminated? Committing murder? Facing federal charges?"

"Purchasing property is not a crime." Connor leaned in to the agent. "I am innocent of killing Howe."

"It is in your best interest to cooperate with the FBI," the agent said. "Lying or withholding evidence is a federal offense."

"No point tossing around the Big Brother factor. I'm here to cooperate."

"Mr. Connor, who took the photos of this boy?" The agent opened a file and pushed a photo of Whitt toward him.

"Don't know."

"Who placed pics of this boy inside Stacy Broussard's Sunday newspaper?"

"I was in custody here Sunday morning."

"Who phoned Stacy Broussard and threatened her?"

He shrugged. "Not me."

"I think you're lying."

"Ending up dead is not in my best interests."

"Isn't that why we're having this conversation? You claimed to have more information. So far, that's not been the case." The agent paused, obviously letting his words sink into Connor's reality check.

He read whatever was written on his notepad. "I'd like information about the dog infected with canine brucellosis."

Connor held up both hands. "I had nothing to do with it."

"Who did?"

"Todd Howe."

"How did he manage to infect the animal with a genetically engineered strain of brucellosis?"

"He worked the biomedical side with the dog. The whole thing was Russell Phillips's idea. He didn't invite me to a strategic planning session."

"You expect us to believe Todd Howe, a restaurant owner, on his own oversaw the development of this disease?"

"It's the truth."

How much of Connor's testimony could they believe? "I see. So how did Howe get the dog to the crime scene on a motorcycle?"

"Not sure."

"What about the quadcopter?"

"I know nothing about that."

The agent pulled Whitt's photo back and closed the file. "We're finished here."

"Why?" Connor said.

"You're withholding information. So the interview is concluded."

"Wait a minute. I can't tell you what I don't know. Ask me more questions."

"Sorry. You're wasting the FBI's time."

"Please. Russell Phillips or one of his men will kill me." A muscle twitched below Connor's left eye.

"What do you know about Todd Howe's murder?"

"Nothing, except Phillips must have ordered it."

"Why?"

"I heard he got greedy. Wanted more money to expand his restaurants nationally."

"You indicated to his widow that whoever popped Todd did the world a favor because he was a worthless idiot."

"Yeah. We'd had an argument, and I was still upset."

"Must have been a big one. Why did you call him?"

"To tell him we were finished doing business together."

"But you claimed to be working with Russell Phillips."

"I planned to resign."

"How do you resign from a man capable of murder?"

"I'd earned the right."

The agent shook his head. "Who was in charge of infecting the dog?"

Connor narrowed his brows. "Already told you Todd's area was the disease portion. He said this woman who lived in the subdivision was a vet. His job was to follow her and plant the dog so she'd find her."

"Her, as in the dog is a female?"

"An assumption since females are the ones most affected by canine brucellosis."

"You're aware of the disease."

Connor shrugged. "I looked it up online when Todd told me the disease had been genetically engineered."

"I'd like to know everything about your association with Russell Phillips."

"I'm telling you, he'll kill me if he learns I've talked." His voice rose.

"How did he initially contact you?"

"Through the man with no name."

"Then how reliable is the name of Russell Phillips?"

"I'm sure of it."

"We could cut you loose—"

"Okay." Connor looked at his hands before beginning. "Russell Phillips is one mean, calculating dude. He planned to move his corporation from California to Houston to save on taxes. He chose an area where the Grand Parkway would soon be constructed, but he didn't want to invest heavily in the land. So he arranged and funded Todd Howe to set up Stacy Broussard with the infected dog, and me with the phony water problem. The subdivision was less than middle class, so an epidemic of flu-like symptoms with a water contamination problem set the stage for a cash buyout at less-than-market-value prices. The driving sales pitch was once the water problem had been rectified, those who owned property would never get what it was worth."

The LA agent repeated a few more questions to which Connor denied knowledge. "A highly respected multimillionaire schemes to buy out a subdivision for building purposes by fabricating a water problem and infecting a dog with a genetically engineered disease that has the ability to kill innocent people?" The agent issued a harsh stare. "You expect the FBI to believe this? Mr. Connor, if you'd like the FBI's assistance, then you'd better come up with valid answers to our questions or you'll be going to jail for a long time."

Connor scratched an ample jaw. "I told you all I know."

"We're finished here. When you're ready to help us, we'll consider your request for protection."

The video ended.

An update from LA flew into their phones: Russell Phillips had been picked up for questioning.

Clearly Connor had lied. All the signs were there, from his denial of critical information to his body language. "What a wild story. And he expects law enforcement to swallow it?" Alex drummed his fingers on the tabletop. "But he wouldn't have laid it out there if some aspects weren't true." He searched online for Russell Phillips and his company.

Ric studied the computer screen. "What more do we have?"

"The company specializes in commercial and residential alarm systems. Been in business for over thirty years. Hold on. I want to see if he's ever been in trouble." He accessed the FBI's secure site. "Phillips looks like a model citizen, gives to charities, is recognized as an outstanding employer to work for. In-house day care for employees' kids. A health facility for employees to work out, complete with a swimming pool. Health insurance is 100 percent paid, and a retirement plan better than any I've seen."

"Sounds like the perfect cover. Who'd suspect him? I agree Phillips doesn't have motive unless there's evidence not yet discovered. Tax evasion. Illegal dealings."

Alex stood. "I disagree. Why oust people from their homes when he has plenty of money? He'd be going door-to-door to explain his business plan and host a barbecue. So why would a lowlife like Connor accuse him of such a scheme?"

"The deeper we investigate Phillips, the more possibilities of motive that we haven't even considered. And we haven't received the full report on Howe's offshore accounts."

"Connor said he and Howe did contract work for Phillips, to get the job done. I realize LA is on this investigation, but Houston isn't their city. I'll concede to your apprehension that he looks too clean. Let's access everything in Phillips's personal and company files." Alex held up a finger. "I'd really like to fire questions at Connor and Phillips."

"Connor's ex might have info."

Alex turned to his partner. "Let's check on flights to LAX."

"I'll make the arrangements."

Alex glanced at the time. "Good. I want to check on Stacy. See when her parents are arriving. She thinks she's getting released."

"Not with what she's been through."

"She's tough. Might just walk." Alex had no clue where his emotions were taking him. He'd been burned and sworn off women. Now he was tangled with a woman, a boy, and a crime. The latter came first. Then he'd concentrate on the future.

46

"**YOU HAVE BRUCELLOSIS,**" Dr. Maberry said. "I cannot take responsibility for your health if you leave the hospital."

"I'll take whatever medicine you prescribe, but this is my choice."

"You live alone. Your temperature could rise. You're weak. Other symptoms that we aren't aware of could surface." He inhaled deeply. "You are risking your life by checking out of the hospital. I'm your doctor, Stacy. Please listen to my counsel."

She'd handled letting down others before, and she'd deal with it again. "I'll take the risk."

"What about your parents?"

"Can't you prescribe antibiotics?"

"You are one stubborn woman. But yes, I can do that. Promise me you'll contact me immediately if your temperature rises even a little. I'll write prescriptions for antibiotics that you must fill before you reach home." Lines deepened around his eyes. "But I'm not signing the release."

"I understand."

"Whitt tested positive for brucellosis. For his sake, cooperate with those seeking him. No shielding him from social services."

The relief she felt in returning home hit void. "Maybe he'll call when he learns I'm home."

"Let's hope he does."

"How are the others doing?"

"Some are improving. Some are not."

She'd find out more later. Right now, she needed to get home.

Midmorning, in front of her little home, Stacy handed Dad her house keys, and he opened the rear passenger door of his rental car and offered her his hand. Earlier he'd driven her truck home, parked it at the curb, and taken a taxi back to the hospital.

Media vans swarmed the street and reporters blocked her drive-way. Weakness assaulted her at the thought of fighting her way through the crowd. How did they know she'd left the hospital?

"I can handle any *pas bon*." He arched his back.

Oh, to hear her father's Cajun, even if he did say he could handle any no-good.

"They aren't going to upset my little girl." He placed a protective embrace around her shoulders and escorted her to the front door.

Reporters and microphones swarmed her.

"Dr. Broussard, how does it feel to cheat death?"

"Have they found the boy for whom you were seeking custody?"

"Are you experiencing any side effects from the antibiotics?"

"What's the long-term prognosis?"

Dad turned and waved his hand over the crowd. "Enough."

A minuscule silence, before the demanding voices began again.

"What about the dog?"

"Do you plan to continue practicing veterinary medicine?"

The length of her driveway seemed to stretch on forever. Dad handed Mom the keys, and she unlocked the door. Stacy breathed in the familiar scent of home, a blend of flowery potpourri. Never had her meager furnishings looked so inviting.

"What a lovely home." Mom wandered through the small living room to the kitchen. "I love the distressed white and the blue accessories. So serene." She smiled at the photos of Whitt. "They will find your boy."

"Not soon enough."

Mom nodded. "I'll go through your kitchen and make a grocery list. Once the buzzards outside leave, I'll have your dad drive me to the store if you feel comfortable alone. Saw a grocery not far from here."

"Thanks, Mom. I have cash in my purse."

"Nonsense. You keep your money."

She recognized Mom's method of handling stress—making sure everyone was fed. "I've missed you."

Mom whisked away a tear. "The past is what it is—gone. We live and love today and tomorrow as part of God's family." She kissed Stacy's cheek. "Need to fatten you up."

While her parents were at the grocery, she flipped on the TV for the latest report, hoping Whitt had been found. The news streamed live.

The antibiotics had helped to reduce the fever for some but not others. Just like Dr. Maberry had indicated.

A woman and two children had died from the human brucellosis.

Eight others hospitalized. Three persons were showing signs of improvement.

Two dogs from her neighborhood had tested positive.

Whitt's parents denied knowledge of his whereabouts.

The critical need for a serum was peaking.

The FBI named Russell Phillips, owner and CEO of Phillips

Security, and Lynx Connor, both of Los Angeles, as persons of interest.

The doorbell rang, and she hesitated to answer. The last thing she needed was a reporter or someone angry about her neglect with Xena . . . or Whitt's parents. A quick look showed it was Alex.

She opened the door and smiled. "I hope you have good news, but even if you don't, I'm glad to see you." She gestured him inside.

"Your parents?"

"At the grocery. Mom wants to fatten me up."

"Good idea." He grinned, and she momentarily forgot the tragedies going on around them.

"Sit down. Would you like coffee?"

"I haven't much time. And I will make or pour any coffee." He brushed a stray hair from her face. "You look better, but your eyes tell me much of it is an act."

How could he tell? "I have a list of things to do."

"Napping had better be at the top."

"Talking to you is first. What have you learned?"

"Bits and pieces. The motivation behind Howe's murder, the unusual relationship between Howe and Connor, and the series of incidents point to a person who is vindictive and calculating. Which brings me to a question. We could be looking at a person who has a history of abusing animals. Does anyone come to mind?"

"My neighborhood is filled with people who hurt humans and animals on a regular basis. The only person who has entered the clinic and threatened me was Ace McMann."

"We're waiting on a report from our behavioral analysts. Another theory is someone with a military background or a felon versed in street and white-collar crime." He forced a smile. "We'll get it nailed. I know you're worried sick about Whitt. Every law enforcement agency in the city is searching for him."

"I know. My faith is taking a beating."

"I wanted to give you a quick update before leaving town. Remember I told you Lynx Connor was arrested in LA? Since then, he's agreed to work with authorities. During an interview, he admitted to some of the goings-on, blamed a few things on Todd Howe, and in short claimed things that require proof. Ric and I want to interview him and the man he's accused of masterminding the crimes."

"A step closer in bringing this to an end." She smiled. "You and Ric will find the answers."

"Hope so. Sorry I wasn't able to meet your parents."

"They're staying awhile. I hadn't seen them in thirteen years, and we have lots to talk about. Someday I'll tell you about it."

"At Starbucks, or we can go riding or fishing. You choose."

She blinked with watery eyes. "Thank you for coming. Don't forget to wash your hands. I'm sure my house is flooded with germs."

"Yes, ma'am. I'd kiss you good-bye, but I'll save it."

"You are crazy."

"True. I'll call or text when I can. I talked to Dexter earlier. He might stop by later. He's a good man, and he's committed to ending this epidemic."

She nodded and watched him leave. His kindness and strength had touched her unlike any man ever had before. What did it mean? Hope for a family? Could the three of them find happiness?

The one thing she grasped was Whitt and Xena must be found. If only she weren't so incredibly weak. For certain she could sleep hours upon hours. But that wouldn't find her precious boy or help others who suffered with the illness or were worried about their pets.

God, please bring Whitt home and guide the researchers to find a cure for this horrible disease.

47

ALL FLIGHTS TO LAX were booked solid except for the last one at 10:30 Wednesday night. That left a good part of the day for Alex and Ric to weed through Connor's accusation of Russell Phillips being the mastermind. They met at Ric's cubicle with one goal: What role, if any, did the owner of Phillips Security play in Houston's crimes?

"Connor represented Walter M. Brown Investments." Alex typed into his phone. "If Phillips and the shell company are connected, we'll soon know."

While they waited for findings, they watched the initial interview with the multimillionaire.

"His baseline questions laid a good foundation for his truth signals," Ric said. "His eye contact is good. Voice inflection doesn't raise. Speaks clearly. Uses hand gestures appropriately. Doesn't touch his face. Of course he's a successful businessman, trained to read others and provide body language that doesn't give away his motives."

Alex replayed Phillips's responses and made notes. "Several significant statements caught my attention. His denial of knowing

Howe or Connor appears sincere. He admits his intentions to move his company to Houston but hasn't located a building site. He refuted the accusations of a water scheme or injecting a dog with a life-threatening disease and claimed no knowledge of how the powerful strain of brucellosis was developed. He offered to sign whatever was necessary for the FBI to search his personal and business records. But what I'd like to research is his possible connection to the stolen quadcopter."

"Give me a moment," Ric said, typing on his computer. "Phillips Security manufactures drones under a subsidiary company called Drone Devices. Primarily government contracts." He held up a finger. "Bingo."

Alex typed a request to the FIG and waited. The results caused him to straighten. "The quadcopter was manufactured by his company."

"Right. Coincidence, or is Phillips lying through his teeth?"

The FIG's report sailed into their phones. The paper trail for Walter M. Brown Investments led straight to Russell Phillips. Just as Lynx Connor had claimed.

Alex gazed into the dark eyes of his partner. "Have LA hold him until we arrive for further questioning."

Shortly after midnight on Thursday morning, Alex and Ric viewed the lights of LA from the air. They'd managed a few hours' sleep on the plane, but they were tired and wired—at least that's the way Alex described his physical and mental condition. He hadn't eaten since lunch, and his stomach grumbled nonstop.

As soon as the agents landed and the plane taxied to the gate, they learned Lynx Connor had given another statement. "Interesting hours ahead," Ric said on the way to hail a taxi.

"I'll reserve my opinion until we have a face-to-face."

They were alerted of a woman's death, and three more people, two of whom were children, had been admitted to the hospital. One child wasn't expected to last the night. Another child showed improvement. Fury stormed though Alex's body. A steadily worsening situation. En route to the FBI office on Wilshire Boulevard, they continued to scroll through reports.

At LA's FBI office, Alex and Ric were given a transcript of Connor's updated statement as of an hour ago along with Russell Phillips's recent interview. They reviewed both before entering an interview room where Phillips awaited them. The older man with red hair lightened by gray sat quiet, unmoving. As he should be. Lines fanned from the corners of his eyes, and his two-hundred-dollar silk tie lay loosened against the open collar of an overly starched white shirt. He'd requested his attorney, and the middle-aged African American woman, dressed in a dark pantsuit with a white blouse, joined him.

Alex extended his hand, and the man and his attorney stood. "Mr. Phillips, I'm Special Agent Alex LeBlanc and this is my partner, Special Agent Ric Price. We're from Houston, Texas, where we've uncovered a series of crimes."

Phillips introduced his attorney. "I understand in Houston there's been a murder, a downed stolen quadcopter with potential to take down an aircraft, a land scheme involving a subdivision's water supply, and a dog carrying an infectious disease. Many victims. In short, you think all of that is somehow related to me, and I've been accused of directing this operation, which I deny. I want to offer my assistance in every way possible."

"We appreciate it. What is your connection to Houston?"

"As I told the LA agents, my company is contemplating a move there. I was enticed by the tax breaks coupled with the near proximity of my wife's family. Nothing's been signed. I don't have a site analysis completed yet."

So far this matched Connor's testimony. "When was the last time you were in Houston?"

"New Year's to visit family." He turned to his attorney. "Please give the agents my itinerary from January."

"Are you working with a real estate firm?"

"Not yet. We're in the preliminary stage, which means I want my people researching the best site before going forward."

"Who's 'we'?"

"Those within my company who are on my board of directors."

"We'd like their names."

Phillips turned to his attorney. "Add this information to the agents' list."

"Are the names Lynx Connor or Todd Howe familiar to you?"

Phillips neither blinked nor moved a muscle. "The names were mentioned by the other agents. Haven't you read or seen the interview?"

Alex ignored him. Everyone teetered on frustration. "What about Dr. Stacy Broussard?"

He shook his head.

"Has anyone proposed a specific area for your relocation?"

"Not to my knowledge. I asked for our search team to narrow their findings and report to the board before approaching a commercial real estate company. I've not negotiated with anyone to buy or procure a building site in an underhanded or illegal manner."

"Why would Lynx Connor name you as the mastermind?"

"I've asked my staff to determine if Mr. Connor ever applied for employment. At present, we have no one within our company by that name. We also have a photo database of our employees, and none of the images match his." He dipped his chin and glared at Alex. "The FBI has the ability to view security cams. Check LA and Houston, and you'll not find a thing incriminating me or my company."

"You're confident of your innocence."

"I am. Although my attorney advises me to request search warrants, I'm relinquishing my right in order to validate I'm above reproach in my personal and business practices. Agents here claim Walter M. Brown Investments, a shell company, has my name on it. That, gentlemen, makes me furious. I have in no way ever put together a front or investment or tax haven company. Search deeper, and you'll confirm my innocence." Again, Phillips hadn't touched his face, mouth, or throat. He neither repeated a phrase when responding to a question nor displayed emotion that didn't match his gestures. Deceit wasn't there.

"Thank you. Do you own a dog?"

"I haven't the interest or the time. However, my wife has a miniature poodle, a lapdog."

Alex was ready to link Phillips to more components of the crime. "We understand you own a subsidiary company that manufactures drones."

"Yes. Drone Devices, but you gentlemen are aware of it."

"We'd like to hear about the business from you."

"The majority of our work comes from government contracts. We also use drones to conduct testing on our alarm systems. We have recently begun manufacturing them for large farms and ranches for added security measures. The owners also use our drones to check fence lines and feed and water levels where it's too costly to run wire or hire manpower. And . . . we've developed a quadcopter for the same use."

Could the man be innocent? "Did you murder or order the death of Todd Howe?"

"No."

"Why would Lynx Connor claim he and Howe worked for you?"

"No idea."

"Why would Connor implicate you in a series of crimes?"

Phillips's face flushed. "I'd like to pose your question to him myself."

Alex focused on Ric. "Would you show him the signed statement from Lynx Connor stating Mr. Phillips hired him to acquire property in northwest Houston by spreading a disease via a dog, claiming it was an issue in the water supply, and then offering cash at a substantially low price to the home owners? It also claims Mr. Phillips engaged an assassin to kill Todd Howe for an undisclosed reason."

Ric handed Phillips the document. "This was signed one hour ago."

Phillips read the affidavit. The longer he read, the more he reddened and his body stiffened. "Where is this liar?"

"He's in custody," Ric said. "He fears his life is in danger."

"And he should," he mumbled. "I know exactly where I was during the crimes listed on the FBI's report. Pathetic. If I conjured up a preposterous document like this, I'd hope somebody would put me out of my misery."

Ric lifted a brow. "Are you threatening Mr. Connor?"

Phillips's attorney touched his arm.

"No. I'm merely saying those who pass off untruths that endanger the reputation of law-abiding people should be careful." His nostrils flared. "I've built my business on a foundation of honest work and integrity. Connor has taken a couple of facts and twisted them into a horrendous crime. The spectrum of incidents is so incredible that if my name wasn't on it, I'd laugh." He pressed his palms onto the table. "Have you investigated the man behind the accusations? What does he have to gain with these outrageous allegations? How do you account for my LA location during critical happenings?"

Not a muscle moved on Ric's face. "He didn't claim you killed Todd Howe. But ordered the crimes. Big difference."

"What's my motivation? I have plenty of money without committing crimes to obtain more. If I didn't know better, I'd swear this entire allegation is nothing more than a theatrical stunt to discredit me. But who or why?"

Phillips's attorney cleared her throat. "My client has offered to cooperate with law enforcement in good faith. Instead, you have brought him here under the false pretense of serious charges, including murder. We have nothing more to say."

Ric rose from his chair. "Russell Phillips, you are a person of interest in this case as well as Lynx Connor."

Anger flashed across his eyes. "Trust me, I'll have my own investigators getting to the bottom of this with facts, not fabrications."

Alex captured his eye contact. "My partner and I will be at your office in the morning to continue our discussion. If you need a warrant, we will have it." He scrolled through his phone and showed him the photos of the deceased woman and lingered on the two children. "Dream about these. Because of this *stunt*, they're sick and she's dead."

48

SHORTLY BEFORE 5 A.M. Pacific time on Thursday, Alex and Ric discussed the interview with Russell Phillips. He'd sworn his innocence, but that was to be expected. Ric studied the video of the proceedings, no doubt looking for body language or a twist of words.

"What's your analysis?" Alex said.

"His body language was mostly open and direct until he mentioned his board. I noted a few seconds' lapse in responding. My first reaction is he's hiding something or holding back information. I want a search warrant before we walk into his offices."

"For a company of his size, it will take a few days to run backgrounds and image files." Alex paused. "I doubt he's behind it, but stranger accusations than this have proven true. Something's not right about this case, and it's driving me nuts."

"Me too. We're missing a segment that ties it all together."

Alex's cell phone rang—Dexter.

"Have you caught any sleep?" Dexter said.

"A few hours on the plane. My guess is I had more than you."

"I'm heading over to Stacy Broussard's home around eight."

"Any word on a cure for the brucellosis?"

"The research might take months or longer. The situation has the public in a panic, and I can't blame them. We're looking at stats on a relatively rare disease, and only a few of the hospitalized victims are responding to treatment. Everyone is working around the clock with the health department to reach out to the community and search for a solution. None of us here are resting until we have this under control."

"Any luck in finding Whitt?"

"Not yet. I've never seen such a twisted case," Dexter said. "With the years spent in the CDC and now my current position, I shouldn't be shocked at what people do in the name of causing others pain or gaining a sense of control."

"I'm right there with you. Locating the developer of this strain could lead to a cure. I want an opportunity to punch his lights out. That's my playbook."

Stacy let the shower pour over her. She'd risen early to get started on the day, knowing her body would force her to relax as the hours slipped by. Having Mom and Dad here soothed her heart in ways she never could have imagined. The gap had been closed. Closing her eyes, she thought of Alex in LA. Did they have a future when this was over? When Whitt was found safe?

She turned off the water. No wasted tears. Just move forward.

Over a cup of coffee and sweet conversation with Mom and Dad, the doorbell rang. As usual, she feared the worst. Where was her optimism?

"I'll get the door," Dad said. "You sit tight."

She watched and listened.

"I'm Dexter Rayken, a friend of Dr. Broussard's and the director of the Laboratory Response Network."

"It's okay, Dad. Alex told me to expect Mr. Rayken."

Dad ushered him inside and invited him for coffee while Stacy introduced her parents to the director of Houston's LRN.

Dexter shook their hands. "My pleasure, and I'd like some coffee. Smells good."

"Dark and rich. Do you need breakfast?" Mom said. "Have grits, broiled boudin, and eggs."

Stacy smiled. If only food could fix the world.

"I'm good, ma'am. But thanks."

Dad cleared his throat. "Stacy, if it's all right, your mother and I will take a stroll, not far in this neighborhood. Let you two discuss things."

"Thanks, that would be great. Then I want to work on what we can do in conjunction with the health department for the community."

"I'm thinking on it."

Once they left, Mr. Rayken sat across from her at the kitchen table. He took a long drink of coffee as though considering his words. "I wanted to check on you."

A kind gesture, but she'd not reveal how bad she felt. "I'm doing much better. A little weak. Headache. Taking my meds. Close call for me. Not so fortunate for others."

"You're probably thinking I'm doing this because of Alex, but I wanted to see you for myself too. Can we talk a bit?" He fidgeted.

"What is it?" Worry for Whitt consumed her.

"A few things. The older gentleman who passed?"

"Mr. Parson."

"Yes. We've requested an autopsy, and his family agreed. We want the cause of death, specifically whether it was human brucellosis."

She dug her fingers into her palms, and the tears flowed. "I'm so sorry."

"None of this is your fault. You are the victim."

She rubbed her palms. "I took in a stray dog and was negligent. I should have done blood work to ensure Xena was healthy. Not sure how I'll ever be able to forgive myself."

"You were set up."

"You sound like Alex."

Dexter smiled. "Who do you think mentored him? He's like a son."

Now she understood Alex's respect for Dexter. "My biggest concern is finding Whitt. He has no chance without antibiotics."

"We'll find him." He sighed, a burdensome sound. "I keep wondering what we've missed in our search for the boy and his dog and how far the disease has spread through his body. Is there a place Whitt would hide?"

"Not that I know of."

"I've been trying to put myself in his shoes, even quizzed my grandson about it. A relative? Neither of Whitt's parents were any help. They were too preoccupied with their other problems. Does he like to camp? Would he run to a friend's house?"

"He has few friends, and he's never had the opportunity to venture far from home. His deceased grandfather spent time with him, but I don't know where. Whitt's intelligence and size aren't a good mix for the average kid. He's bullied a lot. But he's resourceful."

"You mean in securing a place with the dog?"

"I'm sure Xena was an afterthought. You've heard Whitt is running from social services, and that's true. He's had this escape route planned for weeks. He had a bad experience in a foster home, so add trust issues, and he's running scared."

"I studied his background. He missed nurturing from the moment he entered this world. His basic needs were seldom met, leaving him immature, frightened, and mistrustful. His IQ combined with his inability to understand his feelings has him confused."

"True, and he's nearing the age that I have to not only make up for what he lost, but also coach him for the future. Until he gains trust in others, he'll have a difficult time with decision making."

"A huge job." He sighed. "I don't need to say what you already know about how the disease affects the body."

An idea rolled into her mind. "I gave him my laptop, and it's in the guest bedroom closet. We could search through every document and his browsing history. We can only hope he forgot to delete something. He sleeps on my couch and not in the spare bedroom, but he could have hidden something on my laptop. Give me a moment." She walked into the bedroom where her parents had slept the previous night, climbed onto a chair, and searched under a pile of books. But the laptop wasn't there. Whitt had apparently hidden it. But where? She walked into the hallway and an idea sailed into her mind. Dizziness assaulted her, and she waited until her head cleared before calling out to Dexter.

"Can you give me a hand here?"

He emerged from the kitchen. "Sure. What do you need?"

"The laptop isn't in the guest room, and I've been trying to figure out where he put it."

"And?"

She pointed to the pull-down attic stairs. "I never go up there. Everything is stored in the garage. Whitt knows I don't like traipsing in the insulation. But he might have put the laptop up there."

"One way to find out." Dexter gently brought the ladder to the floor. Stacy flipped on the light switch in the hall and he climbed up.

She waited while he seemingly vanished. Dirt and dust fell to the floor. Maybe this wasn't such a good idea. Her head pounded.

"Found it," Dexter said and proceeded down the ladder. "Whitt hid it under some loose insulation."

Stacy smiled her thanks. A few moments later they sat at the kitchen table. She powered it on. Nothing. She tried again and groaned. "Oh, Whitt. It won't boot up." She attempted twice more with the same results.

"Would he have wiped it clean?"

"It appears so." She walked to the window facing the street. "His house is padlocked. Parents were evicted. If you could gain access and look through his room . . ."

"Good ideas. I'll pass this on to law enforcement."

"His bike was in the garage when I got home yesterday. Which means he's on foot." She turned to gaze into Dexter's kind face, and a trace of weariness passed through her. She joined him at the kitchen table.

"Public transportation is our guess, but we've found nothing on security footage. Dr. Broussard, the city and state are on high alert to find him."

"I'm Stacy. Any man who helps me find my boy needs to call me by my first name."

He laughed lightly, and she appreciated the gesture despite the grim circumstances. "I'm Dexter. My daughter's name is Stacy."

"I'm sure she's as admirable as her daddy." She took a breath. "Whitt is brilliant. He'd deliberately steer you down the wrong path. I've been thinking. He wrote he was leaving the city, and yet—"

"You think he didn't?"

"By sending authorities to the bus stops and major roads where he might hitchhike, he'd have an opportunity to do the opposite of what others believe. Not sure why I think that. Except . . ."

"What?"

"As much as he fears social services, he wants a home. He had hope with me. Maybe he has access to the news and learned I'm better. And I can see how you'd think otherwise, that he'd head into a desolate part of the country and monitor what's going on here. But he'd do the opposite of whatever the experts anticipate. He'd not abandon me completely. The little boy in him craves a family. I'm not perfect, but I offered stability and unconditional love."

"Food and water would bring him out of hiding."

"He'd already have those things handled. My theory may sound a little wild. But I'm positive Whitt schemed contrary to the typical twelve-year-old."

"Everyone's aware of his aptitude. The FBI has their intelligence analyzing it." He ran his hands through his hair. "We've got to find him. My mind is preoccupied with a boy dying alone. Keeps me moving. The epidemic is increasing. We now have thirteen hospitalized and four casualties. One pet owner who has a female claims the family's dog has been missing for the past two days. A man who tested positively doesn't live in the community where this began. Neither did he attend the subdivision's carnival. Rather he lives in an apartment complex three miles away and runs in the mornings with his dog."

"You have the animal?"

"Yes. It tested positively, the third dog so far. We're looking at blood samples in an ongoing effort to develop a series of more effective antibiotics or a serum. Like you, some of those stricken have responded to antibiotics, and others have not. There's no apparent cure. You and the others whose temperatures have lowered are by no means well. All I have to do is look at your flushed face and red eyes. Praise God, none of the testing has shown humans can transmit it. Although we're still using precautions at the hospitals."

Awareness of the critical situation hit her hard. "No one can give me a guarantee that Whitt will respond to the antibiotics while Xena spreads the disease to the public."

"True." He pressed his lips together. "How long have researchers been working on a serum for canine brucellosis?" When she winced, he continued. "We are conducting resistance-sensitivity studies as well as studying the blood to combat the infection. The more dogs that are quarantined, the less the disease spreads."

She touched his arm. "What about a press conference? A huge appeal from me. Tell Whitt he's tested positive and antibiotics can help. That we need Xena, just to test her blood, not hurt her." Tears pooled her eyes, and she couldn't stop. "Tell him I love him, and we'll work this out."

"I know you'd do anything for him."

"Can we do it?"

Dexter hesitated. "Let me call Alex. Get his viewpoint and see if the FBI can request media coverage."

She swiped beneath her eyes. "I'm determined."

"For the sake of your own health?"

"I love Whitt as though I'd given birth to him."

He nodded and pressed in a number, and she listened to the one-sided conversation. "I'm at Stacy's. She has an idea about how to lure Whitt out of hiding." Dexter explained the proposed press conference.

She wished she could hear every word.

Dexter glanced at her. "I'll alert her to the possible danger and inform her of protection."

She hadn't thought about the danger of going public with her plea. Whoever was part of the crime or even animal activists had valid reasons to be angry. "I've thought this through, and I'm determined."

He set the phone on the table. "Alex is going to work on the plan. Said that he wants Whitt to know if the problem is social services, he could live with Alex until things are settled. He's phoning your attorney with the offer. I know your parents are here, but social services might want to see a somewhat-permanent arrangement."

What a dear man, her Alex. "When will we have an answer?"

"A couple of hours to obtain approval. Then some time for the tech people."

She nodded. "I'll wait for your call."

49

TEN THIRTY THURSDAY MORNING, Alex and Ric walked into Phillips Security armed with a search warrant signed by a local judge. Russell Phillips greeted them at the door, decked out as though he planned to address the nation. Obviously the company's parking garage cams had caught the agents and alerted him.

"Morning, gentlemen. We're working on a sleep deficit, so let's get down to business. I'm ready to have my name exonerated of this ludicrous accusation."

"We have a signed search warrant," Alex said. "LA special agents will be handling that aspect of the investigation."

"I understand." He pointed toward the elevator. "My executives are in the boardroom, ready to answer questions."

The three men stepped inside a marble-floored elevator, trimmed in brass and mirrors. Alex avoided watching numbers on elevators. Instead he took the moment to prepare for what would happen when the doors opened. Phillips no doubt had pulled in his closest confidants long before the agents arrived. They'd strategized what would and wouldn't be said to the agents from Houston. Their discretion meant nothing to Alex. He wanted the truth.

The doors opened onto the third floor, simple yet elegantly decorated. Phillips led them down a hallway to a typical boardroom, where six men sat at a rectangular wooden table. Coffee brewed, engaging his senses. Definitely liquid lighter fluid guaranteed to wake him up.

Each man stood when they entered. All looked to be in their fifties and sixties.

"Howard, would you begin the introductions?" Phillips said. "He's been with me the longest, a longtime friend. Knows more about the business than I do."

Alex made note.

An African American man nodded, his dark stare fixed on the agents with a heavy dose of animosity. "Chief Operations Officer Howard Dottia."

They went around the table introducing themselves.

"Byron Keller, vice president of marketing."

"Lloyd Summers, vice president of sales."

"Karl Wren, vice president of finance."

"Matthew Smythe, vice president of human resources."

"Walter Alms, vice president of purchasing."

"Thank you, gentlemen. You may be seated." Phillips turned to the agents. "Everyone is present except my nephew, Jensen Phillips, who is vice president of research and product development. He had a personal problem at home, so he's joining via audio bridge." He pressed in a series of numbers connecting the room's voice conferencing system. "Jensen, we're ready."

"Good morning," a male voice said, filled with way too much cheer. "You have my full attention. Russell, thanks for this morning. My little girl is doing much better."

"Wonderful. Special Agents LeBlanc and Price will take over as soon as they're ready. Gentlemen, how do you drink your coffee?"

"Black," they said in unison, prompting a laugh from the other men. The tension eased slightly.

Alex needed the stress level to fall a few notches. "I think we've been stereotyped. Is there an empty office for us to use while we're here?"

"There is." Phillips's cordiality bordered on sarcasm. "We have another smaller boardroom. Do you need to see it first?"

"As long as the door closes, we're in fine shape. We want this rectified quickly."

Phillips paced the front of the room. "I understand the disease persists in Houston. Do you really believe the culprit is in LA?"

"All we can say is the investigation led us here."

"I guarantee you the answers aren't at Phillips Security."

"For your sake, I hope so too." Alex smiled at the men. He picked up some hostility, but their CEO was under suspicion for a terrible crime and loyalty was a prized possession. "The questions we have for you will help us find the person or persons who are behind a series of crimes in Houston. Special Agent Price will explain what we've found, and I'll pick up the conversation with specifics." He eased onto a chair.

Ric rose and detailed the initial crime, meticulously outlining the series of events leading from the body, the quadcopter, the dog, the water contamination hoax, and on to the dog's genetically engineered disease. "A man by the name of Lynx Connor was arrested for threatening the deceased's wife. We learned Connor and Howe were working together. Connor claims Russell Phillips is behind the crimes, motivated by the desire for land in Houston to relocate the company. He also claimed Mr. Phillips ordered the death of Todd Howe."

Howard Dottia raised his fist. "That's insane. Have you checked the company's assets?" He leaned toward Ric, his bald head shining in the overhead light. "Phillips Security could have bought them out and not made a dent in the cash flow."

"We've seen the financials," Ric continued. "And you are scouting out a potential building site. Who is in charge of the project?"

"I am, along with Jensen," Dottia said. "We're searching initially online and haven't made contact with a commercial real estate company. Once favorable sites are established, none of which is the property mentioned in your case, we'll present our findings to the board. Subsequent visits to Houston would occur before any finalization or offers are made. Our process for securing a building site and our reputation negate these accusations."

"Whoever is behind this must be aware of your relocation plans. How publicized is the new operation?" Ric's voice held the timbre of one in control. Alex could pick up a few tips when his ragin' Cajun kicked in. "We'd like the names of anyone you've spoken to."

"I'll answer that," Jensen said. "As soon as Russell gave the green light, we immediately informed all the employees. The board's desire, like Russell's, is for everyone to have ample time to decide if they are willing to make the move. Once we have more information, we'll educate employees with options for a retirement package or how we can assist them financially. Unfortunately, that involves a lot of people to interview."

"Thank you." Ric produced the photos of Todd Howe and Lynx Connor.

Russell texted the photos to his nephew.

None of the board recognized the two men.

"Special Agent LeBlanc and I will now meet with each of you privately. Do not leave the city until everyone is cleared. We apologize for any inconvenience." Ric addressed Russell Phillips. "Your nephew needs to come in as soon as possible. I understand his daughter is ill. We can conduct most of his interview via the audio bridge, but a face-to-face is necessary."

"I'll be at the office in the morning," Jensen said. "I want this settled too."

"How long will the interviews take?" Dottia said.

"Long enough to pose questions and receive acceptable answers."

"I have a meeting in an hour."

Alex cleared his throat while reaching for diplomacy. Didn't these men realize the serious nature of these crimes? "Agent Price, we can begin with this gentleman. Sir, give us a moment to set up."

Russell Phillips led the way into an adjoining room. After showing them the lights, he left, closing the door behind him. Ric and Alex spent the next few minutes searching for cameras and recording devices. Satisfied none existed, they invited Dottia inside and seated themselves across from him at a rectangular table. They opened with simple questions to ease apprehension before moving toward the critical topics.

"Mr. Dottia, how long have you been with Phillips Security?"

"Little over thirty-six years. Russell and I are old friends. Go back to when we were kids."

"Then you feel you know him well?"

"Like a brother, which makes this whole interrogation utterly appalling."

"In looking at Mr. Phillips's file, we see nothing to implicate him in these crimes. However, he was accused."

"Liars avoid the truth. It's who they are." His eyes narrowed. "I'd like to say I've seen Lynx Connor or Todd Howe and end this nonsense. I'm sixty-six and sharp as a tack. My memory surprises me. But, gentlemen, I've never met or seen them before."

Alex saw no reason to doubt the man. Later he and Ric would compare notes. "I have a couple more pics." He scrolled to those of

Bekah Howe and Stacy. Dottia exhibited the same scrutiny as with the others and denied recognition. Additional probing and body language implied an honest man.

"Thank you for your time." Alex gave him his card as well as Ric's. "Feel free to contact us with questions or information."

They shook the man's hand and proceeded to the other executives. The results were the same. Although Jensen Phillips responded by phone, his responses imitated the others.

After examining the LA FBI's reports and reviewing interviews, Alex and Ric left Phillips Security. They ordered backgrounds on the executives and a dozen other officers. LA agents were imaging files and conducting backgrounds on the employees, but it would take several days to compile their full report. Connor's accusations appeared unfounded, but the investigation wasn't concluded yet and neither was the day over.

50

STACY INSISTED the press conference be held at her clinic. In her own environment among the reminders of her dear animals, she could relax and share her heart with viewers and more importantly Whitt. Far too many people were suffering, a tragedy she might never force from her mind. While camera lights flashed hot against her face, she pictured her boy . . . healthy and strong. She'd do anything to find him, even if it meant exposing her vulnerability to the world.

A young woman with turquoise hair applied Stacy's makeup. A little color was a good thing considering her stint in the hospital. Media had cooperated by telling Whitt's story to the public while the FBI updated electronic billboards with his picture and the critical situation hammering the city.

Dexter Rayken smiled, her support and encouragement. She called him friend. He and Dad seemed to have formed a bond and talked fishing lures and hunting stories. Proof a little Cajun existed in every person.

Facial masks were offered to those involved with the production. Two cameramen chose to use them, and one woman wore a hazmat garment.

Kathi Scott, the reporter who'd brought the Channel 5 van to her clinic, waited to conduct the interview. She declined a protective mask. "If I wear one of those, the viewers will lock their minds to her plea. We already have history where I failed her, and it won't happen again. She's a courageous woman to make this appeal. I must do my part."

Stacy reached for Kathi's hand and squeezed it lightly. "Thank you, my friend."

Earlier Kathi had prayed with her as well as Dexter. A cameraman said Christians crawled out of the woodwork when crisis hit. Stacy told him Christians weren't roaches.

How comforting if Alex were standing before her, but his work in California was bringing the epidemic and host of crimes closer to an end. He'd made a huge sacrifice in stepping forward to care for Whitt, causing her to feel more for him.

A text notification sounded. It was from Alex.

Thinking of u. Will call 2day.

She took a deep breath and lifted her gaze to Kathi. "I'm ready when you are."

"We're live in two minutes. I'll make the intro. Speak from your heart." At the proper cue, Kathi smiled into the camera. "We're reporting live from Pet Support Veterinary Clinic in northwest Houston where veterinarian Stacy Broussard serves pet owners in her community. Recently she contracted human brucellosis, the disease of epidemic proportions sweeping across the area in which four people have died and thirteen others are hospitalized. The outbreak began when Dr. Broussard took in a stray dog. The animal had been injected with a genetically engineered strain of canine brucellosis.

Since then our city's law enforcement officials, including Houston's police department, the FBI, and state investigators have been searching for the person or persons responsible for this act of terrorism. The health department, medical officials, and the Laboratory Resource Network, a branch of the CDC, are working around the clock to help individuals who are stricken with the disease and answer questions. A combination of antibiotics has proven successful for some cases. There is no serum for the infected animals or humans.

"The story with Dr. Broussard goes deeper. When she fell ill, she was in the process of petitioning to obtain custody of a twelve-year-old boy. The boy, afraid of the future, has run away with the infected dog. Health officials say the boy tested positive for the disease, and the dog is needed to study its blood for a way to stop the senseless outbreak. Dr. Broussard is appealing to anyone who knows the whereabouts of Whitt McMann to phone the number at the bottom of the viewing screen." Kathi gave Stacy the mic.

Nervous, she prayed for strength. "Whitt, please phone me or contact a law enforcement officer immediately. We're concerned because the disease is in your system. Xena will not be hurt. The researchers need only to draw her blood, not hurt her or any other dog that tests positive. We simply need to quarantine them. Our hope is when a cure is found for us, it will cure dogs too. In the meantime, you need antibiotics to fight the fever. Please . . ." She swallowed the ever-thickening lump in her throat. "Whitt, let us help you. You know how to reach me. I'll be home or here at the clinic assisting others to end this horrible outbreak."

She took questions from various reporters.

"What can people expect from your clinic in the midst of this tragedy?" a woman said.

"Questions answered. Their pets tested, and the health department will also draw blood from anyone who is concerned about their health. All clinics and kennels have been instructed to disinfect their facilities and have their dogs tested. Those dogs that receive a negative test will be issued certificates. Many veterinary clinics and kennels in the area are extending their hours and will have information on the canine and human brucellosis in their offices. The health department also has information on their website."

A young man sought her attention. "The canine version causes female dogs to abort. What about women who have the disease?"

The question hit her hard. She hadn't considered her own inability to carry children. "I'm not a medical professional qualified to answer your question. I'm sure as studies are completed, the findings will be released to the public."

A man spoke. "Looks like you're avoiding the reality of this epidemic. A female dog who has this disease is a danger to those around the animal. Will the animal be euthanized?"

She had expected this reaction. "The dogs will be quarantined until we find a treatment. Permanent decisions will be the owner's decision. I'm an animal lover, sir. I care about their welfare and want to offer compassionate treatment. Those of us who love dogs think of them as our children. They are like two-year-olds, eager to learn, receive and express affection. Does that answer your question about how I feel about ending the life of any animal?"

An older man raised his hand. "For those who want to volunteer in aiding the speedy testing of dogs and humans, how do we register?"

She smiled. "As soon as we're finished here, we'll begin registration for volunteers. Those viewing the program can use the phone number listed for more information. The volunteer process will be an event many clinics and kennels will put into action."

The press conference ended, and although exhausted with the

stress, she'd helped take a step forward in finding her boy and protecting people and animals.

A man in jeans and a dingy T-shirt approached her. He looked familiar from her subdivision, but she couldn't recall the pet. Unshaven. His face drawn. "Stacy Broussard?"

"Yes."

"My daughter may die because of you." He moved closer. "Your fault." His dull eyes alarmed her.

"Please. I'm sorry." She pushed back.

"Sorry doesn't make up for her suffering." As though in slow motion, a fixed-blade hunting knife in his hand sliced through her lab coat. No pain. Blood coated her lower right arm. She must be in shock.

A police officer rushed to the man's side and grabbed his wrist, forcing the knife to the floor of her clinic.

"This won't be the end of those who blame you." The man spit at her. "Someone will get to you."

"Killing me won't undo a thing. The damage's been done." She'd not stop trying to help others, moving forward to bring this horrible ordeal to an end.

Alex grabbed the phone and saw it was Dexter. "I just read what happened. Stacy okay?"

"She's okay. A few stitches. More determined than ever. She responded well and is even more determined to see this through."

"Protection detail intact?"

"Yes. FBI and HPD are on it."

Alex unclenched his fist. "Is she nearby?"

"Not at the moment. The clinic is receiving nonstop calls to volunteer, and she's in the thick of directing people to facilities near them."

Alex let out a breath. "I'll contact her later."

"Progress on your end?"

Alex chose his words carefully. "We've interviewed many people."

"What about the two men?"

"Nothing substantial yet. Connor is still in custody. I believe the answers are here, and I intend to stay until proven right or wrong. People are dead, and others are suffering. Ric and I are among many agents working to find who's responsible."

"And you will. Alex, you never give up."

He thanked him and texted Stacy.

Alex excused himself from the interview room where he and Ric had talked throughout the day. In the men's room, he closed the door to a stall. Not the best place to have a come-to-Jesus meeting, but matters of the heart didn't need an elaborate location. Learning about Stacy's heroic plea for Whitt to surface and then her knife injury showed him his relationship with God needed to be cemented. Dexter had told him that God would touch his life when he didn't expect it.

Moments later, he rose from his knees and glanced at his watch before joining Ric. Thirty minutes until he and Ric would head out to talk to Connor again. If the man in custody was really afraid of Russell Phillips, why hadn't he told the truth from the start? The more Alex processed what they'd learned, the more Connor looked guilty of murder.

His phone alerted him to a text from the LA office.

Lynx Connor found dead in his cell. Unsure of cause of death. An autopsy ordered. Should have prelim results by end of day. No visitors on record. Interviewing guards.

Until Alex and Ric viewed the findings on Connor's cause of death, they'd talk to the ex–Mrs. Connor.

✳

Alex and Ric parked in front of the apartment building where the woman lived. Dressed in jeans, a skimpy top, three-inch earrings, and four-inch pink heels, she received the news of Lynx's death with a sardonic laugh. She'd taught kindergarten in the past—obviously she'd experienced a career change.

"Lynx the jinx finally kicked it, huh?" she said. "Too bad he didn't follow through while we were married." She smacked a generous lump of bubble gum.

"We'd like to talk to you," Alex said.

She stepped outside the door of her apartment. "Okay, but I haven't seen Lynx for about two weeks."

"Were you aware of his illegal activities?"

"There's a reason his friends called him Con."

"Is the name Todd Howe familiar to you?" Alex said.

"Let me make one thing clear, agents. Lynx and I saw each other socially. Period. In the three years we were married or afterward, he never discussed how he made money."

Alex found it difficult to believe her. "I thought his friends called him Con."

She rolled her eyes like a fifteen-year-old. "You know he did time. Are we finished?"

"Not exactly. He was charged with murder and fraud. What do you know about this?"

"Honestly, I have no idea."

"Is there anything you can tell us?"

She blew out a sigh. "Lynx wanted to get back together."

"You were against it?"

"I hadn't decided."

"Do you have any suspicions about his death?"

"All I can tell you is at times depression hit him hard. Lately it had gotten worse, but he promised me he was taking an antidepressant. His mother fought depression, and he showed the same severe lows."

"Do you know which medication he took?"

"Zoloft. Not aware of the dosage. Think about it, though, guys. If I thought someone was behind his death, would I put my life in danger by giving you information?"

The agents hadn't said anything about possible foul play.

Ric gave her his card. "We're able to offer protection."

"That's rich. Like you did for Lynx?"

"I believe you know more than what you're telling us."

She shook her head while her lips trembled. "He was always looking for an angle to make money."

"You indicated you knew nothing about his activities."

"I don't. But he bragged about getting rich." She glanced away.

Alex saw a shadow pass over her face. "You cared about him."

She stared at Alex, as though wrestling with something. "I did care," she whispered. "Would you like to come inside? I know little, except he told me he was in far too deep."

Alex and Ric accepted her invitation. The ex–Mrs. Connor implied murder and hid behind a persona of tough living.

"I have fresh blueberry pie," she said. "Baking helps me work through stress, especially when I haven't heard from Lynx. He called every other day, like clockwork. Then it stopped."

She shed tears as she pulled out a scrapbook of the two when they were first married. Young and happy, Lynx was in shape, and she looked the role of a kindergarten teacher. "I wish I'd been able to conceive. He chose the divorce. Said it was best for both of us."

"But you were having second thoughts about the arrangement?" Ric's compassion skills always outdid Alex's.

"I miss him."

"I understand," Ric continued. "Excellent pie. Right up there with my mom's."

"Thank you. Lynx's favorite."

Ric leaned back in his chair. "Are you sure he never mentioned anyone? Or a place he frequented?"

She shook her head. "During our marriage, he changed. Money became more important than our relationship. Even when he was dealing in land fraud, he still had time for us. He wouldn't introduce me to his friends or give me their names. Said it was better I didn't know, that ignorance was safe. I couldn't handle the uncertainty. Lost my teaching job, and the only job I could find was at a bar."

"You really believe his death wasn't natural?" Ric said.

"Without a doubt. Yes, he dealt with depression. But his health was fine. A little overweight but no high blood pressure problems or other problems." She shrugged. "As I said earlier, he told me he was in too deep with something. When I asked him how he could get out, he said it was impossible."

Shortly afterward she crumbled, no longer able to keep up the act.

They waited until she phoned her sister, neither agent willing to leave her alone.

51

WHITT THRASHED THROUGH THE WOODS. During the night, Xena had deserted him, and he had to find her. They needed each other. They were partners. Tears flowed, and he blinked them back to no avail. He dared not call out her name. Law enforcement could be combing the woods and hear him. The idea of looking for a spot where he could get a WiFi signal seemed important but not at the risk of getting caught.

If Xena came in contact with others, they could get sick. Die. If she were recognized by the authorities, she could lead them to him. Worse yet, the wrong people might have her euthanized.

And Whitt's head and back hurt.

Unexpected nausea shot up from his stomach, and he lost control. Dizziness pressed down, and he struggled to keep from falling. No reason to fool himself—he had human brucellosis. Holding on to a small tree, he glanced behind him. Oh no. He'd left a clear trail for anyone to follow. Only one thing for him to do—backtrack to the campsite. Maybe Xena would tire of roaming and find him there.

Grabbing a broken limb, he forced resolve into his muscles and covered the vomit and the path he'd forged. The chore took much longer than he'd calculated, and he was forced to rest along the way. Not even the right words for how he viewed himself and the surrounding world entered his brain. All along, he'd believed his intelligence would save him, as though impregnable against the forces of the world.

But now he had doubts.

The Tylenol and Pepto-Bismol tablets in his backpack had no impact on what raged through his body.

Fever weakened him. Chills in June?

A churning stomach made it difficult to move.

His worst fear unfolded. Worse than losing Miss Stacy or being placed in a foster home, he'd set the stage to die alone. Even Xena had abandoned him.

Stacy viewed the late-night news on her sofa. Mom and Dad had gone on to bed, but she absorbed updates like a sponge. Lynx Connor, the man arrested in Los Angeles for suspected murder and his involvement in the brucellosis epidemic, had been found dead in his cell. No reason given for his death. The FBI were awaiting an autopsy.

Stacy stared at the screen. Had he not been able to face his accusers? In many people's minds, his death sealed his guilt. What about Russell Phillips? The crimes hadn't made sense from the beginning, not from what she'd seen, learned, or experienced.

She debated calling Alex. He had responsibilities beyond her, a job to complete that would help stop these atrocities. She missed him and wished she could snap her fingers and he'd be there. A bit selfish but true.

Her role was to help find Whitt. Each time she recalled how

seriously ill she'd been with antibiotics pumping into her veins, she feared for her precious boy, who had nothing to fight the attacks against his body. Mom and Dad had contacted their church to pray for Whitt and the other victims stricken with the disease. She longed to be helping Dexter's team with the research, but her skills were lacking. Why hadn't she sought to add a PhD in veterinary research after her name like she'd planned?

She knew what happened . . . She'd met Whitt, and her desire for motherhood outweighed the time and effort to obtain another doctorate.

The mother of the twins from her subdivision who'd initially contracted the human brucellosis volunteered to help with the testing of dogs. One of her daughters had recovered and the other was responding to the antibiotics. Fortunate. Those were the kind of people Stacy admired—the givers.

Her cell rang. Alex. She laughed at how much she'd wanted to phone him. Muting her TV, she greeted him. "Good evening, Special Agent LeBlanc."

"Is this the TV personality? The one who almost made headlines after being knifed?"

"None other."

"Then I have the right number."

The sound of his voice soothed the stress. "Thanks for taking time to call. How are you doing?"

"You're the one with stitches."

"Tylenol is my crutch. Now you?"

"Just got word on a preliminary cause of death for Lynx Connor."

"How tragic for someone to die while in custody. What happened?"

"Arsenic-coated Zoloft."

She startled. "How did that happen in jail?"

"Good question. We're on it. An interesting piece of evidence was just released to the media. His body held traces of human brucellosis."

"His visits to the clinic put him in touch with the infection. Looks like his activities caught up with him or killed him." A chill snaked up her arms. "What more can you tell me?"

"Bekah Howe received the report on Todd's tox screen. His body was free of drugs."

"I'm glad for her. She's been through a lot. Any more news?"

"Honestly? Nothing."

"You're incorrigible."

He chuckled. "I've been called worse. Seriously, when I can, I'll give you more info. Any news about Whitt? With the press conference, I'd hoped for something by now."

She sighed, feeling the familiar ache for her boy. "I keep expecting him to come through the door."

"Stacy, I'm praying."

"I know, and I appreciate all you've done."

"If I were there, I'd be searching to find him." He paused. "Please don't overdo the search. A relapse could be . . . serious."

"I'm following the doctor's orders."

"You and I know differently. Are we still on for a trio coffee date?"

"Yes." A thousand and more. "Will you promise to be safe?"

He laughed lightly. "We are stubborn Cajuns. I need to go. Hearing your voice is—"

"I feel the same. You take care of the investigation. That's your specialty. Bye, Alex." She laid her phone on the end table before she revealed her heart. How selfish when her boy was in danger.

Each moment he had to be growing weaker.

"I believe in you, Whitt," she whispered. "You are destined for great things. Not this. Not a death sentence."

52

FRIDAY MORNING, Alex and Ric waited for Howard Dottia to join them for a seven thirty breakfast. He'd requested the meeting but hadn't revealed why. Alex respected the man's bluntness and loyalty to Russell Phillips. If Dottia's body language had been interpreted correctly and the background checks reported accurately about his contributions to the company and community, he valued integrity.

Once they finished breakfast, they'd meet with Jensen Phillips. The nephew sent a few red flags waving, and Alex had requested a deeper probe. He glanced at his phone. "My battery's low, and I left my charger at the hotel."

"We'll get it later. Mine's charged up," Ric said.

A text arrived from the ASAC in Houston. "Read me what it says," Alex said. "Need to save my battery."

Ric appeared to scan the message. "Okay, the missing man from the CID's investigation has been found dead near Little Rock,

Arkansas. Estimated time of death looks like prior to arresting the partner, Private Wilcox."

"As in the man in custody could have murdered him."

"Possibly. We'll see what the CID uncovers. More than one variable here with Phillips Security the parent company in manufacturing drones and filling government contracts for them."

"A coincidence considering the volume of business or a link to our crimes?" Alex spotted Dottia entering the restaurant. Shoulders erect. "He's here. Let's see what he wants to talk to us about."

The three were seated for breakfast. A young woman brought them coffee and took their orders.

"Gentlemen, we aren't sharing omelets and pancakes because we're hungry," Dottia said. "I'm here to speak on Russell's behalf. His impeccable reputation is at stake, and I want to know what I can do to hurry along the investigation."

Alex stared at him. "Why?" Could his original assessment of Dottia be wrong? Was the man covering up information?

"I'm his friend, like a brother. I despise whoever has conjured this crazy scheme."

Unusual loyalty or hiding something? "I understand," Alex said. "We're here to learn the truth."

"Lynx Connor, who accused Russell, is dead. What or whom do you suspect?"

"Special Agent Price, could you give Mr. Dottia answers?"

Ric shared the same skin color as Dottia, so the man might open up to him, which gave Alex an opportunity to make observations. His gut told him the source of the crimes ran through Phillips Security, and Dottia might not realize he had answers.

"Agent Price, our skin may be the same color, but that doesn't mean I'm going to have sudden recall about this unfortunate set of circumstances."

Ric lifted a brow. "If that was my line of thinking, I would have left Agent LeBlanc sleeping at the hotel."

Dottia smiled and took a sip of coffee. "I pride myself on an infallible memory, and Connor isn't there. I regret the man was killed, but I can't say I'll miss his negative impact on my good friend's life."

"The executives at Phillips Security have tenure except Russell's nephew, Jensen."

"Correct. The rest of us began on the ground floor when Russ conceived the idea of a security business. Back then it was residential. When that took off, we expanded to commercial."

"Did you have any idea the business would grow nationwide?"

The waitress delivered breakfast before Dottia responded.

"Back to your question. In the beginning, Russell designed the equipment. We assembled the systems, sold them, serviced them, all 24-7. We paid the bills and if there was any left over, we celebrated with hot dogs." He poured a generous flow of syrup over a waffle before continuing. "I miss those days, the optimism of youth. The energy. Creativity. Doing much with little and being happy. The wife and I lived on rice and beans in those early years."

"Worth it?" Alex said.

"Without a doubt." He met Alex's gaze. "Hard work and determination instill a sense of satisfaction, a work ethic that is impossible to duplicate, only experience. Why are you two men committed to the FBI?"

"Same reasons," Alex said.

"What about Jensen?" Ric reached for the Tabasco sauce. "Where does he fit?"

He hesitated, and Alex made a quick mental note.

"Russell never had a child, and his wife died of a stroke. Jensen's parents passed within two years of each other from cancer. He's all the family Russ has left, and he's been groomed from the ground up to one day take over the company." A spark of anger burst from Dottia's eyes.

What did the anger mean? Was Dottia motivated to get rid of both Phillips men?

Ric pushed forward. "Sir, in the event Russell was no longer in the picture, why not have the remaining board members run the company?"

"The bottom line is it's his company. We're getting older, and young blood is needed to fuel changes and make updates in technology."

"What's your opinion of Jensen, especially since you two are working together on the relocation project? After all, he may one day be your boss."

"Why do you want to know that?"

Ric stopped eating. "Sounds like he isn't your top choice for a CEO."

The man sliced up his waffles as though he was taking out his frustration on them. "He's capable and extremely intelligent. Innovative ideas, and plans to have feet on the ground to view various property sites soon."

"You're not going with him to Houston?"

"Jensen seeks an opportunity to prove himself."

"I see. Flaws?"

Dottia focused his attention on Ric. "Jensen's odd, but we all have our idiosyncrasies."

"How so?"

"You aren't giving up." He finished his coffee. "This has nothing to do with your investigation, and I shouldn't have labeled Russ's nephew. But since I already hung myself, I'll finish. Jensen thinks more of his dog than his uncle or wife and stepdaughter. Certainly more than the company. When you two visited the office and he spoke about his little girl feeling better, he meant his dog. She accompanies him everywhere, and if the animal isn't permitted, then he doesn't use the establishment."

"A service dog?"

"I suppose."

"Physical or mental issues?"

Alex gave Ric credit for not abandoning the topic.

Dottia smiled. "The most creative of minds may not have people skills."

"So he's not your choice for a company leader."

"Do you really think I'd answer?"

"My job is to ask pointed questions. Is the animal licensed or certified?"

"I have no idea. Jensen claims the dog isn't a pet. It's a peculiar trait on his part. No big thing."

"I see," Ric said. "How does Jensen view the business?"

"It's his cash to play the game."

Alex bolded Dottia's response in his mental log of the interview.

"So he doesn't share in your commitment to Phillips Security?"

"He's young."

Ric chuckled. "Are you making excuses for him?"

"Just telling you how it is."

"Am I correct in assuming if you distrusted any of the board members, it would be Jensen?"

"You're putting words in my mouth that aren't accurate." Annoyance flashed over his face.

Ric leaned toward him. "We have a murder to solve along with fraud and the source of a deadly disease. People have died. Did I mention a stolen military-grade quadcopter? We will probe until the truth surfaces."

Dottia tossed a twenty on the table and stood. "We're finished here."

Alex watched his rigid form exit the restaurant. "Loyalty blinds the strongest of men."

"Russell is his friend, and Jensen—"

"I want to talk to Jensen Phillips now. Call Phillips Security and make sure he stays put. But first I need my phone charger."

Outside, an explosion rocked the restaurant.

53

ALEX AND RIC bolted out the front of the restaurant and on to the parking lot. Blue smoke rolled from the rear of a vehicle, indicating the possibility of a tailpipe bomb. The smell of burning rubber met their nostrils. A closer view showed the driver trapped inside a burning Lexus. No one else appeared to be injured.

Ric raced to the scene and attempted to open the door, jerking back on the obviously hot metal.

The threat of another explosion spurred Alex's adrenaline. "Let me help you." He ripped off his jacket as he raced to the car to pad the handle. Giving it to Ric, Alex peered inside. Howard Dottia slumped against the steering wheel. The smell of gasoline burst into his senses. "It's going to blow."

Ric jerked open the door and felt for a pulse. "He's alive."

"Let's get him out of here." Alex swung the man's legs around and picked them up while Ric released the seat belt and reached to grab Dottia under his arms. The injured man's phone fell from his jacket pocket. Alex kicked it and hurried backward. He'd retrieve it once they were all safe.

A fiery burst of heat and metal propelled the three backward. He held tight to Dottia, and the injured man landed on top of him, face-to-face. Ric flew to the right on the pavement. Ears ringing, Alex lifted Dottia from him, blood pouring from the man's head and neck. Eyes vacant.

Alex turned to Ric, who had blood dripping down his arm.

"I'm okay." He struggled to his feet. "Dottia?"

"He's gone." Sirens pierced the air against Alex's ringing ears. He focused on Ric's blood-soaked arm. "You need that looked at."

"It's a surface wound."

"I'll remind you of those words when you have a blood transfusion."

"Bro, the deeper we get into this case, the more bodies."

Alex waited in the emergency room of Good Samaritan Hospital while a doctor placed fifteen stitches in Ric's upper arm without numbing meds. Ric said he was allergic to an ingredient in pain-killers and numbing agents. After a nurse gave him a tetanus shot, they made their way to the LA office, located a short distance from the hospital.

"Nothing about Dottia appeared vindictive," Ric said, pale and weak.

"Right. Someone wanted him out of the picture."

"That person was afraid he'd given us information?"

"Obviously a dead man can't testify," Alex said. "At the restaurant, we infuriated him. Where was he going, to the office?"

Ric drew in a sharp breath, no doubt hit by a surge of fire. "He knew the big dog in this mix of crimes."

"Has to be a member of the board."

"One or both of the Phillips men. They're in this together."

That didn't sound like his partner, the man who observed before he judged. Pain seemed to be doing the talking. A bomb squad would determine the type of device used and if the explosions were triggered remotely, as well as other means of identifying the person. "We haven't talked to Jensen. I want to know where every member of Phillips's board was this morning, staff too. Anyone who had eyes and ears on this investigation."

Ric clenched his injured arm. "You have Dottia's cell phone, right?"

"In my pocket." He grasped the man's phone and checked the call log. "Last call was to Russell."

"Was he warning his old friend we were about to arrest him or Jensen?"

"Or was he telling him he knew who'd orchestrated the crimes?" He pressed in the man's private number and learned he was with the Dottia family near the Bel Air area. Without hesitation, Russell gave Alex the address.

"Jensen never made it to the office this morning," Russell said. "I intended to call you earlier, but then I received the news about Howard. Jensen's wife hasn't seen him since yesterday morning."

"When did his wife contact you?" Alex said.

"A text while en route here. She wanted to know if I'd heard from him."

"We're headed your way." Alex pressed End and called the LA office, relaying the conversation and asking for Jensen to be picked up. He slipped the phone back into his pocket. "Jensen Phillips is our person of interest."

"You don't think the Phillips men are in this together?"

"Russell has nothing to gain. Jensen stands to inherit a conglomerate. Money says it all."

"Then why aren't we looking for Jensen instead of talking to Russell?"

"While the LA team is running him down, Russell may know where he's at or have the information we need to end this."

On the way to the prestigious area where the Dottia family lived, the LA office forwarded the restaurant's security cams. Alex pulled the rental car into a convenience store parking lot. They watched footage of a man wearing a loose jacket and a Dodgers baseball cap pulled over his face approach Dottia's car. He pulled something from his pocket and placed it under the car. He kept his back to the camera.

"There's our bomber," Ric said. "Caucasian. Trimmer build than Phillips. Spry too, indicating a younger man."

"Like Jensen?"

Ric's silence on that point said it all. "With the timing, the bomber must have followed Dottia here. Russell knows more than what he's saying, and he's got to be covering for his nephew. Those two will have an alibi for this morning because neither would soil his hands."

Ric spoke through his pain. "I disagree," Alex said. "Nothing's indicated Russell was preventing us from being informed of his staff's actions. If I'm right, he'll be honest about his conversation with Dottia." Alex scrolled through the dead man's previous calls. "He called his wife twice before that."

Ric's face tightened, and he grasped his wounded arm.

"Can you take anything over-the-counter for pain?"

"Nope. Ice works. I'll pack it later. I want to talk to Mrs. Dottia and Russell Phillips."

54

ALEX DROVE inside a gated community to where a Spanish colonial with a tiered fountain entry and stone courtyard reminded him of Howard Dottia's success story. The man had stressed hard work and sacrifices to build Phillips Security into the business it was today. Those around him would reap the benefits. Alex vowed that his killer would not be one of those people.

Parked in the massive stone driveway were a Porsche, an Escalade, a Mercedes, a Lamborghini, and two BMWs. Dottia had lived well only to have someone murder him. Maybe a friend.

The agents walked past mature landscaping and flowering bushes to a massive carved double door entry.

"I'm ready to cuff Russell Phillips," Ric said low.

Alex studied his wounded partner. "You're not thinking clearly. Have you considered Russell Phillips could have been set up? Hold off judgment until we question him. Find out what Dottia said."

Ric moaned. "You could be right. I'm reacting to my arm instead of my brain. I'd think modern medicine would have found a pain-killer I could take by now."

"We'll finish here and get back to the hotel. By then we should have heard from Houston. Maybe they've changed their mind about the return home tomorrow. You know how I feel about that."

"Running with our tails between our legs."

"And nothing to show for it but two bodies and few answers." Alex zeroed in on their fact-finding mission. Two possible witnesses were dead, and someone definitely wanted them off the case.

Alex rang the doorbell, and an African American woman in her early thirties responded. With reddened eyes, she introduced herself simply as Howard's daughter.

"We're FBI agents. Russell Phillips is expecting us," Alex said.

She welcomed them into the home. "He'll meet with you in Daddy's study."

"Please, give our condolences to the family," Alex said.

She pointed to Ric's arm. "An agent from the LA office told us what happened. I'm so sorry." They walked down a wide hallway to a stone-and-wood study. It opened onto a flowering courtyard filled with light and color. "I'll tell Uncle Russell you're waiting. Can I bring you anything?"

"No thank you," Ric said. "Who is taking care of you while you're managing everyone else?"

She hesitated. "Only one thing keeps me going, and it's justice. You're FBI. Find out who killed my father. He was the most giving, honorable man who ever walked the earth." She lifted her chin and left them alone.

Alex believed a lot could be told about a man from his office, and the same proved true of Howard Dottia. A leather-bound Bible sat on the right-hand corner of his desk with a worn copy of Oswald Chambers's *My Utmost for His Highest*. Beside it were two photographs—an older woman, who must be his wife, and the young woman they'd just met. On the left side was a framed photo of him and Russell on a ski lift. Behind his desk rose a bookcase crammed with a mix of business, marketing, classics, and biographies of people throughout history who'd contributed to the world's betterment.

"He wasn't a killer or responsible for these crimes," Alex said. "I'm sure of it."

"Howard was my best friend."

The agents turned to find Russell Phillips standing in the doorway. His eyes were red and his face was blotchy.

"You suspect me in Howard's death, but he was closer than a brother. I want his killer found and prosecuted." He drew in a deep breath and appeared to regain his composure. "Agent Price, how's the arm?"

"It'll be fine."

Russell walked to the bookcase where the biographies were shelved. "We shared many a late hour discussing these, from Josephus to Franklin D. Roosevelt. Howard was what we call a prayer warrior. Said he always had my back."

"We're sorry for your loss." Ric's tone held more compassion than prior to entering the home. "I'm sure you understand we need to ask a few questions."

"Of course. When I first heard of the absurdity of crimes that brought you to LA, I told Howard your investigation was a waste of taxpayers' money. Sure you've heard the line before. Now I'm ready to dip into my own funds to arrest who's responsible."

"LA's FBI is outstanding, but Alex and I have a personal stake in this. We understand you spoke to Mr. Dottia before he was killed."

"I might have been the last person who did." His jaw tightened. "It's obvious, don't you agree? Whoever planted the bomb feared Howard had figured him out."

"Would you know why?" Ric said.

"He called me on the way to the parking lot after you had breakfast. Claimed you and Agent LeBlanc challenged his self-respect. He'd spent time thinking through various events and conversations and concluded he knew who initiated the crimes in Houston, and we both knew the man. His words were he'd 'connected the dots.' We were scheduled to talk once he arrived at the office."

"Did he give you a name?"

"Refused, and I was rather insistent."

"Whom do you suspect?" Ric said.

He moistened his lips. "I repeatedly demanded the man's identity. But Howard wouldn't continue the conversation over the phone." He bit down on his lip. "The man who killed Howard and tried to kill you has to be someone I trust. Truth has a way of sucker punching a man. My misjudgment of character got my best friend killed. And I think I know who."

"I understand betrayal," Alex said. A call from Houston's FBI seized his attention—his and Ric's ASAC. Since the trip to the ER, Alex had Ric's cell phone. He excused himself, went into the hallway, and stood beside a huge window that faced a pool and gazebo.

"This is Agent LeBlanc."

"Tried to call you."

"My phone's dead."

"How is Ric holding up?" their assistant special agent in charge said. "He went through knee surgery a few years ago, and I remember he can't tolerate painkillers."

"Fifteen stitches, and he's managing. Rest will help when I can get him to slow down."

"Good luck."

"Will do my best, sir."

"Two things," their ASAC said. "In view of Ric's injuries and the ongoing investigation here, we need you two leaving LA today. We have you booked on a 3:55 flight this afternoon. Be on it. Got a red flag here. Remember Doug Reynold? Hold on while I take this call."

"Sure." Kingpin Doug Reynold had been on the FBI's watch list for the past three years after two police officers were found murdered five miles from his farm. Reynold claimed law enforcement were the gophers of a corrupt government and deserved whatever happened to them. He went by Commander Reynold, and two of his so-called soldiers were arrested for the murders. The men were later released when two women came forward and offered alibis for them.

"Alex, I'm back." The ASAC returned to the line. "Reynold bailed Ace McMann out of jail."

"Are they holed up at Reynold's compound?"

"If so, no one's budged."

The wheels in Alex's head sped forward. "The only use Reynold would have for McMann is access to Whitt and the dog."

"You might be right."

Alex was starting to have mixed feelings about staying in LA. "I'll forward a pic of Reynold to Bekah Howe and Dr. Stacy Broussard."

"Keep me posted if either woman recognizes him. The call I just took was from the CID. Private Wilcox, the man in custody regarding the stolen quadcopter, said the buyer represented an extremist militia group southwest of Houston. He and his partner transported it to Little Rock, Arkansas, where a man paid him, then pulled a gun. Shot at both of them. Killed his partner. Wilcox couldn't give us the shooter's name and claims he doesn't remember what he looked like."

"Reynold's group is in Fresno, same location."

"Connor never mentioned him."

"His killer made sure he didn't say anything more. When you and Ric interviewed him, were there any signs of suicidal tendencies?"

"Not to my knowledge. Connor fought depression according to

his ex-wife, which makes taking Zoloft believable if it wasn't for the arsenic. LA is conducting guard interviews."

"And LA can handle that and Connor's death. The hows and whys are their job. I need you and Ric here today."

"Yes, sir."

"I'll see you and Agent Price at IAH. I want to be briefed on every detail of what you've learned."

"Yes, sir." Alex dropped Ric's phone into his jacket pocket, torn and dirty from the bombing. Answers were here, and he despised the idea of flying home. Ric met him in the hallway.

"Was that Houston?"

"The ASAC." Alex told him what their boss had revealed.

"I regret leaving here with unfinished business," Ric said.

"Right there with you. Whatever Reynold and Ace McMann are up to, the ASAC wants us on it."

"Reynold connected to the quadcopter, the murder, or involved with the disease makes sense." Ric stole a look at his watch. "We need to get back to Russell."

The two men stepped into the library and closed the door. "Thanks for waiting," Alex said.

"Before we were interrupted," Ric said, "you were about to tell us whom you suspected in the murders."

Russell sighed. "The person behind this is insane. Why go to the elaborate scheme for a plot of ground I've never seen? None of my employees would have passed my stringent background checks if anything had been amiss in their records. But maybe I've ignored the warning—"

"Who?"

"My nephew, Jensen." The words were spoken barely above a whisper, as though the sound made the accusation true. "He earned a doctorate in veterinary medicine and completed a postdoctoral degree program in clinical pathology. He focused on research in animal diseases, particularly dogs at a veterinary research facility." Russell paced the room. "He invested years of education and training before embarking upon a future at Phillips Security. I thought my company was what he wanted." He shook his head. "Right now I feel pretty stupid. He started in the basement and worked his way up to the penthouse. Gentlemen, he stands in line to have it all. He worked with Howard Dottia in searching for property in Houston. If the evidence hadn't led to Phillips Security. If Connor hadn't sworn the mastermind was there. If Howard couldn't tell me over the phone. If Jensen didn't have the knowledge, maybe I wouldn't be so sure. Never thought him capable of murder."

Ric's face was etched with the obvious anguish of his wounded arm. "If Jensen is behind these crimes, how do you explain his motivation to infect a dog with a powerful bacterial strain when he's attached to his own animal and is a veterinary pathologist?"

"I don't know how his mind works."

"We need to see his office," Ric said.

"I'm going with you." His drawn features and slumped shoulders revealed his grief. "I should have seen the warning signs. Known this."

"I'll ride with you," Ric said. "In my opinion, your life is in danger too."

Ric had changed his mind about Russell, or was he seeking the man's confidence? "Are you sure you're up to it?" Alex said.

"I can still shoot straight."

After offering condolences to Mrs. Dottia and her daughter, the agents and Russell left for Phillips Security.

After parking, Russell led the way to Jensen Phillips's office. The blinds were closed, and Russell opened them. "Jensen is my deceased brother's only child, and I have no heir. I've always thought of him as my own. What has this stupid old man done?"

Alex raised his hand. "Love is blind. I made a colossal mistake once that almost set a guilty person free. A woman."

He absorbed every detail in the room. A glance at the credenza behind Jensen's desk revealed an eleven-by-fourteen photograph of a man posing with a yellow Lab. Truth gripped him like a vise. The answers were here all along. Smaller individual photos of a collie, a boxer, a cocker spaniel, and a beagle were nearby. Howard Dottia said Jensen was odd . . . the first indication of a depraved mind.

Alex pointed to the photograph of the Lab and the man. "I assume the photo is of your nephew?"

Russell nodded. "With his dog Sophie. She's with Jensen constantly, a 24-7 friend. Brings her to the office. Does magic tricks to amuse her."

Unusual for a huge conglomerate, but Dottia had indicated Sophie was a service dog. "Tell me about his wife, family."

"They have a beautiful seven-year-old girl." He pressed his lips together. "Who am I fooling? I'm making excuses for him. Jensen ignores his stepdaughter and his wife. He's a dog lover. They've been married over four years. I kept hoping he'd grow into being a husband and a father."

"We received the initial autopsy report from Lynx Connor," Alex said. "It revealed traces of human brucellosis, but he died of a lethal dose of an antidepressant coated with arsenic."

"Whoever is behind this doesn't have a problem with murder."

"Or unleashing a deadly disease upon innocent people."

"Do you think Connor and Jensen were working together? Howard shouldn't have died in an effort to expose the truth. I'll not rest until I learn why." Russell eyed him squarely. "And if it's Jensen, God have mercy on his soul." He shook his head. "And mine for not suspecting him."

55

FRIDAY AFTERNOON, while the tantalizing scent of chicken creole filled the house, Stacy searched the extra bedroom for anything the investigators might have missed about Whitt. Nothing surfaced. She lowered herself onto the bed, exhausted and aggravated at her lack of strength. She'd delayed decorating the bedroom until she gained custody, which would allow Whitt to design his own room. Even then she hesitated with the need to sell the house. A tear slipped down her cheek, and she despised that too.

"Hey." Dad sat beside her and wrapped an arm around her. She hadn't noticed him entering the bedroom. "I should have knocked."

"The door's open, and you're sleeping in this room." A gnawing thought settled over her. She'd wakened this morning with her door open. "Tell me you slept through the night instead of taking turns checking on me."

"Can't."

They'd sat vigil for KaraLee all those years ago. She leaned into his strong frame and sobbed. "I thought I was made of better stuff than this, but I'm afraid. I want to break down and cry until there's nothing left inside me."

"*Cher*, God gives us tears to wash our souls free of sadness."

How many times had she heard him say this while growing up? "Since I rode into the clearing, life keeps getting worse. If only Whitt would surface, I could relax a bit. He's bound to be deathly ill. I love him, Dad. I want to provide a home for him, show him everyone isn't like his parents. Teach him how to trust."

"Don't give up. Keep praying."

She drew in his faith. "God and I have been talking nonstop. I trust and believe He has a plan, and I hope it's not like the situation with KaraLee."

"I pray the same for both your sakes. Has Whitt ever talked about going to a special place or mentioned where he'd like to visit?"

"We've talked, but nothing definite. He's extremely intelligent, interested in science and philosophy, not sports and normal kid interests. The wildest conversation was about him learning to play the violin."

"Hunting? Fishing?"

"We've gone fishing, a lake north of town. Nothing remote about it. No place for him to hide."

"Good folks are searching. No one's giving up. I believe things will work out. You've always been my adventuresome child, independent—becoming a vet, moving to the big city by yourself, and now being a foster mother to a boy others wouldn't think of befriending."

"You know my taking care of him started out because of KaraLee. When I realized I truly cared for him, my heart opened to heal. I wanted to see you and Mom, but I feared you'd written me off."

"Never. You're a strong woman, mentally and spiritually." He kissed the top of her head. "And soon to be physically."

"So many things I want to do in my life. Having you and Mom a part of it is a real blessing."

"That works both ways."

Her phone alerted her to an incoming text. She pulled it from her jean pocket.

Sending a pic. Do u recognize him?

She studied the photo of a middle-aged man. Hooded eyes. Grim. **No. Sorry.**

Thanks. Will be home late 2nite.

Arrests?

No. Whitt?

Not yet.

Folks will find him.

I believe so. C u soon.

She placed the phone on the bed. "That was Alex, the FBI agent."

"Can a caring dad ask if he's special?"

Her heart softened. "When I told him Whitt and I came as a package, he didn't run. We don't know each other very well yet."

"I look forward to meeting him."

"He'll be back from LA tonight. He's Cajun too—New Iberia."

Dad laughed. "I like him already."

She did like Alex. Very much. His calls were a highlight to an otherwise-dismal situation while she waited for news about Whitt. How serendipitous when Dexter told her he and Alex were friends.

"We have a big day tomorrow. Can't imagine how many dogs will be at your clinic. Media coverage too. Sure glad you agreed to police protection in case any other idiots crawl out of the swamp."

"Yes, sir. Guess what? Soon as my favorite Cajun restaurant heard about what was going on, they offered to cater lunch."

"Don't tell your mother."

She smiled. "I wouldn't dare."

"Stacy," Mom called from down the hall. "Can you come here a minute?"

She and her dad moved to the other room, where Mom was watching the news on TV. "What do you need?" Stacy said.

Mom swallowed hard. "Just heard that two Houston FBI special agents on assignment in LA narrowly escaped death when attempting to rescue an injured man from a car bombing. One escaped injury and the other required stitches."

"Has to be Alex and Ric. I just texted with him, and he didn't say a word." She picked up her cell phone and typed.

R u ok? Saw the news.

He immediately responded. **I'm ok. Ric has stitches. He's ok.**

When would this be over?

Early Friday evening, Whitt reached for the water canteen and shook the last few droplets into his mouth. Empty, and the body required water to survive. How long until everything shut down? He barely held on to life, and darkness surrounded him inside and out. Xena had returned while Whitt slept. Now she lay with her head on his belly, and the weight hurt. But she was comforting him the only way she knew, like she'd done for Todd Howe.

Dying used to have a frightening sound to it. But the slow walk into whatever the future held wasn't so bad. Sometimes he dozed off only to waken weaker than before. At the rate his body dwindled to shutdown mode, he'd be gone by morning. Miss Stacy had wanted him to grasp the power of God, but he'd clutched restraint like an anchor. He believed a person needed to show he or she was worth eternity. Demonstrate to God he'd taken the brains given to him and made a dent in the depravity of mankind. Now as his body relinquished to its destiny, he wanted to think he'd be good enough. Doubts plagued him. If God took into consideration that Whitt had abandoned Stacy in the hospital, the outcome looked . . . deplorable.

How could he have left her alone? Such a coward.

Worthless.

His parents were such losers. Why hadn't they aborted him? Or did the idea of inflicting physical and mental anguish have a better ring? How many times had the parents insisted he owed them? Right. The only thing they'd taught him was manipulating techniques, and Whitt had sworn off using those tactics.

Or had he? His mind refused to stop its random nonsense.

Selfishness pelted him like rock-size hail. He'd walked out on the only person who'd ever shown him kindness. Teachers had encouraged him, but even they could have ulterior motives. When he performed in class, it offered irrefutable proof their school ranked with the elite school districts.

You're cynical, Whitt. Dying and disillusioned in a world where the strong stepped on the weak. None of the things he wanted to accomplish would happen.

If he could walk out of these woods, he'd turn himself in and apologize to Miss Stacy.

I can conduct myself like a man. Perform one honorable deed for the woman who could have been my mother. Impress God with determination and valor.

The slight movement caused more anguish than he'd imagined. He cried out, startling Xena. But he must try, get to the water supply and purify it with the pills in his backpack. The dog rose onto her haunches, her tender brown eyes urging him to attempt the impossible. He couldn't be angry with the dog when it wasn't her fault she'd been injected with a deadly disease.

God, please help me. I don't want to die without telling Miss Stacy I'm sorry.

56

ON THE FLIGHT TO HOUSTON, Alex's head hurt and his stomach curdled. "Are you feeling okay?" he said to Ric.

"Arm hurts when I breathe."

"What about the rest of you?"

Ric eyed him. "Are you showing signs of brucellosis? Frankly, you look flushed."

"Not sure. Got a huge headache and upset stomach."

"Considering what we've been through, you're entitled. But for the sake of your health, get it checked out ASAP when we arrive in Houston."

"Might have been the burrito at the airport."

"Told you to stick to a burger. You were exposed to Xena more than once."

"We both were." Alex hoped his stomachache was a repercussion from too many jalapeños. "The ASAC won't want to be friendly with a suspicion of brucellosis."

Ric laughed. "Shouldn't have insisted we return home."

In Houston, Alex and Ric were whisked off to the FBI's med clinic near their office. Both had blood drawn. Briefing their ASAC was done via phone. Fortunately the blood results would be available around four in the morning. The agents were ordered to spend the night at the clinic in case they tested positive. Alex's fever registered 102 degrees, and Ric's hovered at 98.9. A combination of antibiotics to stop the spike of fever was administered.

He texted Stacy but avoided the subject of his health.

Shortly before 10 p.m., Alex paced the floor between their clinic beds. Jensen Phillips had seemingly vanished. "If we're delayed any longer than waiting on our blood test results, I might need to check into a mental hospital."

"The good thing is we have all night to piece this together."

"You should try to sleep."

Ric huffed. "Trust me, I can't rest with the steady throb in my arm. You talk and pace, and I'll take one-handed notes." He pulled out his phone. "Ready. Start from the top."

"On a Saturday morning, Stacy is conducting her normal routine of patrolling the outer perimeter of the airport and finds Todd Howe's body, a wounded Lab, and a stolen military-grade quadcopter. In the drone investigation, we look at enlisted men with connections to Fort Benning, where the quadcopter was stolen, which leads us to Doug Reynold and his military antigovernment group.

"Lynx Connor, posing as a rep for an investment firm, steps into the picture and persuades property owners in Stacy's subdivision to sell out. We learn the investment firm is a shell company that leads back to Russell Phillips. Connor phones Bekah Howe and states her husband deserved to die. We go after him. We also discover Howe had a condo and an offshore account in Andorra with over a half million dollars. Was that an investment or a refuge if caught in a crime? Or was he planning to leave his family?

"Stacy is hospitalized. Medical testing indicates she has human brucellosis. The Lab found at the crime site is infected with a genetically engineered disease that infects dogs and people. Whitt McMann runs off and takes the infected Lab because he's afraid of social services sticking him in a foster home. No one can find him, and he tested positive for the disease.

"Connor is picked up in LA. He claims Russell Phillips is the mastermind of the human brucellosis to buy out the subdivision. We fly to LA to talk to Connor and Phillips. Now Connor's been murdered—because someone smuggled poisoned Zoloft into his cell. Obviously someone was afraid he'd talk. Then Howard Dottia phones Russell and tells him he knows who's behind the series of crimes. Unfortunately he's killed in a bombing. All roads lead to Jensen Phillips, but he's conveniently missing. We also learn Jensen has the background to develop the bacterial strain.

"Houston calls us home from LA because Doug Reynold bailed Ace McMann out of jail. McMann is a drunk. Not soldier material, so the only reason Reynold's wasting time with him is McMann has to know where Whitt and Xena are hiding. I hope the boy is still alive." Alex stopped pacing, his body aching with exhaustion. Must be the fever. "What did I miss?"

"That's remarkable for a guy running a fever."

Alex chuckled. "Imagine my output at 98.6. Seriously, the concrete findings are Xena was injected with brucellosis to start an epidemic. Why would Jensen use dogs to accomplish his purpose when he prefers them to humans?"

"If we're freed in the morning, we can dive into what Doug Reynold is up to."

Promptly at 4:05 a.m., a nurse entered the agents' room with the results of their blood work.

"Agent Price, you tested negatively for brucellosis," said the nurse, a petite Vietnamese woman. "Agent LeBlanc, your test is positive. We'd like to keep you until your fever breaks. The combination of antibiotics has reduced it some, but not to our satisfaction. There's—"

"No cure. Take it now."

Alex's temp hovered around 100. What else could go wrong on this case? "When my fever is 99.5, I'm out of here."

"That's not our recommendation," the nurse said.

Irritation rose in defiance like a boil on his behind. "I appreciate your professional opinion. I feel fine."

"Wonderful. Then I suggest you sleep."

"Are you saying my partner is free to go, but I have to hang around?"

The nurse smiled. "Exactly."

Alex fumed. "Only a few hours."

"Stay put." Ric gathered up his belongings from the past few days in LA. "Don't let your pride get in the way."

Logical conclusion, but he had better things to do.

Saturday morning, Stacy opened her eyes to a better attitude than she'd experienced for the past two weeks. She listened to the whirr of grinding coffee beans and pretended it was Whitt instead of Mom. Last night they'd talked in her room, Dad seated on one side of the bed and Mom on the other until she fell asleep. Which didn't take long. But what she remembered was rich and tender. They'd laughed and cried about KaraLee, and the time seemed to heal the lost years.

The coffee grinding stopped, and her mind swept to Whitt again.

Where are you? Are you fighting the effects of the disease?

He seldom spoke of good times with his parents. Ace wasn't such a bad person when he didn't have alcohol in his system. His mother had destroyed any chances of nurturing with her addiction to drugs and other activities. Whitt had reported one trip to the beach and zoo and another to San Antonio. Nothing more Whitt could recall. She texted the information to Alex, who'd know where to forward it. Volunteers to aid in helping pet owners get their dogs tested for brucellosis and distribute facts about the disease planned to arrive at the clinic by 8:00 this morning. She'd open the doors at 8:30.

She glanced at the clock: 6:45. Taking a deep breath, she made her way down the hallway to the kitchen and pretended Whitt was there with Mom and Dad.

"Morning, *cher*." Dad's greeting spread from one ear to the other. "Are you ready for a big day?"

"I'm looking forward to it with my wonderful dad."

"Hungry?" Mom tilted her head. "Grits and scrambled eggs?"

"I love being spoiled." Nobody made grits and scrambled eggs like Mom . . . or Whitt.

Alex had texted last night that he was back in town. She wanted to call, but restraint won out. She'd not interfere with his job.

At 7:35 her cell phone rang with Alex's name shining like a banner on the screen. What a great diversion when her mind searching for Whitt had produced nothing but despair.

"Thanks for sending the info about Whitt. I passed it on."

"Appreciate it. I assume you've been racing since arriving in Houston."

"Not really. I just got my freedom papers."

"Been in meetings?"

"No, quarantined. When Ric and I arrived from LA, we were tested for brucellosis. Ric was the lucky one. But I'm now fever free."

Misery assaulted her. "I'm really sorry."

"I'm fine. Shouldn't have mentioned it. Any word on Whitt?"

"No. I've racked my brain thinking about where he could have gone."

"Has a family member or neighbor ever taken interest in him?"

"The only person was his grandfather, and he died."

"Did they spend time together?"

"He took him fishing, but it was in a public place."

"Where?"

She sighed. "A stocked lake in Montgomery County."

"Anything more specific?"

"Alex, the only person who could give you details would be his dad."

Silence met her ears. "What are you thinking?"

"My agenda for the day."

"What?"

"Adding up what we know. Remember Doug Reynold, the leader of a military antigovernment group in the area? He bailed Ace out of jail. The FBI's watching them, but nothing suspicious. We think Reynold's using Ace to find Whitt and Xena. His chances of figuring out Whitt's location increase with Ace's help. In the wrong hands, Xena could infect hundreds of people."

"Bioterrorism," she said. "Stronger infections and viruses made in laboratories. The outcome would be devastating."

"From your experience, how often have you seen the canine version in your clinic?"

"Rare, and never transmitted to a human."

"Stacy, I need to go."

"I understand. If you find Ace, black both his eyes for me." She dropped her phone into her lab coat, feeling relief that Alex and Ric were back in Houston working the case.

57

ALEX NEVER LIKED TO LOSE. The instinct to succeed gut-punched him every time he thought about the killings and those who'd died from the infection. He wanted to talk to Doug Reynold and walk his property, search every square inch for illegal activities. Reynold had a constitutional right to spout his antigovernment beliefs and to hold military maneuvers on his property. Online chatter indicated they were planning an operation to take down those in power, but did those plans include Todd Howe's murder and a quadcopter?

Alex and Ric labored over paperwork and reviewed backgrounds until nearly noon, when a judge signed a search warrant for Reynold's property based on suspicion of conspiracy—specifically illegal weapons, ammunition, and drones with deadly payloads. Local law enforcement readied for backup.

Ric drove his silver Camaro, although he complained about Reynold and his militia filling it with bullet holes. Three additional vehicles contained agents and police officers. At the entrance to Reynold's property, No Trespassing signs and a chained-lock gate stopped the vehicles. "Call him. He's crazy enough to blow our heads off for tampering with his lock."

Alex read a new sign: *Trespassers' bodies will be shown on YouTube.*

He'd dealt with Reynold in January when a former member of the militia group came forward. A search warrant and a team of agents hadn't discovered the stockpile of weapons and ammo the man stated was hidden there. He was involved in a fatal car accident shortly after the FBI search. Law enforcement officials were convinced the arsenal existed.

Alex exited the passenger's side and pressed in the phone number listed on the gate. "This is FBI Special Agent Alex LeBlanc. I'm at your gate with a search warrant."

"For what?" the man said.

"We have reason to believe you have illegal weapons and ammo on your property."

Reynold laughed, a raspy smoker's sound followed by a cough. "Tried that a few months back, remember? I'm a busy man. No time for government interference in my business."

"Take the time. Either remove the chain or we will, and I'm not alone."

"Oh, I see you. Smile, Agent LeBlanc."

Alex had previously seen the security camera mounted on a pole. "I'm running out of patience."

"Invading private property violates my rights."

"You have ten minutes."

While they waited, agents reported pickup trucks making a fast exodus out the rear of the property. The vehicles were stopped and the drivers and passengers detained for questioning. Ace McMann was not among them.

Eight minutes later, Reynold screeched his rusty pickup to a stop on the opposite side of the gate. Dust swirled behind and above the truck, obviously meant to demonstrate an intimidating force. His six-foot-four lean, muscular frame moved toward the gate as though he were in command of a battalion of fighting men. Which he claimed to be. Releasing a ring of keys from his belt, he unlocked it and spit through the gate's metal railings, the wad landing beside Alex's shoe. Reynold nodded before speeding in reverse along the dirt road to his home.

Alex pushed open the gate and motioned the procession on. The temps were nearing the high nineties, and sweat dripped down the sides of his face. The extra few minutes had given Reynold time to ensure his stash was secure . . . But Alex believed the man always kept his weapons and ammo concealed.

Reynold's two-story stone-and-concrete house resembled a small fortress, complete with iron-barred windows. It had been built about ten years ago when the militia group first started meeting. Reynold had three wives under his belt and hadn't attempted a fourth. Four kids with their mothers, and he didn't pay child support. Rumor was he'd threatened to kill his ex-wives if they took him to court. His tough-guy facade kept those who didn't share his antigovernment beliefs at a distance, but the man had a master's in economics and six years in the Army. Intelligent and belligerent, not a pleasant combo.

Alex walked up the concrete steps to the porch. He'd bet his next paycheck that beneath his feet was concealed what would send Reynold to prison, but as of yet, the FBI hadn't detected an entrance.

Reynold opened the steel front door before Alex knocked. "Let's see what you got." He closed the door behind him. "Agent LeBlanc, you don't give up, do ya?"

"No reason to when a man's hiding what's illegal." Alex handed him the warrant and took in the surroundings. The area looked the same—a shed to the left held a leather and saddle shop, legitimate with its own website and catalog. No weapons in sight. Over three dozen quarter horses and just as many Angus grazed in a pasture behind the house. In the distance, a small herd of Jersey cows supplied milk and butter, or so the website claimed. A creek wove through the property, and a stocked pond kept the occupants in fish. Reynold, and whoever else lived there, grew their own food right down to grain for bread. This afternoon, no one appeared to be working the grounds—they'd taken off.

Reynold returned the warrant. "What's this about?"

"A man at Fort Benning claims he and a partner sold a quad-copter to a military group in this area. The transaction took place in Little Rock. The partner ended up dead. You're the only man who fits the description."

"But you have no name or proof." He sneered.

"The man at Fort Benning has agreed to talk." Which he hadn't, but Reynold didn't know that. "Two men are dead with connections to the device."

"Two dead? How sad the quadcopter didn't inflict more damage."

Alex studied him . . . waiting. Reynold carried a weapon behind his back and probably a knife in his boot. "Bet you'd throw a party."

"All the beer you'd want."

"Why did you pay Ace McMann's bail?"

"My good deed for the week," Reynold said. "Is he dead too?"

"You tell us. What's your interest in him?"

"None. Friend of a friend. That's all."

"We'd like to talk to him," Alex said.

"He's not here. Have no idea where he hightailed to. Look for him all you want." He nodded beyond his front porch. "My buildings are locked. You need me to conduct a tour." Contempt poured over his words.

"Why not hand over the keys and save yourself the trouble? Time's precious for a busy man."

"Have you rob me or plant evidence? Nah, you Feds are all the same. Push your weight around and take respectable citizens for idiots."

Not exactly. No doubt he'd called his lawyer. "We'll be sure to honor your constitutional rights."

"I'll be sure to protect 'em."

Hours later when darkness settled around the property, Alex and Ric closed their car doors and left the area with the other agents and police officers. A surveillance team maintained vigilant watch.

Behind every padlock at the property were items necessary for a working ranch or leather supplies for Reynold's business. Inside the house, a huge refrigeration and freezer unit powered by a generator contained wild game, catfish, and perishables. A large pantry held canned goods, bags of beans and rice, a water purifier, and enough bottled water to last a few years. Agents searched for safe rooms inside the home and the underground storage units outside. Pics were taken from every angle.

Various sizes of boot prints indicated recent activity, but there wasn't even a spent casing or a wrapper from their chew. None of the men leaving through the rear had been armed. Nothing suspicious warranted more of the agents' time today.

"I'm hot and frustrated," Alex said to Ric on the way back to Houston. "One of Reynold's men testified to him storing illegal weapons, bombs, and ammo in some kind of a stronghold. He didn't mention any drones."

"That man got his brakes cut," Ric said. "Reynold has a solid operation. His men are well-trained and keep their mouths shut. Backgrounds state every one of them have served in some branch of the military. All we can do is keep constant surveillance until we nail him."

Alex opened a bottle of warm water from the cup holder. "On the surface, neither Todd Howe nor Lynx Connor are connected to Reynold or any of his known men. We already have him and his officers under surveillance. We'll compare dates and times along with the enlisted men from Fort Benning who might be connected to either man." He paused, remembering . . . "Reynold spouts white supremacy. His principles negate doing business with a Jew, but he wouldn't have a problem killing him. Or anyone, for that matter."

58

LONG AFTER Alex would have, should have, crawled into bed, he and Ric stopped in at the office and learned Russell Phillips had scheduled a late-night interview with the LA office.

Alex logged on to his computer. "Russell will be there in about fifteen minutes. I want to know what's going on."

Ric pulled a chair to Alex's desk with his uninjured arm. "I'm in. The question is did Jensen contact him, or did he have some revelation?"

"I'll take whatever we can get." Alex refused to rest until the mastermind of this case was arrested, but weariness weighed on him. The antibiotics kept the fever down, but the disease zapped his energy, and both sides of his head hammered.

Once the connection was made, they observed a live video stream. The same agents who'd interviewed Connor and Russell in the past handled this one too.

"Mr. Phillips, Special Agents LeBlanc and Price are present in

Houston. They may have questions as we proceed. We understand you have critical information about your nephew, Jensen Phillips," the male agent said.

The professional businessman vanished, and in his wake was a man who seemed to carry far too much weight. "I believe so. Agents, I don't know where Jensen is hiding. What I have to say comes from my association with Jensen. Since spending time with Special Agents LeBlanc and Price from Houston, I've focused on my only living heir and his brilliance. I'm guilty of ignoring the issues in his life, and I'm as guilty as the killer of so many innocent people." He took a deep breath. "I have concluded his preoccupation with dogs and his desire to fulfill his own goals have resulted in the deaths of too many people. One of the victims was my lifelong friend."

"Can you elaborate?" the agent said. "We see in your nephew's background that he has his doctorate in veterinary medicine and completed a postdoctoral degree program in clinical pathology."

Russell nodded. "His passion is dogs and their health. When he was a boy, he had a Lab. The animal was diagnosed with a disease. I don't recall which one. His father, my brother, refused to invest in antibiotics and the precautions needed to continue keeping the dog alive. He had the animal put to sleep. In my opinion, Jensen never got over it. From then on, he was determined to be a veterinarian and focus on canine research. Although his love for dogs seems counterintuitive to his developing a genetically engineered disease, I can see how he could possess the knowledge to do so."

"If you were making an educated guess, what would you say motivated him?"

"If I'd been charged and evidence produced to find me guilty, Phillips Security would have reverted to Jensen's control. He'd have millions of dollars to use for canine research." Russell seemed to age during the conversation. "I understand this may sound ludicrous to you, but I've spent hours thinking through his behavior patterns. Sophie, his Lab, does not leave his sight. He bred her once and had to take a leave of absence from work when her time came to deliver the pup. He was devastated for weeks about the pain she'd experienced and vowed never to breed her again. I learned from his wife that they haven't consummated their marriage. The dog sleeps in a special bed in their room. It's as though he considers himself a guardian for dogs."

Alex zeroed in on the last statement and connected with LA. "Russell, is it feasible Jensen would have developed an antidote?"

He stared into the face of the agent. "I think Alex has made a good point. If Jensen did develop this thing, I want to believe he'd also develop a cure."

"Back to what you said previously," Ric said. "What happened to Sophie's puppy?"

"Jensen's wife said it was a female and given as a gift to someone. She doesn't know the recipient."

"Mr. Phillips, is there anything else you'd like to tell us?" the agent said.

"Not at this time." Russell looked into the camera. "Alex, Ric, whatever I learn, you and the agents here in LA will be the first to know."

The interview ended and Alex turned to Ric. "Xena has to be the missing dog."

"What are the odds Lynx Connor received Sophie's female pup?" Ric picked up his phone. "I'm calling his ex-wife now."

"In theory, Jensen didn't have the patience to wait until his uncle handed over the business. His desire to work with dogs could have motivated his plans."

Ric held up a finger. "Mrs. Connor, this is Special Agent Ric Price of FBI Houston. In our investigation about what happened to your husband, I have a question. Did your husband have a yellow Lab?" Ric nodded at Alex. "Do you have the dog?" A moment later. "Male or female? I see. Thank you for your time." He set his cell on Alex's desk. "Connor was given a female Lab puppy a couple of years ago. When he moved out of the house, he took the dog with him. She has no idea what happened to the animal. Sweet tempered."

"Sophie must not have the disease, but Xena was injected," Alex said. "Would Jensen have vials of the infection or maybe even a serum with him? With airports around the country on alert and his photo on every media's report list, what are we missing?"

Ric clutched his injured arm. "Disguises would give him a head start."

Alex's mind darted in and out of scenarios. "He's killed to protect himself, which makes anyone who gets in his way a threat."

Alex contacted Taylor Freeman at Hooks Airport. If Howe and Connor had used a private plane to cover their covert operations, Jensen Phillips might do the same. He sent the young woman Jensen's photograph with instructions to call or text if he showed up.

Alex stretched out on the floor of his cubicle. A few hours' sleep, and he'd shower at the office and keep working. Ric had concluded the same thing. So much happening on this case that neither of them wanted to return home. If Whitt wasn't found soon, he'd die. His loser dad might be the only way to find him. But from all indications, Whitt wouldn't seek out his dad.

This all began with the murder of Todd Howe and tracking down who'd stolen the quadcopter.

The water hoax and Lynx Connor.

Russell Phillips.

Jensen Phillips.

Doug Reynold.

A text came in from the surveillance team keeping vigil on Reynold's compound. Ace McMann had been spotted exiting a barn. If Ace had been hidden away there, were Whitt and Xena there too? While Alex debated taking a drive back to the compound, Ric approached his cubicle.

"Can't sleep?" Alex said.

A nod. "How did we miss where McMann was hiding?"

"Reynold's smart. He built every structure on that property. Who and what else is stashed away?" Alex weighed his words. "Up to driving to the compound?"

"I'm ready. You drive this time, so hold on while I retrieve my night goggles from my trunk."

Once at the scene, a man on the surveillance team updated Alex and Ric. "We have Doug Reynold and Ace McMann together." He handed the binoculars to Alex. "They're leaving the house through the front door and walking toward a green pickup."

Alex focused on Whitt's dad. Under the inky night sky, Ace climbed into a dark-green pickup on the passenger side. Reynold sped out the rear of the property. Alex handed the binoculars to Ric.

"I'm against stopping them." Ric viewed the truck. "Let's see where they're going."

Alex drove his Jeep with Ric beside him and tailed the truck, staying far enough behind, yet having the FBI and law enforcement in close proximity. Reynold drove north on I-45.

Alex engaged his hands-free device and phoned a sleeping Stacy. "For your ears only. We're following Doug Reynold and Ace McMann north on I-45. Have no idea where this is leading, but I'll keep you posted."

An hour and thirty minutes later, the truck swung onto a remote road in Montgomery County leading into a wooded area. Alex held back until he sensed it was clear to continue. On the left side of the road, the truck sat deserted. Backup teams slid into place.

He phoned Stacy again. "Reynold and McMann disappeared into the woods."

"Where?"

He hesitated to tell her, but if Whitt was found, she'd want to be here. He gave her the location.

"I'm on my way. I'll have Dad drive. I'm calling Dexter. If these two lead us to Whitt and Xena, he'll want Xena."

"This could be nothing, Stacy."

"I have to believe."

Alex ended the call, praying tonight brought Whitt back to Stacy—alive.

59

VOICES MET WHITT'S EARS, and he tried to open his eyes. Was he hallucinating? Had he been found? Awareness filled him with quiet joy. Maybe he'd live, have a second chance to ask Miss Stacy to forgive him. He wanted to believe she'd not despise him for abandoning her. A light shone on him, but he couldn't muster the strength to acknowledge it.

"Over here, Commander," the man said. "Told you I figured out where he'd gone."

Why did the voice sound like his incorrigible father?

"Are you sure, Ace? Black as pitch out here."

Hell could not be worse than this.

"I'm lookin' at him," Dad said. "And the dog's here."

"Best put on a mask. Cash time," the man said.

A second light blinded Whitt. He smelled his dad bending over him, the familiar blend of weed and alcohol oozing from the pores of his skin.

"My boy looks bad."

"He's dying. What do you expect?"

"He's small for his age. Not sure I can leave him alone."

"We came for the dog. Our weapon for power. We'll load the virus into a drone sprayer and show the world we're in control. As long as we keep wearing these masks, we won't get sick." A snap indicated the man had attached a leash to Xena's collar. "Leave the kid. He'll be dead before the night's over anyway."

"He'll die alone in these woods."

"Look, you said you wanted to be one of my soldiers. Fight for our rights and destroy our corrupt government. Live free. That's why I sprang you. As commander, I'm ready to promote you to captain."

"Sounds good."

"Then what's stopping you?"

"Not sure, Commander. I can't leave 'im."

"Either you walk out of here with me to join my men, or you're a coward. My army has only brave men willing to sacrifice for freedom."

Whitt refused to utter a sound. Dad made a choice about him years ago. No reason he'd change his mind.

"Reynold, you came after me when you learned my boy had the dog. I ain't much, but only sorry scum walks away from his own flesh wasting away."

"Suit yourself. When me and my men show this country who's boss, you'll be doing what I tell you whether you like it or not."

The man kicked dirt on Whitt. Whitt opened his eyes through excruciating pain.

I'm not dead yet.

Reynold stomped off with Xena, leaving a trail of curses in his wake. Whitt hoped the dog took a chunk out of his rear.

Dad touched his forehead. So it took dying for his father to show he was human. Dad cursed. Nothing unusual. He slipped his hands under Whitt's body, bringing a scream to his lips. Dad withdrew his arms and sobbed.

"This is my fault. I should have signed papers for Miss Stacy to raise you. Now you hurt too bad for me to get help. I'm sorry. I really am."

"Try again," Whitt whispered. "I won't cry."

"You're awful hot."

"Please." Whitt drew in a breath and braced himself. Dad lifted him into his arms, and a thousand needles pierced his body.

"The law needs your dog too, but I failed there. They have medicines to break the fever, if it's not too late."

He wanted to live, even in a foster home. If medicine had been developed, then Miss Stacy would be fine. Every step Dad took jarred Whitt's insides. At times he believed his bones would break. Raw agony tortured him, sending him in and out of consciousness. Wherever they were going took so long.

Angry voices in the distance disturbed him. The words morphed together, and he caught only a snippet here and there.

"Doug Reynold, drop your gun. You're under arrest."

"Make sure the dog's in the cage."

"Someone else is coming."

"I have Whitt," Dad called out. "He's in bad shape."

"Paramedics, we have the boy."

Dad laid him on what must be a stretcher. Someone took his vitals while another prepared his arm to start an IV. For once, he didn't mind the needle.

"Whitt!"

Was that Miss Stacy? But he was too weak to move his eyes and drifted into blackness.

Stacy rushed to Whitt's side, where he lay still, unable to protest the IV being slid into his vein. She took his limp hand, her tears dripping onto his fingers. His fever-ravaged body shook her. Sobbing met her ears, and she faced Ace, the big man caught up in uncontrollable weeping.

"I'm sorry, Whitt," he said.

"But you found him." She despised the man, yet she pitied him. "No one else could. Thank you."

"Is he dead?" Ace said.

"No, sir." The paramedic worked without looking up. "He's unconscious."

She focused on her dear boy while an agent handcuffed Ace and led him away. Alex had cuffed Doug Reynold earlier, and now Alex joined her with Dad. Her heroes. Ric and Dexter made their way to Whitt's stretcher, where he was being loaded into an ambulance. The road swarmed with vehicles belonging to other agents and Montgomery County police.

"Can I accompany him?" she said.

"Are you his mother?"

"No."

The man offered a grim smile. "I'm sorry. We'll be taking him to Tomball hospital."

She wished she'd lied. Staring into Whitt's face, she prayed for him to survive, to respond to the antibiotics. She bent to his face and kissed his cheek. "I love you," she whispered and released his hand. A moment later, the door to the ambulance slammed shut.

"I'll drive you," Alex said.

"What about Reynold?"

"I want to get you settled, then Ric and I'll interview him."

She glanced at Dad and he nodded. "Go. I'm sure he's had more experience driving at breakneck speeds and weaving in and out of traffic than I have. I'll phone your mother and have her take a taxi to meet us."

"I'll ride with your dad," Ric said.

Stacy hurried with Alex to his Jeep. Whitt's face stayed fixed in her mind . . . the gray shadow of death. "How long until we know if he'll be okay?"

"I have no idea since he's so sick." He started the Jeep and headed toward FM 149 south leading to Tomball Regional Medical Center.

"I was relatively cognizant, and he's unconscious."

"All we can do is hold on tightly to the rope of prayer." He offered a smile. "One of my mother's sayings."

"Sounds like a fine woman."

"She died when I was in college."

"I'm so sorry. Is your dad living?"

"They were both killed in a car accident. Dexter and Eva Rayken were already friends, but then they became my family."

"Alex, I'm really glad they were there for you. He told me about his daughter, Stacy."

"Their only child, except for me."

"In such a short time, I've grown fond of him, and I'm sure his wife is just as lovely."

"Through their prayers, I healed and can now say I'm a Christian."

A comfortable silence fell between them, as though they'd known each other for years.

"Alex, is Doug Reynold the man responsible for all the crimes?"

"Unlikely, but he might have critical evidence to plea-bargain. Doubt if McMann has been privy to anything."

"Good thing the men in custody aren't facing me," Stacy said. "But you can be scary."

He chuckled. "Glad to know I'm intimidating."

She swallowed the acid rising in her throat. "I'm afraid."

"Me too. But I'm planning on Starbucks for three."

His comment lifted her spirits.

In the emergency room, Stacy and Alex stepped into Whitt's curtained area. IVs pumped nourishing fluids and a combination of antibiotics into his body.

"I wish he'd open his eyes," she said.

Alex's phone alerted him to a message, and he read the information.

"Do you need to go?" she said.

"Yes. Text me when he wakes or when the doctor sees him. Or both."

That was optimistic. "I will."

He kissed her cheek, a small gesture that indicated his caring. "Don't lose hope. Lean on those who care."

"Okay." She watched him leave, then stared into her boy's face. "Fight, Whitt."

60

DURING THE EARLY HOURS of the morning, Alex and Ric sat across from Ace McMann at an FBI interview table. According to him, he hadn't seen or heard anything to implicate Reynold in any of the crimes.

"Reynold told me I had the makings of a soldier, and he could use me. The best way to help their cause was for me to lead them to Whitt and the dog." McMann wrung his shaking hands. He was in need of a drink. "What was I thinking? I could have helped the cops find Whitt when they asked." He peered up with reddened eyes. "Is my boy gonna live?"

"We don't know yet. Some victims responded to treatment within hours." Alex bore his stare into Ace. "But the survivors were given the antibiotics in the early stages. What more can you tell us?"

"The one thing I know is Reynold wanted to use the dog's blood to make a virus that a drone could spray into large populated areas."

"How did you feel about his plan?"

Ace shrugged. "He was going to make me a real soldier. Somebody important."

Alex and Ric left Ace with police officers and observed Doug Reynold through a one-way window. He wore a smirk with his arms wrapped around his chest. A tattoo of an exploding cannon burst across a bulging right arm.

Alex opened the door and greeted him. "Mr. Reynold, we just finished talking to Ace McMann, and he tells me you wanted the infected dog for a special project, specifically spraying the disease into large communities."

"You believe a drunk?"

"How's that working for you since you're sitting here with us?"

Reynold cursed. "What do you want from me?"

"Yesterday evening you lied to federal agents about the location of Ace McMann."

"Have no idea how he ended up on my land."

"Really? You two looked real cozy when you left together. For your information, McMann signed an affidavit confirming your plans for the diseased dog."

Reynold sneered. "That'll get thrown out of court, given his record. I mean, he was leaving his kid to die in the woods."

"He carried him out."

"Whatever. He'd never watched anyone die before, thought it would be fun."

"Did you murder Todd Howe?"

"No."

"Do you know who killed him?"

"I never met the man."

At least he hadn't lawyered up. "At this point, you're facing charges of domestic terrorism. I suggest you take up knitting because you're going to have a lot of free time."

Reynold stared into an empty corner. "You have nothing on me but trying to help a man find his son."

"What can you tell us about a stolen military-grade quadcopter?"

A muscle twitched beneath Reynold's eye. "I'm ready to make a deal. But first I want my lawyer present."

"Sure, we'll get your lawyer. One of your rights under our Constitution, the document you claim to despise."

Arrogance seeped from the pores of his skin. "Not a word more."

Alex and Ric stood, but the big man interrupted. "Look, I know what happened to Howe. When my attorney's present, I'll tell you."

Stacy sat beside Whitt's hospital bed and watched his chest slowly rise and fall. The only sound came from the low hum of nurses' voices outside the room and the steady beep of monitors. *God, please take care of him.*

Dad and Mom kept vigil and prayed with her as if he were their own. Whitt's body had taken a beating with the prolonged fever—104.2 when he arrived at the hospital. Monitors kept track of his vitals. IVs transported life into his body.

Whitt. Let me see your eyes.

Mom eased up from her chair. "Cafeteria food is horrible, but I'll pick us up something for dinner. Maybe they have different cooks on the weekend. Any requests?"

When Stacy and her dad ordered only coffee, she left the room.

A perky nurse flitted into the room and took Whitt's temperature. "Good," she said. "His fever is down to 102.5." She replaced an IV bag and checked his pulse.

"When will he wake up?"

The nurse's up mood took a nosedive. "I'm sorry—there's no way to predict that. He's a sick boy. Has your doctor been in today?"

"Yes." Was this a nice way of telling her Whitt might not survive?

The nurse glanced at Whitt's chart. "I suggest talking to Dr. Maberry." She smiled and left the room.

"Hey, little girl." Dad's voice broke the silence. "Dexter tells me researchers are working night and day on a serum."

"The process could take months." She massaged her neck while watching Whitt's face.

He pulled a chair to her side. "Talk to me. About anything. Whitt. The clinic. Alex."

She laid her head on his shoulder. "I'm dying on the inside, a slow bleed."

"Losing someone we love is the hardest test of our faith."

KaraLee. Of course he understood how she felt. "I can't let it stop me from feeling."

"Because if you do, your heart will dry up."

"Is that what happened to you?"

"Yep. Took a long time for me to allow God back in, and once I did, I found peace."

She snuggled close to him while holding Whitt's hand. "Me too. I have no regrets with Whitt. I healed from KaraLee's death through him. But if I lose him, I'm not sure how I'll respond to life."

He squeezed her shoulders. "Promise me you won't abandon God."

Her mind swept over the years of heartache before she inched back to the God who'd never let her go. The misery of living life alone preyed on her heart. "I promise," she whispered.

"That's my girl. Now, we're going to talk about you. *Cher*, I like Alex. He shows his caring."

"We're barely friends."

"That's how me and your mother got started."

"I want a threesome, a family."

"So do I, sweet girl. So do I."

61

ALEX LEANED BACK in his chair and observed Doug Reynold. He'd lawyered up, and now his attorney sat before him and Ric. Once Private Wilcox learned Reynold was in custody, he named him as the buyer of the quadcopter and the man who'd shot and killed his partner. The FBI had evidence that Reynold had contracted for the stolen quadcopter, but additional charges gave him more years behind bars than Reynold had left. But more questions remained: Who'd killed Todd Howe and why?

"Mr. Reynold," Alex began, "you stated during our last conversation that you knew what happened to Todd Howe, resulting in his death."

"Correct. I saw him shot."

"You stood in the clearing and observed the shooting?"

"No." Reynolds rubbed his face.

"Then how did you view it?"

"Computer. At my ranch."

"I don't understand." But he did. Alex wanted him to confess to his crime.

His brows narrowed. "I was monitoring the quadcopter, just to see how it would operate."

"The one stolen from Fort Benning."

"The quadcopter was given to me as a gift. Had no idea it had been stolen."

"Really. The military-grade design didn't raise any red flags?"

Reynold's attorney interrupted. "Agent LeBlanc, my client has stated he didn't know the device was property of the US Army."

"All right." Alex fought to rein in his frustration. He had no intentions of arguing with Reynold since Wilcox had signed a confession. "Through the quadcopter's camera, you saw Howe die."

"I did. It was flying low, losing battery. One man pulled a gun, and a second man held a leash to the dog. The dog pulled and nudged the man with the gun, and he lost balance. The gun fired wildly, repeatedly, and hit the second man in the chest. The animal limped as though it had stepped on something sharp or was grazed by a bullet. Anyway the man kept shooting at the quadcopter and ran off, leaving the body and the dog." He arched his shoulders. "Howe's death was an accident."

Why had Connor called Bekah? It served to lead Alex and Ric to him. . . . Could his mental issues have altered his thinking? Was he tired of working for Jensen? Feeling guilt for killing Howe? Investigators might never know the answer.

While exiting the room, Alex unmuted his phone only to have a text almost immediately alert him. It was from Taylor Freeman at Hooks Airport. He called her back.

"You requested I contact you if I saw the man you're looking for," Taylor said. "I took an extra shift, or I wouldn't be making this call."

All senses fired alert. "You've seen him?"

"Yes, sir. Less than an hour ago, a man fitting the description of Jensen Phillips landed an aircraft here. He had a yellow Lab with him."

"Did you watch him leave?"

"A taxi picked him up, and I have the license plate number. Before you called, I double-checked his photo with what's been posted online."

Adrenaline coursed through Alex's body. He ended the call with Taylor Freeman and fed the license plate number of the taxi through the system with a BOLO.

62

BEFORE THE SUN ROSE, Stacy drove into her dimly lit neighborhood. The clinic caught her eye, and the light she normally left on in the rear wasn't on. Doc Kent had promised to handle her responsibilities until she could step back into her role as a veterinarian, and he must have turned it off. She'd stop on her way out and take care of it. Total darkness invited vandalism.

The more Dad and Mom complained about where she lived, the more she saw her home through their eyes. Not a place to raise Whitt. She struggled for a moment. She'd left the hospital when her parents insisted she take a few hours at home to shower and change clothes. They'd call if any change occurred. She agreed when Whitt's temp dropped to 101.5. The antibiotics must be working, but he hadn't opened his eyes.

If only she felt better. The antibiotics upset her stomach, or maybe it was the brucellosis. Combine that with the headache and exhaustion, and her energy level hit zero.

She pulled into her driveway and stared at her small home with its single garage. Too many things stored there to park her truck inside. Flowers and a green, mowed lawn showed her caring, but not when she needed two padlocks and an alarm system. Grabbing her purse, she felt the weight of the revolver Dad had dropped into it.

Once inside her home, the door behind her secured, she hurried to the bathroom for a shower and to wash her hair. As much as she sensed guilt about leaving Whitt, the water cleansing her body refreshed her. A short while later, she left her home, encouraged and ready to face whatever lay ahead.

She steered her truck to the parking lot of the clinic. A quick trip. Five minutes. That's all.

She released her seat belt, lifted her purse onto her shoulder, and hurried inside. A click of a light, and her world came alive. But she couldn't leave without experiencing it. The faint smells of animals and sterile conditions were like sweet perfume, and no one but a vet would ever really understand. Whitt did. Maybe Alex did a little.

A walk to where she performed surgeries came next. White. Chrome. Clean. Ready to save an animal or give it quality of life. Sighing, she folded her arms and leaned against the doorway. Her passion tugged at her heart.

The next stop was the kennel. Doc Kent's crew had done a superb job in cleaning and disinfecting the area to make it free of all diseases.

A squeak sounded from the reception area, then the distinct click of the door locking from the inside. She whirled around. The light in the waiting area vanished as well as one outside. She chilled. Had she forgotten to lock the door behind her?

The revolver in her purse . . . Could she ever use it on a human being?

"Hello," she called. "Who's there?"

The distinct patter of a dog alerted her. "Do you have need of a vet?"

"I do," a man said.

"I'm closed. Doc Kent about fifteen minutes from here can help you."

The figure drew closer. "I really came to see you." He adjusted what she believed was a backpack on his shoulder.

From the dim light in the kennel, a Lab approached with a man beside her.

"Sophie, this is the lady who's been taking care of your daughter."

Stacy froze. "Jensen Phillips?"

"How did you guess?" He pointed a semiautomatic at her. "I need answers."

A text flew into Alex's and Ric's cell phones with an alert. The taxi driver had dropped off Jensen Phillips at an Avis office in Tomball. According to the car rental business, a man matching Jensen's description picked up a Honda Civic, using the name and credit card of a Jacob Smith.

"HPD is on it," Ric said. "It's only a matter of time until we pick him up."

Alex phoned Dexter. "Be careful. We believe Jensen Phillips is on his way for Xena."

"He won't get past this force. To think, this is about over."

"I'll feel better when he's cuffed," Alex said. "Ric and I are on our way." He ended the call. "Ready?"

"Let's go."

"I'm calling Stacy on the way," Alex said. "Even if I wake her up in the hospital, she'll want to know the update." En route to the parking lot, he pressed in her number. It rang four times and went to voice mail. "Stacy, we have a lead on Jensen Phillips. I'll contact you when I know more."

"Odd she didn't answer." Ric climbed into Alex's Jeep on the passenger side.

A bit of apprehension snaked up his spine and he called her dad. "Sir, this is Alex LeBlanc. Is Stacy nearby?"

"No, she left about an hour and a half ago to take a shower. I expect her soon."

"When she arrives, would you have her text me?"

"Sure."

"How's Whitt?"

"Temp is 101.5, and he's sleeping."

"All right. Talk to you soon." He attempted to contact her again. Nothing. "Stacy is at home. I don't like this."

"Bro, drive her direction."

He blew out his fears and drew in agent mode. "Have I lost it? With Stacy as hostage, he can gain access to Xena."

"Jensen's unstable and could do anything."

Alex turned onto the 290 and headed north. "To think we agree."

"Phenomenal. But I'm right there with you."

He swung his Jeep into the subdivision. Stacy's truck was the lone vehicle in the clinic parking lot. He'd not relax until he had eyes on her.

63

HOW COULD STACY talk down this madman who was pointing a gun at her chest? Jensen Phillips loved dogs. According to Alex, he treasured them more than humans. She understood.

"I've heard you have your doctorate in veterinary medicine. Possibly a postdoctoral degree program in clinical pathology?"

"I do."

"Congratulations. I hope to one day have the same expertise."

"Clinical pathology?"

"I want to be a front-runner in extinguishing animal diseases." She sighed. "One of the reasons I despise what happened to Xena."

He twisted his head in question.

"Sophie's daughter. We named her Xena. It means 'hospitable' in Greek."

"Fits. Never knew what Connor named her."

"Did he inject her with the brucellae?" Stacy forced indignation into her voice and clenched her fists.

Jensen nodded. "But I gave it to him."

"Why?"

"A temporary situation to accomplish my purpose in life."

"I'm not following you."

"My actions have destroyed my uncle's business. Although his attorney will manage to exonerate him, too many other things point to his unscrupulous activities."

"You mean when you killed Howard Dottia?"

"He got in my way. Uncle Russ is too stupid to plan the perfect crime. That's why it was so easy to set him up. I'm leaving this country as soon as I have Sophie's daughter. Overseas, I'll be able to continue my life's work. My canine vitamins are the best available."

She touched her chest. She needed to keep stalling him. "Then you must have a serum?"

"I do." He patted the backpack on his shoulder. "And it works. Connor received one of the three doses. He was my human guinea pig. But he had to be eliminated before he talked. His depression was ruining the mission. Guards are so easily bought."

She wanted to end the discussion about whom he'd killed before he pulled the trigger on her. "Thank you for developing the serum."

"Actually I stumbled onto the strain while perfecting the cure. I kept modifying the bacteria and testing it with my serum. My findings are revolutionary."

"I know Xena needs it, but I don't have her here."

"I'm fully aware of where she's being held. You're going to help me save her from those insane researchers."

"How, Jensen?"

"I can see straight through you, Stacy. You're on their side."

"I'm on the side of every hurting animal."

"I have no reason to trust you. Unfortunately, you'll be eliminated when I have Xena. Might even keep the name."

"Since you plan to kill me, how did you mastermind all of this? The water hoax. Walter M. Brown Investments. My clinic tapped. The photos of Whitt in my newspaper."

"Sure, I have nothing to lose. Blaming the water for infecting people was a no-brainer. People here don't use a doctor unless they're dying. Rather ironic, don't you think? Connor took the photos, but I flew in and placed them in your paper." Jensen's tone remained calm, controlled. "In short, I had a plan. Howe and Connor were college buds who knew too much. Howe was becoming too ambitious, demanding more money to go nationwide with his pitiful restaurant business. Said his family deserved the best. Connor started to slip with mental issues, making serious errors. But anyway, we started working together in our days at Purdue."

"Doing what?"

Jensen's eyes narrowed. "A fraternity wouldn't let us in. We weren't good enough. So I figured out how to steal a few things. Never got caught." He grinned. "Loved the thrill of it."

"I can see you're brilliant," Stacy said. "What else have you done?"

He snapped his fingers. "I set up Walter M. Brown Investments. My uncle will be in prison for a long time."

"Won't the stocks dwindle when the company's reputation is ruined?"

"I outlined every step. I'd buy the stocks when they were low and then rebuild the company."

"A win-win situation."

Jensen smiled. "Later I'd sell and have all the money I'd ever need for research. No more shoddy laboratory equipment. I'd build the finest research facility in the world. Others could study there too."

"Amazing."

He laughed. "Telling you the plan is refreshing. I'm brilliant. Thanks for building up my ego." He patted Sophie. "All I ever wanted was to research ways to better the lives of dogs."

Stacy studied the man before her. Pity with a huge dose of fear trickled through her. Jensen's intelligence could have been an asset to mankind. Had he been eager to learn like Whitt? Had his attachment disorder always been there?

Her phone rang for the third time.

"I'm tired of whoever's calling you," he said. "Answer it. Don't try anything."

She lifted the phone from her purse and her fingertips met the gun, but Jensen had his weapon within inches of her. "This is Stacy."

"We're outside the clinic."

"Hi, Dad. I'll be there shortly."

"Jensen's with you?"

"Yes, I had my shower and grabbed a couple of things. See you soon." She ended the call and stared into Jensen's face.

"Good girl. We're walking out of here to your truck. Your job is to drive Sophie and me to Xena." He gestured down the hall. "In another life, we could have been colleagues. Can't have it now. I have a car parked down the street. We'll look real cozy."

Stacy moved toward the entrance with Jensen a few feet behind her. She unlocked the door and stepped out with Jensen and the Lab. How could Alex stop him?

Alex stood to the side of Stacy's truck, and Ric concealed himself at the corner of the clinic behind him. Until a moment ago, a potential hostage situation hadn't been verified. A SWAT team and negotiator were on their way, but with Stacy and Jensen leaving the building with the dog trailing after, it wouldn't be in time.

"Jensen, this is FBI Special Agent Alex LeBlanc. Put down your weapon." Alex stepped into view. Stacy stood between him and Jensen.

"I don't think so." Jensen sneered. "Looks like I have all the aces. You're a fool if you doubt I'll kill her. My track record speaks for itself."

"Not when you're surrounded."

"I go, and the lady vet gets a bullet to the head." He held the weapon's barrel against her ear. "Call off your big boys. The lady and I have plans."

"What if one of them shoots Sophie?"

Jensen tensed in the darkness. "You wouldn't kill an innocent dog. That's murder."

"Makes me no better than you, right? There's no reason for anyone to get hurt. Why not lay the weapon on the pavement, and we can talk. I know you're angry with Russell. Don't blame you. He destroyed everything you ever dreamed of doing."

"We talk and you'll call off the shooters aimed at Sophie?"

"Sure. Hey, guys, relax a bit until Jensen and I work this out."

Jensen pushed Stacy toward the truck. "Open it, and get inside with Sophie."

She obeyed, pressing the unlock button twice. Had Jensen detected both doors were unlocked? Stacy and Sophie climbed inside. Ric stole around the corner of building toward the passenger side of the truck. Good, he could help her.

"Tell me what you need, and I'll do my best," Alex said. "Providing Stacy is unharmed."

"Let's make a deal, huh? Xena and a path clear to fly out of here from Hooks Airport."

"I'll need time to make it happen."

The passenger door opened, diverting Jensen's attention. Alex grabbed the man and pushed him backward onto the pavement. His weapon dropped with him.

"Sophie!" Jensen struggled. "Don't hurt my little girl. I don't care what you charge me with. Just don't hurt her."

Alex cuffed him. "Your dog's safe."

"I want Sophie. Please, let me hold her." He sobbed. "She's all I have."

"You don't deserve Sophie. You don't deserve anything but a padded cell." He whirled around to Stacy. "Are you all right?"

"Yes. He confessed everything to me."

He wanted to hold her, make sure she hadn't been harmed. Later, he told himself. Later. Instead he yanked Jensen to his feet. "Jensen Phillips, you are under arrest for the murders of Lynx Connor and Howard Dottia, for spreading false information and hoaxes, for weaponizing a dog to be used as a weapon of mass destruction, for framing Russell Phillips for the crimes listed, and for anything else we discover."

Jensen stiffened and offered no response. He swung around, his cuffs flying off, and landed a blow to Alex's face. Ric rushed toward Jensen, but he grabbed his gun and aimed it at both men. "I always have a plan B. Move away from the truck. Stacy, put Sophie back inside and toss me the keys."

"The keys are in my purse." She reached inside. In a flash, she fired into Jensen's right arm, forcing him to drop his weapon.

Stacy reached for the backpack. "Don't mess with a Cajun," she said. "The serum inside here will save countless lives. You could have done so much good with your life."

Alex grinned. He'd never let this woman go.

64

STACY BREATHED IN the impatience of waiting. Dexter and the LRN had worked eight hours diligently testing Jensen's serum. Within his backpack had been a thumb drive detailing his research and the amount given to Lynx Connor, a half-strength dose with the instructions he'd need at least one more. In truth, Jensen used the dosage as a means of manipulating Connor.

An hour ago, Whitt pioneered the hope of so many people and received an injection of the serum. Machines monitored his vitals. His temp dropped to 100 degrees, and his blood pressure rose to 85 over 54.

She and Alex, along with her parents and Dexter, stood vigil. Many others flooded the waiting room, including church members, the media, and those who'd volunteered when the crisis was at its worst.

Alex held her hand with the strength she'd come to respect.

Whitt's eyes fluttered. "Miss Stacy."

Stacy thought her heart would surely burst from her chest. "Oh, Whitt. You're awake."

His gaze took in the people gathered near his bedside.

"It's okay," she said. "I'll introduce you to everyone in a minute. Just understand these are people who care."

"How did I get here?"

She drew in a breath, taking in every inch of him. "Your dad found you."

"I don't remember much."

She could barely control her excitement. "We have great news, Whitt. You're going to be fine."

"A cure was found?"

"Yes, an immunoglobulin, genetically altered to attack your infection."

"You're okay too?"

She brushed his blond hair from his forehead while tears of happiness flowed unchecked. "We are survivors."

"Xena?"

"She's been given a serum like you."

A faint smile met his lips. "Dad found me?"

She nodded.

"Grandpa McMann used to take me to those woods. Where is my dad?"

Dare she reveal the truth? "In custody."

A cloud passed over his face. "Guess that part was real." He glanced at Alex. "I didn't deter you."

Alex laughed. "Nope."

"Mr. Rayken, I'm surprised you're here. Thanks."

"Wouldn't have missed your recovery."

She kissed his forehead. "I have two people I want you to meet." She turned to Mom and Dad and gestured for them to join her. "Mom, Dad, I want you to meet a very special young man."

"Since when did I hit the importance radar?" Whitt said.

"When we realized how much we love you," she said.

EPILOGUE

SIX WEEKS LATER

"Move it an inch to the left," Stacy said. "This is one of my favorites." She stood back and admired the reception area of her new clinic.

"That's what you said about four others." Alex pushed the framed picture of mustangs to where Stacy wanted it hung.

"It's not centered," Whitt said.

"Leave it to you," she said.

Whitt centered the picture. "There." Alex stepped aside and Whitt hammered in a nail. "Glad this is the last one because I'm famished."

Alex laughed. "I'm just hungry. Burgers and fries are calling my name."

Whitt turned and grinned. "Two of each and a double-chocolate milk shake."

The two argued about the best burger place while taking the small toolbox back to Alex's Jeep. Ever since Whitt's hospital stay and Jensen Phillips's arrest, Alex had spent every spare moment with them. A threesome just like she'd dreamed. They'd ridden horses, fished, gone to the shooting range . . . and drunk lots of Starbucks coffee.

"Xena, Sophie, come on, girls. We'll check out the kennel," she said. "The men need sparring room to figure out lunch."

In quiet moments, Alex had told her about being betrayed by a woman who lied to him about her illegal activities, and she told him about KaraLee. The judge had awarded her custody of Whitt, and Whitt's parents had signed over their parental rights. Her boy was debating visiting them in jail, and she encouraged it—when he was ready. Mom and Dad loved Whitt and wanted him for a weekend all to themselves. Dad promised to take him fishing in the bayou, and Mom would cook everything she could think of.

Her life was coming together.

She accompanied Whitt to a Christian psychologist's office twice a week, and sometimes Alex joined them. Her precious boy was working through years of hurt and emotional scars. It might take a lifetime, but he wanted healing.

Stacy stood back and drank in her new clinic's surroundings. Larger. Cleaner. Newer equipment. Nothing she could afford on her own, but she'd swallowed her pride and allowed Mom and Dad to invest in her and Whitt's future. She'd repay every penny, despite their protests.

"Hey, Doc."

Alex's voice sent shivers through her. She'd not admit it just yet. But soon. She turned to him. "Did you send Whitt to McDonald's?"

His brown eyes sparkled the way she remembered the night he showed up at her front door with yellow roses and popcorn Jelly Bellies. "I wanted some alone time with the prettiest vet in Texas." He opened his arms and she gladly stepped into his embrace.

"Got a call late last night from Russell Phillips. Jensen had a complete breakdown. His attachment disorder goes deeper than what was originally diagnosed. He's reportedly catatonic."

"All stemming from his father euthanizing his dog?"

"Appears so. The things parents do to their children."

"Sometimes unknowingly." Like poor Whitt, but he was making progress. "I saw the stocks dropped on Phillips Security."

"But Russell and the board are holding on. Providing funds to manufacture the serum has helped rebuild his stellar reputation."

"Some will always criticize him for not recognizing Jensen's instability." The guilt of her own mistakes would stalk her for a long time.

"That's a fact of life when a person is in the media forefront. I was remembering something Russell said when we were in LA about Jensen performing magic tricks to entertain Sophie. I should have asked if one of those would be slipping out of cuffs. But my girl had my back."

"Lots of law enforcement had you covered that night." She took a deep breath. "Never thought I could aim a gun at someone until I saw your life in danger."

"Hey," he said, lifting her chin. "We won, remember? We have the means to cure the disease, and the developer is in custody." He pulled her closer. "Will you be too tired for our dinner tonight?"

"I'm looking forward to it. Sorta like being with my two favorite guys."

"Just checking. With house hunting yesterday and the clinic opening on Monday, I don't want to wear you out."

"I'm fine."

"Dexter and his wife are good people," he said. "Their grandson will be there. A possible friend for Whitt. I see progress. The other night he opened up to me about his grandfather. Together, we'll show him what real love is."

She loved the *we* term and snuggled closer. "I'm really glad. Ric and Taylor joining us?"

"Yes. I might have fixed him up with the right woman this time."

"Thanks for being you."

"It goes both ways."

"Hey, I have an announcement too. I'm helping Bekah and her sons find a puppy. Whitt's researching the best breeds, as though I might not have any knowledge about the matter."

He laughed, a deep-throated sound she'd come to appreciate. "Are we surprised? You've invested a lot of time with Bekah and her boys."

"I enjoy her company. Eventually I want to talk to her about Jesus. So proud of her taking over the Green-to-Go restaurants." Bekah had reached out to the employees, asking for their input on policy and customer relationships. Many were staying on to help her.

"She has strength, just took a tragedy for it to surface."

The dangers and the unpredictability of the future were certain, but she wanted to share every minute with him. She kissed him lightly. "I wanted to sneak that in."

"I plan to collect many of those for a long time."

"Is it the gumbo or the woman?"

"Oh, it's the woman and her sidekick, who's smarter than both of us combined."

"You crazy Cajun *couillon*. How long is a long time?"

His lips met hers. "How about a lifetime?"

A NOTE FROM THE AUTHOR

Dear Reader,

Deadly Encounter took me on an amazing journey of discovering characters and exploring motives. The story idea came from a friend who is a Houston airport ranger. She wanted a book that spoke of their volunteer work. She's from Louisiana and works with animals—like Stacy. I thought about the plot and a special heroine for months. Passion for the story would not let me go.

I met Special Agent Alex LeBlanc when he entered the scene after Stacy rode onto the tragedy that put the story into motion. Hard not to like him with his Cajun charm and brown eyes.

Whitt was birthed in my heart out of caring for every child caught up in lack of nurturing and subjected to bullying. He refuses to abandon Xena because he understands rejection.

Canine brucellosis is a real disease that affects dogs, but the genetically engineered bacterial infection of my story is fiction.

My characters learn to cast aside pride to know a God who is able to meet every need. We're all guilty of thinking we can live life on our own until we discover the Creator of the universe has a divine and eternal plan that is perfect and beyond our imagination.

Be blessed, my friends,
DiAnn

DISCUSSION QUESTIONS

1. Stacy cares deeply for animals, even acknowledging that she prefers them to most people. Can you relate to Stacy's love for animals? Has an animal in need, like Xena, ever worked its way into your heart?

2. Though he's attracted to Stacy, Alex is wary about beginning a romance after his last relationship broke his heart and damaged his credibility as an agent. Has a past hurt ever held you back from starting something new?

3. Stacy and Alex quickly bond over their Cajun roots, even as they clash over the case. How connected are you to your hometown or state? How much has it shaped who you are?

4. Whitt's high IQ often makes him sound like an adult, even a "little professor," but his emotional immaturity can also make him seem younger than his age. Where do you see this tension as he makes decisions? What challenges do you think this will pose for Stacy as his foster mother?

5. Stacy is torn between a desire to serve and improve her neighborhood and a desire to give Whitt a safe home. Would you have encouraged her to stay or to move? Why?

6. Alex once had a relationship with God but has been distant from Him for some time. Stacy has a more active faith but still realizes she's not as close to God as she used to be. How do both characters change over the course of the story? Has there been a time in your own life when you found yourself distant from God? What happened?

7. Long before she began the legal process to adopt Whitt, Stacy took care of him when his parents abused and neglected him. In a similar way, Dexter and Eva Rayken stepped in to care for Alex after his own parents died. Is there someone who has served as a surrogate parent or mentor in your own life—whether in place of your parents or alongside them? How has that relationship benefited you?

8. While Stacy has living parents who love her, their relationship is still slowly rebuilding after a long-ago breach. She believes that forgiving her parents is "a choice, an act of obedience." Do you agree? Whom in your own life have you struggled to forgive?

9. Whitt struggles to believe in God as a loving heavenly Father. Why is this concept so difficult for him to accept? How does Stacy's role in Whitt's life impact his view of God?

10. What do you think is ahead for Alex, Stacy, and Whitt? Imagine their lives a year after the story's end—what do you see?

ABOUT THE AUTHOR

DiANN MILLS is a bestselling author who believes her readers should expect an adventure. She currently has more than fifty-five books published.

Her titles have appeared on the CBA and ECPA bestseller lists; won two Christy Awards; and been finalists for the RITA, Daphne du Maurier, Inspirational Reader's Choice, and Carol Award contests.

DiAnn is a founding board member of the American Christian Fiction Writers; the 2014 president of the Romance Writers of America's Faith, Hope & Love chapter; and a member of Inspirational Writers Alive, Advanced Writers and Speakers Association, and International Thriller Writers. She speaks to various groups and teaches writing workshops around the country.

She and her husband live in sunny Houston, Texas. Visit her website at www.diannmills.com and connect with her on Facebook (www.facebook.com/DiAnnMills), Twitter (@DiAnnMills), Pinterest (www.pinterest.com/DiAnnMills), and Goodreads (www.goodreads .com/DiAnnMills).